"Marvelous . . .
the best of its kind since *Rosemary's Baby*."
—Mary Higgins Clark on *The Unborn*

Soft, so soft. The sounds were distant, yet close at hand, clearly perceived, like that peculiar state of being so familiar to mothers at slumber when their babies cry. Yet now Jordan was unable to move. It was a strange paralysis, an intolerably heavy inertia. She felt as if she were floating, in a dream that wasn't a dream—not quite awake, yet not quite asleep.

She knew neither who she was nor where she was. All was cotton and fluff, an endless gossamer veil that unfolded toward the horizon. In that satiny near-consciousness, the touch of Dr. Hobson's hand was distant and electric. Her mind had sudden life, unexpected vibrancy. At a moment when everything seemed indistinct, she positively knew, with absolute, immutable clarity, that the man who was speaking was lying.

"The scariest novel we've seen in years . . . lock your
door . . . and start reading."
—*Cosmopolitan* on *The Unborn*

TERMINAL CONDITION

DAVID SHOBIN

St. Martin's Paperbacks

For Steve and Mark—
    Who played a large part in the boy
    That I was, and the man I've become

TERMINAL CONDITION

Copyright © 1998 by David Shobin.

ISBN: 0-312-96622-9

Printed in the United States of America

St. Martin's Paperbacks edition / November 1998

10 9 8 7 6 5 4 3 2

Acknowledgments

Thanks to Drs. Ken Hirsch and Bob Bloom for technical assistance, and to the staff of Metropolitan Hospital.

Thanks also to Jerry Levin, Bob Kaplan, John Franco, Kevin Vesey, Chuck Bleifeld, Jerry Garguilo, Marie Hoenings, Bob Riley, and Jim Byrne for help with personal dilemmas.

Continued thanks to Henry Morrison for ongoing advice and support.

Prologue

SHE FELT AS IF SHE WERE FLOATING. HER EYES WERE closed, and everything about her felt soft, a luxuriating fluffiness like the satin down comforter Grandma Thelma used to have. She thought she must have been sleeping. There was a not-unpleasant heaviness to her limbs, like the time she could finally sit down after standing in church for nearly six hours at Vernon's funeral. Then her brain started to focus in a peculiar sort of way, powerless over thoughts that surfaced unbidden. Jamal suddenly came to mind—how he had gotten her this way, and how she longed to tell Mama, but couldn't. Mama . . .

As her consciousness began to return, she tried without success to open her eyes. Something tight and sticky was holding her lids together. Now she *knew* she was sleeping. She'd felt that strange paralysis before when, wrapped in layers of gossamer dreams, her legs turned to lead as she ran from shadowy pursuers, and her eyes became inert shutters. She was scared. What frightened her most was her breathing. It was tight and raspy, a controlled wheezing like when she had asthma. Growing panicky, her hand went to her mouth, where she found the tube.

Oh Jesus, she thought. Sweet Jesus . . .

Her heart was thunderously racing, filling her chest with explosive fear. She blindly pulled at the tube, ripping it from her throat, gagging violently as it made her gasp and choke. But finally, *finally*, it was free, and she flung it far away. She took a long and calming breath, filling her shuddering lungs with cool air, and then went to work on her eyes. She found strips of tape holding her lids together. She plucked at them in pecking, crowlike motions, first freeing the edges, then the entire strip. Now opening her eyes, her vision exploded with the brightness of a thousand suns.

The dazzling image of a woman loomed up darkly before her. She tried to focus. It was a white woman—a big woman in a white uniform, glaring at her imperiously.

"Why, you little shit," the woman snapped, clamping her hand fiercely over her mouth. She forced her down flat as she reached for a syringe. "Thought you'd make a break for it, huh? No one gets out of here, sweetheart. *No one.*"

Her struggle was brief. As her vision began to blur, she pictured Jamal for a moment, then Mama.

And then there was nothing.

Chapter One

STEPPING OUT OF THE SHOWER, RITA DRIED OFF, TUR-
baned her hair, and sat on a plastic stool before the
vanity. She looked down pensively, rubbing both hands
over her swollen abdomen. After eight months, she'd
grown so used to being pregnant that she wondered
what it would be like to have a flat belly again. She
would find out soon enough; she was due in three
weeks. There came a familiar tapping from within her
as Adrianna began to kick. Rita spread her fingers and
smiled, holding her hands in place. She never tired of
feeling the baby move.

"Everything okay in there, Reet?" called her husband.

"Fine. I'll be out in a jiff."

"You really don't have to go to this thing, you
know. Maybe you should take the night off. Those
kids'll survive without you."

"Jeffrey, I already told you. I *want* to go. I'm only
going to pass this way once."

"Promise you won't stay long?" he asked.

"An hour, tops. I'll be home before you know it."

She couldn't blame him for worrying. This was the
first pregnancy for them both, and her due date was
right around the corner. Indeed, she'd gotten a late start
at childbearing. At thirty-five, Rita Donninger had her
hands full as a first-time mother-to-be and third-year

medical student. The "kids" her husband referred to were her classmates who, on average, were ten years younger than she was. But she was as eager as anyone to celebrate at the class party.

If only she weren't so tired. These days, she could rarely stay up past ten. Was it the pregnancy, she wondered, or her age? Or both? It was a heavy tiredness of leaden eyelids and swollen ankles, of aching joints and shortness of breath. Sometimes all she wanted to do was sleep. Yet she not only wanted to attend the party, she knew it was expected of her. Her younger classmates looked up to her for advice and encouragement.

There would be drinking, of course, and probably drugs. She was happy to let others partake without her. She hadn't consumed alcohol or a mind-altering substance in over a year, since she first started trying to conceive. Not that she'd always been a teetotaler; in fact, in the eight years following her graduation from Barnard, Rita worked hard and played harder. Drinking had been an integral part of her social and business life, until she'd gone to med school.

She finished putting on her makeup and got up, frowning. Her back was aching again. The intermittent lumbar cramping had bothered her for nearly two days. She had to go to the bathroom a little more frequently than usual, and her urine had a slight odor. Ah, she thought to herself: the joys of motherhood. And although she'd already diagnosed it as a muscle spasm, she'd mention it to her obstetrician at her weekly visit tomorrow.

In the bedroom, she slipped out of her robe and put on her bra and pantyhose. Out of the corner of her eye, she saw her husband watching her, a concerned expression on his face. Rita smiled and shook her head.

"Give it a rest, Jeff. You worry more than my mother."

"I'm not worried," he said matter-of-factly.

"Then why the long face?"

"It's lust," he said. "I was thinking how hot you look."

"Get real."

"How much do you weigh now, Reet?"

"One thirty-seven, I think," she said. "Do you think I look heavy?"

"Can I get back to you on that?"

She stuck her tongue out at him. "You beast."

In fact, Rita *did* look hot to him. At five-seven, her long, slender legs and full breasts were enhanced by the pregnancy. Her straight black hair and large, brown eyes had always been striking, but now, with her high cheekbones softly rounded, she seemed more desirable than ever. "Well," he conceded, "maybe I am a little worried. One of us has to be. I mean, nothing ever fazes you. Not your grades, the pregnancy—nothing."

She sat on the bed beside him. "Come on, Jeffrey," she said softly. "You know that's not true. I just hide my fears a little better than you. It's a control thing. When I was out there in the business world, too much fear and self-doubt could be crippling. I might have felt it, but I learned not to show it."

He nodded, knowing she was right. His wife's gutsy assertiveness and bold self-confidence were traits that had attracted him from the start. He couldn't picture Rita afraid of anything. "All right, you're on. Name one thing you're worried about."

For a long moment, she considered it. "Well, I'm worried about the delivery."

He stared at her, perplexed. "I thought you were looking forward to it!"

"Yes and no," she said. "I've enjoyed almost everything about this pregnancy. The way my body's changed. The amnio, when we learned it was a girl. When she moves inside me. As for the birth itself, no sweat."

"So?"

"It's the hospital, Jeff," she said with a shiver.

"You remember when we talked about a home birth? Maybe I didn't articulate it very well then. I guess what I was really saying is that there's something about medical technology that scares me."

"But you were always in favor of medical advances."

"Yes," she said, "progress saves lives. I realize I'm a med student who works in a hospital, but the part that really frightens me is being out of control."

"You? Come on! You're more in control than anyone I've ever known."

"Not about this," she said. "Labor's so damn unpredictable. But I'm really looking forward to delivering Adrianna, because I know I can handle it. It's all the other things that worry me—the IVs, the monitors, and being at the mercy of someone else's decisions. As advanced as medical technology is, I'm scared to death about being on the receiving end."

"Poor baby," said her husband, putting an arm around her shoulders, nuzzling her cheek. "Don't worry, it'll never come to that." He touched her forehead. "You okay, babe? You feel kinda warm."

She pulled away and stood up. "There you go worrying again. You're impossible."

Rita left moments later, smelling of freshness and bath oil, her kiss still warm on her husband's cheek. He watched her go through narrowed lids, tight-lipped with concern.

For Jordan, the question wasn't whether or not to go to the party, but how long to stay. She took her studies very seriously. Although she had the next day off, she still had plenty of work to do that weekend, and she didn't want to tackle it with a hangover.

Earlier that Thursday, Jordan and other third-year medical students had taken part one of the boards, the exam given in either June or October by the National Board of Medical Examiners after the second and fourth years of med school. Now it was time to celebrate. But at twenty-six, Jordan was two years older than many of her fellow students, and centuries more mature. While she would have been content to kick off her shoes and relax to soft jazz with a glass of red, they were intent on heavy partying.

It wasn't that she was a killjoy; Jordan liked a good time as much as the next person did. Rather, she had different values from her classmates—at least, most of them. The person with whom she was most in sync was Rita Donninger. In many ways, they were soulmates. More worldly and reality-based than their peers, Rita and Jordan were no-nonsense women who knew precisely where they were headed. Their practical approaches made them respected and admired. Jordan hoped Rita would be at the party.

During the cab ride, Rita had to shake her head, amused by her husband's solicitude. Ever since she'd become pregnant, Jeffrey had become a doting husband. It hadn't always been like that. They'd gotten married two years before, right after med school began, but she'd known him for five, ever since the last summer she had a beach house in Westhampton. Her midnight-to-dawn parties attracted a cast of thousands, Jeffrey among them.

In those days, he had a hard-drinking, fun-loving, devil-may-care attitude. But then, Rita had also been different. As a driven real-estate executive, she'd successfully made her mark in the high-priced market of Long Island's East End. Thanks to perseverance and high commissions, Rita was financially comfortable by the time she was thirty, with an adequate retirement nest egg. Having made her mark in the business world, Rita decided to finally take up something she'd always dreamed of: a career in medicine. She abandoned real estate and returned to school to fulfill her pre-med requirements.

Her future was now that of a loving wife, dedicated physician, and, in a few weeks, nurturing mother. Warmed by the thought, Rita rested her head against the cab's backseat and closed her eyes. As soon as her back stopped aching, everything would be all right with the world.

The party had begun the instant the exam was over, with drinks at an East Side pub. They soon adjourned to the apartment of one of the students. Jordan, who was exhausted when the exam ended, went home for a well-deserved nap. By the time she arrived at nine, the celebration was still in full swing.

As she rode the elevator up to the apartment, Jordan fretted that Rita might not come. She could understand if Rita decided to stay home. Jordan herself found the long days taxing, and in Rita's condition, she needed the rest as much as anyone. Still, they both knew that in a few weeks, Rita would have even more on her hands.

The party spilled over into the hall, which was a constricting sea of arms and torsos. The wall-to-wall people appeared dimly through a smoky haze redolent of cigars, cigarettes, booze, and reefer. Although some students acknowledged her presence, others were too wasted to notice.

"That you, Jor?"

"Hey, Julie," she said, waving her hand to clear the air. "Guess you made it here, huh? I can't see a thing. Is this still the northern hemisphere?"

"Yeah, right. I suppose it is a little thick in here," said her roommate, taking in Jordan's black slacks and sweater, a form-fitting combination. "Now that's attire with an attitude."

"You think so?" said Jordan, secretly flattered. "And I thought I was underdressed."

"Any more underdressed and you might as well be naked," said Julie, pausing to drag on a Montecristo.

"Want a cigar? Rob brought a couple boxes of Cubans."

"No thanks. I'll settle for a beer."

The two of them squeezed from the hallway into the apartment. People were everywhere, in varying degrees of repose, lounging on furniture, against the walls, or on the floor, spilling from living room to dinette to kitchen. Two kegs of beer were on tap by the door, and a cloth-covered folding table sported an array of liquor bottles. A low coffee table held a pastiche of consumables: open pizza boxes, designer beers, and various prescription medications. Jordan recognized capsules of Marinol, the hot drug on campus. A pill form of marijuana, it was intended as an appetite stimulant for severely debilitated patients. It was no wonder most of the pizza boxes were empty.

Jordan helped herself at the keg, then retreated to a bare spot against the wall. She wondered what the public would think if they stumbled upon tomorrow's medical giants at play like this. Her attention was momentarily diverted by shouts of concern. Across the room, an inebriated student stumbled into the vertical uprights of a wall-mounted shelf display. But before any of the heavier items could topple, someone quickly bolstered the supports, a makeshift solution. Jordan suddenly felt warm lips graze her cheek. Startled, she turned to see a buoyant Rita smiling at her.

"Rita! When did you come in? You sneaked up on me."

"Been here long?"

"A few minutes. Is everything okay?" Jordan asked, noting the redness in her friend's cheeks. "You look kind of flushed."

"I'm fine," Rita said. "Just a little tired. Did you check this place out? Everyone looks so wasted."

"That they are. You're not drinking, are you?"

"Not till the baby's here," Rita said. "But I could

go for an iced tea or something. Hold down the fort until I get back, okay?''

With a smile and a reassuring wave, Rita headed for the refreshments, pushing her way through the crowd. A moment later, Julie returned.

"So what're you doing tonight?" Julie asked. "Wanna go somewhere quiet?"

"I don't think so, Jules." She smiled at her roommate. Although Julie wasn't a med student, Jordan often invited her to their get-togethers. "I'm still a little beat. I'll probably just go home soon. Kick back, maybe watch a little Leno."

"Your call," Julie shrugged. "Oh Jesus, look who's back."

Jordan followed her friend's gaze toward a middle-aged man who was smiling broadly as he made his way through the room. Wearing an oversize cardigan and smoking a pipe, he seemed to brighten when he spotted the two younger women.

"Who invited God's gift to women?" Jordan asked. "Any way we can make a graceful exit before he reaches us?"

"Not a chance. The guy just won't take no for an answer. He spent half an hour hitting on me before you got here."

"Are you serious?"

"Serious as a stroke, girl. God, look at him," Julie said under her breath. "Still got that drooling problem." She forced a smile. "Hi, Professor!"

"Hello, girls," he said. "How's the party?"

"It was great, until a minute ago."

"Julie!" Jordan hissed.

"Y'know, I think someone's calling me," Julie said. "Gotta go. Have fun, kids." Looking away, "Auntie Em!"

The man watched her slink away. "What was that all about?" He put his hand on Jordan's shoulder. "You by yourself tonight?"

Jordan looked at him with strained patience. She supposed he might be considered attractive. He was even a fairly competent biochemistry teacher. But he could not evade his reputation as an incorrigible womanizer. Without taking her eyes from him, Jordan gently pried his fingers from her shoulder.

"If you don't mind, Professor Gregory. It's been a long day."

"Precisely. You should unwind, relax. In fact, we can relax together. What is that old expression? About how love is wasted on the young?"

Jordan had to shake her head. "You never give up, do you, Professor? I think a more appropriate expression would be 'old soldiers never die.'"

"Ha!" Still smiling, he raised a now-empty liquor glass. "True, but they occasionally have to reload. Can I freshen up yours?"

"I don't think so. Professor, maybe I'm not making myself clear. Let me spell it out for you—"

"Spelling's not the issue, Miss Ross. It's more an equation," he said hopefully, once again reaching for her shoulder. "A 'you-and-me-equals' kind of thing."

"That's lame," she said, jerking her arm away.

Her forceful wrench carried her backward. Off balance, she reached for the nearby wall to steady herself, her outstretched arm striking the now-precarious shelf supports. They quickly gave way, and so did she, falling heavily to the floor, where, a fraction of a second later, an upended VCR thudded sickeningly into her head.

Chapter Two

SIRENS WAILING, THE THREE AMBULANCES ARRIVED within seconds of one another. The grim convoy pulled to a halt and parked three abreast in the roped-off courtyard at the emergency room's entrance. It was nine P.M. on an October evening, and the weather was still hot. So, too, was the ER staff. They had been expecting one ambulance. Three were a prescription for chaos.

The ER was already swarming with cops, whose patrol cars were parked haphazardly outside. Forty-five minutes earlier, a gas main had blown up in the basement of a nearby apartment building. A Thursday night explosion was a magnetic attraction for keepers of the peace. In addition, the hospital was still coping with the first of the pre-weekend walk-ins who glutted the place until midnight. In the courtyard, the first stretcher was offloaded and hurriedly wheeled through the electronic entry doors. Nerves frayed, the harried medical staff struggled to practice medicine and crowd control.

"Not in there, for Christ's sake!" shouted one of the nurses. "Take her into the trauma room!"

"It's a him, hot lips," said the EMT. "And unless you get a clamp on his carotid, it's going to be an ex-him."

The paramedic, holding a crimson-soaked dressing to the patient's neck, was jostled by a bystander. As if to punctuate his remark, a thin geyser of arterial blood spurted into the air, much to the surprise of two nearby police officers, whose faces were spray-painted scarlet.

One of the physicians stepped forward. "Move it, people!" he urged, parting the crowd with biblical authority. He was young, about thirty, and his crisp, starched, white jacket and slacks weren't stained yet. His name tag bore the words TODD LANGFORD, M.D. "Just keep up that pressure until we get him onto the table," he said to the EMT.

"You got it."

"Somebody open the vascular tray and find me a rubber-shod clamp!" Then, returning to the paramedic, "Talk to me, pal. Dispatch said we were getting a woman."

"Hey, don't blame me. Lenox Hill's packed, and Sinai's blocked by traffic."

"Just tell me what you've got," said Todd.

"Looks like blast and debris. Abdominal crush, maybe some chest wall. Unconscious when we found him. Homeless guy, mid-to-late twenties."

"Vitals?"

"B.P. was sixty systolic until it bottomed out. Last pulse was one-fifty and thready."

They were now inside the trauma room, leaving the mob scene behind. The hastily assembled trauma team worked together as an efficient unit, lifting the victim from the stretcher to the trauma table and cutting away his tattered clothing with heavy scissors.

"How long's he been in respiratory arrest?"

The paramedic was startled. "He was breathin' when we pulled up!"

"Get me anesthesia, stat!" Todd barked toward the door. "Anybody got that clamp yet? I want a large-bore IV, crystalloid, a Foley, bloods, blood gasses, and X ray. Now, people!"

A male nurse anesthetist burst into the room. "What do you need, Todd?"

"A new BMW'd be nice, but I'll settle for getting this character tubed."

The anesthetist readied a laryngoscope. "Is this the guy from the explosion?"

"One of three," said Todd. "Jesus, where the hell's that clamp?"

"Lacerated carotid," the anesthetist mumbled, shaking his head. "Just great."

One of the nurses slapped the arterial clamp into the physician's bare palm. Gowning and gloving were a luxury he didn't have time for. Another nurse assisted with the sodden dressing until he was poised above the patient's neck. When he nodded and said, "Go," she removed the dressing.

The crimson stream spurted over his shoulder. Oblivious, he worked deliberately, by sight and touch. The gaping wound in the man's neck had a sharp, almost surgical edge. His fingers probed the warm, moist laceration, searching for the pulse. Finally, he found it; and with tactile precision, he placed the jaws of the clamp around the proximal limb of the vessel. The bloodletting immediately lessened to a more manageable ooze.

Meanwhile, the nurse anesthetist, who had paused just long enough for the artery to be clamped, returned to work on the intubation. Laryngoscope in one hand, he eased open the patient's jaws and was immediately greeted by gobs of pinkish froth bubbling up from the man's lungs.

"Suction, I need suction!" Someone handed him a clear plastic catheter, and he quickly aspirated the bubbly fluid. "Jesus, he's drowning in this stuff. What the hell happened to this guy?"

"He's got a flail chest," said Todd, visually assessing the injuries. "I'd guess his abdomen took a bad hit, too. Spleen, aorta, I don't know. Just get the tube in already."

Ninety seconds later, the as-yet-unidentified man lay

on the trauma table, stripped of his torn clothing, looking much like a laboratory preparation. His twisted
body was a study in deformity, with an obviously fractured right arm and left tibia, a misshapen, protuberant
abdomen, and mottled, pale skin covered with innumerable ecchymoses. A silver vascular clamp projected
oddly from his neck. Nevertheless, a large-bore IV was
started, the first unit of O-negative blood was being
hung, an indwelling urinary catheter was inserted, and
the endotracheal tube was hooked to a respirator. The
bloods had been sent to the lab, and the X-ray tech was
preparing to take the first of her films. With a great
deal of luck, the patient *might* survive another ten
minutes, until the trauma team had a better idea of what
it was up against.

The general surgeons arrived and prepared to take
over. This sort of cut-and-paste work was their baili-
wick, turf they shared with the orthopods. The ER staff
was merely fighting a holding action. After quickly
briefing them, Todd backed off. Two other patients had
come in on the coattails of the first, and he hurried to
the next exam room, where the second blast victim had
been taken.

The scene outside Exam Room Two was frenzied but
organized. Nurses and techs scurried in and out in an
orderly stream. There were few shouts or raised voices,
and the efficient, hivelike activity gave the impression
of an emergency under control. After just one glance,
Todd knew why.

The patient on the exam table clung to life by a
thread. The right side of his face was virtually gone.
Something appeared to have struck his head between
maxilla and mandible, evulsing the lower jaw, which
was nowhere in sight. In its place was a ragged scarlet
crater, rimmed on top by exposed molars, whose white-
ness seemed out of place. But although the patient's
life was threatening to seep out of the hole, Todd
watched the man hovering over the table and knew it

would not, because Dr. Hobson was one of the fore-
most practitioners of emergency medicine in the city.

Chief attending physician in emergency medicine,
John Hobson was in his late forties, short but
distinguished-looking, with a long face beneath a receding hairline. He was the kind of physician most of
the program's residents aspired to be. Always in con-
summate control, his soft-spoken voice rang with authority. Hobson was determined to save the patient
beneath him, as he issued crisp orders in a precise,
almost military, cadence.

"Nice job with that Philadelphia collar," he said to
one of the physicians. "It's really critical to properly
immobilize the neck in cases like this. You ordered a
cross-table lateral to X-ray his cervical spines?"

"Well, I—"

"Don't worry," said Hobson, signaling to a waiting
X-ray technician, "we'll get it done. But as important
as immobilization is, don't forget the ABCs, starting
with Airway and Breathing."

The resident seemed puzzled. "Sir?"

"Your patient's blue. He just stopped breathing."

"Jesus Christ!" the resident said, eyes flitting about
the tension-filled room. "Where's the intubation set?"

"No time for that," Hobson said coolly. "With this
kind of trauma, his upper airway's probably swollen as
hell, and full of clots. A laryngoscope would be a struggle. This is what you do."

With utmost calm, he took a sixteen-gauge angiocath
from a nearby IV tray along with some Betadine swabs.
Instructing the young doctor to stabilize the patient's
neck, Hobson quickly cleansed an area just below the
patient's thyroid cartilage. Without hesitation, he
plunged the needle-like angiocath through the skin and
cricothyroid membrane until its tip was within the tra-
chea. When the inner stylet was removed, the patient's
lungs immediately contracted, expelling trapped air

with a forceful *whoosh*. His skin color improved almost immediately.

"Now," Hobson continued, "you can take your time. Try a careful intubation, or do a trach around the angiocath. Either way, just keep an eye on his breathing."

Under Hobson's tutelage, IVs were started, dressings applied, and the patient's head further immobilized. It was order shaped from chaos, the height of skill and compassion. Todd walked into the room and slowly shook his head in admiration. He never ceased to be amazed by Hobson's ability.

"Need anything, Dr. H?"

Hobson looked up. "We're good here, Todd. How're things next door?"

"Stable, for now. The surgeons are working him up."

"Then take a break. I'll call you if I need you."

Todd retreated to the solitude of the ER locker room, where he rinsed the blood off his hands and face and changed out of his stained whites into more utilitarian green scrubs. Then he took a deep breath, finger-combed his hair, and walked out to rejoin the fray.

Dr. Todd Langford was chief resident in emergency medicine at New York's Metropolitan Hospital Center, a four-hundred-bed teaching hospital in upper Manhattan. At just under six feet tall, he walked with a lanky stride. He was a solid one-eighty, and his athletic build filled out the scrubs well. Pausing by the door to the trauma room, he noted that the life-threatening situation was as under control as it possibly could be, so he went to the third exam room, where the last blast victim had been taken. He was less seriously injured than the first two, and the crew inside had everything in hand.

He turned and went to the lounge, where the luke-warm coffee was rancid but strong. He poured himself a cup, needing the caffeine more than the taste; ten hours remained in his shift. Carrying the coffee to a central workstation, he could survey the goings-on as he began the lengthy paperwork for the first trauma victim. Twenty minutes later, with the frenzied pace winding down, he was joined by Josh Meyerson, one of the first-year residents.

"Hobson's unbelievable, isn't he?" said Meyerson.

"*Doctor* Hobson to you, young fella."

"Ooh, a little touchy, aren't we?" asked Josh.

"No, it's just that he doesn't get the respect he deserves," said Todd. "The guy's here till all hours of the night, way after he should've gone home. We should all be that dedicated. And skill? Forget it. You saw what he did with that neck. Meanwhile, get some coffee. I have a feeling we're going to have our hands full this shift."

"Could be a busy night," said Josh.

"Hope you weren't counting on too much rest," said Todd.

"Yeah, I get it. You never slept much as a first-year, so why should I?"

"You know, I've got this dog," Todd said. "An old German shorthair. Can go twenty-four, forty-eight hours without human companionship. Lets himself in and out through one of these pet entrances, feeds himself, you name it. And you know, this dog never complains. Soon as I get home, he just lays down at my feet, grateful for what he's got."

"So if I learn to drink from the toilet bowl and let you scratch behind my ears, I'll get gratitude for working my ass off?"

Just then, the doors to the ER swung open, bringing in yet another patient on a stretcher. Langford shook his head and pointed in that direction. "Fetch, boy." The first-year resident sighed and walked off. Langford had to smile. Meyerson was a good doctor—bright, with a sharp sense of humor. They had worked together all summer and were growing to be friends. Knowing

Meyerson would call him if needed, Langford left the ER to look up some charts in medical records.

Returning half an hour later, Langford found Meyerson in Exam Room Four.

"What've you got, Josh?"

"Seems like a bad bump on the head," he said. "At least, I hope that's all. Twenty-six-year-old white female, unconscious, a big left parietal lump. Preliminary skull film's negative. Vitals are stable and her crit's thirty-four. Assorted dents and dings, but no other obvious trauma. Responds to pain, but not much else."

"What happened to her?"

"Get this—a VCR fell on 'er," Josh said.

"A VCR? What was she doing under a VCR?"

"Beats me. Maybe she works at Blockbuster."

"You page neuro?" asked Todd.

"They were just here. Her exam's basically negative except for some pupillary asymmetry. CT will be ready for her in about ten minutes."

Todd studied the patient. She had no obvious external injuries, and she was surprisingly attractive, with delicate features and slightly wavy, shoulder-length auburn hair. He lifted one of her closed eyelids.

"Green eyes," he said softly.

"What?"

"Just checking her pupils. What do we know about her?"

Josh handed him the clipboard.

Langford studied the ER face sheet. "Georgia Parker-Ross," he said. "Does she look familiar to you?"

"Not really," said Josh. "Why?"

"I could swear I've seen her before. Check out front and see if anyone's with her."

"You got it." Meyerson headed for the reception clerk.

Langford began a rapid but thorough exam, focusing on her vital signs and neurological reflexes. Everything seemed to be in order. He was just finishing when Josh returned.

"Would you believe she's a student here? Third year, just finished part one of the boards today. Got clunked on the head at a party. Half a dozen of her friends are outside."

"A student, huh? I thought she looked familiar." Langford slowly ran his fingers through the woman's hair, searching for the lump on the side of her head. The lesion was huge, the size of a lemon, but without the bony fragments associated with a depressed fracture.

The door swung open, and Dr. Hobson walked in.

"What've you got, Todd? Are we running a special tonight?"

"Looks that way, Dr. Hobson. It's nonstop patients, the usual Thursday night mayhem."

"Any candidates for the study?"

"Maybe the guy that was in the trauma room," said Todd. "If he makes it through surgery."

"What about this patient?" Dr. Hobson asked.

"I doubt it. Looks like a bad concussion, but we'll know more after the CT."

"Just as well," said the older man. "We're getting a bit crowded upstairs."

"You mean with patients for the new drug study, Dr. Hobson?" asked Meyerson. In addition to being chief of the ER, Hobson had a special interest in chronic neurological diseases, especially Alzheimer's disease. He was also working on a variety of new drugs.

Hobson nodded. "We recently got investigational approval for a new drug, an alpha blocker. We already have eight patients enrolled. This particular drug might have some minor CNS side effects. Dizziness, dysphoria, things like that. Since the company likes the work my group does on the neurological aspects of internal medicine, we got a nice grant for a clinical trial. But to tell you the truth, I have mixed feelings about it. Much as I'd like to see what the drug's got, everything comes with a price.'' He lifted the unconscious woman's arm, pausing to check her pulse. ''The last thing I want is for another poor unfortunate to need our services.''

Soft, so soft. The sounds were distant, yet close at hand; clearly perceived, like that peculiar state so familiar to mothers at slumber when their babies cry. Yet Jordan was unable to move. It was a strange paralysis, an intolerably heavy inertia. She felt as if she were floating in a dream that wasn't a dream—not quite awake, not quite asleep.

She knew neither who nor where she was. All was cotton and fluff, an endless gossamer veil unfolding toward the horizon. In that satiny near-consciousness, the touch of his hand was distant and electric. Her mind sprung to life with an unexpected vibrancy. At a moment when everything seemed indistinct, she positively knew, with absolute, immutable clarity, that the man who was speaking was lying.

By eleven P.M., the ER waiting room was largely deserted except for a handful of visitors, who huddled expectantly together. The flickering light from the overhead fluorescent bulbs was a pale reminder of mortality. Rita sat at the center of a group of med students. They were looking to her for advice and inspiration, but at the moment, she didn't feel particularly inspired.

In fact, she was downright despondent. As she watched Jordan's accident, Rita's heart had been in her mouth; the blow to Jordan's head was potentially lethal. Rita was also starting to feel physically ill.

Even before she arrived at the hospital, her whole body began aching with painful muscle spasms. The discomfort in her back was now a relentless throbbing, and she developed an unbearable headache. She felt feverish and light-headed. Across the room, Rob, the cigar aficionado, emerged from the interior of the ER.

"Any news?" Rita asked.

"I spoke with Dr. Meyerson, one of the first-year residents," he said. "She's still unconscious, but she's stable. They think it's only a concussion."

There was a collective sigh of relief. Rita closed her eyes and said a silent prayer. "Thank goodness. What's going to happen now? She's admitted, right?"

"They'll probably want to do some imaging studies," another student suggested.

Rob nodded. "Meyerson says she'll have a CAT scan."

"A precaution, I guess," Rita agreed. "If it's just a concussion, it probably won't show anything. But they've got nothing to lose." She let out a slow, pensive breath. "Well, I suppose we've done everything we can. Julie'll call Jordan's parents. The rest of you guys might as well take off. I'll stick around until the scan results are in."

"I'll hang out with you, Rita," said Rob, as the others rose to leave. "You really don't look so hot."

"Honestly, I feel fine," she lied, getting up to say good-bye. Around her, the room was starting to spin. A blizzard of flashing dots exploded across her retina. "It's just . . . I think it's just . . ."

All of a sudden, her eyes rolled back into their sockets, and Rita collapsed heavily onto the waiting room floor.

In the nuclear medicine suite, Langford flicked bubbles out of the fifty-cc syringe. For a CAT scan of the brain, he'd need about a hundred ccs of Omnipaque, requiring him to make two injections of the non-ionic contrast material. On the stretcher, Jordan remained unconscious.

"You sure you don't mind giving the injection,

Todd? Dr. Weber should be here in half an hour.''

"I don't *have* a half hour, Stacy. I don't need to interrupt his Thursday night, and we caught a little lull downstairs.''

"Okay. Bring her in.''

He wheeled Jordan into the CT booth. An IV of Ringer's lactate was dripping into her left forearm. Once the stretcher was locked and in place, the technician indicated that she was ready. Langford rubbed the IV's rubber hub with an alcohol swab, inserted the eighteen-gauge needle, and slowly began injecting the contrast material. Minutes later, he finished the second syringe and left the booth, joining the tech at the control console. They both eyed the patient.

"Must have been one enormous VCR,'' she said.

"You heard about that?''

"How come she doesn't have a private attending?''

"Because they brought her here, haven of the welfare world.''

When the scan was finished, Langford hung the films on the X-ray view box. There was no sign of a subdural hematoma or major intracranial bleed, but he thought he detected a slight hemispheric shift, suggestive of a subtle neurologic injury. He'd have to discuss it with the neurologist on call. The important thing was that she didn't require surgical intervention and would probably survive with little more than a bad headache. He handed the films back to the technician.

"You think they'll be officially read tomorrow morning?''

"I don't know. Most Friday mornings, no problem. But I think radiology has some all-day conference tomorrow. They might not get read until Monday.''

"Where should I put them?'' he asked.

"Over there,'' she said, indicating a pile of manila X-ray folders beneath a sign marked MRI/CT—TO BE READ.

"You can leave them out like that all weekend?''

"What're you worried about? Who's going to sneak off with an X-ray folder?"

Langford wheeled Jordan back to the ER holding area. What to do with her was becoming a problem. She couldn't remain in the emergency room indefinitely. She wasn't sick enough for the ICU, but neither was she well enough for a bed on an ordinary med-surg floor. Everything would be much easier once she came to—which she presently showed no sign of doing.

As the clock clicked toward midnight, Langford felt pressed to make a decision. The flurry of evening activity had considerably lessened, and he could take a short break, maybe even grab a snack. He spotted Pedro Gonzales, a forlorn first-year resident who always looked a little harried.

"Pedro, let's take a trip to the ICU. Give me a hand with this stretcher."

"Sure. Is this one of Hobson's study patients?"

"Royce and Hobson's," he said, referring to the chief of staff. "What do you know about it?"

Gonzales took up the rear. "Just that it's a new drug. An alpha-blocker, right? And they're getting their patients from the ER."

"Right, and we don't take American Express, and we discourage DNRs," Todd said, referring to the 'Do Not Resuscitate directive. "Royce and Hobson want us to keep these people alive at all costs. Doesn't matter if they're brain-dead, or great organ donors, or someone who's already been resuscitated two or three times. Our job's to keep their hearts and kidneys going."

They wheeled the stretcher onto the elevator. "What for, if they can't be salvaged?" Pedro asked.

"Their theory is that his new alpha blocker needs to be tested in these really borderline situations to get a clear idea of whether or not it's useful. So *everyone* gets it. Mainly ER patients in critical condition, but also some patients on life support. They're already on a shitload of other meds, but the computer will sort that out when the results get analyzed. I don't completely understand it, but Royce and Hobson are smart. If they say it's important, believe me, it's important.''

Pedro nodded seriously.

''But as far as I'm concerned, it's a mixed blessing,'' Todd continued. ''I'm responsible for resident education. And at this time of year, all you new guys could use a little ACLS training.'' Proper training in Advanced Cardiac Life Support was essential in a large urban hospital. ''But come December, pumping all those lifeless chests will get a little stale.''

When they reached the ninth floor, the elevator doors opened. ''Then what's with all the spinal fluids?'' asked Gonzales.

''You heard about that, too, huh? Dr. Hobson asked me to do spinal taps on all patients in the study. Supposedly, after the lab's done with 'em, he's sending all the fluid collections back to the drug manufacturer to check on metabolites. It's kind of hush-hush, but . . . I mean, everybody's heard about it, but they're not really advertising it, you know what I mean? What the hell. Money in my pocket. He pays me a hundred bucks a week to do the taps.''

In the ICU, the charge nurse approached. ''This your head trauma, Todd?''

''Meet Georgia Parker-Ross,'' he said. ''She's a third-year med student here. The police are still trying to locate her family. Her CT's in the folder.'' He looked around the unit. ''Christ, this place is packed. How many study patients are here?''

''Including the two who came in this afternoon, nine.''

Langford did a rough calculation. It seemed that Hobson had been collecting an unusually large amount of spinal fluid recently. Suddenly they heard the alarm of a cardiac monitor.

"Hell, not again!" said the nurse. "He coded right before I came on duty!"

They rushed to the bedside of a man swathed in bandages and sticky with salve. Already intubated, the patient was attached to a respirator. Langford's practiced eye appraised the man's injuries. With over eighty percent of his body covered with third-degree burns, he hadn't a prayer of surviving. But he was a study patient, and they had their orders. An alert desk nurse notified the switchboard, and overhead, the cardiac arrest was announced. Within sixty seconds, the unit would be swarming with young doctors. But they didn't have sixty seconds to wait. At that moment, they were the frontline troops.

"Start pounding his chest, Pedro! Get me a rhythm!" shouted Langford. As the junior resident went to work, he glanced at the IV tubing. "What's in the bottle, Jen?"

"Lidocaine drip." She hurriedly plugged in the defibrillator.

"I need drugs, guys! Where's the crash cart?"

"Right here, Doctor."

"I want intracardiac epi, and get an amp of bretyllium ready! Break those ribs if you have to, Pedro—but get me a pulse!" He eyed the cardiac monitor, whose squiggly line showed the deflections of ventricular fibrillation. "Ready to shock, Jen?"

She held up the paddles. "Just about."

"Okay if I give it a try, Dr. Langford?" asked Gonzales.

Langford looked at the eager but struggling first-year resident. "Sure, why not? Just don't get upset if it doesn't work," he said, as the nurse handed over the defibrillator paddles. "Most of these characters are terminal, just circling the drain."

Chapter Three

SHE SAW IT AS A DISTANT WAVE, MOVING DARKLY
through her head. Its ominous approach was frightening. The vast incoming tide swept relentlessly her way
until it rose up in a menacing gray wall. The roiling
wave crests became white with froth, and just as they
threatened to engulf her, the spume turned to silvery
hair.

Before her marched a phalanx of old and gnarled
men. They scowled at her, glowering defiantly through
unforgiving eyes. When she realized they were going
to do something to her, she grew terrified. On their
shoulders were the gleaming scythes and axes they
used. They came until they towered over her, peering
down menacingly from on high. When they reached for
their tools, the spindly tendons of their forearms protruded cadaverously.

They were looking down into her mind, studying her
soul. Something was broken and needed fixing, and
they were the repair crew. They nodded solemnly to
one another and rolled up their sleeves. She felt a moan
rising in her throat. They lifted their axes, preparing to
cleave her brain. The wail started slowly, then built up
and leapt to her tongue, the prelude to·a scream . . .

Jordan awoke with a start before the scream escaped
her lips. Trembling and breathless, she didn't know
where she was. Her lungs heaved, and her heart was

pounding. She lay there in wide-eyed terror, staring apprehensively at the darkened ceiling. It took several minutes for her shaking to cease. She realized it had only been a dream, but she was frightened to her core that something was seriously wrong.

Six floors above the ICU, the animal labs were located on the twelfth floor in a recently renovated area. The area smelled like a zoo—a pungent mixture of animal chow, urine, and disinfectant. The hospital dealt only in small animals, such as mice, rats, guinea pigs, and rabbits. The neurobiology lab occupied twelve hundred square feet on the floor's southeast corner, a priceless piece of medical real estate overlooking the East River.

The lab's staple research animal was the white rat. Rats were low-cost, easy to sacrifice, and possessed a straightforward neuroanatomy. For the past two years, the lab employed a strain of genetically obese rats known as OB/OB. Researcher Donald Fletcher, head of the lab, used them because of their predictable response to the Breen-Richter test.

Animal testing had come a long way since the days of the maze and the rotating squirrel cage. The basic piece of equipment used was a modified Skinner box, originally designed to measure positive and negative reinforcement. The goal of any test was to gauge how much an animal's response deviated from norms, or standards. Rather than determine how fast a rat negotiated a prescribed course in search of food, the Breen-Richter test added an element of sophistication, using computers.

Although the test had several variations, the basic procedure called for the rat to be placed on a foot-square tray and immobilized in a harness. Once in position, it faced straight ahead, with little room to move. Simultaneously, at the end of its boxy cage, computerized graphics appeared on a flat screen. The images showed various types of food familiar to the rat. A small optical sensor beside the screen tracked the movement of the rat's eyes.

Ordinarily, once the rat grew accustomed to the harness, its eyes became riveted on the pictures of food. Its small whiskers quivered, its nose twitched, and it began to salivate. Time would pass. But inevitably, when there was no reward, its attention would wander. The rat's gaze would drift upward, downward, or sideways. Curiously, when its eyes moved away from the images a sufficient number of times, it would be rewarded with a real food pellet that dropped from the top of the cage.

The computer would measure the rat's response to determine how quickly it learned. The standard image-to-food interval for OB/OB rats was sixteen minutes. Then the computer would vary the necessary response. For example, rather than requiring the rat to move its eyes twice to the right, the animal would have to turn its vision once to the left in order to be rewarded. The test could be further modified by administration of drugs. However much the average image-to-food time was altered was taken to be a measure of drug effect.

Donald Fletcher, Ph.D., had several experiments ongoing in the lab. All of them involved agents known or suspected of having a neurological effect. As often as not, these agents were derived from purified extracts of human cerebrospinal fluid. Purified CSF was a good medium with which to work because its basic ingredients were neutral, not interfering with the agents added. Drugs could accumulate unmetabolized, microbes could grow and multiply, and toxins could be concentrated.

In Fletcher's current test protocols, samples of human CSF extracted by spinal tap were delivered to the lab. Each was appropriately labeled and identified as to source and patient condition. Then, by referencing the patient's ID number from the hospital computer, all the variables that might affect CSF constituents were purified and analyzed, in order to precisely determine what each CSF extract contained. Tiny amounts of the extract were then administered to the rats by injection.

The laboratory workday was largely complete by five P.M. The last person to depart checked the temperature control, turned off the lights, and left. No one would return until seven A.M. the next morning. The caged animals were left to their own devices.

OB/OB rats were an indolent strain. They did little more than eat, drink water, and occasionally—with considerable effort—breed. They generally moved little, preferring to conserve their energy. But at approximately midnight on that lazy October night, several of the rats in one particular cage showed unusual activity.

They appeared to work in tandem. Two of the Fat Rats, as they were affectionately known, scurried to the cage's door. Its metal lock was a simple sliding horizontal latch. One rat remained motionless while the other climbed up its tail and onto its back. Then, rising to its full height on its rear legs, the second rat stretched out its forelegs until its claws touched the metal bar. With a sideways swatting motion, it dislodged the lever. Then it returned to the cage floor, where both rats nudged open the unlocked door with their snouts.

The first rat scurried to the test apparatus. Slowly it wormed its way into the harness, a difficult feat without human aid. Then it remained motionless for several seconds, staring straight ahead. The optical sensor's on-off switch was slaved to a pressure gradient within the harness. Soon the computerized testing apparatus clicked on.

In the darkness of the lab, the food images seemed to flicker. But the rat appeared to pay little attention to the pictures that normally attracted it. Rather, its gaze shot upward, downward, and sideways in seemingly random movements. Yet within seconds, it was rewarded with a food pellet, which it eagerly devoured. Then it repeated the whole process until rewarded a second time. Finally, in an unheard-of feat, it lowered its shoulders and deliberately inched backwards until it was freed from the harness. Then it retreated to a corner of the cage to defecate.

The companion rat took the place of the first, with similar results. By two A.M., each of the special cage's twelve lab animals performed the test protocol several times, each time being duly rewarded. Soon all the corpulent rodents huddled together in one corner. They rubbed noses and nuzzled one another in some sort of communing process, until they slowly drifted off to sleep.

What the Fat Rats accomplished had never been described in the annals of laboratory research. They showed a cognitive ability, a means to intuit, to perceive and learn, that was positively remarkable. It was the laboratory equivalent of the three-minute mile, a trip to Mars, a hundred-homer season. At that moment, only Donald Fletcher suspected the reason behind the Fat Rats' performance.

But it was all dutifully recorded on a miniaturized video camera built into the test apparatus.

Chapter Four

IN THE HALL OUTSIDE THE FOURTH-FLOOR DELIVERY suite, the crowd of med students had grown. Alerted of Rita's collapse, their number quickly doubled until more than a dozen students paced dejectedly back and forth. Someone had notified Rita's husband, Jeff. He sat on a bench by himself, head lowered in his hands, mumbling over and over that he should never have let her go.

Inside the delivery room, Richie Silver was the senior OB resident on call. He stood at the bedside of the most baffling case he'd yet come across in his young career, eyes flitting from the chart to the unconscious patient to the nearby fetal monitor. Everything about the case was confusing, It wasn't often that an apparently healthy thirty-five-year-old patient three weeks from term collapsed for no apparent reason. Complicating matters, she was a private patient, scheduled to deliver at another hospital. And most explosive of all was the fact that she was a third-year medical student, one of their own. A junior resident ran up and handed Silver a slip of paper.

"These her latest labs?" Silver asked.

"Yeah, and they ain't good."

Silver studied the numbers. "Jesus, her platelets are down to sixty thousand! What were they before?"

"Ninety-two. Did you do the gram stain?" the junior

resident asked, referring to a microscopic exam of the patient's urine.

"Sheets of white cells and gram negative rods."

"E. coli?" said the junior resident.

"Probably. Christ," he said, shaking his head, "we need this like a hole in the head! I wish her private OB would have taken her."

"When did he call back?"

"Around five minutes ago," said Silver. "I ran the case by him, and he claims Mount Sinai won't accept a transfer of an unstable patient."

"But we're not trying to dump someone. It's his own patient!"

"I know, I know," Silver said. "Maybe it's a liability thing. Where the hell is that ID guy already?"

When on night call, fellows in infectious diseases took calls from home. Ten minutes later, Dr. Mitchell Rowe, the senior ID fellow, finally arrived from his residence in Queens. Getting him out of bed in the middle of the night had been difficult, but Silver finally prevailed when he stressed that the patient was a student there. Rowe strolled over to them looking dour and annoyed.

"This better be worth it," he grumbled.

"You be the judge," said Silver, nodding toward the bedside. "Meet Rita Donninger, a third-year student here. She was down in the ER visiting a friend when she collapsed. She's thirty-five, first pregnancy, due in about three weeks. According to her private OB over at Sinai, she's had an uneventful antenatal course so far."

"No complaints, no symptoms?"

"The best I can get from some of her friends is that she felt tired. Not unusual for a pregnant patient near term. Some people thought she looked flushed. And in fact, her temp's one-oh-three."

"You said her pressure's low?" asked Rowe.

"*Was* low—eighty over forty. Now it's shocky," he

said, indicating the blood-pressure monitor. "The highest she goes is sixty systolic."

"You maintaining her volume?"

"We're pumping fluids in like crazy," said Silver, "and we might even be getting overloaded. We need a wedge pressure. The critical care fellow's on his way in to place a Swan."

"How's her urine?"

"She's not producing much," said Silver. "Take a look." He held up the plastic tubing from an indwelling urinary catheter. A few drops of cloudy, tea-colored urine dribbled into a collection bag. "That's all she's put out in over two hours, barely thirty ccs. And I think it's the cause of her problem. Her gram stain's on the 'scope in the lab."

Increasingly solemn, Rowe hurried off to review the microscope slide. On the nearby fetal monitor, the unborn child's heartbeat indicated worsening fetal distress. Richie Silver stared at it in mounting helplessness, aware that the already dire situation was growing more critical by the minute.

After studying the slide, Rowe did a cursory exam on Rita, evaluating her head, heart, and lungs. The case seemed depressingly straightforward.

"I'd say E. coli, all right," he said. "With her pressure where it is, this is the worst case of septic shock I've seen in a long time. You better do something fast."

"I've never seen septic shock in an OB patient," Silver said nervously. "I'm open to suggestions. What bug killer do you recommend?"

"Since it's not hospital-acquired," Rowe said, "triples should be fine, say amp-clinda-genta Q six. But the way I see it, antibiotics are secondary to perfusion. The cytokines from her bacterial endotoxin are going to screw up her organs pretty soon. Unless you get her tissues perfused fast, she's not gonna make it."

Silver looked grim. "We're going to throw her into failure with all these fluids."

"Then you better give her pressors," Rowe suggested. "I know you'd like a Swan, but I don't see how you can wait any longer. Is dopamine okay for the baby?"

"Good question," Silver said wearily. "I've never seen it used in an OB patient before. Let me examine her again."

He pulled a unisize latex glove from a nearby box and put it on. Daubing his fingers with lubricating gel, he gently examined the unconscious patient, carefully assessing her cervix. The exam took no more than ten seconds. But when he withdrew his hand, his fingers were dripping wine-colored blood. Rowe gaped in astonishment.

"Do all pregnant patients bleed like that?"

"No," said Silver, "it's much too heavy for bloody show. And I don't like the color."

"Could it be related to these petechiae?" asked Rowe.

"Where?"

Rowe pointed to Rita's trunk and abdomen. Tiny pepper-size red dots had broken out on her skin since they last examined her and appeared to be spreading. Silver gaped in astonishment.

"Jesus, she's bleeding into her skin!"

"How're her coags?" asked Rowe.

A clearly rattled Silver handed him the lab slip. "Her platelets are way down."

"No kidding," said Rowe, studying the results. "What about her FDPs?"

"Let me see that," snapped Silver, taking the report the junior resident held out to him. As he read it, he grew pale. "Christ, look at her FDPs! Her pro time's up, too, and she's got no fibrinogen!"

"What's that all mean?" the shaken junior resident asked.

"It means she's got DIC," Rowe said tersely. "Her blood's not clotting. And unless you guys do something heroic, she's going to bleed to death right in front of us!"

Langford helped Gonzales with the paperwork. Whenever a patient expired, there were countless forms to fill out. Across the room, an LPN tagged the patient and wrapped him in white bedsheets, awaiting transport to the mortuary.

Langford was distracted. A hospital was a small world unto itself, and word had quickly filtered throughout the wards about a pregnant med student who was critically ill on the obstetrics floor. He wondered if he could be of service. He knew a great deal about emergencies, but his knowledge of obstetrics was limited. From the page operator, he learned that Richie Silver was the senior resident on call. After a moment's thought, Langford decided to sit tight. Silver might be a little tentative about making decisions, but he was certainly bright enough.

He was sure Silver had the situation well in hand.

Silver was incredulous. This was the most disastrous night of his obstetric career. He could hardly believe the horror of what was happening to Rita Donninger. Disseminated intravascular coagulation, DIC, was one of the most feared complications in obstetrics, potentially leading to unstoppable hemorrhage and organ failure. Rowe was right: unless they intervened dramatically—and very, very soon—Rita was going to die.

Silver immediately paged the hematology fellow to help with blood management. The junior resident finally got through to their attending, whose phone had been inexplicably busy for an hour. After some momentary grumbling, the attending promised to come in shortly. Meanwhile, the critical care fellow arrived, short-tempered and bleary-eyed. Middle-of-the-night emergencies left everyone in a foul mood. But within seconds of realizing the seriousness of the situation, the fellow immediately settled down to work. In a short while he inserted what was known as a central line, or Swan-Ganz catheter, to aid in fluid and blood-pressure management.

Within minutes, the primary problems were dealt with, as adequate oxygenation was ensured, cardiac output was effectively monitored, and broad-spectrum antibiotics administered. But the respite was temporary. It was soon obvious that Rita was bleeding from everywhere, including all IV sites. And if that were not enough, the unborn child was in profound fetal distress.

Silver faced a frightening dilemma. His patient was in labor, but at barely four centimeters dilated, she wouldn't deliver for hours. And at the present rate, there was no way the distressed fetus could survive that long. In fact, he doubted the baby would make it for another hour without suffering significant neurological impairment. Ordinarily, the situation called for immediate cesarean section. But this was no ordinary situation; operating on a patient whose blood didn't clot might kill her. Silver looked at his watch. The attending was expected to arrive within thirty minutes—thirty minutes Silver didn't have.

Pressured to do *something*, Silver looked helplessly at his patient. Her pale, underperfused skin was dotted with tiny hemorrhages, as if she'd been splattered with red paint. She was on a respirator, but the tube in her lungs could barely provide enough oxygen for her and her unborn child. She had IVs in both arms and a central subclavian line beneath her clavicle, all their puncture sites oozing unclotting blood. Her urinary catheter had turned red from submucosal bladder hemorrhages.

Rita Donninger was living out her worst nightmare: trapped on the receiving end of advanced medical technology, she was being kept alive by machines, gadgets, and sensors, all of which beeped without feeling from one heartbeat to the next.

She saw the light and moved toward it. Someone was whispering her name. She was in that nether state, just below the surface of consciousness, where the senses are heightened but one is unable to act. With a great effort, she forced her eyes open.

"It took a couple hours," a voice said, "but welcome back."

Jordan pursed her lips, but all that emerged was a feeble moan. Her heart raced, the recent dream still vivid in her mind.

"You're in a hospital, Miss Ross. You had a bad bump on the head, but you're going to be fine. Can you hear me?"

The speaker's face slowly swam into focus. It was a man, a handsome man, dressed in a beige shirt, white lab coat, and striped tie. He was leaning over her, intently studying her face.

"I . . . a hospital?"

"That's right. One of New York's finest."

"How did I get here?" she whispered.

"Ambulance. Do you remember the party?"

"What party?"

"Guess that answers that. I'm Todd Langford, one of the hired help around here."

"Are you a doctor?"

"Some would debate it, but yes. Chief resident in emergency medicine. You don't remember me, do you?"

"Should I?"

"Maybe not. I've seen you during rounds, or on the wards."

"What am I doing here?"

"Well, the way I understand it, you got clunked on the head. But so far, all your tests are negative. It looks like just a concussion. But I'd like to do a spinal tap."

He checked his watch. "Look, it's three A.M. now. I'll come back when it's light, after shift change."

"A spinal tap?"

"Just a precaution," he said. "It's important to find out if there's any blood in your spinal fluid." He paused. "Do you remember anything?"

She concentrated, but nothing came. "Not really."

"Don't worry, that's normal. In time, everything'll come back. Get some rest, okay?"

He smiled and touched her cheek, a soft touch. Her mind was mush, a thick gruel. It was frustrating trying to remember. She knew her name, but that was about all. Rather than fight it, she just let it go. She leaned back against the pillow, exhausted. The young doctor had a kind, pleasant face. And soft brown eyes.

"I'm sorry, Mr. Donninger," said Silver. "I wish there was an alternative, but we don't have much choice. Or much time."

Jeff was hopelessly beside himself. "I . . . I don't know what to say."

"You've got to say something. We can't perform the surgery without your consent."

Slack-jawed, it was all Donninger could do to shake his head indecisively from side to side.

"What exactly is Rita's condition now?" one of her classmates asked.

"Extremely critical," Silver replied. "She's in septic shock with severe DIC and what looks like ARDS," he said, referring to adult respiratory distress syndrome. "She's getting blood components, antibiotics, and fluids. It's touch and go. But we've got to operate to save the baby."

"And this is all due to a stupid urinary infection?" asked another student.

"It's pyelonephritis," said Rowe, "a severe kidney infection. The E. coli that's causing it produced an endotoxin that led to septic shock."

"Pyelo's not all that uncommon in pregnancy," Silver explained. "What's unusual is her body's response. But whatever the cause, we need an answer. It's your call, Mr. Donninger. The surgery's a risk, but without it, the baby has no hope." He paused, letting his words sink in, as he looked Donninger straight in the eye. "What would your wife have wanted?"

There were tears in Jeffrey's eyes, and his chin was quivering. "Go ahead," he said. "She desperately wanted that baby. But I'm begging you, please, bring Rita back to me!"

The ward on fourteen ran north-south. The brittle wall tile, once a fashionable lime, was discolored by years of neglect into something resembling puce. The overall effect was drab, befitting the environment—this was the neurology floor, where chronically ill patients clung to life in varying degrees of pre-terminal melancholia.

It was two-fifteen A.M. At that hour, most of the patients not in a coma were asleep. Medications were dispensed every four hours, at ten, two, and six. The mind-numbing routine of tinkering with IVs and forcing pills into barely responsive gullets took over an hour. LPN Juanita Farber, the night-shift charge nurse, was assisted by a nurse's aide. After several years together, they were a smoothly functioning team, saying little, anticipating what needed to be done. Farber heard what sounded like a door closing and looked up.

"That you, Connie?"

There was no answer. Farber frowned, replacing the bottle of Aricept on the meds cart. Could it be one of the security guards? She walked out of one of the four-bed rooms and into the dim corridor, looking left and right. No one was there. She suppressed the involuntary fear that accompanies strange sounds on dark nights. Walking purposefully to the next room, she found the aide securing a patient's wrists with leather straps.

"Did I just hear you out in the hall?"

"Wish I was," said Consuelo Torres. "Old Reggie here decided to test his restraints again."

"I guess." Mollified, Farber returned to her cart. This wasn't the first time her ears had played tricks on her.

Fifty feet away, a man emerged from the shadows in the utility room. He was of indeterminate age, somewhere between twenty-five and forty-five, with a medium complexion and slicked-back blond hair. His most conspicuous feature was the long white lab coat ordinarily worn by physicians. A hospital ID badge gave his name as MICHAEL SCHWARTZ, M.D.

Gaining access to the ward had been child's play. At night, no one looked twice when a properly ID'ed white male breezed through the ER entrance. Nor was he given a second glance when he took the elevator to fourteen. Once he was there, however, the game changed. Even the most dim-witted nurses would look askance at his unexpected appearance. He couldn't simply show up unannounced and perform minor surgery in the middle of the night.

The ward's entrance was a painted metal door, which had a large glass window. Once he'd exited the elevator, Schwartz clung to the shadows, watching Farber and Torres from across the hall. He was waiting for them to begin medication rounds. Once they were occupied with the patients, he cautiously went through the door and hid in the utility room, awaiting his opportunity.

His destination was the first four-bed patient room beyond the nurse's station. Once satisfied that the nurses were back at work, Schwartz crept from his refuge and stole soundlessly onto the ward. Inside the room, he quickly looked around. The four patients were over sixty, all male. Two were on respirators, one was asleep, and the fourth worked his gums while staring sightlessly at the ceiling, thumbs dancing in a Parkinsonian pill-rolling tremor.

Schwartz silently approached the patient on the respirator in the far corner of the room. Despite the darkness, he drew the bedside curtains, more for peace of mind than privacy. He temporarily detached the respirator. Turning the unconscious man onto his side, he positioned the patient on his back, knees drawn up in fetal position, before reattaching the tracheostomy tubing.

He carried everything he needed in the deep pockets of his lab coat. First he removed a small penlight and held it in his teeth. There was no need for antisepsis or sterile drapes. He unwrapped the twenty-gauge, three-and-one-half-inch spinal needle from its plastic package. Lifting the patient's gown, he felt for the vertebrae. Fortunately, the man was thin, and the bones of his spine protruded like pushbuttons.

He located an interspace and carefully inserted the needle. He had no qualms about hurting the patient, but he wanted to avoid a traumatic tap, in which the specimen would be contaminated with blood. Feeling the needle pierce the ligamentum flavum, he withdrew the stylet and checked for flow. Within seconds a drop of glistening fluid appeared at the needle's hub. He uncorked a glass test tube and held it beneath the needle. In the intense but narrow beam, the emerging drops of spinal fluid seemed almost crystalline, liquid jewels that fell like pearls into the vial below.

He'd been told that all he needed was three ccs. But as this patient's fluid was more precious than gold, he waited an extra minute to fill the ten-cc tube halfway. Then he replaced the rubber stopper, pocketed the vial, and withdrew the needle. In another minute he was gone, creeping away as silently as he had come.

At forty-two, Mrs. Rivera was one of the senior members of the housekeeping department, having been a hospital employee for eighteen years. With her tenure, she worked the day shift—mopping, sweeping, and taking out the garbage. Days had always been more stable and predictable than either evenings or nights.

It therefore wasn't often that she worked at night, but she did so on occasion, pitching in for sick co-workers. That night, as she brought all the bagged garbage down to the collection area for pickup, she paused to watch the big trucks roll in during the pre-dawn hours. There were different trucks for different purposes, from red-bagged infectious waste to sorted recyclables to routine kitchen refuse.

Leaning against her broom, Mrs. Rivera saw a large garbage truck backing into the hospital courtyard. The name Aiello & Scarpatta Carting was painted on the side in large yellow letters. The driver and his passenger got out and lit cigarettes as they lowered the rear-loading ramp. Moments later, the night shift head of housekeeping emerged from the shadows and walked toward the truck. He was accompanied by a well-built man in his twenties who wore a white lab coat. He looked familiar to Mrs. Rivera, but she couldn't place him. After saying a few words to the garbage men, a small envelope changed hands.

Mrs. Rivera frowned and shook her head from side to side. Payoffs weren't uncommon in the carting industry, but the man from housekeeping was a union shop steward. There had been talk that the Mafia was increasing its involvement in day-to-day hospital activities, but she thought the talk had been just rumors. Until now.

No matter. It was best to turn a blind eye to such things. She had a sick husband to tend to, and a family to care for.

The interior of the obstetrical OR was a carefully orchestrated frenzy. Nurses, students, and aides scurried about making final preoperative preparations. In addition to OB and neonatal residents, hematologists, anesthesiologists, critical-care specialists, and infectious-disease specialists swelled the ranks to fifteen. It was time for the case to begin. The OR doors swung open to reveal the attending obstetrician, his upraised arms still bubbly with lather.

"What've you got hanging?" he asked the anesthesiologist.

"Lactated Ringer's. We're maintaining her wedge pressure around twelve."

"And the other bags?"

"This is her eighth unit of platelets," said the anesthesia resident. We're KVO'ing her central line and peripheral IV with normal saline. Over here we've got two grams of ampicillin, and that's a dopamine drip."

"Want me to get started?" asked Silver.

Dr. Randall Jenkins, the attending, glanced at the patient, wishing he'd had more time to assess the situation. Sterile blue drapes or antiseptic covered most of the patient's skin, but here and there he saw a patch of marbled skin with its worrisome bruises. Time was a luxury he didn't have, and on top of that, he had received an urgent call from the dean's office just as he was leaving the house. The last thing he wanted was extra pressure. As he toweled dry, he nodded to Silver. "All yours."

Two minutes later, the exposed uterus protruded into the surgical incision, its grayish-purple mass slick and glistening. In the glow of the overhead spotlights, the OR had become unbearably hot. The building's air conditioning had recently been shut down for the season, and the ambient temperature had risen to nearly ninety degrees. Every member of the surgical team was sweating. Although they were working fast, the innumerable stainless-steel clamps used to control the bleeding hindered their progress.

"How's the fetal heart?" the attending asked one of the neonatologists.

"Low and unreactive. Down to the upper fifties."

"Is that a dopamine effect?" Silver asked Jenkins.

"Could be," said the attending. "At these doses, uterine flow is pretty restricted. This kid's going to be hypoxic and acidotic as hell. Keep your eyes open, Richie. See if you can get that bladder flap down a little more."

As Silver dissected the peritoneal fold, a red warning light suddenly flashed on the fetal monitor.

"We've lost thc fetal heart!" shouted the neonatologist.

"Oh, shit!" said Jenkins. He would have loved to continue their methodical pace, but each second was now critical. If the baby had any chance of resuscitation, it had to be delivered immediately. Frantically he grabbed the scalpel off the Mayo stand and made a hurried nick in the lower uterine segment, quickly widening the incision with his fingers. Burgundy-colored amniotic fluid gushed over his gloved hands. Beneath the incision, the mottled flesh of the baby's pale cheeks lay waiting.

Without hesitation, Jenkins thrust his hand into the pouchlike lower uterus. His fingers slid under the fetal head, which he cupped in his palm. As he lifted upward to dislodge the vertex, the head made a moist, sucking sound. He quickly maneuvered the head into the incision, then repositioned his palms, placing one on each fetal cheek. Meanwhile, Silver hurriedly severed the wires securing the fetal monitoring clip to the scalp.

Jenkins gently lifted the head up and out of the uterus, until the entire baby was delivered. Silver quickly suctioned blood-tinged mucus and amniotic fluid from the baby's mouth. Jenkins smoothly double clamped the umbilical cord, cutting it with a heavy scissors. Then he handed the newborn to a waiting neonatal resident. From the moment the cardiac arrest was detected, the remainder of the delivery had taken only forty seconds.

"A girl, right?" asked the anesthetist.

Jenkins nodded. "If she survives."

The child was pathetically limp. Placed back down on the resuscitation mattress, she resembled a broken rag doll that someone had thoughtlessly discarded. The baby was uniformly gray and lifeless. She had been clinically dead for sixty seconds.

The neonatology team immediately set to work. The senior resident briefly listened to the baby's thorax with a stethoscope, then began newborn CPR, rhythmically depressing the infant's sternum with his thumbs. Meanwhile, his co-resident tilted back the baby's slack jaw. Using a pediatric laryngoscope, he quickly inserted a number three-and-a-half endotracheal tube, attaching its end to an ambu bag, he turned the respirations over to a neonatal nurse while he focused his attention on the clamped cord. He catheterized the umbilical vein and administered several ccs of bicarb. But time was passing. It was now more than two minutes into the arrest, and the little girl's heart still wasn't beating. A thick air of desperation dogged the team's efforts.

Jenkins and Silver had problems of their own. The situation was desperate. After they delivered the placenta, blood began welling up within the uterus, a steadily rising tide. They administered Methergine and oxytocin to contract the womb while Silver massaged the uterine muscle with his fingers. The predicament resembled a complication called atony, in which the postpartum uterus wouldn't contract.

Although the uterus finally firmed up, the bleeding continued unabated. Jenkins hurriedly injected a mixture of dinoprostone and vasopressin directly into the placental bed and uterine edges. Nothing worked. The blood welled up like groundwater.

"Hot moist laps!" Jenkins barked. He quickly packed the uterus and wrapped the sterile pads around it, hoping that pressure and thermal effect would accomplish what medications did not. At the very least, the procedure was psychologically effective, for with the uterus hidden from view, the bleeding had an out-of-sight, out-of-mind quality. But the tactic could not succeed for long. "Can't we give individual clotting factors, like factor eight?" Jenkins asked the hematologist.

"We can't get hold of the individual factors at night. They come from the city blood center, and all we can give is what's in our own blood bank. We're already giving platelets, cryoprecipitate, and FFP. If you can keep her alive another hour, her liver will produce all the factors she needs.''

"An hour?" Jenkins asked incredulously. He glanced at the lap pads, which were quickly becoming saturated. "At this rate, she won't even last thirty minutes! Can't we at least give her blood?''

"No problem," said the unnerved hematology fellow. "She's O-positive. We can give all you need."

"Then get at least ten units ready! If we can't stop this goddamn bleeding, we can at least keep up with what she loses! I damn well don't want to be the first attending to lose a med student in his own hospital!''

The atmosphere in the overheated OR crackled with tension. The apparent futility of their best efforts was placing everyone under a tremendous strain. One life was apparently unrecoverable; the other seemed to be seeping through their fingers. But just when the situation seemed bleakest, the neonatal nurse warbled excitedly.

"We've got a rhythm!"

Everyone momentarily fell silent, and all eyes turned toward the oscilloscope. Jagged fluorescent waveforms of cardiac activity suddenly danced brightly across the screen—a hundred and ten beats per minute, then one-twenty. The infant's heart had finally begun beating on its own.

Wasting no time on self-congratulation, the neonatology team continued to work like a well-oiled machine. They immediately hooked the small ET tube up to an automatic respirator. Pediatric doses of cardiac and metabolic drugs were administered through the umbilical line, and an IV was begun. The little girl was identi-banded, wrapped, and carefully transferred to a nearby mobile warmer for transport to the neonatal ICU. In all, the resuscitative efforts had taken four and a half minutes.

They prayed they'd brought her back in time.

Chapter Five

THE SANDS POINT ESTATE OF SALVATORE AIELLO occupied three tastefully landscaped acres overlooking the Long Island Sound. It was nearly daybreak. Soon the rays of morning sun would be dancing across scalloped wave tops, and the view from the master bedroom's bay window would be spectacular. But the seventy-two-year-old Mafia don was no longer able to appreciate it. Nor could he appreciate any of the mob's recent successes, such as infiltrating the health-care industry. He had grown increasingly forgetful in his presenile dementia. That morning, he awakened before sunrise and gazed up at the ceiling, unable to recall where he was.

"'Morning, boss," said his bodyguard. He crossed the room and opened the curtains. "You're up early. Going to be a beautiful day out there. You could see clear to Mamaroneck."

Aiello's vacant stare continued. His mind sifted through stray thoughts, and his lips pursed, searching for words. "What hotel is this? How much we payin' for the night?"

"It's your place, Sal," said Joey, grown accustomed to such nonsense. "The old homestead. Now, you gotta get dressed. Big day today. You remember who's coming over?"

"Who?"

"Mario. He's got a line on the indictment."

Aiello's expression remained blank. "Mario?"

"Come on, boss—*Mario*. You know, your attorney?"

But even if the don did know, he couldn't remember. He narrowed his eyes and looked away, embarrassed by his forgetfulness. He was still alert enough to realize his mind was slipping, and it disturbed him to no end. He threw back the covers.

"Oh, sure. Mario."

He stared at Joseph. Something was troubling him. Sitting up, he swung his feet onto the floor, palms on his pajama-covered knees. Joseph got a robe from the closet and brought it over, holding it open for Aiello.

"Up and at 'em, Sal. We got work to do."

Salvatore Aiello looked up at his bodyguard of twenty-five years, his rheumy eyes still heavy with sleep. After a long and penetrating look, he said, "Do I know you?"

The battle for Rita's life assumed heroic proportions. Time after time, her blood pressure became almost unregisterable. Due to the septic shock, what little blood she had left was pooling in her peripheral vessels; and due to its inability to clot, what she did have oozed out through every cut and pore, a thin, scarlet testimony to her overwhelming infection. After tying off her uterine and infundibulopelvic vessels, her surgeons abandoned trying to stop her bleeding and instead concentrated on replacing the blood.

But the loss was outstripping the gain. Rita produced no urine; her kidneys had completely shut down. Using their hands, the anesthesiologists literally squeezed in plastic bags of transfusable blood, their fingers supplying greater pressure than the less-powerful automatic pumps. Rita's blood was pathetically acidotic, and its lack of oxygen was a major threat to her brain. At one point, her heart went into ventricular fibrillation. But the quick-thinking critical care fellow had anticipated that. Using a waiting defibrillator, he successfully cardioverted her.

It was approaching six A.M. They had been at it for nearly three hours, forcing in twenty-six units of blood, adjusting IVs and fluid volume, and tinkering with life-saving medications. Time was a double-edged sword: the longer their efforts went on, the greater the possibility of significant brain damage; but the more they persevered, the greater the liver's chance to regenerate essential clotting factors. Everyone in the room was dripping with sweat, their scrubs soaked. The OR resembled a battle zone. Blood splattered the floor tile, the ceiling, and the walls. Saturated pads formed a two-foot mound on the floor, and the ripped-open debris of sterile plastic and paper packaging was several inches deep.

For what seemed the hundredth time, Jenkins rewrapped the exposed uterus in a sterile, saline-soaked lap pad to keep it moist. He glanced at the blood, which pooled beneath the still-gaping incision. He blinked, then peered closer. To his admittedly fatigued eyes, for the first time the blood seemed slightly gelatinous, as if starting to congeal. Were his eyes playing tricks on him? He dipped a thumb and forefinger into the liquid pool, pressing their gloved edges lightly together, then slowly inching them apart, looking for telltale adhesiveness. To his amazement, a barely perceptible stickiness clung to the glove.

"God in heaven, she's starting to clot!"

Everyone held their breath as more tubes of blood were drawn. Within five minutes, the onset of coagulation was confirmed. It appeared that Rita's platelets were steadily rising, her fibrinogen was stable, and her pro time was reaching acceptable levels. Jenkins and Silver quickly set to work closing the incisions. This time, when they ran the uterus with a continuous suture, the blood no longer seeped out between needle puncture sites. Minutes later, they had closed the fascia and stapled the skin.

The mood in the room turned jubilant. Although everyone was exhausted from the pace and strain, they were suddenly energized by the unexpected success of their efforts. It seemed like a miracle. Fifteen minutes earlier, they had expected the worst; it seemed only a matter of time before Rita went into irreversible cardiac arrest. But owing to the vagaries of fate and time, the tables had been turned, and they snatched victory from the jaws of defeat by saving one of their own.

Or so it seemed.

Fifteen minutes later, Rita was in the OB recovery room, still too fragile to be transferred to the ICU. Her vital signs were critical, but significantly better than they had been in hours. Her color had improved, and her skin was now a pale but perceptible pink. She was still unconscious, on a respirator, and swathed in bandages, with tubes protruding from every orifice, as well as from numerous man-made openings. But amidst the smiles and kudos, the critical care fellow and recently arrived neurology chief resident remained grim. Using a portable EEG, they carefully attached leads to Rita's scalp and switched on the machine. Thirty seconds later, they had a preliminary printout, but they didn't have the heart to tell anyone.

For all intents and purposes, it looked like Rita was brain-dead.

The hospital cafeteria was in the basement, adjacent to the kitchen. The kitchen prepared over two thousand patient meals per day and food for the five hundred or so hospital employees, who ate cafeteria-style. Breakfast was by far the busiest meal. Langford patiently waited his turn in the crowded line, selecting a tasteless omelet, raspberry yogurt with granola, and a large coffee. Carrying his tray past the cashier, he scanned the room for a familiar face.

He spotted Donald Fletcher sitting alone at a small

corner table. Fletcher was a researcher in neurobiology. Balding and bespectacled, the forty-year-old scientist had an unkempt look which led many to consider him eccentric. He never wore a tie. His casual attire rarely varied: battered high-top sneakers, khaki pants, and a short-sleeve, open-collar denim shirt. His nearly bald head was ringed by long, unkempt, grayish-brown locks, which fell to his head like an electrified wreath.

Moreover, Fletcher's odd mannerisms often put people off. But not Langford. He enjoyed the researcher's peculiarities.

"Greetings, Herr Fletcher," he said, pulling up a seat. "I see you managed to keep the crowds away."

"All part of my charm. Why are you in such a good mood?"

"Good hygiene and proper diet," he said, indicating the omelet. He inspected Fletcher's tray. "And what did mommy put in your breakfast pail today? Looks like tofu, bean sprouts, and what—O. J.?"

"Carrot juice. Need something to coat my stomach before my health shake."

"Just the ticket!" said Todd. "Guaranteed to send your testosterone off the chart. And so sickeningly healthy. How can you eat that stuff every day?"

"My, you are spunky as a puppy," Fletcher said.

Langford sat down and took a large swig of coffee. "So what're you up to today?"

"The usual. Neurotransmitters and lab rats. Royce and Hobson's study has been keeping me busy for a few months now, as you well know. What about you?"

"I already told you—I'm devoting all my spare time to the Royce thing. It's far more lucrative."

"Don't tell me the dedicated young clinician is succumbing to a crass profit motive."

"Perish the thought," said Langford. "I just need the extra hundred bucks a week."

"That's what Royce pays you for doing the spinal taps, huh?"

"Yeah, for about a half dozen a day. There are two control groups, remember?" Langford said. "One is made up of non-critical ER patients who get the drug, and the other is non-critical patients who don't."

"And for this you're getting all of a hundred bucks a week?" Fletcher said. "Let's see . . . Six per day, that's around thirty a week. In private practice, they get at least two-fifty a tap. Times thirty, that's seventy-five hundred a week." He eyed Langford. "I'd say you're underpaid."

"Fletch, I'm just a humble, overworked resident—"

"You know," Fletcher continued, "there's a lot of money in spinal fluid. Biological gold. I might get something out of this spinal fluid study myself."

Langford leaned forward, surprised. "How much is in it for you?"

"Well, it's more the academic glory than the money. I'm going to get some great research papers out of it."

"I'll be damned," Langford said with a sly smile. "What is it?"

"I really can't say. It's sort of hush-hush."

"Don't give me that! Nothing's hush-hush in this hospital. Come on, this is me, your old pal Todd."

Fletcher smiled. "Sorry, old pal. I can't talk about it. You'll know, when the time's right."

Langford sat back, deflated. "Here I am, your very best friend in the world, the guy you break bread with all the time, and you're holding out on me."

Smiling but tight-lipped, Fletcher finished his carrot juice and stood up. "All in due time, very best friend. Remember what curiosity did to the cat." He picked up his tray and walked away.

Langford shook his head, feeling his irritation melt into amusement. Fletcher had never been reluctant to discuss his work. In truth, he had few people to discuss it with. He wasn't married, and his eccentricities left him with few friends, outside of Langford. All of which made Fletcher's silence the more unusual. He was not a man given to secrets unless the stakes were high. Whatever Dr. Fletcher was working on, it must be very, very big.

For a fully conscious patient, getting sleep in the ICU was a virtual impossibility. By definition, care was intensive; it was also continuous. Nurses hovered about the bedside, checking on their charges. The innumerable monitors and alarms hummed together in a discordant mechanical symphony. Only drugged or comatose patients stood any chance of escaping the sights and sounds of constant activity. But Jordan was neither. During the early morning hours, the nurses explained what happened to her. No one mentioned anything about Rita. Jordan realized that, had her injury been a little more serious, she might have died. As dawn approached, she was painfully aware of everything around her. And it was frightening.

In the six weeks since the start of her third year of med school, she'd been on her internal medicine rotation. It was a sobering, eye-opening experience. These were real people, not mere paragraphs in textbooks, their flesh and blood very much like hers, suffering from a variety of potentially fatal diseases. They were in distress, in pain, and in despair. And on more occasions than she cared to remember, they had died. The idea of just how close she came to being among them made her tremble.

Toward seven, the day-shift nurses began to filter in. As they were taking report and talking excitedly about a patient in obstetrics, a cardiac monitor sounded shrilly. Some twenty feet from Jordan's bed, an elderly black man went into cardiac arrest. As the medical team went to work, protective screens were placed around his bed to shield the other patients from the critical activity. But an opening remained. Through it, Jordan had an unobstructed view of what was going on.

She watched their ministrations with a mixture of

detachment and fascination. This wasn't her first exposure to real-time CPR. But it *was* the first time she'd witnessed it from her own hospital bed. Her sense of powerlessness added a macabre note to their caregiving. She wanted to get out of bed, to go over and lend a hand—to *do* something. But as a patient, she was utterly helpless. Head propped on a pillow, all she could do was observe.

From her new perspective, everything seemed artificial, oddly mechanical. It was as if the team wasn't caring for a person, but for an object, a thing. As she watched, team members alternately pounded on the patient's chest, gave IV medications, or administered electroshock. Nothing worked.

The seconds, then minutes, ticked by. Some twenty minutes into the arrest, Jordan detected a new tone to the team's speech. Earlier, their feverish intensity had given way to annoyance, and finally to frustration. Now, however, as more junior caregivers pitched in to help, it developed overtones of a game. It was a curious "if that doesn't work, let's try this" approach. Like pinch hitters, they all stepped up to give their best whack; and when one struck out, in stepped another. They seemed determined to keep the patient alive, as if death itself were a dare.

To a certain extent, Jordan could understand. The list of newer life-sustaining drugs at their disposal was legion. If something didn't work, they had another state-of-the-art potion to try. To those raised in the computer generation, advanced life support had familiar elements of a video game: press here, fire there, and try to elicit a response. But in this case, *nothing* worked. Finally, one of the residents persuaded the others to let him crack the patient's chest.

Dry-mouthed, Jordan couldn't take her eyes off what was happening. Across the room, everyone stepped back as the resident hastily donned gloves and readied a scalpel. Then, in one lightning stroke, his blade

slashed across the frail, bare chest. In less than thirty
seconds, he'd whittled through muscle, rib, and cartilage, until the pale-blue pericardium glistened before
him. He quickly grasped the lifeless heart in his fingers,
trying to coax it back to functioning. But inevitably,
this attempt was no more successful than its predeces-
sors.

When Jordan finally averted her eyes, she was
drenched in perspiration. Spent, she closed her eyes as
her head collapsed against the pillow.

Compared to the previous night, this morning the ER
was considerably quieter. Patients arrived at a manageable rate. The nurses and residents easily attended to
the handful of minor cases. The only life-threatening
emergency, a car-crash victim, was stable and in X ray.

When Todd began his final year of medical school
in Baltimore, he was certain he wanted to become a
general surgeon. He was good with his hands and liked
the idea of critical timing and crucial judgments. But a
month in the shock-trauma unit changed all that. Having been a city-dweller all his life—born and raised in
Baltimore, attending college at Penn—he was accustomed to being where the action was. And among all
his clinical rotations in the last two years of school,
nothing seemed more compelling than the instantaneous decisions required for traumatized patients, or those
in shock. He decided on big-city emergency medicine.

He might have remained in Baltimore—and almost
did—until his two-year relationship with a pediatric
nurse ended abruptly in early May, a month before
graduation. Langford felt an overwhelming need to
leave the area. But he had already landed a slot at Hop-
kins in the residency match, and he felt obligated to
live up to his commitment. Yet by skillfully tiptoeing
through the Internet and logging dozens of hours bill-
able by AT&T, he found a last-minute opening for a

first-year emergency medicine position in the Big Apple. He signed on without ever looking back.

As ER chief resident, he also played an administrative role. He handled disputes and juggled the on-call rotation. He reviewed interoffice mail and signed off on supply requisitions. And he compiled the weekly ER statistics: number of visits, case type, admissions, and utilization of services. By seven forty-five this morning, he was finished. There was even a little time to do a few spinal taps.

First was Georgia Parker-Ross. As a med student, she had a great deal in common with him. But professional similarities aside, he was aware that his interest in her largely stemmed from her appearance. She was young, attractive, and had a nice figure. In an ideal world, he should treat her like any other patient. But Todd Langford knew himself too well. He couldn't help it if he was attracted to intelligent women, especially when they were beautiful.

In the ICU, the nursing staff was preparing to transfer the patient to a step-down unit. They were also getting ready to receive an unusual transfer from the obstetrics unit. Off critical, Georgia no longer needed intensive care. Langford watched her from the nursing station. She was sitting up in bed, looking somewhat pale, checking her reflection in a flip-up mirror built into the tray table. She gave her head a shake, then brushed back her hair. Its auburn color had soft orange highlights. He walked toward her and smiled.

"How're you feeling?"

"Much better, thanks. At least, physically." A look of fear clouded her eyes. "The first time I came to, I didn't know where I was. I'd just had this awful nightmare."

"What about?"

"I dreamed something was wrong with my brain, that something had to be hacked out." She nervously looked at him. "Be honest with me. *Is* there something wrong?"

"No, it's just a concussion," he reassured her. "Forget about the dream."

She looked away and shivered. "I can't wait to get out of here. There was a code here a little while ago," she said, pointing shakily toward the now-empty bed. "He didn't make it. I know I should be used to it, but . . . it was horrible."

"Sick people die."

"That's not what I mean." She went on to describe the unsuccessful resuscitation attempt. "The thing is, he didn't stand a chance. I realize they have to go through the motions anyway. But it seems to me there comes a point when they should say, 'Enough already,' and call it off."

He understood. "Let me tell you a little story. I went to med school in Baltimore. This was a few years back, and things have probably changed a little. But I remember our physiology lab. We were studying pulmonary function—compliance, vital capacity, you know? Anyway, they brought in this big load of dogs. They'd all been anesthetized, I think with barbiturates. They were on a flat cart, heaped on top of one another, kind of like Auschwitz. I looked at them, and I felt sick.

"I love dogs. Always have. I even once thought of becoming a veterinarian because I hate to see animals suffer. So the sight of them piled up like cordwood tore me up. But I knew they were there for a purpose, and I knew I was the student. So four of us—we worked in a team—got a dog and went to work. We did a trach. Hooked its airway up to machines. We tested its breathing, measured all its respiratory parameters, found out what made its lungs tick. Every time it started to wake up, we gave it more drugs. In the end, we even opened its chest to watch things firsthand."

"And then what?"

"There was no saving this animal," he said with a forlorn shake of his head. "We injected it with a big air bolus, and it arrested. Look, I'm not proud of what we did. I think they do it differently now. But the point is, I remember everything vividly. I'll never forget what I learned that day. I don't want to get into whether it was right or wrong, but in a way, the dog served a noble purpose. And the same thing is true of that man. This is a teaching hospital. Almost all of our patients are on welfare. There aren't many private attendings, and God knows, no lawyers. And it's a great place to learn. There aren't as many people looking over our shoulder as in a private hospital. One year teaches the next, and they pass it on to the students, and so on. I'm not saying it's an ideal system, or even the right system. But that patient's life, however grotesquely prolonged, will wind up saving other lives."

What he said made sense, but it was an issue Jordan was still going to have to grapple with. "What happens now?" said Jordan. "With me, I mean."

"As soon as I do your spinal tap," he said brightly, "they're going to transfer you out of here. They told me you signed the consent. So are you ready for this, Georgia?"

"Jordan."

He leaned closer. "Sorry?"

"Nobody calls me Georgia, Doctor. Call me Jordan."

"You bet, as long as you call me Todd—okay?"

"Deal."

He sat on the edge of the bed. "When did you start to think straight?"

"Right after you left. It was good to wake up from the dead."

"I can imagine. How's your memory?"

"What memory?" she deadpanned.

"Well, I—"

"Just kidding," she said, a twinkle in her eye. She

lightly touched his knee. "Sorry. I couldn't resist. I remember just about everything now."

"Great. Tell me about yourself."

She arched her eyebrows. "What do you want to know?"

Everything, he thought. "Does anyone know you're here? Family, friends?"

"Only my classmates. I tried calling my roommate, but she's not home. My parents are in Maine for a few weeks."

"Where do you live?"

"A walkup in SoHo."

"So how was the party? Before you decided to rewind tapes with your head?"

She had to laugh. "It was okay."

There was so much more he wanted to ask her— about her work, her studies, and her career. And especially about herself. Captivated by her astonishingly green eyes, he could have talked with her for hours. But now was not the time. "Time to get down to business. Are you still pumped for that spinal tap?"

"As much as I'll ever be. Might as well get it over with," she ventured gamely. "I have to admit, I'm a little nervous. I have a rough idea of what you're looking for."

In fact, she had much more than a rough idea. Now well into her third year as a med student, Jordan had witnessed dozens of spinal taps, and even assisted on a few. Although the procedures were usually uneventful, they were not without potential dangers. There could be serious consequences. Nonsterile technique could lead to crippling meningitis, and a wayward needle tip could traumatize the cord, resulting in paralysis. The thought of complications was frightening.

"Could you just talk me through it?" she asked.

"Hand-holding's my specialty." Drawing the privacy-assuring curtains around the bed, Langford slid over a chair and opened the carefully wrapped lumbar puncture tray.

He had Jordan sit upright, dangling her legs over the bed. Her gown was open to expose her back. He carefully palpated her vertebrae, noting the appropriate spaces between them. Using his thumbnail, he indented her skin at the level of L-4 to serve as a mark. Then he donned sterile gloves and daubed her spine with applicator sticks soaked in iodine-based antiseptic.

"Sorry that's so cold. Can't be helped."

"I'll survive. Just let me know before you stick me."

"I will." He verbally walked her through the procedure, numbing her back with local anesthetic, repositioning her, and preparing the needle. Holding the four-inch needle between his thumb and forefinger, he pierced the skin and slowly advanced its tip, feeling for obstructions. Sensing when the needle reached the ligament, he lightly pushed it forward, through the epidural space. He stopped every few millimeters to remove the stylet and check for flow. Finally, a glistening drop of fluid appeared at the hub. He sensed her muscles stiffening.

"We're in, Jordan. How're you doin'?"

She no longer heard him. Doctor-in-training though she was, being on the receiving end of medical care was both humbling and intimidating. Moreover, ever since she'd injured her back in a childhood swimming injury, she'd harbored an illogical fear of something happening to her spine. As she fully accepted what was being done to her, her mind retreated to a refuge bounded by panic and terror. She suddenly saw herself partially paralyzed, or a cripple. Mere inches away from her, a doctor she didn't know from Adam, no matter how seemingly capable, pleasant, and good-looking, was in the process of plunging an enormous needle through her back. To get her spinal fluid. Near her spinal cord. And if—

After what seemed like an interminably long time, he finally withdrew the needle. "Okay, all done." He removed the sterile drapes and gloves. "I'm going to want you to lie flat for a couple of hours."

Jordan slowly exhaled, immensely relieved. "I was really hoping to get out of here soon."

"Let's wait until a little later, okay?" He helped her swing her legs up and over the mattress as she reclined. "You were out of it for a couple of hours, and we'll want to keep an eye on you for a while. Your preliminary labs should be back by then."

"And if they're normal?"

"If they're normal, which they probably will be, you're outta here. Now get some rest, okay?" He smiled and turned to leave.

She reached out and took his hand, grateful for his reassuring patience. "Thanks for making it easy for me, Todd."

"My pleasure. I'll stop by and check on you around lunchtime."

She followed him with her eyes, wanting very much for that time to arrive soon.

Suddenly, Jordan was tired. The nightmare of several hours before was gone but not forgotten. Afterwards, she'd been afraid to go back to sleep. But now she was exhausted. It had been a long night and an eventful morning. She lay back and closed her eyes. In a corridor nearby, not quite out of earshot, two young nurses chattered away, about, of all things, Todd Langford.

Feeling drowsy, Jordan halfheartedly listened to their banter. Soon her mind began to drift, gliding lazily toward sleep. In the last vestiges of her consciousness, with slumber softly calling, she dimly heard one of the nurses say, "Sure, he's handsome, but I wouldn't want to go out with him." Somehow, Jordan immediately knew the woman was lying.

Her eyes flashed open, and she bolted upright in bed.

Heart again pounding, she felt her whole body begin to tremble. She was terrified something horribly wrong was going on inside her skull.

My God, she thought, what's *happening* to me?

Chapter Six

DR. FLETCHER WAS THE FIRST TO ENTER THE LAB AT seven A.M. He put his briefcase on his desk and leaned toward his computer monitor.

"Now, where were we?" he said, gaze narrowing. "Aha!"

He emitted a high-pitched cackle and rubbed his hands excitedly together. Fletcher was a man given to emotional extremes, and his eagerness often carried a frenzied, overly excited quality, which could be frightening. He was dedicated to his research, and after he began a project, he was committed to seeing it through.

The phone rang. He frowned, annoyed at the distraction. Never much of a conversationalist, he preferred to have his assistant take messages. But it was early, and his lab tech hadn't yet arrived. He picked up the phone with exasperation.

"May I speak with Dr. Fletcher, please?" a voice said.

He couldn't place the accent. "Who's this?"

"My name is Scarpatta, and—"

"Scarpatta?" he asked, wondering where he'd heard the name before.

There was a pause. "This *is* Dr. Fletcher, isn't it?"

"You got it. Think you could you call back later? I'm a little tied up right now."

"If you don't mind, this will only take a moment.

I'd like to arrange a meeting, Doctor. To discuss something beneficial for both of us.''

''And what might that be?''

''What you found in your research. With the rats.''

Fletcher tilted his head into the phone, as if to keep the conversation from being overheard. His voice lowered to a whisper.

''Exactly what research are you talking about?''

''Your experiments with the new compound. The one that improves their performance.''

Fletcher's eyes widened. Stunned, he straightened up, nostrils flaring. ''Everything that goes on in this lab is confidential. How do you know about that?''

''I won't betray your work, believe me. But what you discovered is far too important to be shared just yet. Which is why I called—''

''It is *Dr.* Scarpatta, I hope?'' Fletcher asked, annoyed.

''Does that matter? Please be patient, Dr. Fletcher. This will prove mutually beneficial. The arrangement I propose—''

''You better believe it matters. If you *are* a doctor, which I doubt, talking about capitalizing on an unpublished research project is damned unethical. And if you're not, we shouldn't even be talking. Now, tell me how you found out about this!''

''Good day, Doctor.''

The caller rang off. Fletcher stared at the phone, then back at his monitor, before hanging up. The source of the leak was obvious.

''Damn computers,'' he mumbled. ''Nothing's safe anymore.''

One of Fletcher's most endearing qualities was his out-of-sight, out-of-mind mentality. No sooner had he hung up than the phone incident was relegated to some obscure part of his cerebral cortex. He returned his attention to the video monitor.

During the night, he had run a special program to

verify all the results of the spinal fluid study he'd been working on for months. The program relied on data supplied by a unique piece of medical equipment, a new autoanalyzer. The prototype machine, the only one of its kind in existence, combined the techniques of biodiffusion, gas chromatography, and gel electrophoresis to determine "unknowns" in CSF samples. During the past few weeks, Fletcher had grown more and more curious about something he was detecting in the CSF of patients in the Royce and Hobson study. He'd already reached preliminary conclusions, but he had to verify everything before allowing himself a pat on the head.

His discovery dovetailed with the same study Todd Langford was getting paid for, to do spinal taps. What he'd discovered was that a particular group of patients—critically ill trauma victims, often on life support—seemed to secrete a highly unusual chemical in their cerebrospinal fluid. At least temporarily. He'd injected the rats in cage twelve with small aliquots of CSF extract derived from trauma victims. Within twenty-four hours of injection, something astonishing began to happen. The usually lethargic animals became much more active, moving vigorously and behaving like their less obese cousins. But more significantly, they demonstrated remarkably heightened cerebral abilities. Simply put, they seemed *smarter*.

At first, he thought it was an error. Yet it wasn't just one rat that had heightened faculties; it was every one in the cage. Every one that had been injected. Their performance on the Breen-Richter test was striking. Suspecting an inherent flaw in the test, Fletcher subjected the rats to half a dozen standard psychological tests over the ensuing few days. Each time, the rats' performances were remarkable.

It soon became apparent that something astonishing was happening to the experimental animals, something he could only attribute to the injection. The objective then switched to determining precisely what had occurred. The most likely conclusion was that the rats' enhanced performance was due to the new drug, the alpha blocker given to Royce's study patients. Yet when Fletcher analyzed the data further, he found that it wasn't.

Notably, however, not every patient in the study received the new alpha blocker. All were supposed to, but occasionally, due to pharmacy error or clerical slip-up, some did not. Even more important were the findings when Fletcher took the next logical step, injecting a different group of test rats with nothing but the drug itself. Not one animal in the group exhibited increased deductive powers. In fact, several became sleepier and confused, a common side effect of that class of drugs.

No, what had been happening to the Fat Rats in cage nine was something different. It was something bizarre and heretofore undescribed, something that pertained to trauma victims in the CSF study. But what? He wasn't familiar with any known biologic compound—compounds such as epinephrine, cortisol, or endorphins—which could cause such behavior. No, it had to be something new. Something different. Something as yet unreported.

That was where the new autoanalyzer came in. After centrifuging off cellular constituents such as white cells and microbes, the machine painstakingly identified each component of the test subjects' CSF. Drugs and chemicals were patiently identified and isolated. Electrolytes were quantified. Potentially neuroactive compounds, like cytokines and prostaglandins, were recognized. In the end, what remained was precisely what Fletcher hoped to find: a molecular breakthrough in neurobiology.

The prototype analyzer was equal to the task, proving its worth when Fletcher saddled it with the advanced biochemical assignment of molecular identification. After an arduous thirty-six hours, the ma-

chine produced a printout of the new compound, three-
dimensionally depicted on the computer monitor. It was
a large peptide, one hundred seventy-two amino acids
long. Fletcher was amazed something that size had
eluded the biochemists. For a few moments, he delib-
erated what to name it. Finally, because it gave his
experimental animals heightened cognitive abilities, he
called it cognopsin.

As the results of the verification program appeared
on his monitor, Fletcher finally allowed himself an easy
grin. This was everything he dreamed of. Beside the
monitor was a VCR with a built-in seven-inch screen.
He popped in the previous night's video and hit the
PLAY button. As they'd done every night for the past
few weeks, the injected Fat Rats worked their Breen-
Richter magic. His eyes alternating between the screen
and the monitor, an enthusiastic Fletcher let out another
maniacal cackle, absolutely elated about what the discovery would mean for mankind.

At seven-thirty, his lab assistant arrived. Twenty-five-
year-old Michael Molloy was a doctoral candidate in
neurobiology. Dark-haired, of medium height and
build, he had an acquired nerdiness that belied his earlier years as a competitive gymnast.

"We're done, Mike," Fletcher said, trying to sound
matter-of-fact. "All the results are verified."

Molloy's eyes widened. "You're kidding!"

Seeing Molloy's reaction, Fletcher abandoned his attempted nonchalance and smiled broadly, brimming
with enthusiasm. "Can you believe it? All these weeks
we suspected we were onto something big! But in the
back of my mind, I was always afraid the final computer analysis would come up with something wrong.
But it didn't, Mike!" Fletcher said, eyes blazing. "We
actually did it!"

Now smiling himself, Molloy rushed over to pump
his boss's hand. "That's fantastic, Dr. Fletcher!"

But Fletcher couldn't linger on self-congratulation. His smile disappeared as he suddenly recalled his earlier phone conversation. "Mike, does anyone outside the lab have access to our data?"

"Which data? The Fat Rats?"

"Right."

Molloy considered it, then shook his head. "I haven't mentioned it. Have you?"

"Not to a soul."

"You haven't left your computer on, have you? When we're gone?"

"Well . . ."

"I told you about that, Doc. Now, what's the problem?"

"Oh, nothing." He waved his hand, not wanting to discuss it. After all, he had nothing concrete to worry about, only snippets of a conversation with an unknown man. "All our data's rock solid. We're really onto something here, Mike."

"You sold me on that, Dr. F." He smiled and shook his head. "Next thing you know, those fat little furballs will be doing the *Times* crossword. I bet this is Nobel Prize material. You're going to get a great research paper out of this."

"Many, *many* papers. This is the discovery of the decade, my friend. Not to mention an award-winning thesis for you. You honestly haven't mentioned this to anyone, right?"

Molloy put a finger to his lips. "Mum's the word, Dr. F. But didn't you say you were going to tell Dr. Royce today?"

"Have to. He's chief of staff."

It was mid-morning when Langford was beeped. Picking up the nearest phone, he dialed the extension.

"Todd," one of the nurses said, "sorry to be a bother. But I want to touch base with you on a patient you admitted last night. A woman named Parker-Ross."

He was instantly alert. "Is there a problem with her tap?"

"No, that went fine. But she started acting a little strange after that, sort of freaked-out. Something seems to be scaring her, but she won't open up about it."

"Did someone tell her about that pregnant classmate of hers?"

"No," said the nurse, "we all agreed to keep quiet about that for now."

"Did you talk to the resident in charge, Dr. Minkoff?" he said.

"We asked her if she wanted us to page him, but she said if we paged anybody, she'd prefer it were you."

"Tell you what," Todd said. "Just calm her down, and I'll speak with Minkoff. If it's okay with him, I'll be up to see her later."

They met in the administrator's office at noon. The impressive professional group included the administrator, the hospital counsel, the director of nursing, and the chiefs of obstetrics and neurology, all seated around a conference table. When Jeff finally showed up he was wearing faded jeans and a stained white dress shirt. He looked exhausted, bedraggled, and forlorn.

"Thanks for coming, Mr. Donninger," said the administrator. "Sit down, please. I know this is a difficult time for you. I understand the baby's doing well?"

He nodded. "They just took her off the respirator," he said. There were dark circles under his eyes, and the lines in his forehead were deep. "It's a little early to tell, but they think she's going to be okay." He stared at the administrator for a long moment. "What do you want?"

Around the table, everyone shifted uncomfortably. Finally, the attorney cleared his throat. "It might be premature, but we'd like to know what your intentions are."

Donninger eyed them peculiarly. "My intentions? You mean, whether or not I'm going to sue the hospital?"

"Now wait a minute," cut in the chief of OB. "We've done nothing—"

"Hold on, Martin," interrupted the administrator, raising his hand. He looked at Jeffrey with an expression of compassion. "Look, Mr. Donninger. Jeff. May I call you Jeff?"

"No."

"Fair enough. The way we see it, you have every right to be angry. Even resentful. What's happened in the past twelve hours has been a nightmare."

"Get to the point," Jeff said impatiently.

"All right. So far as a lawsuit goes, that's certainly your prerogative," the administrator said. "If you choose that route, the hospital will defend itself vigorously. But believe it or not, we feel almost as badly about this as you do. It's not every day that two of our finest students wind up critically ill in our own institution. But that aside, what we'd really like to know is how you want to proceed in regard to your wife's condition."

"What the devil are you talking about?"

"We're referring to your wife's clinical state," said the attorney.

"What are you guys doing, sitting here pontificating? My wife's upstairs on a respirator, and she might not get off it alive!"

"We're all aware of that," Connie Swenson said calmly. Dr. Swenson was chief of neurology. "You see, that's precisely the point. We can't make an exact diagnosis on her for about another eighteen hours— say, six tomorrow morning."

"What do you mean, exact diagnosis? Isn't what happened to her obvious?"

"Not exactly," Swenson explained. It was only six hours earlier that Swenson had received a call from the med school dean, asking for assistance with a critically ill third-year med student. "You're an intelligent man, Mr. Donninger. I won't mince words with you. Right now, for all intents and purposes, your wife is brain-dead. Clinically, it appears that she's infarcted her brainstem from the severe shock. But a diagnosis of brain death isn't usually made until twenty-four hours elapse, which brings us to tomorrow morning. Even though that's a little while off, we'd like to get a feel right now for how you plan to handle it."

"You're talking about codes, DNRs, stuff like that?"

"Exactly."

"So you've written her off, is that what you're saying?" There was anguish in Jeff's voice. "It's completely hopeless? There haven't been any cases like this where the patient comes out of it?"

"Well," the neurologist said with a sigh, "I have seen it happen. Maybe once every two or three years in situations like this. But I've gone over all her data very closely. Realistically, Mr. Donninger, for your wife to show any kind of improvement, it'd take nothing short of a miracle."

The door to Fletcher's lab swung open. A man dressed in a starched white lab coat swept in. There was a no-nonsense air of authority about him. Tall and distinguished-looking, he had an aquiline nose and long, slightly wavy gray hair just going to white, brushed straight back atop a broad forehead. His keen gray eyes held an intelligent look, and his voice was deep and resonant.

"What's this about a discovery, Dr. Fletcher?" Royce asked. "You said it was urgent, that it concerns the study."

"Well, yes and no. I mean, it does. Indirectly."

Dr. Royce smiled inwardly at the researcher's eccentricities. Fletcher wasn't being evasive; that was just the way he spoke. "I'd appreciate it if you got to the point," Royce said.

"Sure. You see, it's like this. In the weeks since the study began, we've been analyzing CSF extracts of study patients, as you know. Anyway, about a week ago, we began to get some very interesting data on rats injected with the extract."

"Interesting? What kind of data?"

"Behavioral stuff, the way they acted. It was, well, spectacular."

Royce's lids narrowed.

"The rats we use are a particular strain called OB/OB," Fletcher went on. "We call them the Fat Rats because they're genetically obese. They're pretty slow and dull, but easy to work with. But after we injected them, their behavior went straight off the charts."

"I'm still not following you."

"You've heard of the Breen-Richter test?" Fletcher said.

"I'm familiar with it."

"In these rats, the onset-reward time is usually around sixteen minutes. But within a day of getting injected, the rats learned how to earn a reward within fifteen seconds."

"Fifteen seconds? That's unbelievable."

"Take a look at this." He led Royce to his desktop VCR. Over the next few minutes, he played before and after tapes of the Fat Rats, ending with their previous night's performance. The chief of staff looked on in silent astonishment.

"See that?" Fletcher continued excitedly. "A quarter minute! That's absolutely phenomenal! It's an increase in their cognitive ability no one would have thought possible. And after running a computer analysis of all the variables, the only explanation is that their performance was related to something in the injection.''

''This is incredible, Fletcher.''

''Now, we inject rats with CSF extract all the time, and none of them has ever showed anything *remotely* like this. So the question was, what was causing it? What was so unique about this extract from critically ill trauma patients? Naturally, the first thing I thought was that it was due to the study drug.''

Royce slowly nodded. ''A side effect, yes. Interesting.''

''Only thing was, it wasn't. The drug had nothing to do with it.''

''How can you be sure of that?''

''Simple. Sometimes, for one reason or another, the drug wasn't given. Clerical error, whatever. Yet even when the drug was omitted, the results were the same— provided the fluid came from critically ill trauma patients. So, if it wasn't the drug, what was it?''

Royce continued to be amused by Fletcher's enthusiasm. ''I presume you're going to tell me.''

''To make a long story short, these trauma patients seem to be producing something novel in their CSF. Something which makes the Fat Rats smart and peppy.''

''Really, Dr. Fletcher,'' said Royce. ''That's reaching a bit, don't you think? Human CSF has been closely studied since the middle of last century. The only thing unique about it might be the presence of a new infection or drug metabolite. Believe me, everything about human CSF is already known.''

''Not quite, Dr. Royce.'' Fletcher handed him a computer printout.

''What do you have here?''

''Something never before discovered. An absolutely fascinating neuropeptide called cognopsin.''

''Cognopsin? I don't think I've ever heard of it.''

''Of course not,'' said Fletcher, with a modest smile.

"That's just the name I gave it. It'll take an international committee on standardized nomenclature to figure out the precise biochemical name for all those amino acids."

"Let me see if I understand this," said Royce, his own enthusiasm mounting. "You're saying that you've discovered a compound in the cerebrospinal fluid extracts of trauma patients—"

"—Critically *ill* trauma patients. That's an important distinction."

"And it's a compound that enhances the cognitive function of a group of fat white rats?"

"Physical functioning, too. And it not only enhances, it makes them near geniuses!"

"That's a rather bold claim, Dr. Fletcher. Assuming that what you say about your experiments is true, what I don't understand is this. As good as everyone knows you are, there are a few other pretty sophisticated neurobiologists in this world, all with the latest equipment. How is it possible that they all overlooked a compound like this?"

"That's the sixty-four-thousand-dollar question, Dr. Royce. I had trouble figuring that out myself. The way I see it, no one has checked the spinal fluid at the most critical time."

"And what time would that be?"

"When they're moribund, on respirators. Sometimes barely resuscitated. You know Todd Langford, chief resident in emergency medicine? Todd told me how his end of the study works. And according to him, tapping patients in that condition isn't done all that often."

"That's not true. A spinal tap in severe neuro cases is absolutely indicated."

"But I'm not talking about just bad neuro cases. I'm referring to things like gunshot wounds, or messy car wrecks. Langford says these patients get tapped too, even if they've just recovered from a cardiac arrest."

Royce nodded. "It's part of the study protocol we

worked out with the drug manufacturer.''

''I'm not questioning whether it's wrong or right. I don't give a damn about that. All I'm saying is, it's unusual. It's an area that hasn't been studied a lot, right?''

''Agreed.''

''And if it hasn't been studied, how could it be found? But to my way of thinking, that's only part of it. I think another likely reason it hasn't been discovered is that the compound doesn't stick around very long. I'm no biochemical expert, but I'd wager it's pretty rapidly metabolized.''

''What makes you say that?''

Fletcher pointed to aspects of the compound's structure. ''See these methylated ends, and those hydroxyl groups? I could be wrong, but they're usually found in compounds that are quickly degraded. Neurotransmitters, for example. If I'm right, cognopsin is metabolized almost as rapidly as it's produced. Unless you look for it at precisely the right time—which is where Todd comes in—it just ain't there.''

''So nobody discovered it before because the patients weren't tapped at the right time—they were tapped too late, or because this cognopsin's not present when they *do* look for it?''

Fletcher nodded.

''But that begs another question, doesn't it?''

''Its function?''

''Exactly. What kind of purpose could such a transiently produced compound have?''

''I don't know,'' Fletcher said, shaking his head. ''We don't have any data on that yet, but I've got some theories. We start with a neuropeptide that's basically produced only when patients are near death. If you administer that compound to a bunch of fat, lazy rats, they become smart and robust. To me, that suggests two target organs: the heart and the brain. Those are the systems ultimately responsible for physical and mental activity. They're also the two organs that absolutely have to be kept alive in times of dire physical crisis. With me so far?"

"Keep going."

"What I'm saying is, in a near-death crisis, the body produces a new compound intended to keep the heart and brain alive. If enough is produced, those two organs survive, and the peptide's quickly metabolized. If not enough is produced, if the injury's too great, or if it's metabolized too fast, the organism succumbs." He nodded to himself. "Q.E.D."

Royce pursed his lips, deep in thought. "That's a fascinating theory, Fletcher. Remarkable, really. It would be wonderful if it turned out to be true."

Fletcher waved a hand toward the cages. "The proof's in the rats, Dr. Royce."

"Maybe, maybe not," said the chief of staff, ever the pragmatist. "If it's so rapidly metabolized, why isn't it rapidly metabolized in your experimental animals?"

"I'm not sure. I just know it isn't. It could be that cognopsin's only rapidly metabolized in the critically ill, the same as it's only produced in those patients."

For several minutes, Royce was silent. Hands clasped behind his back, he slowly began to stroll through the lab, his pensive gaze directed toward the ceiling. "I congratulate you on your fantastic work. But this will have to be tested, of course. Any theory's just fancy rhetoric until proved beyond a doubt."

"I couldn't agree more."

"I certainly hope it pans out, Fletcher. Wouldn't it be remarkable if this cognopsin worked in humans the way it does in rats? Think of what miracles could be accomplished!"

A suddenly animated Fletcher rose from his chair. "I *have* thought about it, Dr. Royce! I was thinking about it all night! I was just waiting until I verified the data. But now that I have, there's no *way* I can keep

this quiet any longer!'' His earlier disturbing conversation with the man called Scarpatta flashed through
his mind. He debated mentioning it, but decided against
it for now. "A discovery like this is much, much too
important to bury in some obscure research paper until
it's published.''

"What do you suggest?"

"I say we go public! Maybe hold a press conference,
I don't know. You know more about that stuff than I
do. As chief of staff, you're much more credible than
I am. I mean, look at me. Who are people going to
believe? Me, the weird scientist, or someone with a
reputation like yours?''

Royce chuckled. "You're far too modest, Dr.
Fletcher. But tell me. Who else knows about this discovery?''

"Just me and Mike," he said, gesturing to his assistant. He again decided not to bring up the possible
computer eavesdropper. "And now, you.''

Royce struck a conciliatory posture. "I understand
your excitement, Doctor. And your eagerness. But in
my position, I've been down this road before. Trust me
on this: there are times to be generous, and times to
husband one's resources.''

"But—"

"We *will* go public, I promise you that. A few days,
a week at the outside. Let's get all our ducks in a row
first, shall we? Dot the i's and cross the t's, make sure
we don't make fools of ourselves in front of CNN?''

Fletcher sat down with a sigh. "If that's what you
think is best.''

"I do. Let me iron out the kinks. Just get everything
down for me on paper . . . It is on paper, right?''

"On computer disk. And I keep a log.''

"Right. Very good, then. You really have done a fine
job here, Fletcher. First rate.'' He turned to go, then
paused. "It's just the critically ill patients, then? You
haven't found anyone else who generates cognopsin?''

"Pretty much. There is one other possible patient I just started working on. Got her fluid just a little while ago." He picked up a piece of paper. "Some woman in her twenties with a concussion. Not critical, going home today. I'd say she's a possible."

"Any explanation for the cognopsin in her CSF?"

"She doesn't fit the profile, but I'm still working her up."

"Good. Keep me posted." Royce turned away in a regal swirl of flying coattails.

Chapter Seven

"HEY, ANTHONY, YOU GONNA SIT DOWN WITH US OR what?" said Vito.

Anthony covered the receiver with his hand. "Gimme a second, I got Joey on the phone."

"I tell ya, it don't look good," Vito directed to the man beside him. "We don't need to be shown up like that. Our own *union*, for chrissake."

"They better show a little more respect. I'm gonna have a talk with them."

"Yeah, they better," said the olive-skinned Vito. The man who was on the phone rejoined them at the lunch table. "They gotta watch their mouth. You hear that, Anthony? The great Dominic Merendino's gonna talk with those fuckin' union clowns."

"Is that right? About time. I don't care if they're hospital workers or not. They don't run the show, we do."

The three men returned to their pastas. The dilemma with the union was typical of the problems encountered by the mob when it tried to involve itself in the business side of medicine. For months, the Manhattan leadership of the hospital and health workers' union had been making waves. Unaccustomed to such dissension within the ranks, the mobsters felt something had to be done. The only question was what. But right now, as they lunched at a Garden City clam house, they had more pressing matters on their minds.

"Was Joey with the boss?" Vito asked Anthony.

"He just came from there. Says the old man's babbling again."

"That ain't good," Vito said, shaking his head. "What happened to my grandmother, first she was talkin' nonsense, y'know what I'm sayin'? Soon she didn't know her own kids."

"I don't believe it," said Anthony.

"Well, believe it," said Vito. "That's how the freakin' disease works."

There were frowns and lowered heads around the table. What was happening to their boss was unthinkable. Salvatore Aiello had been don to their family for fifteen years, and he had more secrets in his head than any of them could ever hope to acquire. Unfortunately, he had just been indicted on a federal racketeering charge, and the odds were better than even that he was going to go away for a while. The idea that his growing dementia might inadvertently lead him to betray mob confidences was unacceptable. Something had to be done.

"This new stuff, it really works?" asked Anthony.

"That's what our hospital contact claims," said Dominic. "We're running out of options."

"But shouldn't we test it or somethin'?"

"It's like this," said Anthony. "The other night, Vinnie—you remember Vinnie?"

"Lotsa muscle, used to go to med school in Milan?"

"Right. Last night, he did a spinal tap on some skeevatz who produces it. He's purifying it now. We should have a dose ready soon."

"That gives me the creeps," said Vito. "Ain't there another source, like someone healthy?"

"Now that you mention it," said Merendino, "there just might be."

*   *   *

"What I find remarkable," said Dr. Royce, "is just
how little we really know about the human brain. Every
breakthrough shows more gaps in our knowledge."

"It's one of the things that got me interested in this
field in the first place," agreed Hobson. "The search
for answers never stops."

Although Drs. Royce and Hobson shared similar professional philosophies, they were hardly cast from the
same physical mold. Royce was the more statuesque of
the two, possessing a tall, distinguished bearing, con-
trasted with Hobson's shorter, more rotund appearance.
There was no doubt who the leader was. Although
Royce could be very soft-spoken around patients, he
was indisputably the more dignified man, with a com-
manding presence and occasionally imperious tone. But
philosophically, they were somewhat conservative, although this was not to say that they were old-fashioned.
Medically, their approach to patient care was quite
liberal, even *avant garde*. They were champions of innovation and newer medical techniques. And both were
also superb physicians.

"Indeed," said Royce. "Speaking of answers, I just
want you to know that the building's repairs are moving right along."

"Good. I never thought we'd find a use for that decrepit old place."

Trained as geriatricians, they'd made their reputations investigating the neurologic aspects of various
chronic diseases, particularly Alzheimer's Disease.
Royce, in particular, had garnered nationwide renown
for pioneering breakthrough drug treatments for the de-
bilitating condition. They had risen through the ranks,
until Royce was chief of the medical staff, and Hobson
was head of emergency medicine. Now they were alone
in the chief of staff's rear office. Hobson filled Royce's
cup with coffee, to which the taller man added artificial
sweetener.

Hobson sipped his coffee. "The building seemed

like a good investment at first, but until recently, I figured it'd keep collecting dust forever."

"And it might have, if this opportunity hadn't come along," said Royce. "It's perfect for what we have in mind. I think we can turn it into a first-rate facility. It's one thing to use it to store all our research materials. But to turn a dilapidated warehouse into a modern clinical center? That calls for a whole new interior design."

"What's the latest on how long the renovations will take?"

"They should finish the cleaning and re-framing this weekend," said Royce. "After that, ten days. A week if we're lucky."

"Are all the estimates in?"

Royce nodded. "Just about. They're pretty steep. This project would normally take months. For the kind of twenty-hours-a-day rush-job and triple work crew we want, it's going to cost us."

"We figured it would," said Hobson, pursing his lips. "We've got to get the first patients there as soon as possible. Now, what about Dr. Fletcher? He's not aware we already knew the results of the Fat Rats study?"

"Doesn't have a clue. Totally in the dark. If he has the slightest inkling how truly earth-shattering his discovery is—from a financial standpoint—he certainly doesn't let on. It's amazing someone who works in this hospital actually thinks he can keep secrets from us."

"What do you suppose he wants?" asked Hobson.

"Fletcher is an excellent researcher, but hopelessly out of touch. He's saddled with that ridiculously egalitarian notion of share and share alike. He doesn't realize that in today's medical climate, that just doesn't cut it. These days, no matter what the quality of medical care, the bottom line always wins out over fairness," said Royce.

"Let me tell you something about Donald Fletcher," said Hobson. "I've known him for at least ten years, and he's one of the most brilliant researchers on staff. He's done a great deal for this hospital. Eccentric, yes. But he's also a complete idealist, and to my way of thinking, that's something this world could use a little more of.''

"Idealism has its place," Royce conceded. "But to tell you the truth, it scares the hell out of me. His scruples make him a loose cannon. Unfortunately, he's not the practical type who'd want to come on board with us. Look, we can't have him running around shooting his mouth off before we know precisely what we're dealing with. The discovery's his, sure. But at this point, a whining do-gooder could ruin everything.''

"Do you think he was serious about going public?" asked Hobson.

"I know he wants to. But I think I persuaded him to keep quiet, at least for now. I just hope he doesn't have a change of heart.''

"I'll tell you what," said Hobson. "I know him better than you do. I'm sure he'll listen to reason. Let me have a talk with him and go over the need for a low profile, at least for now. I think he can be convinced that when the time is right, we'll issue a joint announcement that'll please everybody.''

Throughout the hospital, they prayed for Rita's miracle. They prayed in groups and individually; in corridors and conference rooms; in the ORs and on the wards. Toward the end of the day shift, virtually no one who worked in the hospital was unaware of Rita's tragedy. The situation was dark and depressing. The only saving grace, it seemed, was the gorgeous little baby Adrianna, who was fast becoming everyone's favorite in the NICU.

Karen Schroeder was distracted. The thirty-two-year-old nurse's mind was on the after-hours drinks she'd be having with a fireman she'd met earlier in the day.

Not that she didn't enjoy her work. An RN "float," she worked wherever she was needed on the med-surg wards. For the past week, she'd been assigned to the neuro floor.

What could try the patience of others proved rewarding work for her. By and large, many of the patients were older and handicapped, victims of stroke or chronic neurological diseases. Some reminded her of her grandfather, an eighty-year-old retired carpenter with whom she had a loving relationship. Thus she lingered by the bedside of a man in his seventies, a patient suffering from both Alzheimer's and Parkinson's disease.

"Just one or two spoonfuls, Mr. Stampf," she cooed, mixing sugar into the oatmeal.

"Sure."

She eyed the old man. He usually said almost nothing, and what he did was often unintelligible. Most of the time he just sat there staring vacantly ahead, his body moved by little tremors. Today, however, he was looking at the food rather eagerly. Although his hair was wild and unkempt, his blue eyes glinted with uncharacteristic awareness.

"Even one word's a mouthful for you, isn't it?" Karen said. She leaned over and adjusted his pillow, fluffing it up behind his head. "You must've had one helluva nap this morning."

"Yep."

"Pretty good, Mr. Stampf. You're becoming a regular conversationalist. Soon I'll know everything about you. Why don't we do something? I'll ask you questions, and you try to answer me. Even if you can't, maybe you can just nod, okay?"

To her absolute astonishment, he smiled and winked at her. It was a warm and charming smile, a rascal's wink. She sat up straight and stared at him, a bit unnerved. Had they changed his medications? She'd have to check the chart. "If I didn't know better, I'd think you were flirting with me."

He let out a throaty chuckle and arched his eyebrows. Then he looked at his food and silently opened his mouth.

"Now that's more like it," Karen said. She wasn't sure what was happening with this patient, but she was more comfortable dealing with his silence than his replies. She stirred the cereal and placed a spoonful in his mouth. "There. How's that?"

"Not bad," he said. "Considering."

She stopped what she was doing and looked at him. To her surprise, he was looking back at her with disturbing clarity. He seemed to be taking stock of her. She suppressed a shiver, feeling her heart beat faster. Her voice was tremulous.

"Considering what?"

"Considering that it tastes like shit, and that you've got my arms tied down in these goddamn restraints."

Karen's eyes went wide, and her jaw dropped. The bowl fell from her trembling fingers and shattered on the floor. Her face ashen, she pulled away and leaped out of her chair. "Jenine!" she shrieked, racing toward the nursing station. "Oh my God, Jenine!"

Chapter Eight

WITH AN INFLUX OF MEDICAL CHAOS, LANGFORD'S AF-
ternoon proved emotionally brutal. Fortunately, however, the afternoon was also busy. The city took no
hiatus from carnage, and the emergency ward was
crowded. He found the pace a welcome distraction. By
two P.M., few of his colleagues, other than Meyerson,
continued to notice or comment on his mood. As he
was about to go up to see Jordan, he was approached
by one of the nurses.

"What's going on, Todd? Do you feel all right? If I
didn't know better, I'd think you were sick."

"It's been a real rough shift." He looked away and
shook his head.

"I know something that'll cheer you up," Jenine
said. "You remember Albert Stampf, a patient you admitted about two weeks ago?"

"Stampf?" He furrowed his brow. "Oh, yeah.
Funny little guy. His family dumped him. Alzheimer's,
right?"

"That's him." She nodded. "Anyway, the weirdest
thing happened a little while ago. Karen was feeding
him, okay? Usually, Albert just sits there sucking on
his gums, rolling his fingers, and staring off into the
distance. But this time, she was about to give him his
cornflakes, when he starts having a regular conversation with her."

"The Albert Stampf I admitted could no sooner have a conversation than he could do the Macarena."

"That's what I thought. But you should have seen him, out of bed, walking around like a twenty-year-old. At first I thought he was going to have a heart attack, I never saw someone his age with so much energy. It was wild!"

"Did they change his meds or something?"

"I don't think so. It was really incredible. It was like his Parkinson's was gone. And his Alzheimer's? He was no more demented than you are."

He smiled and shrugged. "Who knows? Maybe someone's come up with a new cure for old age. Funny. Renee, on seven, told me something just like that. There was this woman I admitted maybe ten days ago in CHF. Big beer drinker, with a wet brain, terminal alcoholic psychosis. I was ready to write her off. But Renee tells me that yesterday, the patient was suddenly bouncing around like a woman twenty years younger. Her lungs were dry, her head was clear, and her edema was gone. It was like she'd had some kind of a transplant. No one can figure it."

"You think that's related to Stampf?"

He shook his head. "I doubt it. The way I figure it, it's just a couple of goners having a good day. Stranger things have happened." But despite his protestations, he felt a lingering sense of curiosity—and of concern.

Mike Molloy was off on his lunch break when the call came in to the lab.

"Dr. Fletcher, this is Scarpatta again," said the voice. "I was wondering if you had a chance to reconsider my suggestion."

Fletcher was instantly unnerved. "I told you before— I don't know who you are, or what you want," he said tremulously. "But whatever goes on here is confidential. You and I have nothing to talk about."

"Really, Doctor, I think you should reconsider. The

benefit to both of us could be enormous, and—"

Fletcher slammed down the phone before the man could continue. He had no idea what was going on, but he was definitely worried. First this man Scarpatta, and then Dr. Royce's implication that he keep his mouth shut . . . or was he imagining it? Unaccountably nervous, Fletcher's eyes flitted about the lab. He knew he had no reason to feel guilty, but for some reason, he couldn't shake the feeling that he was being watched.

Metropolitan Hospital was a hotbed of people who played the numbers. This was especially true since the mob had begun infiltrating the ranks of hospital workers, and the daily winning numbers were often chalked inconspicuously on little-noticed blackboards throughout the building. It wasn't long before enterprising capitalists began taking bets on Rita's survival. The going odds were a hundred-to-one against. By late afternoon, a cottage industry had sprung up. Money changed hands in locker rooms, hallways, and parking lots. It wasn't long before ten thousand dollars had been wagered, less than ten percent of it directed toward Rita's survival.

Langford finally had time to go up to see Jordan. Outside the lobby elevator, a heavyset woman of about forty greeted him. He recognized her immediately: Mrs. Rivera, a member of the housekeeping department.

"How are you today, Dr. Langford?" she asked, smiling radiantly.

"I've had better days, Mrs. Rivera. But I'm hangin' in there. How's the family?"

"Jes' fine, thanks to you," she said. Langford had diagnosed a virulent form of tuberculosis in her husband a year earlier. "Reynaldo is finally off his medicines, and feelin' good."

"Has it been that long already? Man. And the kids?"

"Good, real good. My baby Conchita's seventeen now."

"Some baby." Entering the elevator, he threw her a wave. "Be good, Mrs. Rivera."

"You take care, Doctor."

When Langford reached Jordan's floor, she was packing. In the morning's flurry of activity, he'd nearly forgotten the nurse's page about Jordan's fears. Now, contrary to what he expected, she seemed to be in an upbeat mood. Her hair was brushed, and the dark unwashed denim mini looked very hip on her hips. The cropped denim vest, over a plain white tee, was casual without being sloppy. She smiled at his approach. Obviously, no one had told her about Rita.

"Hey, partner," he said, with ersatz cheerfulness. "Where'd you get them duds?"

"My roommate, Julie. She's down in admitting, doing my paperwork."

"You can only afford one night in this motel?"

She laughed. "I can't say it hasn't been great. But if I have to spend another night on this mattress, I might develop some serious health problems. How were my tests?"

"Fine. At least, the last I heard." He paused, studying her. "The nurses said you were upset about something this morning."

She waved it off with a dismissive shrug. "It was nothing. I just want to get out of here."

"What did Dr. Minkoff say? He's the resident in charge of the ward."

"He didn't say too much. He was here about an hour ago, but he got called away."

"But he didn't sign you out, right?" Todd asked.

She made a face. "I don't suppose you could do it for him?"

"Tell you what, give him half an hour. If you're not checked out by three, I'll come back and do the papers myself. Then your roommate can take you home."

"I might have to take a cab," she said. "Julie's boss has this silly notion about actually having to work in the afternoon."

"I'm getting off soon. If you still don't have a ride, I can give you a lift, if you want."

She did and told him so. Langford smiled, leaving Jordan with the not unpleasant thought that she just might hang around until he got back.

Throughout the afternoon, Rita's clinical condition varied little. She remained in a coma. She did, however, emerge from shock. Her blood pressure rose to an acceptable ninety over sixty, and the cliplike pulse oximeters attached to her body indicated good oxygenation. Her kidneys, however, remained shut down, and giving IV fluids without overloading was a technical challenge. But most troublesome of all was her neurological status. Predictably, the waveforms of her twelve-channel EEG remained flat. Her doctors and nurses were losing hope.

Friends maintained a constant vigil. The day after the NBME exam, there were no classes for junior med students. Some of them stopped to visit Jordan Parker-Ross, although, at the suggestion of one of the senior psychiatrists, no one mentioned Rita.

At the center of the group sat Jeffrey Donninger, his haggard face a mask of fatigue and despair. He had lost hope. The twenty-four-hour mark, and what would prove to be his wife's final EEG, was rapidly approaching.

Jordan couldn't wait to get out of the hospital. The events of the night and early morning frightened her, and there was nothing she wanted more than to curl up in the secure warmth of her own bed. Jordan was surprised she hadn't heard from Rita. Rob poked his boyish face into her room. Behind him were several classmates, all smiling halfheartedly.

"God, do I look that bad?" Jordan asked. "I'm okay, really. Why the long faces?"

"You look great, Jor," Rob said. "We heard you're being discharged, and we thought we might miss you. We just wanted to catch you before you left."

She gave him her most focused stare. Rob averted his eyes, shifting his weight nervously. As she gazed at her friends, they all shared a sheepish expression, unable to look directly at her. "All right, what's going on? What aren't you guys telling me?"

But other than make evasive comments about her health and appearance, no one said a thing. After a self-conscious sixty seconds, they lofted their farewells and slunk from the room. Jordan sat there, annoyed and concerned. Did they know something about her condition that the doctors hadn't told her?

A compulsive personality, Langford was largely a creature of habit. He worked and felt best in a regularly structured environment. Long blocks of idle time left him edgy and unfulfilled. Besides, he was hungry and tired, and he knew if he slowed down, he'd fall asleep. Thus, when he left Jordan's bedside, he had a little time to kill. He hadn't yet eaten lunch. Deciding on a late snack, he avoided the elevator, took the stairs, and headed down to the cafeteria.

Soon, tray piled high with pasta dishes, he left the lunch line and looked around for a familiar face. As he scanned the room, he felt a nudge from behind. He turned and saw that it was Fletcher.

"I gotta talk to you about something," Fletcher said.

"Sure. You in a hurry?"

"Not here." He furtively looked around. "Not in the hospital."

"What's going on?"

"Do you know someone named Scarpatta?"

"Scarpatta? There are dozens of Scarpattas in the Big Apple. Does he work here?"

"I . . . I don't think so," he said, *sotto voce*. "He called me early this morning in the lab, and then he called again about an hour ago. Wanted to talk about my research, but I put him off."

"So, what about your research?"

"I really can't talk about it now." His eyes continued to dart about. "Can you meet me later on at my place?"

"Come on, Fletch. Paranoia's not your style."

"There's something else going on, an ethical thing. I'm getting bad vibes about it."

"God, you're cryptic. About what?"

Fletcher took a calming breath. "It's about the study we're working on, okay?"

"Royce and Hobson's CSF study? What about it?"

Fletcher glared at him, lowering his voice to an insistent whisper. "I told you, not here! First this Scarpatta character, then Dr. Royce came to see me. Maybe I'm overreacting, but I feel like I'm being pressured to . . . Look, we'll talk it over at my place. When do you get off?"

Langford mulled it over, thinking about his promise to Jordan. "I'm off now. I guess I could be there around five, depending on traffic."

"I'll be waiting. This is really important, Todd. And don't tell anyone I spoke to you about this. *No* one. Understand?"

Before Langford could reply, Fletcher turned and walked away. Todd was confused, and a little worried. To be sure, the scientist was always eccentric, but Langford had never seen him spooked.

He didn't have time to dwell on it before his beeper went off. Sighing, he put down his tray and picked up the nearby wall phone. Within seconds, he was dashing from the cafeteria, abandoning both his tray and his worries about Fletcher.

In the ER, the ward clerk directed, "In Three, Dr. Langford."

He headed for Exam Room Three and its flurry of activity. Two nurses and two physicians were frantically attending to a young patient on a stretcher. The patient was a black female, perhaps fifteen or so, with strong features and shoulder-length black hair. Although she was slight of build, her face was swollen, and her puffy eyelids were the narrowest of slits. She appeared to be either unconscious or comatose, he couldn't tell which. One of the nurses was cutting through a rock group logo on the patient's smudged T-shirt. Beneath it, a soiled white bra restrained her breasts.

"OD?" he asked.

"Don't think so," said one of the residents. "Fourteen-year-old, helping mom start supper. Said she didn't feel good and went to sit on a couch. Collapsed nibbling on Fritos."

"What's with the swelling?" he said, moving to the bedside.

"Good question. The mother said there's no cardiac or renal history. The edema began two or three days ago," he said, readying an IV. "No other history."

"No drugs? What about sibs?"

"No drugs, no booze, no smokes. An older brother and younger sister are fine."

Langford joined the team fluidly, comfortably sliding in to do an exam as the others performed pre-assigned tasks in a flawless orchestration of movement. As one resident started the IV, a nurse readied test tubes with different-colored stoppers. The other resident was preparing EKG leads, while yet another nurse wheeled in a crash cart for possible CPR.

"What've we got for vitals?" Langford asked.

"No temp yet. Pulse one-oh-eight, respirations eighteen. BP two-sixty over one-forty."

"Say again?"

"You heard me right. Sky-high, stratospheric numbers."

"How're her pupils?" asked Todd.

"I didn't check yet."

Langford removed a penlight from his jacket pocket and leaned over the young patient. "Anybody know her name?"

"Shaheena Jackson."

"Okay, Shaheena honey," he said, not knowing if she could hear or not. "Let the sun shine in." He clicked on the light and shined it into her left eye. The pupil constricted, albeit weakly. "A little sluggish, but reactive. Let's see the other side." Lifting the right lid, he directed the beam from outside to the center, then repeated it. "Oh, shit."

"No reaction?" asked one of the residents.

"Very widely dilated. Asymmetric. I think we're talkin' intracranial, folks."

"An aneurysm? You think she popped a berry?"

"Could be. Kind of young for your standard bleed, though." Without prompting, he removed a reflex hammer from his pocket and tapped her knees. One leg shot out briskly, an exaggerated response, while the other didn't move at all. "Not good. I wonder if she's hemiparetic. You got that IV in?"

"Just about. D-five, half-normal. You want Narcan and fifty-percent dextrose on her?"

"Can't hurt, but a CAT scan'd be better. Can somebody call X ray? Let's get these pants off. We need some cath urine."

With the help of a nurse, he tugged at her skintight jeans. He noticed that the front zipper was partially open, and the waist snap wouldn't close. Finally they had the jeans off. A different nurse brought over a bladder catheterization tray. As the team slipped off the patient's underpants and spread her thighs into frog-legged position, Langford was distracted by her abdomen. The skin was smooth and tight, the muscles slightly protuberant. There was a thin pigmented line running vertically up her belly. Langford concentrated.

Something about that line, her abdomen's shape, the large breasts . . .

"Bring me a Doptone from the OB room."

A nurse scurried from the room. She returned seconds later with a plastic box the size of a cigarette pack, to which a slender microphone was attached. Langford squirted clear acoustic gel onto the patient's abdomen and pressed a button. Almost instantaneously, the room was filled with the rapid, unexpected beep of a fetal heartbeat.

"Can you believe that?" said Langford. "Who's on call for OB?"

"I'll check." A nurse rushed toward the phones.

"So much for confiding in mommy," said one of the residents.

"She's going to confide in a priest soon if we can't get her pressure down. We got a tracing yet?" he asked of the resident monitoring the EKG.

"Sinus tach."

"Marge!" Langford shouted to the ward clerk. "Call ultrasound and tell them to get here stat!"

"How far along is she?" asked a nurse.

"Who knows? When these kids want to hide it, they can really suck it in. She could be full term, for all I know."

"You think this could be eclampsia?" said a resident.

"Yeah, maybe. Somebody get some mag sulfate in case the OB guy wants it."

"Forget the mag!" shouted the other resident. "She's in V-fib!"

"Oh, Lawdy," Langford groaned. "Call a code! Give me the paddles!"

For the next few minutes, the cubicle was a beehive of controlled chaos as the team struggled to restore a heartbeat. An anesthetist arrived and prepared for intubation. Mindful of the proper procedures in advanced cardiac life support, the nurse in charge of the cart readied a syringe of intracardiac epinephrine and prepared a lidocaine drip. Langford positioned the paddles and pressed the button, watching the torso temporarily go rigid. His first attempt at cardioversion was unsuccessful, but the second shock restored some semblance of a rhythm. The teenager had also stopped breathing. Once the heart was beating, the anesthetist quickly inserted the endotracheal tube and ventilated the young patient. It was forty-five seconds into the arrest.

Langford stepped back to take stock, his own heart beating wildly, his senses heightened. He wasn't an obstetrician, and the fact that he had *two* patients under his care was an awesome responsibility. The burden was worsened by uncertainty. Although he knew exactly how to proceed with the mother, he wasn't quite sure what to do for her unborn child. As he weighed his options, the sonogram technician arrived, wheeling in a portable sono unit. OB resident Richie Silver was close on her heels.

Richie couldn't believe he was getting sucked into this. He'd been on call for thirty-two straight hours without sleep, and he was tired beyond belief. The nightmare with Rita Donninger had been exhausting, and he wanted nothing more than to go home and get some rest. He was in the hallway leading to the building exit when the ER paged him. But looking at the patient before him, he wondered if they'd made a mistake.

"Whoa," he said, intimidated by the resuscitative paraphernalia. "Are you sure you paged the right service?"

"Don't go anywhere," said Langford. "This is your baby. Literally. Our patient's fourteen years old and pregnant, we don't know how far. There's a three-day history of progressive edema, and then she suddenly loses consciousness."

"That's eclampsia, until proven otherwise."

"That's why we paged you. Her BP's off the chart,

a one-forty diastolic. But she also has asymmetric reflexes and one dilated pupil. Can you get that in
eclampsia?''

''Not that I've seen. They usually just have little ret-
inal hemorrhages.''

''How about a CVA?'' asked Todd.

''That's more likely, I guess. Did you page neuro?''

''On their way. But just before you got here,'' he
said, pointing a finger, ''the kid coded. We got a
rhythm back, but I have absolutely no idea what to do
with the pregnancy.''

''Is she in labor?''

''She certainly could be,'' said Langford.

''I can't do anything unless I know her gestational
age.'' He walked to the left side of the bed and gently
palpated the abdomen. ''Here's the vertex right here,''
he said. ''I'd say at least seven months. Hand me that
ultrasound transducer.''

The sono tech gave him a rectangular probe with
insulated wiring. He lubed the abdomen with transmission gel and slowly moved the transducer back and
forth in the patient's suprapubic area. On the nearby
monitor, a real-time image of the fetal skull was sharp
and distinct. He froze the picture and measured the di-
ameter of the fetal head with digital calipers.

''Thirty-two weeks,'' he said. ''Two months from
term.''

''So it's viable?''

''You bet. This kid'd have a real good shot outside
the uterus. But there's a catch. If the diagnosis is
straightforward eclampsia, we'd stabilize her, get her
ready for surgery, and section her. But if she has an
intracranial bleed, all bets are off. That might take pre-
cedence. I need the neuro resident to tell me if the
surgeons have to go right in.''

''What about fetal distress?'' Langford asked.

''It's there, all right. Any time there's reduced blood
flow to the uterus, the fetus is in trouble. I'll need a

fetal monitor to tell me exactly how bad, but they're all up on the unit. But the quicker this kid's delivered, the better. There are enough patients in Royce's study already. You get any more vegetables out of this room, you could open a farm stand.''

"Sounds to me like we should get her up to the OB suite.''

"Yeah. I think that—''

"V-fib again!'' yelled the resident.

"Start with three hundred joules!'' Langford shouted. "Run that lidocaine in, and keep the epi ready!''

"What about the baby?'' someone asked.

As he reached for the paddles, Langford stared insistently at the OB resident. "Do your thing before we lose them both!''

"Right *here*?''

"Of course right here! Someone get him a scalpel, for Christ's sake! Okay, people. Clear!''

He placed the paddles on the teenager's chest and depressed the trigger. There was an audible thump, and her upper body rose fractionally off the table. He nervously eyed the cardioscope.

"What've we got?''

"No dice,'' said the resident.

"Shit!'' Langford screamed. "Give me that epi, and spray some damn Betadine on the belly for him!''

While Langford prepared the intracardiac epinephrine, a nurse quickly doused the abdomen with brownish antiseptic. Someone slapped a scalpel into Silver's palm. With thoughts of Rita Donninger fresh in his mind, he looked up rather sheepishly.

"Are we doing the right thing, Todd?''

"Go!'' Langford shouted. "Go, go, go!''

Spurred on by Langford's urgent tone, Silver made a bold vertical swipe through the abdominal skin. The teenager had precious little subcutaneous fat. The incision was so generous that it pared through fascia, muscle, peritoneum, and the outer covering of the uterus. Silver wore only sterile latex gloves, more for his own protection than for antisepsis; and as he hurriedly operated, droplets of blood went flying, splattering his white jacket with scarlet flecks.

Langford, meanwhile, located the proper space between the ribs. Angling the long intracardiac needle, he plunged it into the patient's quivering heart. He aspirated several dark and sticky ccs, then injected the epinephrine. Above him, the anesthetist had momentarily stopped bagging the patient. When he saw Langford withdraw the needle, he quickly resumed breathing for the teenager.

The room was a frenzy of desperate activity, and an icy tone of despondency hung in the air. Both patients were in dire straits, and time was now the team's main enemy. Langford pounded the teenager's chest with the heel of his hand, then resumed external cardiac compression. Meanwhile, Silver quickly widened the gash in the uterus. But his overly generous incision had sliced through the amniotic membranes and nicked the fetal body within. Undeterred, he reached into the gaping womb, cupped the as-yet-unborn child's skull in his palm, and lifted it up into the world.

It was a small and fragile head, wet and dripping, with pinkish mucus exuding from its nostrils. A nurse reached over with a suction bulb to aspirate the mouth and nose. The chief OB resident grasped the fetal cheeks and lifted up and out. The shoulders rose through the incision, quickly followed by the body and feet. He handed the slippery bundle to the nurse, who held an open blanket out to him. Then he quickly clamped and cut the cord. The entire delivery had taken less than a minute.

Moments before, the ward clerk had the good sense to stat page the pediatrics resident. He quickly took the infant and placed it on the newborn resuscitation cart. After wiping the baby dry, he inspected its pharynx, preparing to intubate, while a nurse listened for the baby's heartbeat with a stethoscope.

"We've got a pulse," she announced.

Just then, the tiny child grimaced. Its face contorted, and its dainty lips retracted. After a long moment, it loosed a wet and spluttering cough. Then its small chest started to expand. Seconds later, it let out a weak but heartfelt cry.

"I'll be damned," said the pediatrician.

"What is it?"

"A little girl."

Silver breathed a sigh of relief. But he hadn't finished his work; he couldn't leave the patient wide open. "I'll need something to close," he said to a nurse. "Get me a suture set and some zero Vicryl."

Langford, meanwhile, paused in his CPR. All eyes were on the cardioscope.

"We've got a heartbeat," the anesthetist announced.

"About time," Langford said. "Can't keep this up forever. I just hope we can keep her alive."

Chapter Nine

TEN MINUTES LATER, THE THREE-POUND INFANT WAS out of the cubicle, carefully wrapped and transported to the newborn ICU. Miraculously, the teenager was holding her own. Working from the inside out, the obstetrician was finally up to the skin, completing a hasty closure. Langford stood vigil by the bedside, arms folded across his chest, taking everything in. His emotions were mixed—he was relieved that the premature baby was alive and well, but concerned that the teenager might never leave the room. At present, she was little more than a laboratory preparation, endlessly circling the drain—yet another terminal patient marked for inclusion in Dr. Royce's study.

While waiting to be signed out, Jordan grew restless. As a properly ID'ed medical student, she was free to roam the wards. She thought a look around might take her mind off her classmates and what they might be hiding from her. She decided to take a walk to the newborn nursery. Her next rotation would be pediatrics, and watching the infants was heartwarming.

As she approached the nursery, she saw three gowned staff members coming her way, pushing an enclosed infant warmer. Jordan greeted them with a wave, and they smiled at her noncommittally. At least one of them, she thought, looked unnerved by her approach.

What was *with* these people? she thought. Glancing through the warmer's Plexiglas, she saw a beautiful young baby lying contentedly on its stomach, oblivious to the wires attached to its body. The warmer's gender-coded ID card listed the child's name as Adrianna. Jordan thought the name sounded familiar, but she couldn't place it.

At the nursery's observation window, she saw a young doctor and nurse remove another baby from a warmer. The infant seemed unusually small, but it was crying vigorously. Its face was extremely ruddy, and an occasional streak of unwashed blood moistened its skin, testimony to the birthing process. The physician looked up at her for a moment and smiled. After saying something to the nurse, he walked outside toward Jordan.

"Thinking of having one yourself, Miss Ross?"

"Do I know you?"

"Josh Meyerson," he said, holding out his hand. "I helped Todd Langford admit you last night. How're you feeling?"

"Pretty good." Jordan studied his smiling face. Meyerson had a lively expression and playful eyes. "Did you just deliver that baby?"

"No, I brought her up from the ER." He briefly replayed the drama that occurred downstairs. "At least the kid'll probably make it," he concluded, looking at his watch. "I'm not so sure about the mother. Hey, I gotta get back. Maybe you should, too. I think Todd's coming up to see you soon."

Conchita Rivera stood outside the clinic, nibbling on her nails. Her mother worked at the hospital nearby, and Conchita was terrified of being spotted. Her once-long fingernails were bitten down to the quick. Such behavior was out of character for her, for she had always been conscious of her appearance. At seventeen, she had a beautiful *latina* face, a shapely figure, and radiant, long black hair. Yet it was that same appearance which had landed her in trouble: by the time she'd entered puberty, she was already attracting stares from men of all ages. For a troubled young woman from Spanish Harlem, that proved a difficult burden; and before her sixteenth birthday, she had already mothered two children out of wedlock.

Fortunately, she came from a caring, committed family. With the undying love of her parents, Conchita managed to turn her life around. She returned to school and even made the honor roll. Her mother's heart swelled with pride when Conchita began talking about college; higher education had always seemed beyond the Riveras' reach. Now, however, as she leaned against the wall outside Planned Parenthood, her life seemed as dirty and cluttered as the streets around her.

She was pregnant again. She'd known it from the day she missed her period last July. That in itself was shameful enough. But her boyfriend Roberto had sounded serious when he talked about making a life together, about raising a family, caring for all three children as if they were his own. She could even attend a special educational program for pregnant teens and not miss a day of school. Now, however, Roberto was gone.

The clinic personnel were supportive, but not terribly helpful. She was already four months along, and they didn't perform terminations past twelve weeks. She'd have to find another facility on her own. Even worse, she was told the procedure could cost a thousand dollars. Although she held a fairly regular after-school job, she gave most of the money to her parents, keeping only pocket change for herself. She knew she could always keep the baby, but having another child at her age would break her parents' hearts. And so Conchita continued to bite her nails, not knowing what to do, or where she could turn.

*   *   *

It was after three forty-five when he finally finished up. Langford was looking forward to the opportunity to spend time with Jordan. When he reached the ward, he thought she'd be relaxing and watching TV. Instead, she stood in a corner of the room, arms folded across her chest, looking annoyed and impatient. Todd apologized for getting tied up.

"Don't worry, better late than never," Jordan said. "I was just down at the nursery, having a chat with your sidekick, Dr. Meyerson."

"Josh? Better keep your eye on him. He only recently discovered women. Is everything okay with you? You look a little antsy."

"I am. There's something going on in this place that's annoying the hell out of me," she said. She went on to relate her classmates' uncharacteristic evasiveness, and the way everyone who saw her seemed to avert their eyes. "It's like they're afraid to tell me something."

He looked at her for a long moment. "Maybe they are."

"What do you mean, Todd?" she said with a frown. "Don't tell me you're holding out on me, too."

"Maybe it's for your own good."

"My *own good*?" she said. "That's pretty patronizing. What am I, a four-year-old kid who can't take bad news? What is it you're not telling me?"

"Don't worry, Jordan. It has nothing to do with your own health."

"Then level with me, for God's sake!"

"All right, I will. But let's get out of here first. Let me scribble a note on your chart. It'll only take a minute."

"Dr. Minkoff already signed me out."

"Really? Do you still need a lift?" he asked.

"Todd . . ."

"In that case, what're we waiting for?" He led her out of the room, past the nursing station, toward the bank of elevators. "How'd your tests turn out?"

"Why are you changing the subject?"

"Like I said, wait till we leave the building. Humor me."

Jordan sighed in exasperation. "All right, we'll do it your way. Minkoff said everything was okay. All I have to do is make a follow-up appointment with a neurologist in a week. I guess I have a hard head."

"Thank goodness for that. It was a pretty serious concussion, considering. You don't have any nausea or headache?"

"Not a blessed thing. But he suggested I take it easy for a week. I'm not sure I want to miss my classes."

They took the elevator down, went through the lobby, and headed for the staff parking lot by Draper Hall.

The blond-haired man immediately spotted them as they left the hospital's First Avenue entrance. As the couple crossed the street toward the parking lot, the man glanced at the photo cupped in his palm. There was no doubt about it. It was the girl, all right. Quickly but unobtrusively, he retreated to his car, preparing to follow them.

Health-conscious as he was, Dr. Fletcher hadn't used a mood-altering substance in years. The last time he consumed alcohol had been a glass of wine celebrating the birth of his sister's son a decade before. Now, however, he desperately needed a drink. The events of the day left him with an all-consuming anxiety he couldn't escape. Talking things out would be helpful, and he both valued and wanted Todd's perspective. But Todd wouldn't arrive for another hour, and Fletcher's apprehension was overwhelming.

The bourbon was fiery in his throat. He couldn't imagine how such a noxious taste could be considered so appealing. At his second sip, he gagged repeatedly, but managed to hold it down. Somehow, the addition of ice cubes seemed to make the substance more palatable. In five minutes, he began to feel the first soothing fingers of light-headedness. Soon, the amber liquid didn't seem so bad. He finished the first drink and poured another.

From the time he'd been a child, he had never been one who could tolerate social pressures. One of the reasons he went into research was to remain above political and financial considerations. It was enough for him to do the tests; let others reap the glory and the reward.

Which was why the day's mysterious phone calls—and Dr. Royce's admonition to remain silent—were proving more than he could bear. He knew he might be overreacting, but he couldn't help it. He doubted the two phone calls were related to what Royce had said, but he couldn't be sure. It wasn't that what was suggested was wrong, so much as he didn't know how to handle it: deviousness and bending the rules were as foreign to him as breathing through gills.

Perhaps a bath would help. The idea of immersion in a tub full of warm water, Wild Turkey at his side, suddenly seemed very appealing. And so Donald Fletcher went into the bathroom and turned on the tap, unaware that someone was carefully inserting lockpicks into his front door.

Jordan's fourth-floor walkup was a study in casual chic. It was an uncluttered floor-through, wide and breezy, with tall scheffleras and tasteful ferns backlit by recessed lighting. There were stark rice-paper prints on the walls, and a couple of Warhol reproductions. Between pieces of solid oak furniture, there were wall units with an elaborate sound system. She clicked on the CD player and inserted a Hootie and the Blowfish disc. Langford looked around, impressed.

"This is quite the place. Exactly where I'd want to drop dead after walking up four flights of stairs."

"Thank goodness I brought a doctor along."

He plopped onto a narrow leather sofa. "What did you say your roommate's name was?"

"All right, I've had it," said Jordan. "My patience is parchment-thin. We had a deal, Todd. I can keep playing the dutiful hostess, or I can hold you to your end of the bargain to tell me what's going on."

"Maybe I'm not telling you for your own good. Okay," he relented. "People *were* withholding something, even though they didn't want to. Given what happened to you, everyone figured the last thing you needed was extra stress."

"Gimme a break, Todd! Do people really think I'm that fragile? Tell me already!"

Looking out across the room, he took a deep breath. "Remember the infant you saw near the nursery? The one whose name you couldn't place?"

"Adrianna?"

"Right," he nodded. "It sounds familiar because it *is* familiar. Think about it. It's the name one of your friends picked out for her baby."

"One of my friends?" she said, puzzled. Suddenly, Jordan fell silent. She had a momentarily distant expression, which slowly left her as her eyes regained their focus. "Rita . . . My God," she whispered. "Tell me what happened to Rita!"

He told her, relating the tragedy as it had unfolded, from the moment Rita collapsed in the ER. The expression on Jordan's face vacillated between pain and incredulity. From time to time, she silently shook her head in stunned disbelief. When he was finished, there were tears in her eyes.

Her voice was weak. "You should have told me. She's my best friend from school."

"It wasn't our decision, Jordan. The order to keep you in the dark came from the chiefs of two departments. They thought the news might be too much of a strain."

"I could've handled it."

"Maybe," he conceded, "but the more I get to know you, the more I realize how strong-willed you can be. I have a feeling that as soon as you heard, you'd have been out of your hospital bed and standing next to hers."

"I suppose," she said, wiping a tear from her eye. "God, there must be something I can do!"

"That's the point—there isn't. We're absolutely powerless over this."

He was right, and she knew it. It was pointless to be indignant. Although Rita would never be far from her thoughts, Jordan could at least try to distract herself. Taking a deep breath, "Did you say you missed lunch?"

"Don't bother," he said with a wave of his hand. "I'll be out of here as soon as I catch my breath."

"It's no bother. Stay put," she said. "I'll be back in a few minutes."

In the kitchen, she took the basil and garlic from the refrigerator and chopped them, then mechanically fed the pieces into a food processor. Willing Rita from her mind, she removed a frozen French baguette from the freezer and defrosted it in the microwave. She added pine nuts and freshly grated Parmesan to the processor, followed by extra-virgin olive oil.

In the other room, Langford leaned back, listening to the high-pitched sound of the processor's electric motor. As the aroma of garlic wafted toward him, he caught glimpses of her preparing the food. He wondered what he'd done to appeal to her maternal instinct. It was pleasant to watch her graceful strides and to admire the long legs that seemed to go through the roof from beneath her denim mini. He watched in silent contentment as she brought the platter toward him.

"You want a Diet Coke?" she asked.

"Sure. What's the green stuff?" he asked, as she headed back to the kitchen. "Guacamole?"

"No, it's pesto. You'll like it." She returned with ice-filled glasses and the drinks. "Dip the cheese in and eat it with some bread." •

He did. The fresh mozzarella was deliciously soft, its flavor blending smoothly with the garlic and basil. "How long've you lived here?"

"Two years. Just before my freshman year in med school."

"That's a long commute up to Valhalla," he said, referring to the New York Medical College campus in Westchester County.

"You get used to it. But for the next two years, all my clinical rotations are here. At Met, St. Vincent's, or Lincoln."

"No main man in your life? You don't look like a social recluse."

"Thank you. No main man. I guess I'm picky."

She was aware, as they spoke, that she was accomplishing her purpose, just as he was accomplishing his. She'd temporarily stopped obsessing about Rita, and her guest seemed relaxed and at ease, content to eat and make small talk. His growing comfort, in turn, comforted her. She freely spoke about herself.

The younger of two sisters, Jordan grew up in Princeton, where her father taught history. She hadn't wanted to be a doctor until she'd nearly finished her senior year at Bates. Her grandfather, of whom she was very fond, finally died after a long illness and toward the end she had noticed that the caregivers no longer seemed to care. It was then that she decided to try a career in medicine. After graduation, Jordan came to New York, where she spent the next two years working and taking required pre-med courses until accepted to medical school.

An hour quickly passed, and she realized that she had been monopolizing the conversation. She refreshed their drinks and steered the discussion toward him.

"What about you? Are you going to stick with emergency medicine?"

"For now," he said. "At least until I burn out. It's pretty demanding. But I feel like I'm addicted to it."

"At least you don't have a demanding family to compete with."

"What makes you think I'm not married?"

She flustered. "I . . . well, it's just that . . ."

He laughed. "Don't worry. I wouldn't be here alone with someone as attractive as you if I had to worry about getting castrated by a jealous wife."

She gave her head a shake. "Do you always make outrageous comments like that?"

"Only to women with concussions."

She had to smile at his wry sense of humor. In the hospital, she'd been taken with his soft brown eyes. Now, as they spoke, she studied his lean frame, expressive face, and thick, dirty-blond hair. And she liked what she saw.

Jordan ultimately got him to talk about his work in the ER—the successes and failures, the emotional highs and lows. It was an occupational form of living on the edge that could easily become addictive. Another hour passed. It was nearly five-thirty when he glanced at his watch. He immediately sat up straight, spilling his soda. How had he forgotten that Fletcher desperately wanted to talk to him?

"God, I can't believe it. What happened to the time?" He put his glass down and got up. "I was supposed to be somewhere half an hour ago!"

"I'm sorry, Todd, I didn't mean to—"

"My fault, I lost track of the time," he said, jumping up. "Look, I've really gotta run. Okay if I call you later?"

It was. She gave him the number and showed him to the door, trying to thank him again for going out of his way for her. But he was already down the hall.

* * *

A mist of steam wafted upward from the bathwater, rising in layers about his head. Fletcher was oblivious. Warmed by the water and the bourbon, his mind seemed to drift away. He sank lower in the tub, closing his eyes as he immersed himself up to the neck.

The bathroom was thick with humid vapor, and visibility was a yard, at best. The intruder slowly turned the bathroom doorknob and cracked the door open an inch. Tendrils of steam uncurled toward him. He held the cord tight in both fists. Obscured by the fog, he crept slowly ahead.

Fletcher luxuriated in the bath water, feeling his knotted muscles relax. The tension was seeping from his body. Behind closed lids, he rolled his head lazily from side to side. The day's events no longer seemed that significant, and his last conscious thought was that he had indeed been overreacting.

Langford took the stairs two at a time. He was annoyed at his own thoughtlessness. At that time of day, he knew traffic would be heavy. He quickly jumped into the driver's seat and angled northwest, weaving impatiently around the Lincoln Tunnel bottleneck as he made his way to the Upper West Side. It took him another half hour to reach Fletcher's apartment, and an infuriating fifteen minutes more to find a parking spot.

He rang the apartment bell, but there was no answer. That wasn't unusual. His friend was often distracted, working at home or listening to New Age music with headphones. Langford rang several other doorbells until he was buzzed in. Undaunted, he took the old and wobbly elevator up to the fifth floor. Fletcher's apartment, one of six on the floor, was at the rear of the landing. Langford knocked. As before, there was no response. He turned the knob.

The door was unlocked. He shook his head and let himself in, never failing to be amazed by Fletcher's poor judgment. Although the neighborhood wasn't bad, it was still New York. The lights were on.

"Fletch?" he called. "You home? It's Todd."

There was no answer. He walked through the living room, where haphazardly strewn magazines and dust-covered chairs made it as untidy as the rest of the researcher's personal life. The bedroom door was closed, and the small kitchenette was unlit. Hearing an indistinct sound coming from the direction of the bathroom, Langford slowly approached it, growing worried.

"Fletcher, you decent? Sorry I'm late. You in there?"

The bathroom door was ajar. He hesitated, fully expecting his friend to be sitting on the commode, absorbed in his earphones, leafing through a research paper. Then he saw the water.

The edge of advancing wetness slowly streamed under the door, winding and serpentine. Curious, Langford cocked his head, listening. The indistinct sound grew recognizable as the splash of overflowing water. Concerned, Langford pushed the door open, anticipating he'd find a stoppered sink with water slopping over the rim. What he saw instead made his heart nearly erupt from his chest.

The water was flowing out of the tub in thin, cascading sheets. The tap had been left on. The water was hot, and thin wisps of steam wafted lazily toward the ceiling. Donald Fletcher was sitting upright in the back of the tub, staring straight ahead.

He was naked. The skin on his arms, which floated weightlessly just beneath the surface, was red and blistered. His mouth was open, lips downturned in an expression of agony. A thick and bulbous tongue protruded from his mouth, and his bulging, sightless eyes were red and inflamed. A severed electric cord was knotted in a tight noose around his neck. Langford's whole body was quivering.

"Oh, Jesus," he managed, his voice forlorn. "Jesus, Fletch."

Chapter Ten

BY EARLY EVENING, RITA'S FRIENDS AND FAMILY HAD begun to drift away from the ICU. Those remaining were simply going through the motions, awaiting the inevitable. But suddenly, unexpected blips began to appear on the EEG machine. There were small alpha waves, followed by theta spikes. The ICU staff began to hover excitedly around the printout. Soon more robust waveforms appeared, and by eight P.M., the tracing resembled that of someone unconscious, but no longer comatose. Word of the dramatic change filtered out into the hall, and everyone held their breath or crossed their fingers.

Rita was quickly and carefully transported to X ray, where an emergency carotid angiogram was performed. Even before the films were developed, the findings could be viewed on the fluoroscope. Incredibly, all cerebral arteries showed good function, with no obstructions to blood flow. What must have occurred, they surmised, was that the profound shock made the brain's arteries go into spasm, leading to the appearance of cerebral infarction. Once the shock was corrected, blood flow was gradually restored. It appeared Rita wasn't brain-dead at all.

The news spread like wildfire. Knowing Jordan was safely recovering at home, Rob even dared make the call, sharing the glad tidings. Jordan was overjoyed.

Outside the ICU, a cheer quickly went up, reverberating through the hospital. Although still critically ill and hardly out of the woods, it appeared that Rita Donninger suddenly had a chance for survival.

The unlikely miracle they'd all prayed for had arrived.

Langford stood in the hall outside the apartment, leaning against a wall, arms crossed over his chest. His expression was grim, and his lips were pressed into a dispirited line. It had been an hour since he'd called 911. Although the patrol cars had responded quickly, the detectives had been slow in arriving. One of the officers was roping off the apartment with yellow crime-scene tape. The forensic unit had yet to show up. The detective who questioned Langford reviewed the entries in his notebook.

"You're certain you didn't touch anything but the phone?"

"I'm positive. That and the doors. The front door, and the door to the bathroom."

"The bathroom doorknob?"

"No, the door was open. I just gave it a push."

"What about the hot water tap?"

"Yeah, I guess. That too." He grew impatient. "Can't you take him out of the tub now?"

"Not until the ME gets here. Look, Doc, I realize this guy was a friend of yours, but we got procedures, you know? Just be patient."

"You know, if I hadn't been running so late, he might still be alive!"

The detective shrugged. "You never know. You say you were supposed to meet him at five?"

He nodded.

"And he wanted to talk to you about something? Something he didn't want to discuss in the hospital?"

Langford silently nodded again.

"Look, Doc. There's gotta be more to it than that.

You see your buddy at lunch, and he won't talk. He's
all worked up about something and says he doesn't
want to go over it in the hospital. Now, this is a guy
whose *life* is the hospital, you say. Only he doesn't
mention a thing. Instead, he tells you to meet him here,
and he's going to spill the beans. You get here, and
he's dead.'' He paused. ''What was so important that
he couldn't talk to you in the hospital? Was it important
enough to get him killed?''

Langford felt as if he'd been struck by lightning.
''You think someone murdered him over what he
wanted to tell me?''

''I don't think anything. I'm just asking. Help me
out here.''

Langford looked away. He vividly recalled the brief
conversation. Dr. Fletcher clearly had been worried,
worried to the point of paranoia. All he had said of
substance was that it had something to do with the CSF
study. But beyond that . . .

Langford shook his head. He saw no point in saying
anything about the study—that would only open a can
of worms.

''What's behind that look, Doc?''

''All he said was that we'd go over it when I got
here.''

The detective studied him for a long and stony moment. ''Your call. The guy was your friend, not mine.
But if something happens to refresh your memory,
you've got my number.''

Joey loved firearms. He adored the feel, the smell, the
added weight a gun lent to his hand. His current pre-
occupation was the new Five seveN pistol, a twenty-
round Fabrique Nationale offering that chambered the
minuscule 5.7-millimeter round. He was busily polish-
ing its Glock-ish contours when Merendino called.

''We're all set up, ready to go,'' Merendino said.
''I'll make the call tomorrow morning.''

"You think she'll bite?"

"Oh, I think I can be pretty convincing."

"This is really necessary, huh?"

"It's like this," Merendino said. "We've got a time problem here. Sal is going fast, agreed? His medications aren't worth a damn, and the only thing that looks like it's going to help is this spinal fluid stuff. It's just a question of where to get it. According to our contact in the hospital, everyone who's got it is on life support, except one person. If we can find that out for sure, we can get it to the boss. I don't see what the big problem is."

"Yeah, I guess you're right," Joey said. "Give me a call when it's all over." He rang off, hefting the pistol in his hand, sighting along the barrel. If things with the woman didn't work out, he'd be happy to escort her into the next life.

When he finally left the scene, Langford was distraught. The day's only bright spot had been the time he'd spent with Jordan. She buoyed his spirits and made him feel at ease. And right now, he definitely needed some cheering up.

So he decided to call her. As soon as Jordan picked up the phone, she told him the fantastic news about Rita. But Langford's own relief was mitigated by Fletcher's death. Hearing the pain in his voice, she asked him what was wrong. Fumbling with his words like a tongue-tied schoolboy, he told her. She immediately insisted they get together. Half an hour later, they were in a coffee shop in Little Italy. Langford told her about finding Fletcher's body.

"Fletcher was a nut, but he was harmless," Todd said. "If you took time to listen to him, he could be an interesting guy."

"Nobody ever listened?"

"Hardly ever. His intensity scared people. Maybe we

were kindred spirits. I really liked him. Fletch told me everything—or so I thought.''

''You think someone killed him for what he wanted to tell you?'' Jordan asked.

He shook his head. ''That's reaching. When the detective suggested that, it nearly jolted me out of my socks. After all, that wasn't the first time I found his door open. Some neighborhood punk was probably cruising around looking for a place to score, and he got lucky.''

''So you think it was a robbery?''

''His wallet's missing, right? What else could it have been?''

''It wouldn't be the first time a homicide was made to resemble a burglary to cover up the real motive. Perhaps the detective was right. Maybe he was killed because he knew something. Something he was hoping to share with you.''

Langford shook his head. ''This is real life, Jordan, not an Alfred Hitchcock movie. And in real life, he lived in an Upper West Side neighborhood swarming with junkies.''

''Why didn't you tell the cop what Dr. Fletcher said about someone named Scarpatta, and about the CSF study?''

''What was the point?''

''Because Fletcher was frightened and wanted to talk to you. What does that suggest?''

''It suggests you have a very vivid imagination.''

''Is it just possible, Doctor dear,'' she politely persisted, ''that he was onto something really dangerous? That he had some kind of information, something explosive, something that would blow your mind?''

''Like what?''

''That's what I'm asking.''

''You mean something so important other people might kill him to shut him up?''

She nodded.

"Anything's possible, I suppose," he conceded. For a moment, Todd wondered if it were feasible. If so, what he found really disturbing was that people in his own world, hospital people, might somehow be involved. The idea was totally unthinkable. Feeling irritable, he glanced at the wall clock. "It's getting pretty late. Maybe we should call it a night."

"It's not *that* late. What do you plan to do now?"

"I'm not sure. Maybe cruise the bars until the wee hours. Drink tequila and listen to Jimmy Buffet until I pass out. Something like that."

"I hope you're not serious."

"If there was ever a night to tie one on, this is it. I'm not too keen on going back to an empty house in Riverdale."

"If you're so intent on drinking, why not do it at my place? My roommate Julie's out with her boyfriend and won't be home until late. If you wind up passing out, I'd rather you did it on my couch than in some gin mill. How about it?"

He brightened. "With a couch as comfortable as yours, how could I refuse?"

Half an hour after they left the restaurant for her apartment, Langford was into his third glass of burgundy. By ten o'clock, he was feeling delightfully mellow. In the wine's embrace, the day's woes seemed to slip away. He was starting to feel amorous. He moved closer and put an arm around her shoulder.

His hand felt wonderful against her skin. She looked into his brown eyes and saw the desire there. Her heart was starting to beat faster, in sync with her own eagerness. Was this what she'd had in mind, she wondered, an ulterior motive behind her hospitality? While she was wondering what to do, he leaned over and kissed her.

His lips were soft and warm, redolent of wine. It was a grazing kiss, a feathery caress. His lips, hot and dry, rubbed lightly against hers, sliding like satin. It was communion, a tender touching without insistence, a let-me-get-to-know-you contact. But soon his lips pressed harder—moving, seeking. His other arm went around her, and he drew her to him in a take-no-prisoners embrace. Jordan felt her body start to respond. But as much as she ached for him, she pushed away, breathless.

"Whoa, I don't know if I'm ready for this."

He looked at his watch. "When will you know?"

"For now," she said, getting up, "let's stick with the game plan and get you some shut-eye. It's late. Why don't you take my roommate's bed? It doesn't look like she's coming home."

"Okay," he yawned. "I don't want to wear out my welcome." Head reeling, he made it to Julie's room and lay back heavily on her bed. Beneath his lids, flickering images danced across his retina. Soon he felt his loafers being slipped off and a cool pillow tucked under his head. As he lay there wondering if he'd died and gone to heaven, he fell asleep.

Throughout the night, Rita's condition continued to stabilize. She'd been breathing on her own for several hours, and her lungs were clear. They removed the endotracheal tube. At three A.M., her status was thoroughly reevaluated. Rita's physicians agreed that her cardiovascular system was in surprisingly good shape, and her shock was a thing of the past. Her infection was treated and under control. The biggest problem was her kidneys, which still weren't functioning. She was definitely going to need dialysis, and preparations for it were already underway.

There was no agreement on when she would wake up. Given the severe trauma to her central nervous system, not to mention the various drugs and poisons still circulating through her bloodstream, the consensus estimates were in the thirty-six- to forty-eight-hour range.

Pedro Gonzales was working in the ICU that night.

A complex medical case like Rita's baffled him. As a first-year resident, he did little more than run errands and hang IV fluids. Before dawn, Pedro had to replace one of the empty IV bags. He took the new liter just delivered from the pharmacy and checked the label with the doctor's order sheet. The orders for the main-line IV called for 1000 ccs of normal saline every eight hours, to which had been added a gram of ampicillin. The bag's label was a match.

Then something on the paste-on label caught his eye. Pedro squinted. Next to the name of the antibiotic, an asterisk was typed in. Pedro squinted. For a moment he considered asking one of the nurses, then thought better of it, presuming it was something he should know. No doubt it had something to do with the severity of the case.

Without giving it another second's thought, Pedro hung the bag.

Outside Jordan's apartment, an early autumn thunderstorm swept through SoHo in a gusty squall. A flash of lightning split the darkness, silhouetting the skyline. On the apartment roof across the street, the blond-haired man leaned against a brick chimney, virtually invisible in his black rain slicker. He was intent on Jordan's bedroom window, and a pair of compact Leica binoculars were fixed to his eyes. Soon, as a clap of thunder rumbled across windswept tenements, he let them fall away.

He'd been waiting there when the young doctor returned unexpectedly to the apartment. That posed no great problem, for he knew that Langford was scheduled to work the next morning. It was important that the woman be alone when their plan went into action. As the heavy raindrops began to fall, he knew he'd have to remain there all night, if necessary, to insure that the woman was by herself.

*   *   *

Alone in her bedroom, Jordan was feeling wonderfully content. With the air conditioner on high because of the humidity, she got into bed, pulled the covers up to her neck, and reclined against a propped-up pillow. Outside, she heard the booming of thunder, and the irregular tapping of windswept rain against her window. She clicked on the TV remote and sighed, crossing her arms over her abdomen. There was no doubt she wanted Todd every bit as much as he seemed to want her. She was a little surprised by the intensity of her feeling. She'd never thought of herself as easy, but she couldn't deny the overwhelming attraction she felt for him.

Suddenly she was drowsy. Her accident and hospitalization were only vague memories. Her nightmare was forgotten. Her fears about her health, she realized, were unnecessary. Todd had been so reassuring about that.

The late news was just coming on. Yawning, she closed her eyes as the anchor read the headlines. Her breathing slowed and deepened.

Jordan drifted off. She slipped into that state of near-weightlessness, the meditative lightness that precedes REM sleep. Totally relaxed, she floated on a wave of buoyant fog. In the background, the newscaster was interviewing a distraught mother whose three-year-old son had been murdered. Just before she lapsed into sleep, Jordan's sensory perception heightened. Her hearing focused on the mother's words—and in particular, her tone. Jordan's auditory cortex keyed into her inflection, volume, and verbal range. And although she was almost overtaken by slumber, she knew, as clearly as she had known with Dr. Hobson and the nurses, that the woman was lying.

Her fear instantly returned, explosive in its intensity. Jordan was jarred awake, suffocated by anxiety. She sat up trembling, staring into the darkness.

*   *   *

After a fitful night's sleep, Jordan got up early to make coffee, thinking about putting her life back together. When the phone rang, she was thankful for the momentary distraction. She lifted the receiver.

"Miss Parker-Ross, please?"

"Speaking."

"This is Dr. Merendino from the radiology department at Metropolitan Hospital. I hope I'm not disturbing you."

"No, I . . ." She held the phone tighter. "What department did you say?"

"Radiology. I'm one of the senior attendings. I've been asked to review your CAT scan from, let's see," he said. In the background, the rumpling of a folder could be heard. "The night before last. How are you feeling, by the way?"

"Pretty good, thanks." The caller had a trace of an accent, definitely foreign-born. "Sorry to call you so early on a Saturday, but yours is one of the first films I've reviewed. I'm afraid it has me a little puzzled."

Jordan felt her pulse quicken. "I don't understand. Dr. Minkoff said all my tests were okay, that all I had was a concussion."

"And it was just a concussion. But a concussion's a clinical diagnosis. The reason they *have* attendings, Miss Parker-Ross, is that some of the more junior people, like Minkoff, can miss subtle radiological findings. But what I see on your films definitely has me worried."

"Worried about what?" Her heart was now pounding. "Is something wrong?"

"Possibly. Look, what I want to say is very important, and I'd prefer not to go into it over the phone. But it's imperative that we discuss what's on your films, and what can be done about it."

Jordan's mouth had become impossibly dry, and she had to squeeze the receiver to keep from dropping it. "Do I have a tumor, is that what you found?"

"Why not come right over to my office, and we'll go over it? I'm in my private office, on East Thirty-ninth. A courier drops the films off for me to read every Saturday morning. How soon can you get here?"

She checked the clock. "I guess in about half an hour. Is that all right?"

"I'll be waiting." He gave her the exact address and rang off.

Jordan tremulously replaced the receiver. In the back of her mind, she'd always been terrified something like this would happen. She was almost positive something was seriously wrong. How naive she'd been, thinking that she could escape scot-free from such serious head trauma. She forced herself to take slow, deep breaths, calming herself, trying to relax.

Bit by bit, her anxiety lessened. She began to hope she might be jumping to conclusions. Maybe, just maybe, Merendino was simply being cautious, obeying some doctrine drummed into physicians' heads by hospital malpractice attorneys.

She half expected Todd to be still asleep in Julie's bed. Instead, she found it neatly made. Lying on the pillow was a piece of paper torn from a nearby scrap pad.

"Thanks for the hospitality," read Todd's hastily scribbled note. "And thanks for listening. Call you later." He signed it simply: T.

She let the note fall. She needed to talk to him. He'd never mentioned his schedule, and she didn't know whether or not he was working. He hadn't given her his home phone, and she didn't even know his address, either. She quickly picked up the phone and dialed the main switchboard at Metropolitan Hospital Center. After talking to the page operator, Jordan leaned against the wall and drummed her fingers, trying to calm her fears. The seconds ticked by with agonizing slowness.

"I'm sorry," said the operator. "Dr. Langford's not answering his page."

Jordan rang off, unnerved. If only Todd were there to answer her questions! Why had they told her everything was all right, when clearly it was not? Struggling to keep her imagination under control, she hurried back to her room to dress.

At eight A.M., the ER was quiet enough for Langford to chat with a friend who came by.

"So pretty soon I'm going to be working for the mob?" Langford said.

"You never know," said Courtney. "You're into pasta, right?"

"Are you sure? Everyone I know in the hospital workers' union is either black or Spanish."

"Those are the grassroots workers. The mob controls the leadership."

Langford thought Courtney's claim unexpected, but not unimaginable. If anyone, Courtney should know. Retired DEA, Tom Courtney still had enough clout to work freelance for his former employer or other federal agencies. He was currently working for the Organized Crime Strike Force, a unit within the Department of Justice.

According to Courtney, the Mafia, and the Aiello mob in particular, was trying to get a foothold in organized medicine, both as a legitimate offshoot of its illegal activities, and to launder money. Using its years in the drug trade as a springboard, the mob also wanted to enter the pharmaceutical and biotech arenas. It did this by exerting its considerable clout with unions. The unions controlled many of a hospital's day-to-day activities, and they could also sway their members into joining one managed-care provider over another. The ramifications of Mafia control of medicine were numerous, not the least of which was access to medical care.

"Maybe it wouldn't be so bad working for a godfather," said Todd, trying to remain unconcerned.

"We'd probably get a helluva lot more done than we do right now."

"But if you didn't," said Courtney, with a laugh, "they'd slit your throat and pull your tongue out through your neck."

Langford listened intently. He'd known Courtney for two years, since the day the agent had brought his fifteen-year-old son in with a drug overdose. Langford worked on him long and hard, saving the boy's life and eventually helping get him admitted to a drug rehab clinic. The agent stopped by periodically after that, sharing news of his son and inquiring about medical matters, both professional and personal. The two men developed an easy friendship.

"What the mob ultimately wants is respectability," Courtney went on. "But they want it on their own terms. They want to be able to say who gets cared for and who doesn't. You think managed care's a problem now, denying specialized procedures and insisting on referrals? Reviewing a doctor's charts, sending him before various committees? Christ, if the Mafia didn't like your results, they'd have an instant twenty-two-caliber solution."

Suspecting that Courtney was joking to hide his concern, Todd smiled. "You don't think they'd make doctors more compliant?"

"The mob's also interested in little things like profit skimming and income tax evasion. That'd hardly be in the patient's best interest. All of which brings me to the reason I came to see you. I want to rely on your capacity as chief rumormonger."

"Me?"

"You saying it's not true? My friend, more secrets are spilled in this ER than anyplace in the city. It's gossip central. Man, if only the walls had ears."

"Well . . ." Langford sheepishly allowed.

"The Mafia has definitely worked its way into your hospital, we know that. So far, it's on a small scale.

The boys at Justice want to keep it from going any further. All I'm askin' you to do is keep your ears open, okay? If you hear anything interesting, give me a call, huh?''

Perplexed and a little worried, Todd watched Courtney depart. When he'd gone into medicine, he thought the closest he would come to a crisis was when a patient didn't respond to treatment. But now the mob was supposedly involved in medicine, and one of his closest friends had been murdered. He was appalled at what was happening to his nice, safe world.

Langford busied himself in the ER. He was grateful that the mind-numbing work kept him from obsessing about Fletcher's death. When the pace slowed around nine, he was surprised at how much he missed Jordan. Unable to get her out of his mind, he gave her a call. He was disappointed when she didn't answer, but maybe he was rushing things. He could always call back later.

Shortly after nine A.M., Rita unexpectedly opened her eyes, a full day before anyone had predicted. Her sclerae were surprisingly clear, and her lids lacked the puffy redness associated with the recently comatose. She was in an amnesiac's temporary funk, and she had no recollection of recent events, particularly her pregnancy, or what happened to Jordan. Rita looked around, trying to comprehend the scene before her. She was unquestionably in a medical environment, but where?

Her abdomen ached. She put her hands on top of it and found dressings. A nurse stood at the foot of the bed, engrossed in paperwork. Rita tried to say something, but her throat was impossibly dry. She coughed and tried again.

''Excuse me,'' she managed, ''but could I get a glass of water?''

The nurse looked up, her eyes going wide. ''Oh my God, you're awake! Don't move, I'll be right back!''

The remark struck Rita as humorous. She couldn't move if she wanted to, and she still didn't know what was going on. But Rita began to smile. She let out a throaty chuckle that soon became a hearty laugh which made her stomach hurt. Soon, her bedside was mobbed. Doctors and nurses surrounded their prized patient, performing status checks and offering words of encouragement to someone still in the dark. Rita's extremely rapid return to almost normal from the near-dead was nothing short of remarkable, yet another aspect of the miracle for which there was no known explanation.

On the ride to the doctor's office, Jordan kept thinking about what the radiologist might have seen on her films. A tumor? The thought was scaring her to death. Then, of course, it might be an aneurysm, or the white lesions associated with multiple sclerosis. None of the possibilities was the least bit reassuring.

Finally, Jordan emerged from the cab. The building was a large henna-colored brownstone with few distinguishing features. It had a below-decks basement entrance, and another door at the top of the stone stoop. Beside the doorjamb was a new black lacquer plaque, whose gold lettering read, ERNESTO MERENDINO, M.D., RADIOLOGY. She took a deep breath and pressed the bell.

Seconds later, there was a return buzz, and she let herself in. The entry foyer was a long, dark, floor-through corridor. There were a number of doors leading off the main hallway, which at one time probably led to sitting or living rooms, but which were now all closed. Jordan thought it a little peculiar that there were no other offices on the floor. Merendino must be a remarkable doctor, or else very well-to-do. His office entrance was at the end of the hall.

The door was open. Jordan entered a spacious, well-lit waiting room. The place looked newly redecorated.

There were no other patients. But it *was* a weekend, and Merendino probably didn't have regular Saturday hours. At the far end of the room, a woman was seated behind a desk.

She wore a white medical pants suit, and she looked up at Jordan's approach. She appeared to be about sixty, with a swarthy complexion, dark eyes, and long black hair gone to gray. Her lips held the hint of a smile, but the remainder of her expression was inscrutable.

"May I help you?" she asked, in heavily accented English.

"I'm Jordan Parker-Ross," she offered. The woman stared blankly at her. "Dr. Merendino called me. About my CAT scan."

"Are you alone?"

"Yes. Is that a problem?"

After a long moment, the woman finally stood up. "Right this way."

What was that all about? Jordan wondered, as she followed the woman into a spacious consultation area, with dark oak-paneled walls. In the center sat a large, antique wooden desk. The man behind it rose to meet Jordan.

He was of medium height and slightly stocky, with radiant white teeth and a thick black mustache. "Ernesto Merendino," he said with a smile, taking Jordan's hand. "I appreciate your coming in. Please," he said, indicating a chair. "Have a seat."

"Thank you. I got here as soon as I could. Am I your only patient today?"

"Oh, I rarely see patients on Saturdays, except special cases. Like yours."

"I don't mind telling you, I'm a nervous wreck."

"Understandably," he said, the smile never leaving his lips. He rose from the chair and walked to an X-ray view box affixed to the sidewall. "Can I get you something, Miss Parker-Ross? Coffee or tea?"

"No thanks. My stomach's doing enough flip-flops without extra caffeine."

"It's decaf. Venezuelan, a special order. It's already brewing."

"I don't think so, Dr. Merendino," she said, growing exasperated. "I appreciate your courtesy, but all I want is—"

"I never take coffee alone, my dear. It will relax you, believe me."

She didn't want to offend him. "If you insist."

"Excellent! Milagros?" he called. "Bring the coffee, for two."

"Is that my scan? Can I see it?"

"Of course. Have you taken radiology yet?"

She got up and approached the viewbox, her curiosity not quite matching her trepidation. "Not yet. I know about X-ray theory, but not any interpretation."

"That requires years of training. Let me come to the point. Take a look up here," he said. "These first images are coronal sections, seen from the top on down. Your cortex appears completely normal, all the way down to here. Ah, thank you, Milagros." He took the silver serving tray, and the woman disappeared. "Let me just get this ready."

As he placed the tray on his desk, Jordan studied the images. The anatomy looked normal. What was she missing? "So where's the problem?"

"In a moment," said Merendino. He paused to open packets of sweetener, which he poured into their cups.

Jordan suppressed a sigh, wanting him to get to the point already. Merendino was too gracious a host. She took a large sip of her coffee. The brew was strong, and rather bitter.

"One develops a taste for it," the doctor said. "Now, where were we?"

"Up to here," she indicated on the film.

"Right. Now, when we get to these cuts, we're mid-brain and beyond. Here's the third ventricle, thalamus, and hypothalamus. Do you see the hippocampus on this side?''

Jordan narrowed her eyes. "I'm really not sure."

"Now, that's the caudate nucleus. Can you make out this little bulge right next to it? The size of a large pea?"

She took another sip of her coffee. "A bulge?"

"Yes, right here." He made a centimeter circle with his finger. "This is the area that concerns me. Notice how it protrudes medially?"

Jordan could see nothing, and she began to feel slightly relieved. She'd been expecting to see an enormous lesion, baseball-size or beyond. Not only was something that large not present, but she couldn't see anything at all. "I'll take your word for it, Dr. Merendino."

"All right." He led the way back to their seats. "It's very subtle, but believe me, it's there."

For the first time, Jordan looked around the room. The walls, however beautiful, were stark, devoid of the usual diplomas. In fact, other than the view box, the room's only furnishings were a desk lamp and a potted philodendron. "I believe you. But what does it mean?"

"Well, it's most likely an anatomic variant. But what disturbs me are recent reports in the British literature, reports describing cases identical to yours. In several cases, the findings were related to neoplasia."

Her heart quickened. "Tumors?"

"Yes, usually benign. But they were often functional, producing hormonal changes."

"My God." Jordan lowered her eyes and calmed herself with another sip of decaf. "So what do I do now? Is there any treatment for it?"

"That's jumping the gun a bit. First we have to determine if you have this condition. Fortunately, there's a very simple diagnostic test."

"An X ray?"

"No, it's blood work. A variation of the petrosal

stimulation test." He watched her intently. "Are you familiar with it?"

"The . . ." All of a sudden, her tongue seemed wooden, impossibly thick. She tried to swallow, but her mouth felt like parchment, devoid of saliva. A wave of nausea swept over her, then vanished. She shook her head. "No, I'm not."

"It's quite simple. Basically, it's an isotope test. We can do it right here, if you like."

Her gaze grew dark around the edges, creating tunnel vision. Her voice sounded tinny to her ears. "Here?"

He slowly nodded, his eyes fixed on hers, like a cat watching a mouse. "If you have a couple of hours free, we can get right to it." He paused. "Are you all right, Miss Parker-Ross?"

She was jolted by an unexpected surge of vertigo, which threatened to topple her from her seat. Her vision seemed to flicker, a chiaroscuro twinkling. Her stomach was threatening to turn over. "Is there . . . your bathroom?"

His reply seemed to take forever, but his smile never wavered. "Certainly. Down the hall."

Jordan rose unsteadily to her feet, gripping the back of the chair to keep from falling. Her line of sight was constricted into a darkened gunbarrel view. She couldn't understand why she felt so light-headed. As she plodded out of the room, the floor turned to jelly beneath her. She felt embarrassed, and more than a little scared. Was her giddiness related to what was going on with her brain? As she negotiated the room's doorway, she had to hold on to steady herself. She wobbled precariously down the hall and spotted the bathroom some fifteen feet away. With the wide, ataxic gait of a drunken sailor, she headed toward it.

As she staggered forward, the nausea rose up, and Jordan had to grit her teeth to keep from gagging. She had gone but several steps when she was distracted as she went by an open room. She caught only the briefest glimpse as she lurched past, but the fleeting image was indelibly seared into her brain. Inside the room stood the white-clad Milagros, her back to the doorway, opening what was unmistakably a lumbar puncture tray, identical to the one Todd used in the hospital.

Jordan wanted to scream. Certain she hadn't been seen, she continued blindly ahead. Her wildly thudding heart felt like it would erupt from her chest. A second later, she reached the bathroom and somehow managed to shut the door silently. She leaned heavily against the wall, fighting a rising tide of nausea, dizziness, and disbelief.

Her breath came in fiery spasms. She momentarily closed her eyes, only to find the dizziness and vertigo increasing. Her brain was turning to mush. Nothing made sense anymore. And yet suddenly, everything made sense: the hastily redecorated, almost empty office with its lack of diplomas; the absence of other patients; the urgent need for her to come there on a weekend; and Merendino's—was that his real name?—insistence that she drink the coffee . . . dammit, *the coffee*! Why were they doing this to her?

She looked around, desperate to find a way out. The cabooselike bathroom was long and narrow. It contained a wide marble basin with bronze fixtures, and an old commode hugged the rear wall. Above the toilet, drawn chintz curtains concealed a small window. Without hesitation, Jordan headed toward it, her only means of escape.

Her dizziness deepened, a whirlpool of purple vertigo that spun about her brain. Jordan knew she didn't have much time before she lost consciousness. That knowledge made her desperate, and the desperation spurred her on. Her coruscating vision blurred, darkening around the edges. An instant later she was standing on the commode, reaching for the curtains.

They came off in her fist. So did the curtain rod, clattering to the tiled floor. She fumbled numbly at the sash's lock, and wooden though her fingers felt, she soon had it open. The window groaned and gave way, rattling upward in a flurry of brittle white paint chips. It rose about a foot when it shuddered to a halt, wedged in by a warped frame. She prayed there was enough room. She wormed her head and shoulders into the opening. Pushing off the commode with her tiptoes, she wriggled ahead, snakelike. Her waning consciousness was like a curtain descending, but she forced herself on. Her waist rested on the sill, and she looked downward.

Some six feet below her, flat concrete beckoned like a darkened sea. Jordan wobbled for a moment, tottering. She could scarcely see anymore. Then she made up her mind and let go, plummeting head-over-heels in a graceful arc toward the ground. She struck the concrete with her shoulders, her upper back cushioning the heavy blow. Rolling painfully onto her side, she struggled breathlessly to her knees.

She thought she was in some sort of courtyard, but she couldn't tell. In was now all Jordan could do to see. She made a bold push to her feet and willed her trembling legs to move. She staggered blindly ahead. In the last vestiges of her consciousness, before grayness turned to black, Jordan was convinced she was going to die, and nobody was ever going to find her.

Chapter Eleven

IN THE FIRST FEW HOURS OF LANGFORD'S DAY, HE HAD DOAs, and a heroin OD was clinging to life. An aura of death hovered about him like fog. He deeply felt Fletcher's absence and couldn't stop thinking about him. Few other hospital personnel even realized the man was dead. The story hadn't yet made the papers, and as an eccentric loner, he was relatively unknown to most of the staff. Moreover, he apparently had no family; there wasn't even a funeral scheduled.

What he wanted to do was check out the nurses' reports about the miraculous improvements in two of his patients, one with Parkinson's disease, the other with alcoholic psychosis and congestive heart failure. Something didn't compute. He thought it highly unlikely, to say the least, that what the nurses suggested was possible. The idea that terminal heart disease could get better on its own, or that a chronic and complex neurological condition could virtually disappear overnight, made absolutely no sense. If there *were* answers, he thought, they might be in the patient charts.

He entered the nursing station at the entrance to the general medical ward and spotted a small stack of charts on a countertop, just returned from medical records, awaiting physician signatures. Langford noticed that Jordan's chart was on top. Curious, he opened the manila folder and started to read.

The admitting note was written by Meyerson. Meyerson's entry was lean and concise. Langford glanced at the notations under PHYSICAL EXAM. The medical shorthand that described the head, eyes, ears, nose, throat, and chest was straightforward. But when he saw what was written next to BREASTS, Langford bristled. He tracked down the resident by phone, finding him in the clinic.

"What's up, Todd?"

"You remember that patient, Parker-Ross? Came in the other day?"

There was an edge to his friend's voice that Josh didn't like. "Sure. The girl with the green eyes."

"I'm going over your admitting note. What the hell is this you wrote next to BREASTS?"

"Next to . . ."

"You wrote, 'nice.' " He paused, straining at the silence. "Maybe you've become a lady-killer since you started working here, but this is bullshit. You know, even the worst malpractice attorney would have a field day with crap like that! Christ, I can't *wait* to see what you penciled in next to PELVIC EXAM!"

"I'm sorry, Todd, I thought—"

"Don't think! Just act a little more professional, for God's sake!"

Langford slammed down the phone before Meyerson could reply. For the next few moments he sat there fuming, perplexed by his own response. Righteous indignation was out of character for him. And Josh, after Fletcher, was probably his best friend in the hospital.

What was he really upset about, anyway? To be sure, the entry was highly inappropriate, but he'd made similarly unprofessional remarks during his residency. No, he concluded, it was something else. It suddenly dawned on him. Where it came to Jordan, he was beginning to feel a disturbing degree of protectiveness.

Unwilling to think about it further, he distracted himself with a review of the charts he came for and was soon engrossed. Albert Stampf, the seventy-two-year-old patient with both Alzheimer's and Parkinson's disease, had been a study in progressive neurological deterioration when admitted. On a scale from one to ten, he barely registered. He had the degree of dementia that quickly led to total incapacity. Too sick for a nursing home, Stampf wouldn't have lasted two weeks in an acute-care hospital. The usually inexorable course would have him quickly succumbing to a stroke, pneumonia, or aspiration. The remarkable clinical about-face was nothing short of miraculous.

Puzzled, Langford pored over the wealth of lab and diagnostic data in the chart, searching for clues. His best guess was that the diagnosis was mistaken—that the patient was instead suffering from an infection, perhaps, like encephalitis, or the sort of demyelinating disease known for its remissions and exacerbations. But the more he searched, the more solid the diagnosis appeared. Stampf had a strong family history of Alzheimer's; and the slowly progressive, well-documented, years-long slide left little doubt that the clinical impression was accurate. Could it have been something in his treatment, or his meds?

Langford reviewed the chart again, paying careful attention to the nurses' notes and the drugs administered. There was no suggestion of the slightest deviation from usual standards. All the care rendered, and all the drugs administered, were standard operating procedure. Finally, he shook his head and moved on to the next patient.

He went up to eight and took Mary Scoggins' chart from the rack. Scoggins was the fifty-three-year-old black woman with a man's appetite for beer. A chronic alcoholic, she consumed upwards of a case of Budweiser a day. Even though she had little money, her whole life revolved around obtaining and consuming six-packs. In one of her more affluent moments, she even had a likeness of the Budweiser frog tattooed on her buttocks.

Her brain was the first organ to go, succumbing to alcoholic psychosis. For the preceding two years, Scoggins had been in and out of numerous hospitals and clinics, suffering from DTs. Ultimately, she passed the clinical point of no return, and when Langford had admitted her, the woman was incoherent and suffering from both heart and liver failure. An enlarged and weakened heart filled most of her chest, and her lungs were filled with fluid. If she ever showed improvement, she might conceivably be a candidate for heart and liver transplants—at least on paper. But her brain would probably never improve.

This time, however, Langford doubted she would leave the hospital alive. Certainly no transplant program would consider her unless she began thinking clearly and entered a recovery program, something she had tried and failed at many times. She was the kind of chronically relapsing alcoholic who seemed intent on drinking herself to death. The best they could hope for, Langford thought, was to stabilize and comfort her.

Leafing through the chart, Langford observed that she'd been treated with a standard regimen of fluid restriction, diuretics, digitalis, and morphine. From the ER, she'd been admitted to the Coronary ICU in florid heart failure. After holding her own for a few days, she began the predictable downward spiral, ultimately lapsing into a coma. But then, for no apparent reason three days ago, she began to improve dramatically. Her bilirubin fell from nine to one-point-six, and her neck veins were no longer distended. Her edema inexplicably vanished, and her heart shrunk to reasonable proportions. Just as significantly, her eyes began to sparkle, and her speech, while still sluggish, became coherent. It was the closest thing imaginable to an act of God.

But Langford knew it was more than that. An hour

later, he slowly closed the chart, more perplexed than ever. No, something had happened to this patient, just as it had to Albert Stampf. Something he couldn't put his finger on. But the clues were there, of that he was certain—if only he knew where to look.

It was a little after eleven when his beeper went off. When he dialed the switchboard, the page operator told him he had an outside call. It was Rick Scott, chief resident in emergency medicine at New York University Hospital.

"I got a real winner here, Todd. Thought maybe you could help me out."

"Nice try, Rick. That's the kind of butt-kissing I hear before the request for transfer. What've you got, some old gork who goes to our clinic?"

"Actually, she's pretty young. I think she's trippin', either dust or ketamine. The EMTs brought her in a few hours ago, passed out somewhere. Now she's really freaked. Before I turn her over to psych, I figured I'd give you a call. We found discharge papers with your name on 'em in her wallet."

Langford was starting to get a sinking feeling. "What's her name?"

"Let's see . . . here we go. Georgia Par—"

Langford had already dropped the phone, and was dashing frantically out of the hospital.

Forty-five minutes later, he and Jordan were in his car, heading back uptown. Jordan leaned her head against the passenger-side door, eyes closed in sullen silence. When he'd first seen her in the NYU ER, she'd been overjoyed to see him, and nearly hysterical. Coming down from being high on something, she alternated between incessant tears and maniacal babbling about a strange physician wanting to do a spinal tap on her. Langford and Scott stared at one another in confusion. The ER had already done a tox screen, though the results wouldn't be available for days. Because Jordan didn't appear suicidal or a threat to others, she was discharged in Langford's care.

In the car, when he asked her what she'd taken, Jordan became enraged. The one man she thought would be there for her was turning on her, treating her like a common drug addict. Light-headed, she kept her eyes closed.

"I can't help you if you won't talk to me," Todd said.

"Help me what?" she said icily. "Get into a seven-day detox?"

"If that's what you want."

"For the last time, I am not some damn druggie!"

"Are you denying that you were high as a kite on something? Are you saying the ambulance crew didn't find you collapsed in some alley? I'd say you're lucky to be alive!"

"Don't patronize me, dammit. I'm not denying anything. I told you, I was drugged."

"By a radiology attending at Met? Some guy named Merendino, who doesn't exist?" She remained silent. "Come on, Jordan! Listen to how all this sounds. What do you expect me to think?"

"Think whatever you want," she said with a sigh. "I'm telling you the truth."

She felt emotionally and mentally drained. Ever since she'd come to, she'd been racking her brains, trying to figure out what had happened to her. She had absolutely no idea who the people in the brownstone were; and although she'd felt certain they wanted to do a spinal tap, she hadn't the faintest inkling why. But her greatest fear was that if they wanted her before, they might want her again.

Langford looked straight ahead, clenching his teeth. Was what she was saying even *remotely* possible? Jordan certainly didn't seem the type to make things up. Yet her tale seemed *so* preposterous, and people on drugs had been known to say outlandish things. Still, he owed it to her, he supposed, to keep an open mind. And he actually wanted to believe her.

"And you're certain you don't want to go back to your apartment?"

"Not till Julie's home. I told you, I'm not going to stay alone. They might still be watching."

"All right, tell you what. You can hang out in my on-call room, get some rest. Let whatever's in your system wear off. That sound okay?"

"Fine."

As he escorted her through the hospital to the on-call area, he got a staf page from the emergency room. The EMTs radioed ahead that they were transporting several shooting victims from an early-morning drive-by in Spanish Harlem. From the description of the injuries, it sounded like the ER would be jumping.

Within ten minutes, the scene was chaotic. Not two, but five patients arrived, four of them in critical condition. The fifth was dead on arrival. Soon the ER was swarming with family members, medical personnel, cops, and reporters. It was a mob scene. The trauma teams quickly found themselves overwhelmed. The minutes turned to hours, and it wasn't until four P.M. that the frantic pace slowed. A second gunshot victim had died, another was declared brain-dead, and the other two were still in surgery.

Finally, Langford retreated to the on-call to check on Jordan. But she was gone. In her place, there was a note.

"Julie finally got home. I'm going to spend some time with her. Thanks for everything," read the simple message. "Sorry I jumped on you like that. I know you were just doing your job. Call me."

When he did, Jordan said she'd just gotten out of the shower. She was glad he called. She agreed that there was a lot they had to discuss, but she asked if it could possibly wait. Todd agreed. Speaking with Jordan was just what he needed, an emotional revitalization. He thought about her green eyes, her hair, and even about what she was wearing.

Sure, it was possible she might be a kook. People with serious drug problems could be very persuasive, and convincing addicts had fooled him before. But his gut told him she wasn't, and he wanted to spend more time with her. He closed his eyes and contentedly lay back on the call-room bed, phone to his ear. But a strident voice and urgent knock on the door soon interrupted him.

Like a storm cloud, yet another emergency was descending on the hospital. He quickly rang off. Once he'd dealt with that problem, another crisis developed. He didn't have a minute to himself until nearly twelve. When he finally had a chance to rest, it was well past midnight. Back in his room, he quickly fell asleep.

Jeffrey Donninger thought his wife looked fantastic. It had been more than half a day since her phenomenal recovery, and she was allowed to sit in a chair for the first time since her surgery. Although she still had one IV, she was permitted sips of water by mouth. Her cheeks were pink, her hair was brushed, and her eyes were glistening. To him, she was every bit as beautiful as when they'd first met.

She'd been slow to accept what happened to her. As her amnesia cleared, Rita recalled being in the ER, concerned about Jordan. After that, she remembered nothing until she'd awakened in the ICU. Once she'd fully awakened, her immediate concern had been for her baby. Jeff explained that Adrianna was fine, in terrific shape. Then, with the help of Dr. Silver, he slowly recounted everything that occurred. Rita was astonished.

Incredulous though she was, her greater interest lay with her child. She hadn't yet seen Adrianna, and everyone's reassurances notwithstanding, she wouldn't stop worrying until she held her baby in her arms. The

time had now come. With her husband at her side, she
watched apprehensively as they wheeled the warmer
across the room. The nurse gently lifted the still-
sleeping child, then handed the baby to Rita.

Rita cradled her arms around the tightly wrapped
bundle with a look of wonder. She didn't know what
to say. A fold of blanket obscured Adrianna's head,
and Jeff lifted it away. Their daughter's face was red
and full and fragrant, and soft, brown hair curled grace-
fully around her ears like fine down. Adrianna wriggled, scrunching up her tiny eyes, pursing her lips.
Rita's full breasts immediately began aching. A smile
of joy and gratitude spread over her face, and her eyes
were moist with tears.

Despite all that had happened, everything was now
right with the world.

"You look great today, Sal. How're you feelin'?"

"Never better, Joey. Like a kid again." Indeed,
Aiello seemed reborn. Back straight, eyes gleaming,
he'd completely regained his vitality.

"That's great, Sal."

"I tell ya, we are gonna kick ass in court! Who do
the feds think they are, screwin' with me like that?
They got nothin' on me, y'hear?"

"I hear ya, boss." Joey shook his head in awe,
astonished by the don's improvement. It had been less
than twenty-four hours since the injection, and the results were nothing short of miraculous. Aiello seemed
to have as much vigor as when they'd first met years
ago.

The problem was, no one seemed to know how long
the effects would last. A week, a month? Would it have
to be repeated? The doctor said they had only the one
dose. The don was a man of fierce determination, but
he was also capable of anger that bordered on rage.
When he discovered his improvement might not be per-
manent, he could turn on them with a wrath that knew
no bounds.

Chapter Twelve

THE NEXT MORNING, LANGFORD SLEPT UNTIL NOON. Although he was off duty at seven A.M., he wasn't emotionally prepared to return to his empty house. Thus, as soon as his relief came on, he retired to the on-call room, physically drained, and sacked out on the unmade bed, still clad in his whites. Sleeping late was a normal practice after a grueling twenty-four hours on call.

As soon as he got up, he started thinking about Jordan. He was concerned about her. The drug should have largely worn off by now, but since he didn't know what it was, he worried about possible lingering effects. He called Jordan.

"Glad you're still home," he said.

"Actually, I just got back. Julie and I took a ride up to see Rita for a few minutes. I'm still too shaky to go anywhere by myself."

"Is your roommate still there?"

"For a little while. She's going out with her boyfriend soon."

"You get any sleep?" he asked.

"Not much. I kept thinking about everything that happened in the past few days—to me, to Rita. Maybe Dr. Minkoff was right."

"How do you mean?"

"He kept hinting that I take some time off. I decided

that I will, maybe a week or two. They can do without me on the wards. And I'm way behind on my reading for internal medicine." She paused. "This might be a good time for me to catch up on my *Harrison*."

He wondered what she was leaving unsaid. "There's more, isn't there?"

"Well . . . Are you doing anything today?"

"Not really."

"How about going for a ride with me? I want to show you something."

Half an hour later, he pulled up in front of her apartment. Jordan bounced out of the building and made a beeline for his car, still looking shaken. "Thank God you're here."

"Where to?"

"Go across Houston, then north on First."

He knew where they were heading, but he wanted her to bring it up. Jordan's face had a worried but determined expression. He distracted her with light-hearted teasing about her collision with the VCR.

"Slow down," she said. "Take a left at the next corner."

They leisurely crept west, across Thirty-ninth. Langford watched Jordan out of the corner of his eye. Her skin had an unhealthy pallor, and her lips were pressed into a thin line. Finally she raised a trembling finger and pointed to a building midway down the block.

"This the place?"

She nodded weakly. "You don't happen to have some sort of weapon with you?"

He knew she meant it. "Come on, we won't need anything like that."

He parked the car and helped her out, holding her hand. Jordan looked scared to death. But her fear was mixed with steely determination he hadn't noticed before. As they crossed the street, she gripped his fingers tightly. Soon they were on the front steps. But as they neared the top, her gait slowed, and her jaw began to drop.

"The name plaque . . . it's *gone*."

"The what?"

"It said, 'Dr. Merendino's Office,' or something like that."

Langford inspected where she was pointing. The only thing there were three bronze street numerals, weathered to a bluish tint. "These look like they've been here for a while. Are you sure this is the right address?"

"I'm positive." Without hesitation, she stepped forward and rang the bell.

"You sure you want to do this?"

"I'm not imagining things, Todd. I was here yesterday morning."

Through the door glass, they saw someone approach. Langford felt Jordan tense. Seconds later, the door eased ajar, and a tall, gaunt man dressed in a butler's attire peered down his nose at them. His voice had a haughty tone.

"May I help you?"

"I want to see Dr. Merendino," she said firmly.

"I beg your pardon?"

"The doctor who works here, for God's sake!"

He bestowed his most patrician stare. "I'm afraid you're mistaken. This is a private residence. There is no doctor—"

"Bullshit!" An enraged Jordan put her shoulder to the door, nearly bowling the man over as she stormed past.

"Jordan!" Langford called, running after her.

She was already halfway down the hall. "He's here, I know it!"

The butler was quickly on their heels. "If you don't leave at once, I'm going to call the police."

"Go ahead, call 'em!" She barged into the area she had known as the waiting room. "It's about time we . . ." Her voice trailed off to a whisper. Jordan slowed down and looked around in astonishment. She was standing in the middle of what was unmistakably an ornate den. Fully stocked bookshelves were everywhere, along with leather recliners and reading lamps. She weakly shook her head, pointing to a spot by the wall. "There was a desk over there."

The butler reached for a telephone. "This goes beyond trespassing," he said, dialing 911. "The police will have their say about behavior like this."

"Whose house is this?" Langford tried politely. "Could I speak with them?"

"No one's home now, and that's really none of your business."

Langford reached for her arm. "I think we'd better split."

She pulled out of his grasp, walking around the corner. In place of the consultation room, there was now a dining area, complete with dinner table, chairs, and a china cabinet. Her voice had grown hollow. "This was his office."

He caught up with her. "Come on, Jor."

But she was off again, heading down the hall to where the bathroom had been. She opened the door and looked inside, crestfallen. The room was a fully stocked linen closet. It was all she could do to face Langford. "I swear to you, Todd . . ."

This time, when he took her arm, she allowed herself to be led away. She felt limp. He put his arm around her shoulder and gently drew her back toward the front entrance. The butler was close on their heels.

"I was hoping you'd stay," he said tersely. "I was looking forward to seeing you both led off in handcuffs."

They lunched on black beans and green wine at the Cafe Brazilia, a small ethnic restaurant in Englewood. The eatery's midday clientele was predominantly Portuguese, with a smattering of Spanish-speaking or Italian patrons. Over platters of garlicky fish and pork, they politely discussed their families and the don before turning to the business at hand. They spoke in modulated tones, as if to keep from being overheard.

"You sure the girl can't cause problems?" asked Joey.

"She doesn't know a damn thing," said Vito. "Even if the cops believe her, there's no way she could finger us."

"The boys did a great job," Anthony Scarpatta agreed, pausing to wipe up some sauce with a thick crust of bread. "You can't believe how they turned the place over in under twelve hours."

"Maybe, but we shouldn't have been in that position to begin with," Joey said to a fourth man. "You nearly blew everything."

"We've already been through this," said Merendino. "Sure, I take responsibility for what happened, but I'm not sure we should have put ourselves in that position. I hate to be locked into a single source of supply. There've got to be better sources. More *plentiful* sources. And if there aren't, we can always get her back again."

"Then we'd better find them," said Vito. "I hear the boss is fumin'. If we don't come up with somethin' soon, all our asses are gonna be in a sling."

Jordan felt as if she were going insane. Here she was, just barely coping with the fact of being drugged and nearly experimented upon, when the office in which it happened literally disappeared. It seemed like some monstrous hoax, a charade perpetrated for reasons totally unknown. But she was also filled with growing self-doubt; and even before she returned to Langford's car, she began to wonder if she imagined the trip to the radiologist's office. Was the nightmarish scenario the result of her head injury, an organic hallucination?

She was still terrified something was seriously wrong with her brain. The man who'd claimed to be a radiologist might have lied about her CAT scan, but that didn't mean it was normal. The residents still could have missed something. How else could she explain her strange dreams, the bizarre thoughts, and the times she felt convinced someone wasn't telling the truth?

Too shaken up to even discuss it, Jordan withdrew, deciding she needed her space. As much as she felt indebted to Langford and enjoyed his company, the air between them was growing tense with acrimony and unspoken accusation. It would be best to take a break from one another for a few days, to mull things over, gather her wits. With any luck, she might even be able to figure out what was going on.

They drove back to her apartment in frosty silence, each absorbed in his or her own thoughts. Jordan asked him to make himself comfortable while she made her calls from the bedroom. Within twenty minutes, she secured both an invitation from her parents to visit them in Maine, and a reservation on a flight out of La Guardia. She quickly packed and accepted Todd's offer of a ride to the airport.

On Monday, Langford's first order of business, as soon as the ER quieted down, was to visit the medical staff office. The computerized name search didn't take long. There *was* one Merendino on the list—an attending in OB/GYN—but none in radiology. He suspected as much. Next, he went to the CAT scan room.

"Hello, Stace. How was the weekend?"

"Same old, same old. How come all the men I meet are such incredible dorks?"

"Would you believe it's God's will?"

"You're being such a skunk today, Todd. Did you come all the way up here to cheer me up?"

"Actually, I'm looking for some films. You remember the scan we did on that med student late Thursday night?"

"The head trauma?" she asked.

"Right. Have they been read yet?"

"I think the residents went over them on Saturday. There was a delay, remember? They'll be officially read this morning by someone in Weber's group."

"I want to take another look at it. Are they in one of these piles?"

"I think that stack over there," she indicated. "Isn't that the CTs?"

He leafed through the dozen or so manila folders. "Yeah, it is." He thumbed through them once, then once more, slowly frowning as he matched the names and dates. "It's not here, Stacy. Is there another pile somewhere?"

"Shouldn't be." She came over to join the search, looking around for stray folders. "Maybe someone signed it out." She looked at the ledger for weekend checkouts.

"Why would somebody do that?"

"Ours is not to reason why, Doctor." She double-checked the logbook entries. "Nope, not here."

"You mean someone just came in and took the damn thing?"

She shrugged. "Happens sometimes. But don't worry, it'll turn up. Always does."

Langford turned away, conscious of a sinking feeling in the pit of his stomach.

As he left radiology, Langford bumped into Mike Molloy on the elevator. The two of them often shared lunch with Dr. Fletcher, and Todd had the impression Molloy had been in awe of his boss. The young research assistant had his arms wrapped around a cardboard box filled with file folders.

"Mike," said Langford, "did the cops talk to you about Dr. Fletcher?"

"Yeah, the day after he died. Was that horrible, or what? I hear you found him."

Langford nodded. "He wanted to talk to me about something, but it was too late when I got there. Any idea why he wanted me to come over?"

"Nope. Dr. Fletcher sometimes played things close to the vest. He was funny that way, even with people he knew."

"I suppose you're right," said Todd, eyeing the files. "So what're you going to do now?"

"Oh, I don't know. I have some loose ends to tie up. It'll take me a week or two," he said, seeing from the floor indicator that the elevator was approaching the lobby. "Then, who knows? Something'll turn up."

"What exactly was it that Fletch discovered?" Todd asked, as the elevator doors opened. "Something about it had him really spooked."

"He never told me," said Molloy. "See you around."

"One more thing, Mike," Langford called after him. "Ever hear of someone named Scarpatta?"

Molloy halted in mid-stride, and for the briefest second his facial muscles had the slightest twitch. "Sorry, never heard of him," he said, walking away.

Josh Meyerson was in a hurry. He was supposed to meet one of the nurses for drinks at a local pub at five P.M., and it was already a few minutes past. Quickly rounding a corner toward the hospital exit, he ran squarely into somebody else, sending the man and his briefcase sprawling.

"Jeez, I'm sorry," Josh said, retrieving the briefcase. "Are you okay?"

The lanky man sat up and put his glasses back on. Gazing at Josh, he eased into a smile. "Meyerson. I might have known. Always in a hurry."

It was Roger Fine, head of the pharmacy. He'd always been amiable toward Josh. "You're right about that, Dr. Fine. I didn't mean to bowl you over, but a great-looking woman's waiting for me. How come you're leaving so early? The past few weeks, you were on the wards pretty late.''

''We were a little short-staffed,'' said Fine, brushing himself off. ''And I'm just about finished with a project I was working on, so now it's back to eight-to-five.''

''It looks like you're okay,'' said Josh. ''Gotta run. You know how women are.''

Fine watched Meyerson depart, shaking his head sympathetically. He never wanted to forget that he'd been young once, too.

Three days into her recovery, Rita was looking forward to finishing her hemodialysis treatment and returning to her hospital room. They had told her she could begin breast-feeding. Her breasts were aching. Most of the medications had to be out of her body before she started nursing. They'd stopped all the IV meds, and she was now only on a small dose of ampicillin, which should have little effect on the baby.

Back on the postpartum floor, Rita smiled to herself, marveling at just how lucky she'd been. She was filled with gratitude, both for the phenomenal efforts of her health-care team, and for all the friends and family who'd flocked to her bedside. Everything about her sickness and recovery was bizarre. She'd come an incredibly long way. Now, apparently the only thing remaining to make her recovery complete was receipt of a new kidney.

And she knew that she would get one, in time. Next to the cornea, the kidney was an abundantly transplanted organ. Her blood samples had already been sent out for tissue typing. The staff told her that she'd probably have the transplant within a few months. No matter. As she lay back in her hospital bed, Rita realized there were more important things in life. Her whole face softened as they wheeled Adrianna into the room.

Even at the comparatively old age of thirty-five, motherhood was proving to be everything she'd wished for.

Rita wiped her hands with an antiseptic towelette. "I'm a little nervous about this," she said.

"Everybody is the first time."

"You think she'll take to the breast? What if she already prefers the bottle?"

The nurse smiled encouragingly. "I guess there's only one way to find out."

Earlier, she'd shown Rita how to prepare her nipples. The baby lay on her stomach in the isolette, sleeping soundly. Propping herself up, Rita untied her gown and undid the clasp to her nursing bra, exposing her left breast. Using a washcloth and warm water, she completely removed the thin film of A & D ointment. Her nipple grew erect and ready. When the nurse picked up the baby, Adrianna gave a little grunt. Her tiny face contorted into a grimace, and a sleepy cry escaped her lips. When Rita heard the sound, she felt her nipple tighten. Milk quickly dripped from its tip. "I guess I'm ready," she said.

Her sleeping disrupted, Adrianna was softly crying. Rita took her from the nurse and held her snugly in her arms. The baby's cheek came to lie against her moist nipple. Feeling its closeness, the rooting reflex kicked in, and Adrianna's head turned into the breast. Her bowlike lips pursed and opened, sucking, seeking. Finally they latched onto the nipple. Rita felt tightness, then a surge as her milk let down. Almost immediately Adrianna was nursing contentedly, her little cheeks contracting in and out. Rita smiled and looked over at the nurse.

"I suppose that answers that."

"It's a great feeling, isn't it?" said the nurse.

Rita nodded. Indeed, it was one of the most satisfying sensations in the world. She now realized this was something she'd always wanted. With her child nursing at the breast, she felt fulfilled, complete. The worst was behind her, and everything was right with the world.

Nothing could possibly go wrong now.

This week, for some undetermined reason, living in the city had grown unusually hazardous for residents of lower Harlem and the Upper East Side, and the ER was swamped with all manner of accident, injury, and illness. Emergency room personnel were becoming particularly good at what they did best, which was keeping people alive. This was especially true of severe trauma and neurological cases. Their often-heroic techniques were practiced over and over again, until they became second nature.

Word of their expertise spread quickly. Already highly regarded in the hospital, the trauma teams garnered a first-rate reputation among public and private ambulance crews citywide. While the emergency rooms at Columbia, Mount Sinai, Lenox Hill, and St. Vincent's were considered good, in a rather short period of time, Metropolitan's ER came to be considered the gold standard. The skill of the health professionals who worked there became a self-fulfilling dilemma; the better they were, the more patients were referred to their institution for emergency care.

In Manhattan's competitive health-care market, this was not all that unusual, for reputations within a given specialty rose and fell as quickly as the stock market. But the upshot was a glut of admissions, especially the critical variety. Unfortunately, there was no place to put them. The ICUs were filled to capacity, and the medical and surgical wards were over census. Plans to downsize the hospital were put on hold. The halls outside the ER were brimming with stretcher-borne coma cases, parked end-to-end like a grisly armada preparing for battle.

But keep them alive they did. Drs. Hobson and Royce were continually after them to try to salvage even the most hopeless cases. The hospital developed a shortage of respirators, which had to be borrowed from other facilities. IV supplies were seriously depleted, until replenished by a rush shipment from Baxter. Yet a diligent Langford persevered through it all, even managing to fit in his spinal fluid studies. He expected that by now, Dr. Royce would notify him about how the study was going, but he hadn't heard a thing. By week's end, he estimated he'd delivered nearly a liter of CSF to Dr. Royce's lab.

The retreat to her parents' house on the Maine coast was just what Jordan needed. Freed from the bustle of New York, her days there were restful and relaxing. Although the weather had turned cool, she spent most of her time outdoors, taking long walks alone. From an idyllic patch of solitude overlooking Penobscot Bay, she could follow the lazy antics of overhead gulls, and she watched the clammers work the mud flats at low tide.

By midweek, her recent anxiety had considerably lessened. She felt refreshed, and she'd stopped looking over her shoulder to see if she was being followed. Although she still wondered about the bizarre incident in the doctor's office, she was no longer obsessed by it. She felt relaxed enough to call Rita every day. At night Jordan slept soundly, without nightmares. Being a practical person, she knew that too much of a good thing could lessen her appreciation of it. Besides, she was a city girl at heart.

It was time to go home.

For Langford, the hectic work was an anodyne. He missed Jordan, and he knew he would've become preoccupied with her dilemma, were it not for his workload. On Wednesday, when he had a slight break, he called Rick Scott at NYU to follow up on Jordan's toxicology screen. Scott told him that the lab was having some difficulty with it, because what they came up with wasn't a standard drug. But they'd finally identified it an hour before.

"You have any metapyrinol cases up there?"

Langford frowned. "I never even heard of it."

"Neither did I, but there are some cases in the southwest. It's brand new, a potent oral opiate-benzo combination. Causes rapid intoxication and sleep, just like you'd expect with a narcotic and tranquilizer."

"Where would she get something like that?"

"Good question. It's years from FDA approval, so the only sources are foreign. In the San Diego cases, it was smuggled across the border from Mexico."

Scott's information certainly raised interesting questions. Either Jordan had stumbled onto a little-known and frightening new street drug, or . . . Unanswered questions were suddenly swirling through his mind like little eddies: a doctor she had called Merendino; a missing X-ray folder; and Courtney's information about Mafia medical involvement. He wondered if any of it could possibly be related to Fletcher's murder, and his friend's mention of a mysterious Scarpatta. None of it made sense to him.

Hoping someone else might help him make sense of things, he decided to run his fragmented thoughts by Tom Courtney. The ex-DEA agent had a mind that was used to integrating seemingly unrelated clues. Before he left work on Thursday, he gave Courtney a ring. His friend promised to check into it.

Friday night, Jordan surprised him with a call. A week with her parents was enough, she said, and she'd be returning to the city the next morning. Did he want to get together that weekend? They made arrangements to meet on Sunday.

Langford was finishing his shift on Saturday when Royce showed up unexpectedly. The chief of staff was generally considered to be a nine-to-five, Monday-through-Friday physician. Langford guessed he must be up to something important.

"Got your hands full, Langford?" he asked, clapping him warmly on the back.

"Yes, sir. It's been hell week here. I don't know where all these patients are coming from."

"Word gets around, I suppose. I just wanted to congratulate you. Your team has been doing a great job. To a man, all the attendings—and the people in administration—are very appreciative. And I wanted to give my personal thanks for your splendid effort on the CSF study. You've certainly been earning your stipend."

"No problem, Dr. Royce. How's that going, anyway?"

"Very well. We should have some preliminary results soon. I'm sorry I can't share them with you yet. The drug manufacturer insists on keeping everything under wraps. Suffice it to say that I'm very excited about what we've found."

"Glad to hear it. Any chance of getting my name on the research paper?"

Royce smiled. "That goes without saying. Look, I've got some good news about the hospital census. I realize the pace has been pretty hectic around here—"

"It's not the work, Dr. Royce," Langford interrupted. "That's our job. It's the conditions. I realize it's a city hospital, and there are financial considerations. But we've got patients in the halls, backed up like freight cars. A lot of them are critical. This place is a disaster in the making. With this kind of overcrowding, we can't give the proper care. And with the patients stacked like cordwood, there's a real risk of an epidemic."

"That's why I'm here. Everyone's aware of the situation. Dr. Hobson and I have spoken with administration, and I think we have a solution. We're putting

finishing touches on a critical-care facility not far from
here to help with the patient load.''

"We? What facility?"

"Hobson, I, and some investors. We realized something had to be done about the overcrowding. We've
owned an old apartment building for a while, just off
First Avenue. Used it for research, storage, and things
like that. We recently fixed it up. Then we got approval
from the city and state health departments. Starting
Monday, eligible patients are going to be transferred
there to relieve the census. We're calling it Eastgate.''

"This is happening awfully fast, Dr. Royce,'' Todd
said. "We've only had this crowding problem a few
weeks. How'd you get all the approvals and put the
place together so quickly?''

"There's a little luck involved,'' Royce said with a
smile. "But basically it's a matter of knowing the right
people. And paying construction men twice the going
rate to work 'round the clock.''

Langford's eyes narrowed. At first blush, it sounded
like a great idea. Royce stood to make money on the
deal, but the older man had a reputation as an empathic
physician, and he doubted the motive was financial.
Moreover, Langford knew the state was putting a priority on moving long-term patients, such as chronic
neurological cases or ventilator patients, out of acute-
care hospitals. But chronic and critical were hardly the
same thing.

"How are you going to manage that? A lot of these
people are just circling the drain, a heartbeat away from
another cardiac arrest. What they need is an ICU, not
chronic care.''

"We've considered that,'' Royce nodded. "No one
will ever be denied an appropriate level of care. But
you know as well as I do that not all of these patients
can be salvaged. Some are rather hopeless. We've developed an airtight protocol to deal with precisely that
issue. Once it's been determined that a given patient

has virtually no chance of being successfully resuscitated—hopelessly circling the drain, as you put it—he'll be eligible for transfer. Under no circumstances will we permit anyone to suffer from what's basically an administrative decision.''

"I don't know," said Langford. "Seems a little risky, from a medical standpoint. You know what they say about something sounding too good to be true."

Royce laughed. "Have faith, my young friend. This is going to work out to everyone's benefit."

Jordan Parker-Ross was never fully aware of the way her hair drew glances from everyone around her. On that October Sunday, her auburn tresses gleamed. She had side-parted, shoulder-length hair whose layered edges curled inward. When she moved her head, each glossy strand, backlit by the sun, seemed to sparkle. Langford stretched out on the picnic blanket, enjoying the way her hair played in the breeze.

His eagerness to see her surprised him, but he admitted he was starting to feel peculiarly incomplete without her. He thought that her buoyant mood indicated she felt likewise. She was full of energy and playful chatter. The week with her parents had obviously done her good, and her long visit with Rita had been reassuring. Before he picked her up at eleven, he stopped at a gourmet deli for picnic fare. Fortified with homemade cioppino, baguettes, and Southwestern fruit salad, they drove to Central Park and found a grassy expanse in the lower Seventies, determined not to spoil the moment by bringing up the unpleasant events of the previous week.

As they unpacked, he told her about his workweek. Jordan listened with interest and consideration, rarely interrupting. It seemed important for him to talk about it. He was especially absorbed in the riddle of the two patients who had miraculously improved. Finally, his voice trailed off.

"Does there have to be an answer for everything?" she asked. "I realize everything's supposed to make sense in medicine, but I bet this happens more often than you think. Why couldn't it just be good luck?"

"Jordan, once you get into your clinical rotations, you'll appreciate that doctors don't put much stock in luck. We're pretty logical people, maybe too logical. For every sign or symptom, there should be a medical explanation. When your professor asks why the patient improved, smiling back and chalking it up to good luck is going to get you nowhere."

"Then maybe it's coincidence," she said. "Was it just those two patients?"

"Two that I'm aware of, but I've heard there might be another three or four. A woman on fourteen with severe aphasia, and a male with unstable angina and severe CHD."

"They're all supposed to have gotten better?"

" 'Cured' is more like it. It's as if they were never sick at all. I'm going to check out the other charts when I get a chance."

"Is there a common denominator, something they all have in common?"

"Not that I can find. I mean, they're all old and sick." He paused, mentally shuffling through the deck, selecting a card. "Well, maybe not. There's supposed to be this nearly brain-dead kid on pediatrics who came somersaulting out of a coma. Head trauma."

"So they're all cardiac or neurology patients."

"No, they're . . ." Again, he hesitated. "I don't know. Maybe they are. I hadn't thought of that."

"Why aren't there any renal or gynecology patients? Could that be important?"

"I doubt it, but you never know. Why do you ask?"

"I had a job this summer working for the city health department. It was all epidemiology and statistics. We looked for common threads, equations, and things that are mathematically precise. The statistician's job is to make sense out of things that at first seem unrelated. So I was just wondering.''

"Maybe you ought to check into this stuff.''

"I wouldn't mind.''

Jordan had already gotten permission, she said, to skip classes for another week. Although she could definitely use the rest, she wanted to keep her mind busy, but not by reading chapter after chapter of internal medicine. To Langford, the idea of having Jordan around the hospital was both delightful and reassuring. He could certainly use a fresh epidemiological perspective on what was going on. They discussed it further, opening a bottle of Portuguese *vino verde* she'd brought, drinking from plastic cups. Under the influence of the food and wine, the day grew languorous. At length they both leaned back, silently enjoying the brilliant summer sun.

This time, she drank more than he did. The wine, besides making her sleepy, was a great social lubricant, emboldening Jordan to inquire about something that interested her a lot: his social life. She knew he wasn't married, but little more than that. Soon they were leisurely discussing their relationships, past and present; their commitments, of which there were few; and their values. Jordan was relieved to find that he was as unattached as she was. Lying flat on her back, she yawned self-consciously and closed her lids, shielding her eyes in the crook of her arm. The warmth of sleep began to overtake her.

"What's the sexiest thing you ever did?'' she asked.

"Did, or happened to me?''

"Your choice.''

Closing his eyes to the overhead glare, he relaxed beside her, their shoulders softly touching. "I guess it would be at this wedding two years ago. A guy I knew from college was getting married. Nice affair up in Westchester, black tie. I went by myself, and I didn't know any people there. Anyway, I wound up having sex with someone I never met before, and have never seen since." Hearing her breathing grow heavy, he glanced her way. "You listening?"

"This is going to be one of those male fantasy things," she managed.

"No, it really happened. The bridesmaids all wore these low-cut, tight, black satin sheaths. One of them was a knockout. Very tan, a bleached blond with a dynamite figure. I remember catching her eye during the exchange of vows. I guess it was just flirting, but it was pretty intense. I remember seeing the blond standing outside on the terrace by herself, looking out across the golf course. For some reason, I knew that was the moment. I got a bottle of champagne, two glasses, and went outside to take my chances."

The lightness of sleep flowed over her like a tide. Warmed by the sun and the wine, she drifted off weightlessly. She could still hear him, but it was far away, a faint and distant perception.

"I don't recall saying very much," he continued. "I held up the bottle, and she nodded. She asked me to light her cigarette. I didn't have a match, so instead I said something very clever, like 'Why don't we take a walk instead?' And that was all she wrote. Before you knew it, we were doing it on the fairway grass below the second tee."

She hovered in that nether place, neither awake nor truly asleep, just below the surface of consciousness. It was that state known to mothers of infants, when they can lie in bed enduring the loudest traffic, yet hear their baby's tiniest cry. And in that peculiar state, Jordan felt it yet again, the feeling of absolute certainty that Todd was lying. Her heart started to pound, and her lids fluttered open.

"I don't believe you."

"Why not?" he asked with a laugh. "You asked me, so I told you."

"But you're not telling the truth!"

"How would you know?"

How *did* she know? She shakily propped herself up on an elbow. Was something terribly wrong inside her head?. "I . . . I just know, that's all."

"But, Jordan, you weren't exactly there."

"Look, I'm trying to explain this, okay?" she began, hesitating. Could she tell him the truth? Would he believe her? "I've always had this, well, what I'd call a knack, for lack of a better word. And lately, it's become something even more powerful."

"I'm not sure I follow you."

"Haven't you ever lied to someone, and then they just stare at you? And without their saying a word, you just *know* they can see right through you?"

He thought about it. "Well, there was this one girl up in Boston . . ."

"You rat! I'm trying to be serious!"

"Okay, okay," he said with a smile. "I guess I have known people like that. It's just that you do it so *well*."

"I know. That's what scares me."

He shrugged. "I wouldn't worry about it. Maybe you're a closet psychic."

In mid-afternoon, they folded the picnic blanket and set out for a drive. Todd didn't know what to make of Jordan's sudden reticence, the lengthening shadow of distrust between them. He drove in silence up to the G. W. Bridge, then west and north, along the Palisades. They took in the scenery without talking.

As they drove along, Jordan's wariness slowly lessened. When she thought he wouldn't notice, she cast sidelong glances his way. She hoped she hadn't insulted him, and his laughing disclaimer had been reassuring. But she couldn't help what she'd done. Her contrary reaction to his tale had been a peculiar and frightening kind of automatic response she didn't fully understand. She hadn't meant to jump on him like that; it was just . . . *reflex*.

In fact, almost everything about him was low-key and playful. She wondered if his frolicsome personality had developed as a reaction to the stresses of his job. She vividly remembered the way he'd kissed her, several days before. Now, despite her anxiety, she desperately wanted to kiss him back. Eventually, they crossed back into New York and retreated south. He skirted across Westchester, winding through Yonkers to the Bronx.

"Hungry?" he asked.

"Not really." She watched him yawn. "Tired?"

"A little." He nodded. "Sorry. It was a long week."

"Maybe you should take a nap."

"Shut-eye behind the wheel is frowned upon."

"No, I'm serious. You live near here, don't you?"

"About ten minutes."

"So why don't we go to your place for a little while? It's only five o'clock. You hit the sack for an hour or two, and I'll tweeze my eyebrows or something. Then we can go out to eat and maybe take in a movie. My treat."

He looked at her and laughed. "This is the first time a date has told me I need some rest. I must be Mr. Excitement."

"More than you know."

His bedroom faced west, and the setting sun cast lazy beams of light through half-closed blinds. He'd been asleep for ninety minutes. In the nearby living room, Jordan turned off the TV and glided toward the bedroom. She knew precisely what she was doing. There was no alcohol now, no excuse, and no distractions. They had only each other. And she wanted him.

Standing outside the bedroom, she heard the soft sound of the window air conditioner. She turned the knob and eased the door ajar. As she let herself in, the hinges made an audible creak. The tiny noise made him stir, and he rolled onto his back, the linen bunching around his ankles. He was wearing only his briefs. Jordan took in his tousled hair, and the straight line of his jaw. In the slatted sunlight, his lean body looked ruggedly handsome.

She took off her shoes and quickly disrobed, tossing her top aside, letting her cutoffs and panties form a pile around her bare feet. Then she sat next to him on the bed and leaned forward until the strands of her shimmering hair played softly about his face.

Emerging from a dream, Langford opened his eyes and drank in her perfume. Highlighted by the sun, her auburn strands took on a surreal look. The nearness of her warm and dappled skin was intoxicating, and when her lips softly grazed his ear, he sighed contentedly. Her voice was husky.

"Is it true that all men have erections when they wake up?"

"I can't speak for all men."

"Then maybe you shouldn't speak at all."

Before he could reply, he was silenced by the light touch of her hand on his stomach. Her nails trailed dreamily through the hairs of his lower abdomen, a hallucinatory caress. Her feathery breath was hot against his cheek. When her fingers strayed beneath the elastic of his briefs, he closed his eyes and reached for her. But she stilled his touch, meeting his hand with her own.

"No," she whispered. "Let me."

Against his mouth, a stiffening nipple. Her breasts moved across his lips in provocative undulations whose tempo matched the beating of his heart. Then she undressed him, deft motions that mirrored her desire. For the first time, he appreciated her nakedness, and his arousal was complete. As she moved atop him with nimble grace, he lay back in surrender.

She kissed him then, a deliberate, delicate kiss that hung there beckoning. When she took hold of him, he could lie still no more. His arms went around her in an embrace, strength mixed with passion. His lips were touched by fire, and his tongue sought hers, reaching, probing. Neither of them could hold back.

Their coming together was a union delayed, a promise fulfilled. They couldn't get enough. Their ardor was deep and mutual, a suppressed hunger they couldn't restrain. Locked in a lovers' embrace, they drank deeply of one another. Finally they lay together, spent, his cheek against hers, not wanting to move.

Hours later, thoughts of a movie forgotten, they lay asleep in each other's arms. When he awoke, Langford carefully disengaged and got up to go. to the bathroom. He returned to lean over the bed and nuzzled her awake, nibbling on the side of her neck. She smiled with eyes closed.

"Is that what you did with the girl at the country club?" she asked.

"Do I look like the kiss-and-tell type?"

"You really didn't make it with her on the golf course, did you?"

"Well . . . How'd you know?"

No, she thought, I can't tell him yet. What happened is still scaring me too much. "I just knew, that's all."

"You little skunk. How could you tell?"

"Trade secret," she said, putting a finger to her mouth. "My lips are sealed."

"Not if I can help it."

He suddenly kissed her firmly, forcibly parting her lips, pulling down the sheets and covering her naked body with his. Their mutual arousal was instantaneous. Soon they were locked in an embrace, each hungrily exploring the other's body, overcome by desire.

He lay atop her, drained. Their dewy perspiration soon cooled in the air-conditioned breeze. Her heartbeat slowed, and he could hear her breathing relax and become more regular. When he was certain she was asleep, he gently rolled away. Replacing the covers, he placed his head on the pillow beside her, his lips next to her ear.

"I really think I love you," he said. "And it scares the heck out of me."

She was in that twilight place again, the arena of inconsistent awareness, hovering before the portals of slumber. Nerve endings discharged and synapses fired as her auditory cortex processed the verbal stimuli. Despite her diminished reactions, her perception was heightened. That part of her brain that constituted awareness was fully operative. Subconsciously, she could gauge his verbal tone, his pulse, and his respiratory rate. And it was good.

Relaxed and contented, Langford tenderly kissed one eyelid, then the other. He was in a playful mood. "If my wife had been that responsive," he said devilishly, "I might have stayed married."

Her eyes suddenly flashed open. Nostrils flaring, Jordan raised her head, her frightened gaze fixing on his. She didn't know how; she just knew. In that moment, Langford also knew. And it worried the hell out of him.

"Excuse me?" the ICU nurse said politely. "*Excuse* me?"

The two paramedics wheeling the stretcher slowly came to a halt by the nurses' station. "Where's bed nine?" one asked. "We're here for the transport."

"Transport? It's three A.M. Nobody told me about a transport."

"Figures. That's why we've got the paperwork." He handed her a sheaf of papers.

"Patient transport?" she mumbled. "At this hour of the night?" But she took the papers anyway. The first was a copy of the face sheet of a patient's chart, containing demographic, diagnostic, and billing information. Then there were EMT routing slips, a business office authorization, and a doctor's order sheet, with the transfer signed by Dr. Minkoff. Finally, the nurse shrugged. "Okay, I guess. Where're you taking her?"

"P and S," said the first paramedic.

"Columbia? What're they going to do with her over there?"

"Lady, we just drive the ambulance." He looked down the ward. "Which bed's hers?"

The nurse hesitated for a moment. She'd never seen these two before, although their manner and appearance were professional. And she'd never heard of a non-emergency transfer during the night shift. She supposed she could call Dr. Minkoff, but . . . After a brief pause, she pointed the way. "Third on the left."

Five minutes later, the two men wheeled the stretcher out the darkened ER entrance. Within thirty seconds, a nondescript van carrying the moribund Shaheena Jackson sped off into the night.

Chapter Thirteen

CONSTANCE SWENSON, M.D., CHIEF OF NEUROL-
OGY, was a small and wiry woman of limitless energy.
Some of that could be attributed to her addiction to
coffee and cigarettes. She was a tireless worker, and an
occasional tyrant to the residents. She listened to Langford's story about Jordan with characteristic impa-
tience, asking questions and punctuating her remarks
with jabs of a cigarette.

"And you believe her?" she asked.

He chewed on his lip. "I don't know what to believe.
But last night, when she finally told me about this, well
'knack' of hers, I could see that she was scared out of
her wits. She's thinking about seeing a neurologist.
She's terrified something's seriously wrong with her
brain."

"Do you think there is?" she asked.

"That's why I'm here. All I know is that *she* believes it. She can be pretty damn convincing. I just
don't see how it's possible."

"You're looking for a medical explanation."

"Connie," he said, "I told Jordan to hold off on
seeing a doctor, and I didn't tell her I was coming here.
I guess I just want a little reassurance. I suppose I'll
settle for a reasonable hypothesis."

"And she claims that until the time of her injury,
she never had this 'knack,' as you call it?"

"No, she says she could always do it, but to a lesser degree. It's just that since the bump on her head, she just does it better. Or more frequently. Or both."

"I take it you believe her. Maybe a part of you *wants* to believe her." She paused. "Are you sleeping with her?"

"Dr. Swenson . . ."

"*Are* you? I have to know where you're coming from."

"What if I am? Okay, so I might not be totally objective. But I'm a cynic at heart. If anything, my relationship with her makes what she says even *more* dubious, not more credible." He looked at her hopefully. "C'mon, Con. I'm after logic here, not psychoanalysis."

Swenson took a deep drag on her Marlboro, lost in thought. "I don't know if conjecture qualifies as logic."

"Conjecture away."

"First of all, people like her aren't that uncommon," she said. "The literature's filled with anecdotes about patients with unusual powers of perception. Everybody knows someone can get amnesia from a bump on the head. The brain's a complex structure, and sometimes its wiring gets jumbled. But occasionally, it does just the opposite. There have been lots of times when a patient winds up with heightened abilities after a concussion, at least temporarily. Head injuries have been known to do strange things."

"So?"

"All I'm saying is, she might be one of those people whose powers of perception are sharpened after cerebral trauma."

"So this knack of hers is refined by her injury?"

"That's the way I see it," said Swenson. "And when she's semiconscious, or drowsy, she can do it even better, because all the conscious interruptions get filtered out."

"I find all this a little incredible."

"I'm not stating it as a fact, Todd. All I'm saying is, what happened to her is medically possible. Does that bother you?"

"Put yourself in my place, Connie. How many guys would be thrilled to find out that the girl they're dating is a human polygraph?"

It was a magnificent early fall morning, crisp around the edges, with brilliant overhead sunshine and a whisper of chill in the air. It was a day to be outdoors. Yet in spite of the favorable weather, the general public largely ignored the Monday ribbon-cutting ceremony. But the press was fully represented, with members of the various media jockeying for position in front of the building's Ninety-fourth Street entrance. Hobson and Royce were present, along with several non-physician investors. The guest of honor was the mayor, who beamed with his trademark toothiness as he stepped up to the podium.

"I'll try to keep my remarks uncharacteristically brief," he said with a smile. "This is a landmark day in the long history of medical care in this city. New York has always been a shining example of medical progress and innovation. We have the finest research and clinical facilities in the nation, bar none. The opening of Eastgate continues that tradition of excellence, but with an important new direction. Across the country, medicine stands at an economic crossroads. We in New York are determined to keep patient care both first-rate and financially viable. Today, the city of New York is embarking on a model partnership with the private sector—a model which will suit both our needs as we move into the next century together." He turned to his side. "Would you agree with that, Dr. Royce?"

"That about says it all, Your Honor."

His Honor then handed a ceremonial scissors to a woman in a wheelchair. Still recovering from severe neurologic injuries, the woman had become a spokesperson for the handicapped. Cameras flashed as she wheeled across the rostrum, where she cut the ribbon with a flourish.

A reporter shouted a question. "Are you already accepting patients?"

"Yes," said Hobson, "we began today."

"When do we get a tour of the facility?"

"We'll have coffee in the reception area when the ceremony's over."

"What about the patient floors?"

Royce held up his palms in a gesture of patience. "All in good time. We'll announce an in-depth tour as soon as the kinks are ironed out."

Mingling easily with the media was a blond-haired bystander, the same man who had followed Jordan from the hospital. Unless they found the other sources they wanted, getting her back again was still an option. Listening intently to what was said, he observed everything that went on.

On West 112th Street, the police struggled to keep the passersby from getting too close. The victim, a twenty-four-year-old black man, was something of a curiosity, inasmuch as he had the front three inches of a meat cleaver buried in the top of his skull. He lay on the pavement unconscious, his head in a congealing pool of blood, as the crowd gawked nearby. In the background, the undulating wail of an emergency services van became louder as the ambulance approached.

Soon the paramedics got out, bearing a collapsible stretcher. They carefully stabilized the victim's head, making no attempt to remove the cleaver. With the assistance of several officers, they eased the man onto the stretcher and then quickly loaded him into the ambulance.

"You guys need an escort?" asked one of the cops.

"Thanks, we're good."

"Where're you headed, uptown or St. Luke's?"

"We're workin' on that now," said the paramedic. "Appreciate your help."

Moments later, they sped off, siren wailing. They headed north, toward Columbia. But then they turned east, going all the way across 125th Street, before heading south on Second Avenue. It seemed an unnecessarily long, circuitous trip.

But the money they were being paid to bring this sort of patient to Metropolitan made it all worthwhile.

The Tuesday morning article on page six of the Metro section of the *Times* was similar to that in other New York area dailies. It warranted a scant two columns, and was largely taken from a press release jointly issued by the New York City Health Department and Medical Partners, Inc. According to the article, the Eastgate medical facility was an interim solution to the unexpected overcrowding that plagued several of the city's municipal hospitals. Intended for the maintenance treatment of severe trauma cases, the clinic reportedly offered state-of-the-art high-tech equipment "for the safe, continuous care of the injured patient awaiting return to an acute-care or chronic medical institution." The article concluded by stating that the first patients had been transferred to Eastgate on Monday.

Safe, my butt, thought Jordan. She put down the paper and shook her head. Todd had told her of Dr. Royce's plans for the clinic. While it sounded great in theory, she was in complete agreement with his misgivings about the riskiness of transferring critically ill patients. But maybe she was being judgmental. For the time being, perhaps she should give the place the benefit of the doubt.

Anyway, she had other things on her mind. She'd made her morning phone calls, touching base with Rita, thrilled by her steady progress. Julie had just left for work, and Jordan was once more feeling apprehensive and didn't want to be by herself. Despite Todd's reassurances, she still wondered if she had a tumor. When she was alone with her thoughts, Jordan was behind enemy lines.

She'd begun wondering again if she was being followed; unless Todd or Julie were around, she had to get out of her apartment. And idleness was a problem in its own right. As a person accustomed to daily mental activity, she was becoming antsy. Although she wasn't ready for the rigors of classwork, she wanted to keep herself busy on the wards. Todd told her that once he got clearance, he'd have her help him with a biostatistical chart review in a few days.

For those who toiled in the hospital admitting office, the opening of the Eastgate clinic was something of a godsend. Even with little public fanfare, the hospital census quickly fell to acceptable levels, a manageable one-hundred-two-percent occupancy. Within several days, critically ill patients no longer filled the hospital corridors. By Thursday, between five and six patients per day were being transferred in a macabre medical exodus.

Langford observed the daily transfers with mixed feelings. A patient with a fractured neck, immobilizing orthopedic halo fastened to his skull and shoulders, would be gently lifted into a transport van, while a patient with terminal Lou Gehrig's disease, comatose and on a respirator, had his ventilator setting adjusted prior to the trip. In many cases, the patient had recently been stabilized, within twenty-four hours of recovering from a cardiopulmonary arrest. So while Langford was relieved that his workload was reduced, he felt intellectually incomplete. His concept of saving patients, of restoring them to some sort of normalcy, was under assault.

The unshakable feeling that something was not quite right troubled him. It wasn't simply a moral reservation about the appropriateness of transferring such sick patients; rather, his suspicions stemmed from little things, such as Royce's glibness, and the suddenness with which events were occurring. Todd recalled feeling the same way when he reviewed the charts of what he now thought of as the "miracle patients." It was an irritation, a mental burr, an illogical itch he couldn't scratch. The root of the problem, he supposed, was that he was being asked to accept something on blind faith, something he could neither understand nor explain.

At one P.M., he was just leaving the library when the overhead loudspeakers blared. "Code ninety-nine, fourteen south. Anesthesia, fourteen south. Code ninety-nine, fourteen south."

Fourteen south was the neuro ward. Langford raced down the corridor to the stairwell, taking the steps two at a time. By the time he breathlessly reached fourteen, he found a trio of nurses quickly wheeling a crash cart to a room in the middle of the floor. Close on their heels, Langford turned into the room.

He was the first physician to arrive. As he skidded to a halt, Langford quickly appraised the situation. Lying on the bed, unresponsive, was a familiar-looking elderly man. His half-opened eyes stared vacantly at the ceiling, and a limp right leg tumbled off the mattress to the floor. The slate-colored skin of his face was mottled, and flecks of frothy sputum clung to his lips like a receding tide. Above him, a nurse with tears in her eyes was pounding on the man's chest.

Langford wiped away the froth with a bedsheet and tilted the patient's head back. "Let's go, I need an airway!"

The nurses rummaged through the crash cart in confusion. "It's here somewhere, Doctor."

He looked on, exasperated. "Come on, this isn't *Rescue 911!*" Unable to wait, he pinched the man's nostrils and opened his mouth, checking for debris. The patient's upper denture had dislodged and was wedged in his throat. Langford plucked it out and quickly removed the lowers. The patient's tongue was already thick and dry. Then he leaned over, sealed the man's lips with his, and forced two deep exhalations. The patient's unshaved stubble grated his chin.

The nurses watched him, aghast. In municipal hospitals, direct mouth-to-mouth was frowned upon. "For God's sake, Todd, what are you doing?"

His eyes flashed at them. "Jesus, don't you guys at least have an ambu bag?"

"Here's the airway."

He quickly slipped the curved piece of plastic over the patient's tongue and into the pharynx. A loud and fetid belch escaped from the man's esophagus. He snugged the rubber mask on the black neoprene ambu bag against the mandible and began bagging, between chest compressions. The nurse pressing on the sternum seemed distraught.

"You okay, Karen?"

With tears wetting her cheeks, she nodded in shaky silence.

"Someone give her a hand already!"

Another nurse stepped in to relieve her, and Karen backed away, bursting into sobs. Langford stared at her, perplexed. As the initial person on the scene, she was the one most likely to know what happened. That information could prove crucial. "Don't quit on me now, Karen. I need you. What's the story here?"

Unable to contain herself, she fled from the room.

"Karen!" he called. "Would someone mind telling me what the hell is going on?"

The other nurses continued their feverish ministrations. "This is Mr. Stampf. An Alzheimer's patient who seemed to get better about ten days ago?"

The name sounded familiar. "So?"

"Karen got real attached to him. Said he reminded her of her father."

"I hate to tell her, but even fathers arrest. Here, let

me work on the IV. Rachel, take the bag.'' They switched places, and he applied a tourniquet, searching for a vein in the man's forearm. ''Christ, this is pathetic. Does *anybody* know what happened?''

The nurses were frantically hooking up the EKG leads. ''At report, they said he wasn't doing too good. A bad night or something.''

''Bad, how? Pain, dyspnea? *What*?''

''I don't know, Doctor.''

Langford found a vein and plunged the IV home. He felt incredibly frustrated. Even in the ER, he got a better history than that. Not that it really mattered; he guessed they were already too late. There came the sound of approaching footsteps in the corridor. Finally, the electrodes in place, they turned on the EKG just as the resuscitation team entered the room.

''Sorry we're late, kids,'' said the anesthesiologist. ''Whose party is it?''

They all paused to look at the EKG, which traced a flat line.

''Thanks for coming,'' Langford said dejectedly. ''But the party's over.''

Fifteen minutes later, when they finally ended the code, Langford sat on the desktop at the nursing station, his arm around a disconsolate Karen Schroeder.

''It's going to happen, Kar,'' he said. ''Nobody lasts forever.''

''Don't patronize me, Todd. I'm not a four-year-old.''

''So why're you taking this so hard?''

''Because it was so damn unexpected. You had to have seen him before he got better. There was nothing, a shell. But afterward, he just . . . I don't know. He was such a nice old guy. Really charming. I guess he became special to me.''

''So what happened?''

''That's just it,'' she said. ''I don't know. I was off for two days. Supposedly, he didn't look so good yes-

terday. Nothing specific—just real lethargic, his color
was bad. But he didn't complain of anything, and there
was nothing objective. And then, according to nights,
he really started to go downhill. He just lay there, not
moving, not talking. When I came on this morning,"
she continued, fighting back tears, "he seemed worse
than when he was admitted. Upstairs, there was nobody
home."

Langford frowned, perplexed. "How could he dete-
riorate so fast, in twenty-four hours?"

"I don't know." She sighed. "He got sick as fast
as he got well. I was hoping you could tell me."

But he could not. Giving her an encouraging squeeze
on the nape of the neck, he promised to keep her
posted. He asked the nurses to hold the chart for him;
he'd write a note when he got a chance. Then he
phoned Jordan and asked her to meet him on the floor
at three o'clock.

After Jordan told him she'd done biostatistical research during the summer, he'd gotten clearance for her
to assist in chart review. The time had finally come to
take her up on her offer of help. He wasn't sure what
she might add, but her biostatistical bias would give
their inquiry a new perspective. Finally, he returned to
the ER to attend to what, for him, had temporarily become the more mundane matters of life and death.

Just before Jordan arrived, Langford overheard
something else shocking. An orderly dropped a bomb-
shell: Mary Scoggins was dead. Langford was dumb-
struck. Apparently, she had expired several days
before. He quickly left the ER and went to medical
records to sign out her chart.

He hurriedly scanned the entries as he took the elevator back up to fourteen. Once in the hallway, he
slowed, rereading the notes more carefully. Apparently,
Scoggins's condition had unexpectedly deteriorated
midday Saturday. She had gone from robust to moribund in a space of sixteen hours, from being nearly

ready for discharge to a terminal cardiac cripple. And then, just as suddenly, she was dead.

Her fate had an uncanny, disturbing similarity to that of Albert Stampf. *Disturbingly* similar, he thought. Both had undergone seemingly miraculous recoveries within days of one another and remained healthy for about a week and a half. And both, just as suddenly, had taken a sudden and dramatic turn for the worse, dying within a frighteningly short time. Except for differences in their symptoms and diagnoses, their clinical courses were nearly identical. But he couldn't see the common thread, if there was one.

Jordan was already sitting at the nurses' station, reviewing Stampf's chart. When no one was looking, he greeted her with an avuncular hug and a peck on the cheek.

"Afraid someone will see us?" she asked.

"Absolutely terrified. If word of this gets around, I'm finished."

"You really know how to flatter a girl. Why the long face?"

He dropped the Scoggins chart on the desk beside her.

"What's that?"

"You read what happened to Stampf?" he asked.

"Not yet. I'm only up to the admitting note."

He told her about both patients. Jordan listened attentively, occasionally interjecting a question.

"Deterioration that fast is pretty unusual," she said. "It suggests major organ system shutdown—like the heart, or CNS."

"That's what you suggested before," he said, impressed. Jordan had a keen mind, and a good appreciation of medical details. Finally, he folded his arms.

"How's that sound so far?"

"You're right, a little too coincidental. Stuff like this doesn't just happen. At least, not naturally."

"Meaning what?"

"I mean there's probably a common denominator. Maybe it'll show up in their charts, maybe not. Are these the only two cases like this?"

"As far as I've heard. I suppose there might be others on floors I don't get around to that often, like GYN or peds. I'll check it out."

She nodded. "We have to think cardiac or cranial, Todd. Those are the two organ systems most likely to be involved. It's a starting place."

With things under control in the ER, Langford logged onto the hospital computer system. He began tracking all patients admitted through the ER for the month of September. The medical software spreadsheet provided daily, weekly, and monthly admissions summaries. By entering the parameters he was interested in, he could eliminate irrelevant variables. He first had the computer summarize all cases whose condition was life-threatening and whose prognosis was very guarded. Next, he sorted the cases by diagnosis, only allowing for cardiac or neurologic conditions. Finally, he analyzed the cases by length of stay, eliminating anyone who hadn't been in the hospital for a week.

Ultimately, Langford discovered that five cases fit his criteria to a tee. As expected, Stampf and Scoggins were on the list. The other three were frighteningly similar, and could have been cast from the same clinical mold. The reason he wasn't aware of what happened to them was because they'd been admitted to non-medical floors, such as surgery or pediatrics.

One was a thirty-five-year-old AIDS patient with cryptococcal meningitis. After being admitted on death's door, he received the standard IV therapies, showing hardly any improvement—until, eight days into his hospitalization, he opened his eyes and literally walked out of bed. The next was a fifteen-year-old girl on peds, who was readmitted in coma after receiving two prosthetic heart valves several weeks previously. The valves had become infected, and she'd developed methicillin-resistant staph endocarditis, with sepsis. She'd hovered near death for two weeks, and received the last rites. No one could explain how she suddenly emerged from coma and returned to being the cheerful adolescent she'd been the month before. The final patient was a fifty-three-year-old construction worker whose skull had been crushed when a masonry wall collapsed. Like the others, his dramatic recovery was totally unexpected.

Yet all three patients shared the same baffling fate as Stampf and Scoggins. Their abrupt deterioration, after everything had been going so well, was both perplexing and heartrending. Their medical care providers could neither explain why they improved, nor why they'd so suddenly died. It was unheard of. One case, maybe, Langford thought . . . but *five*? He phoned medical records, had them pull the three charts he didn't have, and returned to Jordan on the neuro floor.

"Are you always so disgustingly right?" he asked.

"What'd you find?"

"Three more, clones of the ones you're reviewing. All CNS or cardiac. Each nearly dead when admitted, almost pronounceable. And then, a week or more into their hospitalizations, bingo, they bounce out of bed as if they'd never been sick." He shook his head. "I don't get it. They were suddenly so alive, so healthy, with all this unrealized potential."

"Interesting reading," she said, pushing the charts toward him. "I've gotten more medical education in two hours than I could from seeing patients for two weeks."

"Come up with anything interesting?"

"What I'm mainly looking at is patterns, patterns of care. Any discrepancies or deviations they had in common. I'm more interested in *how* something was done, than what."

"And? Learn anything useful?"

"Too early to tell," she said. "Do you need those

three charts? I'd like to see what they have to say."

"All yours, inspector. Just don't take 'em out of the hospital," he said, checking his watch. "It's five-thirty. I'm gonna go home for a while, check on the dog and the mail, all right?"

She nodded. "How late is the library open?"

"Around ten," he said.

"Okay. I doubt I'll be here that long. I'll give you a call when I'm done."

As he left the hospital, Langford's mind was overflowing with the day's events. The shock of discovering so many patients with nearly identical clinical courses was numbing. In medicine, he knew, there had to be answers for everything. There was no such thing as coincidence or happenstance: things occurred for finite reasons, be those reasons microbial, atherosclerotic, oncologic, toxic, or whatever. It was inconceivable that the outcome of those five patients "just happened." No, there was a reason somewhere—a good reason. He hoped Jordan would help him discover what it was.

When Langford got home, his phone was ringing. He picked up the receiver and said hello.

"Todd, it's Tom Courtney. I got that information you wanted."

"Great. I could use some answers. What'd you find out?"

"First," said Courtney, "concerning that new drug, metapyrinol. I checked with the boys at DEA, and Miss Ross's case is definitely the first reported east of the Mississippi. They're worried. They've done pretty good at interdiction, and they thought they had the drug confined to the Southwest. Any word on where she got it?"

"Not yet."

. "All right. Now, about that townhouse on Thirty-ninth Street. It's owned by a nephew of Salvatore Aiello."

"That sounds familiar."

"It should. Remember I mentioned the Aiello mob? Big Sal, as he's known, is head of one of the largest crime families in the East. Justice has been after that guy a long time. He's going to court soon on a racketeering indictment. What's this all about, Todd? What does this woman have to do with a bad new drug and a mob-owned townhouse? Does it have anything to do with those rumors I asked you to keep your ears open for?"

Langford's jaw went slack in openmouthed astonishment. He couldn't believe what he'd just heard. If they'd taken Jordan once . . .

"Todd, you still there?"

"Yeah, I'm here."

"These are very bad guys, Todd. Be careful. Tell your woman friend to stay away from them."

"They won't get near her," Langford said protectively.

"Is that right? You try something stupid," said Courtney, "and they'll kill you both in a heartbeat."

Chapter Fourteen

ROGER FINE LEANED FORWARD, INTENT ON HIS COM-
puter screen. The head pharmacist knew the time had
come to cover his tracks. For weeks, he'd been doing
what they told him. The task had been simple enough:
all he had to do, once he knew the molecular structure,
was isolate the compound, purify it, and prepare it for
intravenous administration. Other than for the very last
patient, they told him who was going to get it and
when, but they left the method of delivery up to him.
That had proved deceptively easy; the compound had
no interactions with other drugs. Since all the patients
in question were on some sort of antibiotic, he'd merely
added it to the infusion.

He hadn't wanted to do this or been trained for it,
but his wife was seriously ill, and he was very much
in debt. The six figures they offered him could go a
long way toward alleviating his financial problem. After considerable soul-searching, he agreed to their prop-
osition. Besides, his involvement wouldn't last very
long.

And now it was over. The experiment completed, it
was time to put the whole mess behind him. Of course,
there was the question of his own record-keeping,
which was the reason he was here tonight. Every time
he mixed up a special infusion, he'd typed an asterisk
next to the antibiotic, entering it into the pharmacy

code on his computer. It seemed such a simple thing when he'd begun, for he'd wanted some sort of backup to his handwritten notes. However, removing the asterisk proved no easy process.

He thought he could simply delete it using the edit mode. But after an hour of trying, he finally gave up. Apparently, the system-wide program he'd been using deposited the data on the hospital mainframe, and removing data from the mainframe would require the hospital's computer engineer. That should prove no great challenge, but it might take a few days. He certainly couldn't do it from his office.

Reluctantly, Fine turned off his computer and left his office. This was a minor stumbling block that would be easy to rectify. Most importantly, his involvement was now over, and he wanted the whole episode to be nothing more than a bad memory.

In the hospital library, Jordan puzzled over the charts. She'd been through all five of them several times. Different teams of doctors and nurses made the entries on different floors. They differed in style, content, handwriting, and clinical course, but the director of medical education would have been proud of the thoroughness of his charges. Their training was solid, their skills sharp. But beyond the obvious differences, there were the distinct similarities she and Todd had discovered earlier. On closer inspection, the cases appeared even more nearly identical. The gravity of their disease states was the same (critical); the suddenness of their recoveries was alike (within twenty-four hours); the duration of their improvement nearly equal (averaging ten days); and the speed of their deterioration remarkably similar (overnight).

As a statistician, it was her job to discern what the underlying similarities were. Even before she'd begun her chart review, she was certain something unusual had happened to each and every one of the five patients.

It was tempting to go for the easy explanation. Perhaps all five went to the same church picnic before they got ill. Maybe they were all included in Dr. Royce's study, or perhaps they all shared a new nutritional supplement. But on closer inspection, Jordan quickly learned that these hypotheses, or a half dozen others that occurred to her, simply didn't pan out. It had to be something subtler, she thought. Statistics were like tight men's briefs, someone once told her: what they reveal is enticing, but what they conceal is vital.

Then it hit her. Other than being emergency admissions in critical condition, what all the patients shared was the commonality of IV fluids. Each received a continuous IV infusion until the moment he got well. The types of fluids, however, were different; sometimes it was five percent dextrose in water, and at other times Ringer's lactate or normal saline or combinations thereof. The patient's condition and diagnosis dictated the type of fluid administered. It wasn't surprising that since their needs were different, the types of IVs used varied. But there were also, Jordan discovered, other substances that were administered intravenously. It was here that her investigation began to focus.

All things the nurses gave by the IV route were supplied by the pharmacy. There was the odd case of emergency IV administration of fifty percent dextrose or Benadryl by a physician, but the days of direct injection of substances through the IV tubing—known as bolus injection—were gone. If antibiotics, analgesics, electrolytes, or other substances were ordered, they were prepared in the pharmacy and shipped to the floor in disposable one-hundred-cc plastic bags. One by one, Jordan checked the infusions "piggybacked" to the five patients, looking for similarities in substance or timing. At various times, the patients received painkillers, potassium, diuretics, or third-generation cephalosporins, each of which was listed by code on the chart's pharmacy sheet. Finally, at nearly nine P.M., the computer spit out what she was looking for.

The piggyback IVs reconstituted in the pharmacy were all marked with peel-off, one-and-a-half-by-three-inch labels. Each bore the patient's name and medical record number, the medication contained, and a computer code. Each of the five patients, Jordan saw, received some sort of piggyback infusion during the night shift prior to their recoveries, generally around midnight. In no case was the IV medication identical, although all were antibiotics. Likewise, the computer codes were different. But in every case, the code ended with a typed asterisk.

"An asterisk?" she wondered aloud.

Jordan puzzled over that, unable to decipher its meaning. She looked back over the pharmacy sheets in the charts. There were pages and pages of entries. Of the myriad medications administered during the patients' hospitalizations, there were only five instances where the piggyback was starred. Perplexed, Jordan called the pharmacy and spoke with the pharmacy tech on duty. Curiously, the tech claimed to have never heard about any starred medications. But she was new, she said, and maybe it would be best to call back in the morning and speak to Dr. Fine, the head of the pharmacy. Undaunted, Jordan spoke with the head nurse on evenings. Yet she, too, was unfamiliar with the starred entry; and even if she'd seen it, she probably presumed it was a typographical error. Finally, near eight P.M., Jordan called Todd and explained what she'd found.

"Beats the hell out of me," he said.

"You and everyone else. But I seriously doubt it's a typo."

"It could be something internal," he said. "Like an accounting thing."

"Maybe. That should be easy enough to find out. All I'm saying is, I'm looking for a common denominator, and this is it. The timing is right. In statistics, there just aren't any coincidences.''

"You know who you might mention this to?" he said. "Josh Meyerson. He's on call tonight, and he's pretty sharp. I already asked him to give us a hand with the chart review."

"I will, if I see him."

"All right," said Todd. "What're you going to do with this coup?"

"Talk with the head of pharmacy, I guess. He works days."

There was a pause. "Hey, Jordan?"

"Yes, my mentor?"

"It's getting late. Why don't you knock off for the night?"

"Okay. Do you want to get together, or something?"

"The 'or something' sounds good. Actually, I want to talk with you about something."

"Oh God," she said theatrically. "Do I still have time to take the antibiotics?"

He laughed. "Nothing to worry about there. Seriously, how about I meet you at your place?"

As she was leaving the hospital, Jordan walked through the ER, looking for Josh Meyerson. She found him in the corridor leading to X ray, one hand holding on to the side rail of a stretcher, the other draped around a shapely nurse. Jordan smiled to herself, amused; Meyerson certainly appeared to be the lady-killer Todd made him out to be. When he saw Jordan, Josh gave her his winningest smile.

"What's up, Jordan?"

"Hi, Josh. I was going over some charts. Could I talk to you for a second?"

"Sure." When Meyerson whispered something in the nurse's ear, she laughed, then departed.

"Did Todd mention this chart review we're doing, on those patients who seem to miraculously improve?"

"Yeah. It's really wild. Is there any way I can help?"

She showed him the papers she was carrying and explained what she'd deduced so far. "You see these asterisks by the pharmacy codes? They've got to be there for a reason, but nobody seems to know what they mean."

"You know who could tell you? Dr. Fine, the head of pharmacy."

"I'm going to see him when he gets in tomorrow," said Jordan.

"Why wait?" Josh asked. "I saw him maybe an hour ago, working late."

Jordan frowned, perplexed. That certainly didn't jibe with what the pharmacy tech had said.

When the decline came, it arrived with virulent swiftness.

With Jeff sitting nearby, Rita was breast-feeding Adrianna, getting ready for the night. Within five minutes, the baby finished nursing. Satisfied, Adrianna closed her eyes and quietly drifted off. Her lids were heavy with contentment, and her tiny lips slipped off the moist nipple as she sleepily relaxed in her mother's arms. Suddenly, Rita felt a wave of fatigue sweep over her like a veil.

"Jeff," she murmured.

"What, hon?"

"Could you . . . take the baby? I don't know what's . . ."

"You okay, Rita?"

But clearly, she was not. Rita's eyes were thoroughly glazed, and she seemed to be staring at some point across the room. Her crisscrossed arms started to sag toward her lap, threatening to topple the baby. Jeff leapt to his feet and lifted Adrianna to safety.

"Rita!" Jeff cried.

Quickly placing the baby in the isolette, he shook

Rita's shoulders—gently at first, then more insistently.
She didn't respond. Her head sagged to the side, and
saliva dribbled from the corner of her mouth. Jeff
jabbed at the bedside buzzer, ringing for the nurse. By
the time she arrived, Rita had slumped over on one
side, unconscious.

They couldn't rouse her. For no apparent reason,
Rita's condition had taken a sudden and dramatic turn
for the worse. The nurse quickly summoned the chief
resident, then set about taking the patient's vital signs.
Various clinical possibilities raced through her brain: a
stroke, perhaps, or a cardiac arrhythmia. Rita's respirations were perceptibly slowing, and her blood pressure was plummeting. What in God's name was
happening?

By the time the resident arrived, Rita had gone into
cardiac arrest.

The resident didn't have time to worry about what
was going on. He immediately pounded on Rita's chest,
coaxing life back into the same heart that had first worried them less than two weeks previously. The nurse
ran into the hall screaming for assistance. Within seconds, the overhead loudspeakers blared out the emergency. Help quickly arrived. In less than five minutes,
Rita was successfully cardioverted, re-intubated,
hooked up to various IVs, and attached to a respirator.

Someone had returned Adrianna to the nursery. Jeffrey Donninger huddled solemnly in a corner, arms
wrapped around his body, grim-faced and tight-lipped.
When his wife had been returned to him, he dared hope
it might be forever. Now fate seemed to be playing a
cruel joke, once again threatening to take away what
he loved most.

On the way to Jordan's apartment, Langford stopped at
a Lower East Side microbrewery for a six-pack. When
Jordan let him in, he held the lager aloft and pecked
her on the cheek.

"In the mood for some premium suds?" he asked.

"Sure, but I'm not much of a beer drinker. I'll get the glasses."

When she went into the kitchen, he sank into the sofa. She soon returned with a bottle opener and two iced steins, which quickly grew frosty at room temperature.

"Thanks. Pretty fancy for someone who doesn't drink beer."

"In fact, I put them in the freezer about five months ago. I hope they don't have that skunky refrigerator taste."

He popped two bottle caps and slowly poured, admiring the beer's color and head. He lifted his mug and took a long sip. "Not half bad." Then he leaned back, wiped the foam from his lips, and gazed at her. She was wearing a chic kind of sportswear—sexy tight jeans and a clingy, black nylon slip top. Braless underneath, it had a come-hither look that left him momentarily speechless. He wasn't sure where to begin. At a loss for words, he simply looked back as she studied him, brushing her hair back with her hand. How flawless it looked, he thought. Her hair seemed to shimmer, gliding weightlessly when she moved her head, bouncing atop her shoulders.

"Well?" she said.

He cleared his throat and smiled. "I was thinking how hot you look."

"Todd . . ."

"Okay, okay," he relented, holding up his hand. "Let me get right to it. At work this morning, I spoke with someone about this knack of yours. A doctor."

"You didn't."

Her vehemence startled him. "Sorry, Jor. I didn't think you'd mind."

"*Mind?* For a while there, I thought I was going crazy!" she shouted. "I was getting paranoid, and I thought I had a brain tumor! But you reassured me that everything was all right, and I was overreacting . . ." Her voice trailed off, and her lips began to tremble. "And now, out of the blue, you talk to some doctor about me behind my back. Why, Todd?"

He reached for her, but she pulled away. "I thought you wanted to find out."

"Find out what? That there is something wrong with me, after all?"

"Look," he said softly, "I *was* having trouble believing you at first. Can you blame me? But you convinced me that your knack, or whatever you want to call it, really exists. I figured I owed it to both of us to try to get some answers."

Still annoyed, she crossed her arms in defensive body language. "Maybe you should've asked me first. Did it ever occur to you that I might not want the whole world to know about this?"

"Not the whole world, for God's sake. There's this great neurologist I work with, a woman named—"

"What about patient confidentiality? Doesn't that mean anything?"

"You're right, it does. Maybe I shouldn't have said anything."

"A little too late for that," she said, shaking her head. She took a deep, calming breath. "All right, what did she say?"

"She had a reasonable explanation." He went on to relate what Dr. Swenson had said. As patiently as he could, he explained the theoretical mechanism behind her heightened perceptions. Yet as he spoke, he could tell she was becoming agitated. She squirmed in her seat and pressed her lips into a tight line. When he was finished, he tried a conciliatory smile, but she wasn't buying it.

"That's just great, Todd! When I get drowsy, I become this human lie detector!"

"But you said you always had this knack," he said calmly. "It's just a little more pronounced now."

"Don't patronize me!"

"Calm down, Jordan. This doesn't mean what you're making it out to be."

"No? I'll tell you what it means! It means I'm a circus freak, a walking sideshow! It means I'm some kind of psychic who ought to have her own 1–900 line! Just ninety-five cents a minute, folks. Give me a ring, and I'll tell you if you're lying!" Her eyes filled with tears. Her voice quivered. "Jesus Christ, Todd."

His arms immediately went around her in warmth and comfort. He held her tenderly, without speaking, until he felt her relax and sink into him. "I don't know what to say."

"Please tell me I'm overreacting again," she said.

"Are you going to believe me?"

"Yes," she managed.

"This ability you have is probably just temporary. It could be gone tomorrow. And there's nothing supernatural about it," he went on. "It's a very subtle response to a very subtle injury. Period. Don't lose sleep over it."

"I won't, as long as you promise not to lie to me as I'm drifting off."

"Deal. Now, there's one other thing, Jordan." He told her what he'd learned from Tom Courtney, going over what he'd learned about metapyrinol and the true ownership of the East Side brownstone.

Jordan listened in stunned silence. Lips pressed into a thin line, she'd begun to tremble again. Relieved though she was by the discovery, her overriding feeling was fear. "What's happening, Todd?" she said weakly. "Why are these people after me?"

"Tom Courtney doesn't think they are," he said reassuringly. "What I'm trying to say is, I'm not completely sure why this happened to you, but I guess I owe you an apology. I believe you, Jordan. Will you forgive me?"

Relieved, she managed a grateful smile. Then she

leaned over and kissed him softly on the lips. "I don't think that'll be a problem."

"Now," he continued, "when were you going to talk to the head of pharmacy?"

"Is tomorrow morning soon enough?"

Chapter Fifteen

WORD OF RITA'S DETERIORATION SPREAD RAPIDLY through the hospital. By midnight, almost everyone knew what happened. Then the calls went out, first to the physicians linked to the case, and then to Rita's classmates. Jordan found out shortly after three A.M. She was instantly awake, heartbroken, yet furious. No one could understand. Everyone was mystified and in shock.

The following day, just after six in the morning, Todd met Jordan for coffee at a run-down deli on Ninety-sixth Street. The interior was decrepit, but the coffee was surprisingly good. Todd hadn't heard about Rita, and he was shocked. For several minutes, they both simply sat there, glum and silent. But Todd's shift started at seven. Pharmacist Roger Fine wasn't due in until eight.

The ER was relatively uncrowded. The junior residents and nursing staff easily handled the patient volume. Langford was just settling down for a long overdue chart review when a nurse interrupted him. A crosstown ambulance was just pulling into the courtyard.

"We've got a passenger-side MVA coming in," she said. "Went through the windshield."

"I didn't hear them radio in," Todd said.

"They called just this second."

Langford got up just as the ER door swung open. The paramedics wheeled in a stretcher covered with blood. The black male patient was wearing a cervical collar, and a MAST suit was balled up around his ankles. Langford had to look no farther than the man's right upper leg to see why the suit hadn't been put on. In the middle of the thigh, the patient's khaki pants were perforated by a compound fracture. A sharp and jagged end of proximal femur protruded grotesquely upward, its ragged white point dangling loose fibers of torn muscle.

From the appearance of the injuries, the patient was already in profound shock. His circulating volume was massively depleted. He would need fluids fast, and probably blood. Meyerson was at the head of the stretcher, pulling it into Trauma One. He turned to Langford.

"Okay if I take this one, Todd?"

Langford figured Meyerson was ready. Treatment of multiple trauma was fairly straightforward: maintain airway and circulation, stanch the bleeding, prevent or reverse shock, draw the labs and get the films, and treat the injuries. Moreover, there were plenty of personnel to assist.

"Okay, Josh. Your call. Go get 'em."

As the team entered the trauma room, Langford pulled aside the trailing paramedic. "Hey, Chico. What's the story?"

"Same old, same old," said the paramedic. "A DWI, guy was in the front seat. The old Chevy hit a pole in front of a bodega. No seatbelt, and boom! Went through the windshield like a slingshot."

"Where was this?"

"West One Twenty-fourth."

Langford frowned. That was thirty blocks away. With an abundance of private and municipal hospitals, Manhattan was divided into emergency catchment areas—ambulance zones, or grids. And while Met had developed an excellent reputation for its ER, an EMS unit was supposed to service cases in its area, delivering patients to the designated nearest hospital emergency room. It wasn't a question of turf battle; it was a matter of safety. It was dangerous to transport a critically ill patient to a more distant facility.

"Isn't that a little out of the way? What the hell are you doing here?"

The EMT shrugged sheepishly, but his eyes sparkled with a cat-who-ate-the-canary expression. "You know how it is, man."

"I give up," Todd said. "How is it?"

"A guy's gotta make a living, right?" He rubbed his thumb and fingers together, and a conspiratorial smile was on his lips. "*Baksheesh.*"

Langford stopped in his tracks. He realized that much of the world ran on graft and corruption, but not when it came to hospitals and lives. All along, he'd assumed that the hospital's rising ER and inpatient census was related to the quality of its care, not to bribery. Could the EMT have been joking?

Curious, Langford approached one of the nurses. Joanne Long was a hard-bitten nurse in her forties. In a field where many people burned out quickly, Long was a survivor. She'd been there, done that, in a career that had seen almost everything.

"Joanne, you see that ambulance attendant who was just here?"

She was rubbing her palms with a hand cream that smelled like insect repellant. "Sorry, lover. Missed him."

"His crew works the West Side, usually out of P and S," he said, referring to Columbia. "The patient they just brought in should have gone there."

"So? Maybe there was traffic."

"Maybe," he said, "but he pretty much implied they were bribed to bring him here."

"You don't say? Wouldn't be the first time it happened."

"What're you saying?"

"Come on, don't be naive. It's been going on for weeks."

"*What* has?"

"Where've you been?" she said. "The word on the street is, take all your severe trauma to Met."

"They told you that?"

"Not in so many words, but you get the drift. Like Clinton's gay policy. Don't ask, don't tell."

"I don't get it," he said. "Who'd bribe an ambulance attendant to bring patients here?"

"How much time have you got? I mean, who wouldn't? Start with a hungry orthopedist who needs the referrals. An administrator who wants to buff the numbers, or get the beds filled. A drug company that wants its new product tested. Why's that so surprising? These days, the bottom line is everything."

He felt deflated. "I guess," he said softly. *Am* I being naive? he wondered. "I just never heard of it before."

"Welcome to the real world, Dr. Schweitzer."

A little after eight A.M., Jordan arrived at the pharmacy. Roger Fine, Ph.D., was seated at a desk in his office. He had thinning, slicked-back brown hair. When he rose to greet her, Jordan saw that he was tall, about six-four. His handshake was cordial.

"What can I do for you, Miss Parker-Ross?"

"I'm a student here, Dr. Fine. Going into my third year. I was wondering if you could help me with a project I'm working on."

"I'm always happy to help students, but I'm a little busy right now, and—"

"It won't take that long," she said. "Just a question or two."

"All right," he said. "What kind of project?"

"Have you been following those patients in the hospital, the ones who come in critically ill, but then who suddenly get better?"

She was watching his face as she spoke. Fine's friendliness suddenly vanished, and he became distant and skittish. At first, there was a telltale blink of his eyelids. But then his expression turned granite hard, blank and inscrutable. "I can't say that I have."

"Well, there are five patients so far. When they were admitted, they were all in serious condition, or on life support. Their clinical courses were pretty similar, and they held their own for a week or two. Then, almost miraculously, they all got better. Virtually overnight. We were wondering if you could help us with that."

"Who's 'we'?" Fine asked.

"A doctor I'm working with on staff."

"Why would you think I'd know anything about it?"

She held out the pharmacy sheets. "I used to do epidemiology research, Dr. Fine. I look for common threads. I've checked out these cases pretty closely, and so far, the only thing they have in common is a pharmacy computer code. I thought you might be able to tell me what it was all about."

His expression didn't waver. He gave her his most indecipherable stare as if to convince her of his neutrality by his unflinching demeanor. "I don't have a clue what you're referring to."

"Right here," she continued, pointing out the codes in question. "These are the codes the pharmacy uses for IV antibiotics. One's for penicillin, two are for cefoxitin, and two are cephazolin. My question is, what's the significance of the typed star after the last number?"

What was most curious, she thought, was that he didn't even look at the pages. But there was a sudden chink in his poker-face armor, a telltale twitch in his left eyelid. "I haven't the faintest idea."

"Couldn't you just look at it, Dr. Fine? These stars right here?" she indicated.

Reluctantly, his gaze shifted to the pages. "I suppose it could be anything."

"But as head of the pharmacy, isn't it your job to know what these things mean?"

He fixed her with a reptilian scowl. "I supervise the workings of a large and busy pharmacy, young lady. When it comes to medications, we know precisely what we're doing. But I'm not responsible for every little comma, asterisk, or printer glitch. So please don't tell me what my job is!"

"But don't you think you should—"

He dismissed her with a wave of his hand. "If you don't mind, I'm very busy."

As she walked away, he glared at her in brooding, stony silence.

"So he wasn't up front with you?" Langford asked.

"Not in the least. He seemed very hostile. Getting information out of him was like pulling teeth."

"What about the asterisks? He didn't know what they meant?"

"He hinted something was wrong with the computer printer," she said. "It was a cop-out."

"He's got to be joking! Who would know, if not him?"

"I don't know, Todd. He got huffy when I suggested that. He was downright evasive."

"Ah, but was he lying?" he asked. "Could you tell?"

"Well, I . . ." Jordan slowly shook her head. "I don't know, not really. Not with the strength of conviction, the certainty I've had before."

"That makes sense. This knack of yours gets stronger when you're in that subconscious never-neverland. It'd be nice to know where he's coming from, though. Too bad you can't do it at will."

She had a pensive look. "Maybe I can."

"You can what? Fall asleep during a conversation?"

"No, you rat," she said. "Y'know, I was just wondering. I might not have been able to read him before, but do you suppose I could through self-hypnosis?"

"Maybe. It's a thought."

"After all, hypnosis is just really deep relaxation on a different level of consciousness."

"You know how to hypnotize yourself?" he asked.

"Sure, they taught it in intro to psych. I got pretty good at it. I use it when I'm tense, or when I want to unwind."

"Hmmm. Maybe we should test it out. Tell you what," he said. "Why don't you hypnotize yourself, and I'll tell you about all the women in my life, and you can—"

"I think we've already tried that. I have a better idea."

They waited until lunchtime to track down Dr. Fine. The pharmacist was apparently something of a recluse, keeping to himself and spending little time with other faculty. He was in his office, brown-bagging it, when they arrived. When he saw them, he stopped eating and put his sandwich away.

"Hello, Dr. Fine," said Langford. "Could I bother you for a minute?"

"Landon, isn't it?" He studied the young physician's photo ID. "Langford. What can I do for you? Please don't tell me you want to discuss what this young woman was badgering me about before."

"Can I sit down, Dr. Fine?" Jordan asked.

"Suit yourself."

Earlier, Jordan had described the layout of the room. While Todd remained standing, she settled into the armchair beside the pharmacist's desk. The hypnotic method with which she was familiar was called the eye-roll arm levitation technique. With Langford continuing the conversation, Jordan closed her eyes and took two cleansing breaths. She placed her arms on the armrests. Using familiar skills, she was quickly able to relax completely.

She breathed diaphragmatically, through her nose and deep into her abdomen. Then she rolled her eyes backwards, into her sockets. Simultaneously, she willed her right arm to become weightless. It soon felt like a feather. It wanted to float, to rise up and drift away. As her body grew heavy, Jordan sensed a change in her consciousness.

"We don't mean to keep pestering you about this, Dr. Fine," said Todd. "But this is important. All these patients who suddenly got better died just as suddenly."

"So?" he said.

"I know, shit happens. But nobody working on these cases can explain either their improvement or their deterioration. Five cases like this can't be coincidence. So we're looking at everything that might be a factor. The only thing we've been able to come up with are these starred entries."

Relaxed, in a different state of alertness, Jordan was nonetheless able to concentrate completely. The focus of her perception centered on the pharmacist's words.

"Who told you to look into this business?" asked Fine.

"Look, nobody told us," said Todd. "Call it scientific curiosity. Maybe the rest of the hospital's too busy to look into this, but someone has to. Level with us, huh? Do these asterisks after the computer codes mean anything?"

"I have absolutely no idea what they mean."

Jordan felt as if a jolt surged through her. She gave a little shudder and slowly opened her eyes. Gazing up, she saw that Todd was looking at her.

"Okay, Dr. Fine," Langford said. "If you say so. Sorry to bother you. Let's go, Jordan." They both turned to walk away.

"If I were you, I'd stick to emergency medicine," said Fine. "You recall what the cat had to say about curiosity."

Langford stopped and looked back. "What's that supposed to mean?"

"Nothing," Fine said obliquely. "Nothing at all."

He waited until they were gone. Then, eyes narrowed and suspicious, the pharmacist slowly picked up the phone.

Traffic was heavy in lower Spanish Harlem at five-fifteen. The man in the car listened to his instructions over the mobile phone one last time. Then he pressed the END button and put the device on the seat beside him. He picked up the pair of compact Steiner binoculars and intently scanned the hospital's side entrance.

He was sitting in a car on the corner of Ninety-ninth and Second, with the engine running. He'd stolen the nondescript blue Toyota off a Brooklyn side street an hour before. Despite the traffic, he had a good view of the building a hundred yards away. His target soon emerged, flanked by other hospital employees. The man in the car glanced at the photo taped to his dashboard, then back through the binoculars. There was no mistake.

When he'd been contacted earlier, the man in the car debated where to do the job. The pharmacist lived on a cozy residential street in Douglaston, Queens. After due consideration, he decided to remain in the city. While a suburb offered convenience and accessibility, a crowded city street had the distinct advantage of helping conceal escape.

The target walked to his vehicle, a late-model Nissan Pathfinder parked in one of the fifty or so reserved spots on the asphalt lot. Across the street, the man gunned the Toyota and pulled away from the curb. He sped across the street, weaving through traffic and pulling into the hospital parking lot. On the driver's seat was a neatly folded Barbour windbreaker. Beneath the jacket was a Ruger MK II Government Model .22 autoloader with an integral Sound Technology suppressor. It was loaded with ten rounds of Eley Tenex, whose roundnose lead, leaving the muzzle at 1,000 feet per second, was more than adequate to do the job.

In his Nissan, the pharmacist put the transmission in reverse and checked the rearview mirror. Some thirty feet away, the man in the Toyota slowed to a crawl. When the Nissan began backing out of its reserved space, the Toyota suddenly sped up. Its left front bumper collided with the Pathfinder's tailgate on the right, shattering the taillight assembly and collapsing the smaller car's fender.

Although only mildly jostled, the pharmacist was startled nonetheless. "Jesus Christ," he muttered. Before he could collect his thoughts, he saw that the driver of the car that had struck him was already out of his vehicle. Forcing a sigh, the pharmacist shook his head and unbuttoned his seat belt.

Behind the Pathfinder, the Toyota's driver had skillfully maneuvered his car so that the two vehicles formed a wedgelike V at the point of impact. The pharmacist got out of the RV and walked to the rear. He studied the other man, who seemed to be surveying the damage.

"I'm so sorry," the other man said. "Didn't see you coming."

The pharmacist studied the other man. He looked vaguely familiar, but he couldn't place him. He had a medium build and was dressed in worn jeans and a white T-shirt. The jacket folded over his right arm looked incongruous on such a warm afternoon.

"You shouldn't even be in here," said Fine. "This is a reserved lot."

The man with the jacket was looking at the passersby. Although initially curious when they heard the collision, they were still New Yorkers. When they saw that nothing sensational had occurred beyond a routine fender-bender, they quickly returned to their business, leaving the drivers to sort things out.

"I don't know this area too good. I think I'm lost," the man said. "But I also think you were backing up too fast."

"Tell it to the judge," the pharmacist scoffed. "I hope you've got insurance."

"And I hope you've got a good mechanic. See what happened?" he pointed, indicating a spot below the trunk. "Looks like a leak."

"What're you talking about?" said Fine, who saw nothing but shattered plastic.

"It's dripping like crazy," the man said. "Sure hope it's not your gas tank."

"Better not be."

The pharmacist bent over, peering under the bumper. There was a sudden pressure on his neck as the man hit him, forcing his head down. Gripping the Ruger under his jacket, he quickly thumbed off the safety. In one fluid movement, he swung the pistol free and brought it up to the pharmacist's head. Fine was just beginning to resist when there were two muted pops.

The pharmacist instantly collapsed to the ground, lifeless. As a precaution, the assassin fired one more round, directly into the target's ear. The body momentarily jerked, then lay still. Using the sole of his shoe, he rolled the body under the Nissan, partially out of sight. Then the shooter hid the pistol under the jacket and casually looked around. As expected, no one was remotely interested in what was going on in the recess between the two vehicles.

He retrieved the three brass shell casings and pocketed them in his jeans. He put on a pair of mirrored, wraparound sunglasses and got back in his car. On Second Avenue, the southbound flow of traffic continued unabated. As he quickly drove into it, the man inhaled a deep and satisfying breath.

"God, I love New York."

Chapter Sixteen

LANGFORD LEARNED OF FINE'S DEATH WHEN HE ARrived at work the next morning. The entire hospital staff was in shock. A passing clerical worker, who at first thought the pharmacist was trying to fix his car, had discovered Dr. Fine's body. The widening pool of blood under his head, however, proved otherwise.

The security guards quickly brought him to the emergency room, more out of a sense of duty than a legitimate hope that he could be saved. A zealous ward clerk had even gone to the trouble of clocking the pharmacist in and preparing a chart. And although the nurses were prepared to go through the motions of resuscitation, an astute senior resident reluctantly pronounced the pharmacist dead. With the patient's fixed, dilated pupils and absence of heartbeat, it would have been hard not to. The hospital-wide process of mourning soon began. Although Fine wasn't the most outgoing or popular person, he was still a colleague, and the savagery of the unwitnessed act left everyone a little numb.

After they'd met with the pharmacist, Todd had the impression Fine was lying, whereas Jordan was absolutely certain of it. But they still didn't know what to make of it.

Today, after he finished work at three, he met Jordan in the ICU, where she was sitting at Rita's bedside.

Before the hopelessness of the situation got to them both, they decided to go out for an early supper.

"Did you hear what happened to Dr. Fine?" she asked.

"Yeah, as soon as I got to work." He nodded. "The whole hospital's talking about it."

"That poor man. Do they have any idea who did it?"

"No, they think it was a traffic argument. Somebody poked him in the trunk while he was backing out of a parking space. A couple of people saw what happened, but they didn't pay much attention. I guess it got out of control."

"And he got shot for that?" she said.

"This is the Big Apple, Jordan. Happens all the time. People have been killed for less. Look what happened to Dr. Fletcher."

"You don't think they're related, do you?"

"No, but I have to admit, it crossed my mind," he said. "Being around me can prove hazardous to your health. Maybe I should wear a warning label."

"Come on, Typhoid Todd, don't be silly. What did you say he was working on?"

"Fletch? The son-of-a-gun wouldn't tell me. It had something to do with spinal fluid."

"What a coincidence."

"What are you getting at?" he asked.

"Just that too many peculiar things are happening at your place of work. First Dr. Fletcher dies, while he's working on something confidential. Then there's this business of all the patients who mysteriously get better, but then suddenly drop dead." Suddenly, she had a faraway expression. "You don't suppose that Rita could be involved in this, do you?"

"How could she? She's an OB patient."

"I know, but she also has a severe neurological problem."

Todd shook his head.

"Anyway," Jordan continued, "nobody has a clue about the others. Finally, we go to talk about it with the one man who might have an answer, and he gets whacked." She paused, hoping to let her words sink in.

He was puzzled by the enigmatic expression on her face—the slightly upturned lips, the twinkle in her eye. He wondered if she honestly believed what she was suggesting. "You've got a vivid imagination, love."

"Think so?" she said. "Did they know one another, Fletcher and Fine?"

"I doubt it. Fletch never mentioned it. They both kept to themselves."

"But there *could* be a connection," she said.

"Well, you're the one with time on her hands. Maybe you can look for it."

"Okay with me. Where do you suggest I look?"

"The lab or the pharmacy, I guess," he said. "Probably Fletcher's lab."

"Why? Less crowded?"

"You might say that. It's closed," said Todd. "Some guys from administration and Mike Molloy, his lab assistant, moved all the animals out, but his data should still be there. It shouldn't be hard getting you in. I know all the security guards."

The guard let her in at six P.M. It was Saturday, and Mike Molloy didn't work weekends. The pretext Langford used was that Jordan had to retrieve some research she'd been working on with Fletcher. Jordan turned on the light and closed the door. The thing that struck her first was the odor. Although the lab animals were gone, their scent remained, a lingering, musky intruder. The empty metal cages with doors ajar bore silent witness to the methods of medical progress. A thin coat of dust was beginning to accumulate on the slate countertops.

Jordan slowly walked through the lab. Cardboard boxes, no doubt packed by someone shortly after the murder, sat on the floor. Wall-mounted shelves were stocked with containers of animal chow, medications, and lab supplies. There were several desks at the far end of the room. On the largest of them rested Dr. Fletcher's nameplate. Jordan sat at the desk, leaning back in the contoured chair.

The desk had a view of the entire deserted lab. As she looked around, she lost herself in reflection. What was it you were working on? she wondered. Why was it such a secret? Come on, talk to me. She tried the top desk drawer and found it locked. So were the side drawers. But she was familiar with desks such as this— low-end products of mediocre construction. As often as not, the legs wobbled, rivets were misaligned, and screws were loose.

Reaching under the central drawer, she located the four small screws to the backplate. Using her nails, she found a bit of play between the backplate and the drawer's sheet metal. Wiggling the plate with her fingers, she slowly worked the screws loose, until she could unscrew them with her fingers. In several minutes, the entire lock came free.

She gingerly slid the drawer open, peering intently over the rim, expecting to be surprised by the volume of its contents. But there was surprisingly little. There were a handful of credit card receipts, stapled together; a dog-eared, five-year-old copy of *Playboy*, which— given what Todd said about Fletcher—Jordan found incongruous; and a thin, blue cloth ledger. Curious, she opened it.

The book bore no inscription. There was no ''property of,'' table of contents, or index. She thumbed through the handwritten pages. If anything, the ledger was a kind of diary. The entries began in August, and all seemed to relate to CG #12, which she took to mean cage number twelve. Most of the entries were a numerical shorthand which appeared to represent times or specific dates. She couldn't tell, however, if 15:29

meant hours and minutes, or minutes and seconds. Above the times was the name Breen-Richter, underlined twice.

She narrowed her eyes in concentration. She thought the name sounded familiar, but she couldn't place it. Toward the middle of September, several of the entries were circled. Also, the numbers became substantially smaller; 15:29 was reduced to 0:18, or a similar number. Some ten pages into the ledger, the entries ended with the notation, "Stop—go to V.VII—new rats." On the following page, the words "purified Cog." were scribbled, followed by the chemical formula for a long, complex organic molecule.

She puzzled over it. The formula didn't represent anything she recognized from her biochemistry course. On the overleaf, the molecule was depicted in graphic chemical form. Some of its constituent parts looked familiar: it was long, like a growth hormone; it had a steroid nucleus; and it had terminal hydroxyl and methyl groups. She had no doubt her biochemistry professor could identify it if she showed it to him.

The next page was dated "21 September," under which was the notation, "purified Cog. 50 mcg." There followed a list of times similar to the first entries she'd seen. But within twenty-four hours, the times again decreased. The ledger continued for the next few weeks before ending abruptly. The final entry alluded to a patient, one G. P., who might have elevated "cog" levels. The date, she recalled, was just prior to Dr. Fletcher's death.

She put the book aside and opened the uppermost right-hand drawer. It was filled with videocassettes, some two dozen in all. Each was labeled with a date. The dates began earlier in the year, and ran up to early October. Each tape covered a time frame of ten days to two weeks. Jordan picked out the final two tapes and put them atop the ledger.

Armed with more questions than answers, she gathered everything up and turned off the light.

An hour later, Jordan popped the first cassette into her VCR, hit the PLAY button, and lay back on her bed. Julie and her boyfriend had gone to an early movie, but they promised to be back by ten. Temporarily alone in her apartment, Jordan's fright had lessened. She knew she had to confront her fears if she ever hoped to defeat them, but she would do so in little bits.

The tapes proved little more than rodent-watching. The date and time were digitally recorded in the right-hand corner of the frame. Somehow, Dr. Fletcher had used a miniature videocam to tape directly into a cage. She could tell it was cage twelve by the identifying plaque on the uppermost bars. Inside were the fattest white rats she'd ever seen. The corpulent fur-balls were the epitome of sloth, barely moving around. Then they were placed in some sort of harness, while the camera recorded a view of their eyes. Jogged by a sudden memory, Jordan pressed the PAUSE button and got out of bed.

She found a psychology textbook in her bookcase. Leafing through the index, she located the entry for the Breen-Richter test. She turned to the page and soon found a brief description of the test, whose methodology corresponded to what she was watching on tape. So that's it, she thought. She *knew* she'd seen the name somewhere. Now, all she had to do was make sense of what she was looking at.

She turned the VCR back on and resumed watching. The white rats' antics were funny, in a way, but also incredibly boring. From time to time, she correlated the entries in Fletcher's log with what she was watching on the screen. Then, just as her interest was waning, something remarkable happened.

Jordan sat up in bed, astonished. She rewound the segment she'd just seen, a segment that corresponded to the eighteen seconds Dr. Fletcher had circled toward the middle of September. She watched the recorded events two more times, unable to believe her eyes. She shook her head, thinking aloud.

"Those fat little tubs just got smart."

Sitting cross-legged in bed, she quickly went to the next tape, labeled VIII. This, she recalled, was with a new batch of rats. After plodding through the test on day one, with predictably slow times, the animals appeared to have been given something Fletcher referred to as "purified Cog. 50 mcg." A day later, their astounding performance on the Breen-Richter test was nothing short of miraculous. Jordan felt a chill.

"So that's what you were working on," she whispered. "Why couldn't you tell Todd?"

He was on call that night. She tried to phone him, but the clerk said he was tied up in an emergency. She hung up without leaving a message. Jordan was tired, and she decided to go to bed early. With the ledger and the tapes secure on the night table beside her, she turned off the light and crawled under the covers. But she couldn't sleep. The events of the preceding two hours kept going around in her head, like a squirrel running on a wheel.

From what Todd had told her, she knew Dr. Fletcher had been working with spinal fluid, and had discovered something he wouldn't—or couldn't—reveal. Todd surmised it was something big. Indeed, now that she'd seen the tapes, she had to agree. Whatever "Cog." was, it had the astonishing ability to turn otherwise dull, corpulent rats into little rodent wizards. But why had it been a secret? What exactly was "Cog," and where did it come from? Most important of all, could Dr. Fletcher's discovery somehow be related to his death? The idea was frightening. She'd felt chilled before. Now her body was as cold as ice.

That night, Jordan slept in fits and starts. The next morning, she was up at dawn, looking for answers.

* * *

Late the evening before, when the suggestion came that Rita be transferred to Eastgate, it was met with mixed feelings. On one hand, Rita was everyone's friend, relative, or colleague, and no one wanted to consciously admit that she'd be gone, sent elsewhere for her care. But on the subconscious level, it was a different matter entirely. As much as everyone denied that Rita was becoming a psychological burden, the tragedy of what was happening to her was exhausting them emotionally. Sending her someplace else—somewhere brand-new and high-tech—offered a convenient excuse, an out-of-sight, out-of-mind mentality that might help everyone cope. But ultimately, the decision was Jeff's.

Grief-stricken as he was, he was initially unwilling to have her transferred someplace he couldn't visit. They assured him it was only temporary—that Eastgate, so recently opened and already flooded with transfers—was currently allowing only staff on-site. What finally swayed him was the wishes of his family. It was obvious to everyone that he was physically and spiritually exhausted, and a few days to himself, relieved of the self-imposed burden of remaining by Rita's bedside, would benefit everyone in the long run.

Thus, he gave his reluctant consent. Rita was transferred to Eastgate just before dawn, without hoopla or ceremony, and largely devoid of honor.

"Listen to what I'm saying, Ray. Just listen! You're playing with people's lives here!"

"Don't lecture me, Doc. I'm just doin' what anybody else would under the circumstances."

"But doesn't it matter to you that some patients might die because of the extra time it takes to get here? I'm not talking about some kid with a hangnail. But if you've got a gunshot or a severe MVA and you're over on Ninth Avenue, how the hell can you justify bringing them all the way over here?"

"Look, Dr. Langford," said the EMT, "nobody's died yet, so what are you cryin' about? We don't break the rules. Maybe we bend 'em a little, but we're professionals. We use our judgment, same as you. I don't see what you're so pissed off about. Most hospitals are screamin' for patients. Especially the critical ones. So, if we make a little money in the process, what's the big deal? Everyone wins."

"You're playing with fire, my friend. Just because no one's died doesn't mean it can't happen ten minutes from now. And what happens when some hungry reporter gets wind of this? We're talking front page of the *Daily News*."

"Mountain out of a molehill, Doc," said the paramedic, shaking his head. "Anyway, it ain't my problem."

As the ambulance attendant walked away, Langford just stood there, glaring at him. He had nothing against free enterprise, or hustling a buck, but when a critically ill patient was transported all the way cross town . . . So far the ambulance crews had been incredibly lucky.

He'd ceased being shocked by bribes, a rumor he'd confirmed by independent sources. But it was just a question of time before disaster struck. He knew it, and he was certain that, despite their protestations, the ambulance drivers knew it, too. The larger question was, who was doing the bribing? So far, no one seemed to have a clue. He wondered just how high up the payments originated. Although it was late at night, he wanted answers.

On the weekends, the administrator on call was often a senior member of the nursing staff. Sue Jacobs, the ADN, or assistant director of nurses, was a battle-hardened veteran of numerous OR skirmishes. If anyone had an inkling of what was going on with the ambulance transports, it was sure to be her.

Langford met her in the nursing office. Jacobs was a chain smoker and preferred the privacy of her own desk and telephone to making walking rounds. In her late forties, Jacobs had a brittle look brought on by years of smoking and sun exposure. As she listened, she smoked continuously. When he finished his recitation, she stubbed out her cigarette and lit another.

"No, I hadn't heard it," said Jacobs. "But it doesn't surprise me. This is a big hospital, with a lot of egos and just as many personalities. A little well-placed money can go a long way."

"But who could be behind it? Most of our patients are indigent. No money, no insurance except Medicaid. I doubt any of the attendings is making a bundle off this." He sighed deeply. "Joanne Long, down in the ER, thought I was being naive."

"Maybe you are," she said. "Or maybe you're just an idealist, like we all were before we burnt out. But you're right about one thing: if this business goes haywire, it could spell real trouble for the hospital. Give me a few days, let me nose around a little. I'll catch up with you the next time you're on call."

New York Medical College had a sprawling campus in Valhalla, in Westchester County. It was a sunny Monday morning, and despite the rush hour, it proved a leisurely drive for Jordan, as she was going against traffic. Shortly before nine, she pulled into an uncrowded parking lot not far from the biochemistry building.

Professor Gregory was just opening his office door. "Miss Parker-Ross, what a surprise! How're you feeling?"

"Pretty good, Professor."

"You look well," he said, looking at her from head to toe. "Fully recovered from your little ordeal? You were quite the talk on campus for a while."

"I didn't realize a concussion would be such a big deal."

"Really, Jordan," he said, moving around the desk toward her. "The academic community is more tightly knit than you think. We're all still in shock over what happened to poor Rita Donninger. But enough of that. What brings you here today?''

As he approached her, Jordan found herself backing away. The man just didn't get it. "Dr. Gregory, I didn't come all the way up here to play grab-ass," she said, holding up Fletcher's ledger. "There's something I want you to look at."

Chastened, Gregory stopped. "Research project, is it?''

"Big time." She opened the book to the page with the molecular formula. "Have you ever seen an organic compound like this?"

Gregory took the ledger and went back to his desk. He sat down, put on a pair of reading glasses, and studied the text. "Cog? What's that mean?"

"I don't know. It's some sort of shorthand. I was hoping you could tell me."

"Can't say that I'm familiar with any Cog," he said. "This isn't your work, then?"

"No," she simply said. "It belongs to someone else."

He gazed at her for a long moment. "I see." Then he returned to the ledger, studying both sides of the page. "A very interesting molecule. I don't believe I've ever seen anything quite like it. Is this theoretical, or does it actually exist?"

"Whatever it is, I'm pretty sure it already exists."

"Hmmm," he said, tapping the page with his finger. "I suppose you're here for my opinion?"

She nodded. "If you would, Professor."

He leaned back in his chair, lacing his fingers atop his abdomen. "All right. From the structure of its terminal groups, I'd say it's biologically active. Moderate half-life, a week or two. The steroid nucleus suggests it's rapidly produced, but more slowly metabolized. And my best guess is that, in humans, it might have neurological effects. How's that?"

"That would make sense, Dr. Gregory. The man who was working on it specialized in neurotransmitters."

"What do you mean by *was* working on it?"

"He's dead. Murdered in his apartment. You heard about Dr. Fletcher?" As he nodded, she took a deep, calming breath. "It's really very complicated. I guess you can say I'm looking for leads."

"You're continuing Fletcher's work, then?"

"In a manner of speaking." She suddenly felt apprehensive, unsure if she'd said too much, or too little. It was time to leave.

Conchita Rivera was terrified. The place wasn't a clinic at all, but a run-down fourth-floor apartment in a decrepit tenement. She had heard about this practitioner from a friend. Although the abortionist wasn't a doctor, he was reputed to handle pregnancies over twelve weeks for a relatively low fee. And all Conchita had was three hundred dollars.

"Come on, come on," he said impatiently. "I don't have all day. Slide down more."

She inched down on the makeshift exam table, convinced she could endure it. After all, she'd gone through her second labor and delivery with almost no medication. She heard the clanking of metal, and something cold was thrust into her vagina, making her wince. She prayed it was clean. "What're you going to do now?"

"Just be quiet and hold still. If you keep wiggling around, I won't be able to do a damn thing. You want me to go through with this, or not?"

She fought back the tears. "Yes."

Something pinched her insides, and then she felt a strong cramp. She bit her lip to keep from moving. There came a pause. Conchita took a deep breath and closed her eyes in relief. Just when she figured the worst was over, she felt a searing pain rip through her lower abdomen.

"It was really uncomfortable," she said, moving her food across the plate with her fork. "I felt like he couldn't take his eyes off my blouse."

"From what you've said, Gregory seems like a harmless lech," said Langford. "At least we found out what Fletcher was working on. I just don't understand why he couldn't let me in on it."

"Todd, you had to have seen the videos. They were so incredible, they bordered on being frightening. It was just *unbelievable* what those porky rodents could do after getting the stuff."

"All the more reason for Fletcher to have told me about it," he said.

"Maybe not. If this molecule, whatever it is, turns out to have human applications, he could have made a mint."

"Fletch?" He vehemently shook his head. "Not that kind of guy. He wasn't interested in money. He was happy with an old pair of jeans, a few throw pillows, and a year's supply of pita bread." He mentally shifted gears. "Let me take a look at his ledger again."

For the next few minutes, Langford studied the nearly illegible notations. Everything was very much as Jordan had indicated, and Todd's conclusions were the same. But the final entry puzzled him.

"Does this refer to you?" he asked. "It must. Your initials, G. P., on the day I did your spinal tap."

"Are you serious? Let me see that!" He showed her the entry, and she suddenly realized he was right. "I read right by it! How could I miss the connection?"

"I wonder what he meant by 'possibly elevated cog levels.'"

"In me?" she said. "It says they were elevated in me?"

"Of course, that makes sense! What do you think

Dr. Swenson would say if she knew about this? It sort of dovetails with what she already said!''

"What do you mean?"

"It explains how your knack, your lie detection, gets improved!" he said excitedly. "If the bump on your head caused elevated levels of cognopsin, and it's no wonder you can tell when people are lying!"

"Dear God," she said, her voice a bird-like warble. "There *is* something wrong with me, I *knew* there was."

"No, you're missing the point," he reassured. "It's going to wear off. It has in every other patient so far."

Jordan bit her lip. "But why's it taking so long? It's been over two weeks since the accident!"

"Ten days was an average. In one of the cases I reviewed, it lasted a little longer. I'm sure it'll disappear in you, too. And until it does," he said, pulling her to him, "I'll be around you almost all the time."

Comforted, Jordan put down the logbook and relaxed against him. "That's a relief." After a moment, "So, if Dr. Fletcher wasn't in it for the money, do you think that maybe he was working for somebody, so he didn't feel he could discuss the discovery with anyone else?"

"And you think this discovery got him murdered?" said Todd.

"I don't know what to think anymore." She speared an asparagus tip. "I guess it's possible. You think we should go to the cops with this?"

"With what? That we think he discovered something so earth-shattering that it got him killed? We don't have any evidence, Jordan. It's pure speculation. They'd laugh us out of the precinct."

"Perhaps. But what about Dr. Fine?"

"What about him?" Todd asked. "All we know is that he lied to you about not being aware of certain patients in the hospital, and he lied to both of us about the pharmacy codes in the charts. Then he goes and gets himself shot after a stupid fender-bender. I don't know," he said, running a hand through his hair. "Nothing makes sense anymore. Two guys working on projects they won't own up to get killed. Ambulance attendants are being bribed to bring certain patients to the hospital. I wonder what's next."

The faraway look in her eyes vanished, replaced by a glint of insight. "Todd, remember when we didn't think Fletcher and Fine were connected at all?"

"What about it?"

"I was just thinking," she mused. "This 'Cog' stuff. Professor Gregory said it might be neurologically active, in humans. Well, in rats, it really perks up their brains. Turns them into near-geniuses. What if it actually *had* already been given to humans?"

He was beginning to see what she was driving at. "Go on."

"Let's say, hypothetically speaking, that it was given to a patient with severe Parkinson's disease. Or Alzheimer's." She let her words trail off. "What do you suppose would happen?"

He felt a sudden pounding in his ears. The spark of realization suddenly blazed through his brain, setting his thoughts afire. His jaw tightened. "Oh, sweet Jesus."

Her green eyes locked on his. "Exactly. It's happening, Todd. Right in front of us!"

Langford was suddenly furious with himself. God almighty, why hadn't he seen it before? All the clues were there, but he'd been too blind to recognize them. He disgustedly pushed his plate away. "I must be brain-dead not to have seen it! What else did your professor say? That the compound probably had about a ten-day half-life? Of course it did! That explains why our five miracle patients suddenly deteriorated after a week and a half."

"There's got to be something we can do about this," she said.

"Oh, you better believe it! And I think I know just where to look."

Chapter Seventeen

SHIFT CHANGE IN THE PHARMACY OCCURRED AN HOUR later than it did in the rest of the hospital. The eight-hour night shift generally began at midnight and ended at eight A.M., every night except Saturday, when it was closed. The brief shutdown marked the hospital administration's concession to the concept of a weekend. The timing worked out perfectly for Langford. Since he was on call that Saturday, his presence in the hospital wouldn't be unusual. The only question was whether the weekend chaos would diminish enough for him to leave the ER and implement his plan.

Friday and Saturday nights could be a nightmare. Despite the local community's best efforts, the barrios of the South Bronx remained a haven of gang warfare and drive-by shootings. Local ERs did a land-office business in gunshot wounds, stabbings, and assorted physical mayhem. Cynical staff physicians wore T-shirts reading, "PAID-UP MEMBER, KNIFE AND GUN CLUB." The glut of homicidal injuries generally decreased by early morning, when they were overtaken by the results of drug and alcohol abuse: the heroin OD, the windshield injury to the seatbelt-less drunk, the paranoia of the addict on crystal meth. But finally, just before dawn, these, too, began to wane.

Langford told Jordan to stay near the phone. He called her at four, just after she'd finally drifted off.

She quickly dressed, flagged down a cab, and was at the hospital within fifteen minutes. She sat patiently in the ER waiting room until Langford called her in. Pretending that she was a patient, he addressed her in garbled non sequiturs as he led her to an exam room. When no one was looking, he nonchalantly steered her toward an exit corridor that led into the hospital.

At that time of day, the non-patient floors were virtually deserted. Still, they couldn't hazard being discovered by an unaccountably motivated security guard. Jordan went inside a ladies' room far from the main lobby to wait. Then Todd ducked into a stairwell and made his way upstairs. He wanted to be as far away from the pharmacy as possible.

On ten, he caught his breath and eased the stairwell door ajar. The ORs were down the hall, in a long corridor at right angles to the elevator banks. There was virtually no activity on the floor, and the hall was empty. Having phoned upstairs just before Jordan arrived, he knew that one of the ORs was still in use, where a sixteen-year-old he'd admitted five hours previously tenaciously clung to life, despite having his torso perforated by four nine-millimeter rounds. Langford stole across the hall and entered the men's locker room.

In the bathroom, he found the sink nearest the overhead smoke detector. He placed a wastebasket on top of the sink and filled it with balled-up paper towels, adding some crumpled plastic garbage liners for good measure. Then he took a pack of cigarettes and book of matches from his breast pocket. He'd pilfered the Newport Lights from a patient. Tearing a paper match from the book, he placed a cigarette at right angles to the matches and closed the matchbook cover, so the unlit end protruded from one side of the matchbook, and the filter from the other. Finally, he struck the match.

He lit the cigarette and dragged on the butt, until

satisfied that his fire bomb would remain lit. With a flick of his wrist, he chucked the improvised incendiary device into the wastebasket. The cigarette would probably burn down to the match heads in about five minutes. Creeping out of the locker room, he retreated unseen to the stairwell and sat down on the top step, checking his watch.

Three minutes later, he got up and patiently descended the stairs. He took them more slowly, one step at a time. In three minutes, he neared the first floor. He halted, wondering if he'd screwed things up. Leaning against the wall, he waited by the interior door, counting off the seconds in his head.

"Code red, ten east. Code red, ten east. Security, ten east."

Overhead, the public address system repeated the announcement several more times. Langford permitted himself a triumphant smile. Then he casually opened the door and sauntered into the hall. From the end of the corridor, a bleary-eyed security guard came into view, followed by another, hurrying to the elevators. Langford forced a perplexed look as they rushed past him.

"Is that a fire on ten?" he called after them.

The first guard repeatedly jabbed the elevator button. "Better not be."

"Oh shit," said the second. "Damn elevators shut down during a fire. Come on!"

The two guards jogged past him into the stairwell. Langford fought a self-congratulatory grin as he headed in the opposite direction. It was a bit too early to gloat, he reminded himself. Reaching the ladies' room, he knocked twice and eased the door open. Jordan appeared, looking apprehensive.

"Did it go all right?" she asked.

"So far so good. Come on, we've got work to do." He quickly led her in the direction of the pharmacy.

"How much time do we have?"

"I figure about fifteen minutes. When they realize
there's no big emergency, they'll probably break for a
smoke and go back to wherever they came from. But
that should give us enough time."

In the hospital, how often the pharmacy was broken
into had become a standing joke. A week before, and
for the third time that year, there had been an attempted
break-in. Although none of the burglaries was successful, the pharmacy was an understandably attractive target, with large quantities of narcotics, including
transdermal and injectable fentanyl; various forms of
cocaine; an inexhaustible supply of tranquilizers; and
neurolept anesthetics like ketamine.

Langford had a twofold reason for choosing that particular night. Not only was the pharmacy unoccupied
until eight, but the pharmacy's dead bolt had been destroyed during the most recent break-in. Thus far, the
lock had not been replaced; and after the narcotics and
other controlled drugs were safely secured in interior
cabinets, the only exterior lock remaining was a simple
push-button affair.

When they reached the pharmacy entrance, the first-
floor corridor remained deserted. Langford took out his
wallet. Jordan tried the doorknob and found it locked.

"I hope you're right about the credit card," she said.

He removed the American Express card. "Don't
leave home without it," he said wryly. With one last
look around, he carefully slid the plastic card between
door and doorframe, working it against the latch as he
gently jostled the knob to and fro. Soon the lock
yielded, and the door eased open. Then he and Jordan
silently ducked inside, closed the door behind them,
and switched on the lights.

They found the door to Dr. Fine's vacant office
locked, as expected. But it, too, had a push-button lock
conquerable by a credit card. Once inside, they shut the
door and paused, looking around. The room seemed
much as they remembered it, largely untouched.

"Any idea what we're looking for?" he asked.

"I figure it's like pornography," Jordan said.

"We'll know it when we see it?"

"Precisely," she said. "I'll start with the desk, you take the shelves."

After several minutes of searching, they came up with nothing. The shelves were lined with textbooks, journals, and continuing education materials. The desk contained invoices, pharmacy documents, and correspondence. But nowhere was there a diary, ledger, or accounting book like she'd found in Dr. Fletcher's office.

"How much time have we got?"

"Maybe ten minutes," he said. "Let's not waste it."

"Let's see what's on his p.c." Fine's computer was a mid-range Digital model. Jordan turned on the power and checked the hard drives. Fine had hundreds of files, which would take hours to review—hours they didn't have. Instead, they decided to look for something significant in the file names. Hunched over the monitor, they studied the titles as she scrolled through the drives. "Research.doc" seemed promising, but when she called it up, it proved to be an old thesis on drug interactions. Likewise, "Animal.ltr" sounded like a possibility, but it turned out to be personal correspondence with the ASPCA. Langford slumped back, depressed.

"Well, that's that. It was worth a look."

"Wait a minute," Jordan said. "Maybe he kept it separate."

"Like where?"

"Like here," she said, pointing at one of the shelves. Between two textbooks was a cardboard box imprinted with the 3M logo. It was the disposable container for a set of ten high-density formatted diskettes. Apparently, Fine used the box as storage for three-and-a-half-inch floppies. Langford took it down and placed it on the desk. It contained nine diskettes, eight of which were video games. The ninth, however, had a simple

stick-on label with the handwritten letter "F." Jordan
lifted it up for inspection.

"I give up," she said. "It could be anything."

"We're gonna have to get out of here. Throw it on
the B drive and let's take a peek."

She quickly booted up, drumming her fingers for the
few seconds the computer required to change drives.
Langford looked over his shoulder toward the doorway
and nervously checked his watch. But then, suddenly,
the screen before them lit up. Jordan's eyes went wide,
and she slowly began nodding her head.

"Jesus Christ, Todd," she said. "Great shot. All
net."

The monitor glowed with the chemical structure of
a long, organic molecule, followed by an equally long
and unpronounceable name. Jordan quickly went to the
next screen, where the molecule was graphically depicted.

"Is that it?"

"Yes, sir, it is," she said. "Paydirt. Same as in Dr.
Fletcher's ledger. Look," she said, pointing to the
screen. "He called it 'cognopsin.' "

"Cognopsin, huh? Fletch, you old hound. For a guy
like Dr. Fletcher, that's pretty damn original. I guess
we don't have to wonder what Cog means anymore.
Come on, Jordan. What else is there?"

When she moved on to the next and final screen,
they both fell silent, gaping in astonishment at the simple, unmistakable entries. Going from one to five, it
was a numerical tabulation of medical records numbers.
Next to each entry were the corresponding patient
names, all of which they knew by heart. And finally,
representing the starred items on the pharmacy computer code, there was the time and date, along with the
amount in milligrams, of cognopsin administered.

"Is that the end?" he asked.

"Just about."

"I suppose we don't have to wonder anymore if they

knew each other. Come on, let's get out of here. Give me the diskette.''

"Hold on, there's one more page."

Jordan hit the PAGE DOWN button. The one-line entry was brief. At the top of the final screen, there was a sixth number, most recently added. And beside it, a name whose familiarity sent a chill through them.

"Rita," he said hoarsely.

Jordan was struck dumb. She gazed in horror at the name of her friend, a friend unwittingly used in some god-awful experiment. Her hands began to tremble.

"Come on, Jordan," he said. "We've got what we want."

"Not quite," she finally managed, switching on the laser printer. "If we get a hard copy, we can leave the diskette here."

"How long will that take?"

"Give me a minute." She entered the edit mode and hit the print command, calling for one copy of the entire document. The printer was old and slow, taking twenty seconds a page. But soon they had the four pages they needed. Jordan tore them off and folded them neatly while Todd replaced the diskette. After turning off the printer and p.c., they exited, leaving Fine's office exactly as they found it. Langford checked his watch: twelve minutes had elapsed. He took Jordan by the elbow, which was still shaking. When they reached the pharmacy entrance, he cautiously peered into the corridor.

The hallway was empty. They quickly ducked outside, locking the pharmacy door behind them. They headed back in the direction of the ER, slowing their pace to a leisurely stroll. One of the security guards emerged from the elevator and headed their way.

"False alarm?" Langford asked.

"Just a brushfire," said the guard. "Some asshole playing with matches. Jesus, some people got nothin' better to do this time of day."

*   *   *

Completely unnerved, they decided to go back to Jordan's apartment. Todd was on call the rest of the night, but he thought he could sign out to someone, if it was quiet enough. Once away from the hospital's chaos they could best decide what to do. But the emergency room had gone berserk. It was all Todd could do to hustle Jordan to the door before one of the nurses spotted him. He promised Jordan they'd get together as soon as he could, though it might take hours.

"Take a look at the girl in four, Todd," a nurse called out to him.

"What the hell happened to this place?"

"We got a private walk-in with chest pain," she said, "then an OD whose buddies dumped him in the courtyard. We've got our hands full, but we were managing, until the third patient showed up. Vaginal bleeding, shocky."

"Is she pregnant?"

"It's hard to get a good history. She's semi-coherent."

"Did you page GYN?" he asked.

She nodded. "Both residents are tied up in a stat section. They said they'd be about half an hour and asked us to hold down the fort. But from the looks of this kid, we don't have that long. I put in an IV and sent the bloods, but she's taching away, and I can barely get a blood pressure."

On the exam table, a slender teenage girl lay on her side with knees drawn up, shivering. She appeared to be about eighteen, with long black hair and a dark complexion. In a nearby corner, a heavyset woman anxiously looked on, fighting back tears. Langford took a close look at her and froze. It was Mrs. Rivera from the housekeeping department. He automatically reached for the girl's pulse.

"Mrs. Rivera?" he said. "What's going on?"

"Oh, Dr. Langford, *gracias a Dios*!" she said, with

a heavy Spanish accent. "She wouldn't let me help her."

"Is this your daughter?"

"Conchita." She nodded. "My baby."

"Is she pregnant?"

"She wouldn't tell me, but I think so. A mother can tell."

"Help me get her in stirrups," he said to the nurse. "And open the GYN pack." To the woman, "Look, *señora*, we're going to do the best we can for her, okay? I'm afraid I have to ask you to wait outside, but let me ask you a few questions first. When did she get sick like this?"

"I don' know, she was gone all day. Then she showed up, like, around midnight, you know? I tried to give her some tea, but—"

"Was she bleeding when she came home?" he asked. "From the vagina?"

"I think so," Mrs. Rivera said.

"Do you know when her last period was?"

"No, I don't know that."

"Does she have regular periods?" he said.

"She did a few years ago, before she got pregnant."

"I thought you didn't know if she was pregnant."

"No, I mean with her other babies," said Mrs. Rivera.

"Babies? How many does she have?"

"You don' remember, Dr. Langford? Two little boys, very healthy."

"How old is she, your daughter?"

"Conchita? She's seventeen. Please, Doctor. Is she going to be all right?"

"I'll do my best," he said. "One last thing, *señora*. Does she use any drugs or alcohol? Does she have any medical problems?"

"Drugs? No. I never seen her drink."

"Okay. Just have a seat in the waiting room, and we'll talk with you soon."

They positioned the patient in the knee-crutch stirrups, drawing her hips down to the edge of the exam
table. The teenager's teeth were chattering. As she
moaned, she kept reaching weakly for her lower abdomen. Her skin was moist and cold. Langford lightly
placed his hand above her pubis, and she winced
through closed eyes. Her abdomen was tense and distended.

"Hemoperitoneum," he said to the nurse. "I'd bet
on it. She must have at least a liter of blood in her
belly."

"You think she's got an ectopic?"

"Maybe. Let's find out."

He took a seat at the end of the exam table and
switched on a lamp. From the patient's vulva, a stream
of painfully thin blood seeped onto the white sheet beneath her buttocks. Langford put on a pair of gloves,
took a metal speculum from the tray, and separated the
labia. He expected the patient to grow tense, but she
became unexpectedly quiet.

"Conchita?" he called. No answer. To the nurse,
"How's she doing up there, Sally?"

"Not good," said the nurse, squeezing the bag of
IV fluid with both hands. "She's losing it faster than
we can replace it."

Even with the speculum open and in place, he
couldn't see anything but red. Watery, purplish blood
filled the vagina, obscuring the cervix. Worse still, the
blood wasn't clotting, leading him to think they might
be dealing with a life-threatening coagulopathy.

"Christ, I can't see a damn thing. Is there a Gomco
in here?"

"No suction at all. The best I have is a sponge
stick."

"That'll have to do." He swabbed at the torrent of
blood, repeatedly wiping away or absorbing as much
as possible. Suddenly, half way up the vagina, he
reached an obstruction. "What the hell is this?" He

removed the gauze from his instrument and opened its jaws, placing the ends around the impeding object, which had a soft, mushy consistency.

The nurse peered over his shoulder. "Is that a clot?"

"No, she's not clotting. It's a wad of some kind."

Pulling steadily on the handle of the ring forceps, the irregular wad was slowly dislodged with a moist, sucking sound. It came free, loosing a sea of blood that surged outward unobstructed, drenching his shirt and pants. Undaunted, he gazed at the sticky object he held in gloved fingers.

"Is she aborting?"

"No, I think it's . . . like a fabric. Some kind of cotton? Jesus, some people will put *anything* up there." Placing the material aside, he loaded the sponge stick with fresh gauze and returned to the speculum. Peering intently, he sponged away the remaining blood. As he reached the cervix, something odd caught his eye. "What the hell?"

"*Now* what?"

"Good question." He adjusted the lamp for better light. "There's some sort of plug in her cervix. Like a cork." Manipulating the forceps, he worked its jaws around the plug. His mind awhirl, he slowly, carefully began extracting it. All of his training was coming to bear as he struggled to figure out what was going on. Clearly, the patient had to be pregnant. The bluish, soft consistency of her cervix, and the fact that something was wedged into it, suggested an act related to pregnancy. But what? He hoped the GYN resident would get there soon. All at once, the woody substance came loose, followed by yet another gush of blood.

He held it up to the light. The foreign object resembled a boar's tusk. An inch thick and about four times as long, its internal end was curved and pointy. Langford touched the tip, worried by its sharpness.

"Is this a fertility thing?" the nurse asked.

"No, it's an abortion thing. I'll bet this is something

used to dilate the cervix, made of wood. There are clinics that use this stuff called laminaria for mid-trimester abortions. It's a kind of sterile seaweed that dilates the cervix overnight, before they do the procedure.''

''A clinic put that in?''

''Not around here, they didn't,'' he said. ''This is no legal abortion, Sal. This kid probably didn't have the money, and went to the local witch doctor. He probably thought he was doing her a favor by shoving that into her uterus.'' He shook his head disgustedly. ''Man, with abortion so available these days, you think the word would get around.'' He stood up to perform a pelvic exam.

''So where's all the blood coming from?'' asked the nurse.

He gently probed inside the patient, the internal fingers of his gloved right hand sweeping from side to side while his external hand felt for the rounded dome of the uterus. He frowned. ''Holy Christ, she must be five months along! And . . .'' He paused. ''What the hell is this?''

Off to the patient's right, a pronounced, doughy bulge indented the upper vagina, beside the lower uterine segment. Puzzled, Langford withdrew his blood-soaked glove. An ectopic? he wondered. No, she had an intrauterine pregnancy. An ovarian tumor? He suddenly picked up the laminaria and held it in the exact position he'd removed it from the uterus. It dawned on him that its pointed end had been angled off to the right. All color slowly drained from his face, and the sound of his voice was painfully pinched.

''I don't believe it.''

The nurse picked up on his ominous tone. ''What's happening?''

''Jesus, what was I thinking? See how this thing is curved? The wacko who inserted it perforated, right through her upper cervix! You asked why she was bleeding? He ripped her uterine artery to shreds, that's why!''

As he disgustedly tore off his gloves, the nurse anxiously checked the patient's blood pressure. The teenager lay morbidly still, appearing to have lapsed into a coma. Langford flung open the door and shouted into the ER proper.

"We need a hand in here! Someone tell one of those GYN residents to scrub out, and we're going to need an OR! Page anesthesia, call the blood bank, and—''

"Dr. Langford!''

He quickly whirled, hearing the urgency in her voice. A stethoscope to her ears, the nurse was frantically listening to the patient's chest. Then her eyes met his, and she rapidly shook her head.

"I just lost her pulse!''

"Oh, marvelous.'' Before he began CPR, he briefly shouted back toward the nursing station. "We've got an arrest in here, guys! And there's still two hours until shift change, in case anyone was thinking about bugging out of here early!''

As a hospital employee, Mrs. Rivera was allowed to remain at the nursing station. Head in her hands, she sat at the desk during Langford's exam, deep in prayer. But when he emerged from the room calling for help, she began to wail—piercing, grief-stricken sobs that reached all the way to the waiting room.

Dr. Royce took the phone from his live-in housekeeper. Dr. Hobson was on the line.

"Still coming for breakfast, aren't you?'' Royce said smoothly.

Hobson was fuming. "I really think you lost your mind this time! I thought we agreed to only transfer a certain type of patient!''

"Get ahold of yourself,'' said Royce. "You're blowing things way out of proportion. This discovery applies to all classes of patients, right? It's really not

necessary that we limit transfers to the impoverished or
derelicts.''

"The point is, they don't have families who call!"
Hobson continued. "Here I go away for two days, and
when I come back, the clinic's answering service tells
me there've been over a dozen calls about this woman
since midnight! Her family wants to see her, visit her!
We can't put these people off forever!''

Royce remained calm. "Why not? No one's getting
in until we let them."

"Look," said Hobson, taking a deep breath, "what
I'm saying is, things have been going pretty well, and
we don't need this kind of complication. Fine already
made a mistake when he gave the woman the compound, and now you transfer her to the clinic. What
the hell's going to happen next?''

"What are you worried about?"

"I'm worried about mistakes! I'm worried about the
Mafia snooping around, nosing into our business! I'm
worried about some ER resident and a female medical
student pulling out charts!''

"Nobody knows a thing, believe me," said Royce.
"The mob might be trying to get into the hospital business, but it has no idea what we're up to. Neither do
the others. Now, do your best to relax.''

When Langford arrived at Jordan's apartment, he finally met her roommate. Julie Kennan was a tall,
flighty blond with abundant nervous energy. After
greeting him, she stepped back and gestured toward her
outfit.

"Does this look all right?" she said.

She was wearing a form-fitting nylon top with flared
stretch pants atop a pair of pumps, all of which she
filled out rather nicely.

" 'All right' isn't exactly how I'd describe it, but
yes. Where are you going wearing that?''

"I'm meeting my boyfriend. He said something

about breakfast," she said vacuously. "Nice to meet you." She breezed by with the effortless grace of someone accustomed to being stared at.

Langford paused in the doorway, watching her departure. Julie had the kind of magnetic, eye-catching body language that would never be lost in a crowd. On his cheek, there appeared the wispy softness of Jordan's lips.

"She does that to people," Jordan said. "No one will ever accuse Julie of being shy."

"You let her go out like that without adult supervision?"

"Oh, I wouldn't worry about it. She can handle herself." She pulled away and looked into his eyes. He looked back, seeing a profound fatigue, and sadness.

"Still thinking about what we learned in Fine's office, aren't you?"

"I can't help it," she said, sagging against him. "Rita's my friend. The idea that she's being used for something is disgusting. I was thinking about it all night."

"We have plenty of time for that. Let's talk about something else," he said. "Tell me about Julie. I never would have figured her for your roommate. How come you don't share the place with another med student?"

"I've known Julie since college," Jordan said. "We decided to room together before I got accepted to med school. Anyway, how was the rest of the night after I left? You look like you haven't slept a wink."

He told her. Jordan could still see the residue of anxiety in his expression, which whitened his face like a layer of dust. His body was ragged around the edges, jangled as if by caffeine from the hours of dealing with life-and-death drama. As much as she realized he loved his work, it would inevitably take its toll. Repeated nights like this would make him burn out early. He desperately needed to relax.

"Would you like a drink?"

"At this time of morning?" he said. "Do I look that wired?"

She nodded. "Like your finger's stuck in an electric outlet."

He closed the door behind him with slow deliberation. His arms went around her, and he drew her toward him. "You know, what I could really use," he said, looking into her eyes, "is a little shared bodily warmth." He took her face in his hands and kissed her softly on the lips.

"Is that what it says in the residents' manual?" Jordan asked.

"Yes. And I always follow the directions."

Jordan disengaged, pushing herself away to arm's length. She was wearing a loose terry robe, tied at the waist. Keeping her gaze on his, she slowly undid the sash and parted the material to reveal her nakedness underneath. She shrugged out of the fabric, letting the robe slide off her shoulders. It cascaded down her legs, forming a pile on the rug.

"Far be it from me to stand in the way of medical education." Then she turned and walked toward the bedroom.

An hour later, they lay on their sides in bed. With his abdomen pressing into her lower back, Langford's arm was slung loosely over her shoulder. His fingers made small circles on the back of her hand. She snuggled close to him, warmed by his body heat. Much as she wanted to remain in quiet togetherness like that, she was nagged by what they'd discovered hours before.

"I can't stop thinking about what we found in Fine's office," she said.

"Me too. It doesn't make any sense."

"Yes it does," she said. "We're just not seeing the whole picture."

"Okay. Lay it out for me."

"Well, to begin with, your friend Fletcher discovered the new molecule. A long organic compound that's neurologically active. When he injected it into a rat, it became Mighty Mouse. A brainy little rodent problem-solver.''

"Why'd he call it cognopsin?'' he said.

"I guess because it improved cognition. It made Fat Rats smart.''

"And people, too?''

"Probably,'' she said. "'Somewhere along the line, he showed it to Dr. Fine. Or Fine got wind of it, whatever. Anyway, Fine takes the stuff, this purified cognopsin, and gives it to humans—first, the five we knew about, then Rita. To sick patients with neurologic problems. And, bingo—overnight, they jump out of bed and shout hallelujah.''

"For a while,'' he said.

"Yep. Ten days, maybe two weeks. Then it gets degraded, and it wears off. They get sick again, so sick that they die. Or they become vegetables, like they were before, and they get transferred to that farm stand called Eastgate.''

"And? What happens after that?''

She sighed. "That's as far as I got. How's it sound to you?''

"Not bad, up to a point. It leaves a lot of questions unanswered.''

"Tell me about it,'' she said. "Like where did Dr. Fletcher get the cognopsin in the first place?''

"Right. We know he was involved in the spinal fluid study, the same as I was.''

She thought about that. "Todd, could it be produced in spinal fluid somehow?''

"I don't know. I suppose so. Most of what he did was a little complicated. But as I understand it, he was studying extracts of CSF.''

"So,'' she said, "maybe the cognopsin was derived from the CSF of other patients.''

"Maybe. Anyway, one way or the other, Fine learns

what's going on in the animal lab. And he does his thing with the patients. The question is, what's in it for him? It's hard to believe he'd do something like that out of scientific curiosity. Fine's not a researcher.''

"What other reason would he have?" she asked.

"Could be something as simple as money or power. Or sex.''

"Do you really believe that?" she said.

He considered it. "Well, probably not sex. He didn't seem the type. But money's a pretty strong motivator. Maybe he was in debt.''

"You know, I really think we're missing the big picture. We know these two people are involved, and they're both a little weird. But what we're overlooking is that they're both stone-cold dead. Someone killed them, and I'll *bet* it's because of their involvement with cognopsin.''

"You're saying someone wanted them out of the way?" he said.

"That's what I'm thinking," she said. "It's too co-incidental to think these were random murders. And if someone *did* kill them, it could be someone who's got the answers to our questions. No, there had to be an intermediary.''

"So you don't think it was just the two of them?''

Jordan suppressed a chill, pressing her body more closely to his. "Absolutely not. There's someone else, or maybe more than one. And that same someone killed them both.''

His heart began beating faster. "I have a real problem with what you're suggesting, Jordan.''

"Why?''

"If there's another person—or people—involved, it has to be someone intimately familiar with what's going on in the hospital. Someone on the inside. Probably someone I know, maybe even work with.''

They both fell silent, digesting the weight of their conclusions. Langford held her close, pressing his face into the cool flesh of her neck. What they were proposing was monstrous. The idea that something so evil and so sinister could be happening where he worked was nothing short of a nightmare.

And it was scaring them to death.

They needed help, and they knew it. They were in way over their heads. But they didn't know to whom to turn. Clearly, it had to be someone who knew the hospital inside and out. They were both familiar with many people on the hospital staff, yet there were few, if any, they trusted unconditionally. Jordan's best friend and confidante—her roommate Julie—wouldn't know one end of the hospital from the other, whereas Langford's closest ally had been murdered. No, they had to come up with someone else.

"What about Dr. Meyerson?" she asked. "You said he was bright."

"He is," Langford agreed. "In fact, he was on call with me last night, and I brought him up to speed on what we know so far. But he has just as many questions as we do. I was thinking of someone with a little more clout than him." He paused. "How about Dr. Royce?"

"I don't know," she said, shaking her head. She told him how, as an ER patient, she'd been convinced Dr. Hobson was lying. "I'm sure it's nothing, but I don't really feel comfortable with either Hobson or his partner, Royce."

But they couldn't come up with someone they both felt comfortable with. In addition, there was the question of murder—*two* murders, and the police didn't seem to have the slightest clue about the deaths of either Dr. Fletcher or Dr. Fine. The scuttlebutt in the hospital was that both cases were being considered simple crimes of opportunity, not of intent. So it was very unlikely the cops would view their theory about the peculiar goings-on in the hospital as anything more than a flight of fancy.

Moreover, neither he nor Jordan had any real contacts in the police department. But then, Langford recalled, there was Tom Courtney. His contacts might
prove helpful indeed.

The high-rise faced east, overlooking Columbus Circle.
It had a magnificent view of the lower park and the
expansive promenade of Central Park South. On that
warm October morning, with the rising sun a welcome
balm on their faces, they breakfasted on the apartment's
balcony and surveyed the scene below. The Salvadoran
maid brought out plates of vegetable frittata with herbs
and goat cheese, then departed, closing the balcony's
sliding glass doors behind her.

"I knew you'd feel better once you thought things
out," said Royce.

"Please, please accept my apologies. I was way out
of line."

"No apology necessary," said Royce. "So, everything considered, how do you think the place is running?"

"I salute you," said Hobson. "I had my doubts in
the beginning, I admit. But you've laid them to rest."

"Thank you. It was a gamble," Royce agreed, "but
someone had to take the initiative. What we're discovering in Eastgate is invaluable. We couldn't possibly
have done it in the hospital."

"I still can't believe what happened to Dr. Fine,"
said Hobson, shaking his head. "Sometimes I hate this
city. And Fletcher? If only I'd spoken to him before
his apartment was broken into!"

"Stop blaming yourself," said Royce. "He was a
victim of his own carelessness. But it's too bad they're
both not here to share this triumph. We couldn't have
done it without them."

"To say the least," Hobson agreed. "How long until
we have enough cognopsin?"

"Oh, we should have a hundred doses by week's

end. That should be enough to continue our research in a more traditional manner.''

''And then we're going to publish?''

''Yes, but without revealing our methods,'' said Royce. ''Being *too* honest could get us into serious trouble. Everyone wants to be on the cutting edge, but no one wants to do what has to be done. We'll give Dr. Fletcher the credit due him, and then turn Eastgate into a true chronic-care facility.''

''What about Todd Langford and that med student? Langford's a top-notch resident. Before Fine was murdered, didn't he say they seemed to be getting pretty close to finding out what we're doing?''

Royce's expression had grown cloudy and distant. ''When the opportunity presents itself, I'll have a talk with him.''

It was easy to tell when Dr. Royce walked into a room, because all conversation stopped. The man had presence. It wasn't just his appearance, which in itself was striking—the perfectly tailored imported silk suit, cut in conservative lines; the bronzed skin, revitalized with alpha-hydroxys and moisturizer; or the highlighted silver streaks in his well-coiffed hair. Rather, Royce had a no-nonsense dynamism in his body language, a charisma of movement.

The next morning, when Royce entered the ER, all heads turned in his direction. It was as if everyone was waiting for him to say something. Instead, he went to the nursing station and pulled several charts from the rack, quietly reviewing them one at a time. Slowly, the pace of activity in the room returned to its previous level.

Langford, whose response to Dr. Royce was as predictably Pavlovian as everyone else, went back to caring for his patient. The twenty-four-year-old woman with a history of psychiatric disorders had come in last night. She was what they called a jumper because she had thrown herself out of a six-story apartment window onto the concrete sidewalk in front of a building on 109th Street. She was an exception to Langford's four-story rule, which held that an unimpeded descent from a height of four stories or greater was invariably fatal. In her case, a clothesline slowed her speed and altered her trajectory, interrupting her fall. Instead of landing on her head, her shoulders absorbed the impact.

As a result, she eluded instantaneous death. But in her case, mortality was merely delayed, not permanently deferred. She suffered a severely broken neck—a complete fracture of C-2, with pulverization of the spinal column, rendering her not only immediately quadriplegic, but unable to breathe on her own. In addition, she had fractures of both clavicles, a broken pelvis, and a compound fracture of her right humerus. The resultant blood loss and effect on her nervous system was leading to irreversible shock.

Still, the trauma team persevered. Although the woman was comatose and unresponsive, they performed a tracheostomy after an unsuccessful intubation, and placed her on a respirator. They started two large-bore IVs, placed a central line, and inserted a chest tube to deal with a pneumothorax. Then they immobilized her fractures, lavaged her abdomen to check for internal bleeding, and drained her damaged bladder. When she suffered the inevitable cardiac arrest, they resuscitated her twice.

From the standpoint of medical education, she was the ideal lab preparation. There was virtually no chance she would survive as a functional human being. Yet her resilient thorax was a worthy platform on which to practice closed cardiac massage. Despite her cardiovascular collapse, she was slender, and the prominent veins of her arms and legs were ripe targets for venipuncture. Best of all, she was young enough to have good vascular tone. Unimpeded by atherosclerosis, her blood vessels responded well to the changing rhythms of ACLS. When her pressure dropped, the trauma team responded with pressors and vasoconstrictors. When her heart failed, they juggled inotropic agents. When her CVP skyrocketed, they switched vasodilators and diuretics. Over the course of two hours, the team administered some twenty-three different medications. Tragic though the case was, the team's best efforts developed an air of dark comedy, which helped insulate them from feelings of helplessness and frustration.

Now, four hours after her admission, Langford stood over the woman's body, deliberating what to do next. She was as stable as she was going to get. Although she was virtually brain-dead, he was aware that some doctors—especially neurosurgical residents in need of training—might make a case for surgical intervention. Critical though she was, she had virtually *no* chance unless her cervical fractures were debrided and her spinal cord decompressed. As Langford looked down in concentration, he became aware of someone standing beside him.

"Looks like quite the challenging case, Todd. I was going over the chart."

"Dr. Royce, I've got a real catch-twenty-two here. This patient will never make it unless they debride the vertebral fragments and clean up her cord. But her neck's so damaged, and her airway's so distorted, that anesthesia says they won't be able to keep her oxygenated on the OR table."

"They give her steroids?" asked Royce.

"Yes, enough to keep the swelling down. But it's only temporary."

"Get used to it," Royce said. "Emergency medicine's full of tough choices. What did your attending say?"

"He left it up to me."

"I'm not surprised. What's the patient on now?"

"An Isuprel drip," said Todd. "Enough to give her a pressure. And she got the study drug."

"Probably the last one to do so," said Royce. "We're calling off the study, as of today. We finally have enough cases to analyze the data and draw conclusions." He paused. "What about the SICU? Can they take her?"

"No, not yet. Same old story, no beds."

Royce thoughtfully pursed his lips. "Well, you can't keep her here forever. If you get backed up, I suggest you transfer her to Eastgate."

Langford suddenly couldn't help himself. "Like Rita Donninger?" he asked.

"She's getting the finest care possible, Langford. All the patients are."

He smiled and walked away with the effortless authority that caused heads to turn. Watching him go, Langford thought back to the frightening dilemma he and Jordan confronted the night before. They couldn't keep their fears to themselves forever. They had to confide in someone—someone in a position of trust and authority. Jordan had vague suspicions about Dr. Royce. But to Langford's way of thinking, there was probably no better choice. He left the bedside and caught up with the older man.

"Excuse me, Dr. Royce?" said Todd. "Got a minute?"

Royce stopped and checked his watch. "Certainly."

"Could we talk privately?"

"Why not step outside? It's a beautiful morning."

Minutes later, holding Styrofoam cups of coffee, they strolled leisurely down Ninety-seventh Street, taking in the sun. Langford knew he was taking a risk, but he felt it was a risk he had to take. As succinctly as possible, he related what he and Jordan knew, and what they suspected. Royce listened patiently, saying nothing and showing little reaction. At the end of the block they turned back. When Langford was finished, Royce clasped his arms behind his back and stopped to look up at the sky.

"You have any proof of this?" Royce asked.

"Just the hard copy from Dr. Fine's computer. The original diskette should still be in his office."

"I'd like to see it. Where did you say the hard copy was?"

"In Miss Ross's apartment," said Todd. "It should be safe there."

"Undoubtedly. And the lab video, and Dr. Fletcher's ledger?"

"Same place."

"I see." Royce gazed into the distance, shaking his head. "This is all rather incredible. If I didn't know you better, I'd say you and the girl have lost your minds. Dr. Fletcher and Dr. Fine both murdered over some experiment, and the police don't have a clue? Anyone else would say that's preposterous! But I think I know you pretty well, Langford. And I don't think even *you* could make up something that far-fetched."

"I didn't make it up, Dr. Royce. All you have to do is look at those five patient charts and match them to the pharmacy records."

"Oh, I will. And the things in Miss Ross's apartment? Could I send someone by later to collect them?"

"Why don't I drop them off at your office tomorrow?" said Todd. "We might want to make copies first."

A brooding look clouded Royce's eyes. "Of course. You know what I find most remarkable about this ... what did you call it?"

"Cognopsin?"

"Yes, cognopsin. If it exists, how could it have eluded the scientific community for so long?"

"I couldn't tell you, Dr. Royce."

"And where does it come from?" asked Royce. "Is it a naturally produced substance, or is it artificially made?"

"Fletcher's logbook doesn't go into that."

They reached the entrance to the ER. "Too bad.

Well, I'll be happy to look into this for you. If you
want my opinion, I think there's probably a logical explanation for everything. If we search hard enough,
we'll find it. I honestly doubt this is the grand con-
spiracy you make it out to be."

"I hope you're right. And thanks for listening."

Royce started to go in, then hesitated. "You haven't
mentioned this to anyone, by chance?"

"Not yet. Jordan has a friend who works for *The
Wall Street Journal*. We might run it by her later tonight, just to get an objective opinion."

Royce's expression darkened. "I don't think that's
very wise."

"Why not?" asked Langford.

"You know how the press can blow things way out
of proportion. Perhaps you could postpone it a day or
two? At least let me review all the information first."

"I'll run it by Jordan, Dr. Royce, but she's a determined woman. Anyway, don't worry about it. At this
point, no newspaper would take the ball and run with
it. And, hey, thanks for your help," he said, extending
his hand.

Royce watched the young physician depart, gazing
after him with narrowed eyes.

Chapter Eighteen

HE KNEW MANY WAYS TO MAKE A BOMB, AND WAS proficient at most of them. The more popular methods, however, were also the ones he was least likely to use. A mixture of fertilizer and fuel oil, like the one used in the Oklahoma City explosion, was cumbersome and messy. Packing relatively little punch for its massive weight, it also stank. Then there was Semtex, the widely used Czech explosive that brought down Pan Am 103. While compact, Semtex also left a distinct chemical footprint. And ever since the TWA 800 disaster, even the least-sophisticated bomb detection unit could identify it. Finally, there were the commercial gunpowders used for reloading ammunition. While these were ideal for making pipe bombs, it was difficult to direct their explosive power.

His personal favorite was used by special units of the Israeli Defense Forces. Called *barak*, the Hebrew word for lightning, it was manufactured in a small factory in Herzliyya. Powerful and compact, it also created an intensely bright flash that would blind those victims not killed outright. The problem was its scarcity. He hadn't been able to get his hands on any in six months. He therefore decided to use something known by the oxymoronic sobriquet of *el gigante pequeña*.

"The little giant," as it was referred to in Colombia, was a favorite of the elite police squads that raided cartel strongpoints. A derivative of American C-4, it was a highly moldable plastique suitable for making shaped charges. It was particularly effective against reinforced doors and locks. Extremely volatile, it required the tiniest of detonators. The package's diminutive size made it ideal for what he had in mind.

Gaining access to her apartment had been child's play. After receiving his instructions, he waited until Jordan left the building. Once inside, he doubted he'd need more than fifteen minutes. He'd already learned that her roommate never returned before six. He also learned a great deal of other information about her, such as phone company records, credit card status, and utility payments. Now it was just a question of putting that knowledge to work.

The set of Monsour Professional lockpicks got him past the upper and lower Schlage locks. He closed the door behind him, drew the curtains, and turned on the lights. The first order of business, he'd been told, was retrieving the tape and the ledger. He had little trouble locating the items in her bedroom clothes closet. He put them into one of the larger pockets in his photographer's vest. Next it was time to more closely examine the apartment.

He was looking for a piece of electronic equipment that guaranteed proximity to its user. The phone was a definite possibility. The Mossad, in its campaign against Hamas, perfected the technique. A tiny charge wedged in the earpiece could decapitate the listener. It had the disadvantage, however, of having to wait for an incoming call. That might not be until tonight, or perhaps even tomorrow—and they told him they wanted the job accomplished as quickly as possible. Her personal computer held some advantages, but it, too, might not be used for a while. Then there was the interior light switch upon entering the apartment. Unfortunately, he didn't know whether she or her roommate would be the first to return and switch it on.

The phone rang in her bedroom. Both women had their own phones, with separate numbers and separate rooms. After the second ring, he heard a voice. He halted, tense and alert. But he soon recognized it as the muted, artificial sound of a recording. It was her answering machine. Walking on the balls of his feet, he returned to the bedroom, only half listening to the caller's voice. The machine was on her night table. A slight smile curled the corners of his mouth, and he reached for his tools. He knew that almost *everyone* listened to their messages the instant they got home.

He turned on the bedside lamp and studied the machine closely. One of the newer Panasonic offerings, it sported some features he wasn't familiar with. He was most comfortable with the Radio Shack model he trained on, but he presumed the internal electronics were similar. Working quickly but carefully, he removed the protective plastic shell and inspected the interior wiring. The circuits were clear-cut and well-marked. After a few seconds' study, he located the playback circuit. After isolating the wiring, he went to work on the explosive.

That afternoon, Sue Jacobs caught up with Langford before he left work.

"Looks like you're right about those rumors, Todd," she said. "The word I'm hearing is that there are bribes galore."

"Who's the money coming from?"

"No one seems to know," she said. "If an ambulance crew brings a bad trauma case here that should've gone elsewhere, they get an anonymous hundred-dollar bill in an unmarked envelope."

"It's gotta originate somewhere," he said.

"I'm still looking into that. But if this hits the papers, there'll be a helluva scandal. It's time I bucked this upstairs."

"Who're you going to tell?" he asked.
"Dr. Royce."

"I just don't trust him, that's all," said Jordan.
"Why not?" asked Langford. "It doesn't matter whether or not he believes us. Even if he doesn't, what's the worst thing he could do—order a psych consult?"
"There must have been someone else you could've told."
"Not with his kind of clout," said Todd. "Royce gets published. He serves on all these mayoral commissions and health subcommittees. People listen to him. If he discovers any hint of scandal, there'll be an investigation."
"What if he's part of it? What if he had something to do with Rita?" she asked.
"Please. He might be a publicity-seeking prima donna, but he's not a weasel."
"I hope to hell you're right."
Langford skillfully weaved through the late afternoon traffic, heading for SoHo. They planned to hang around her apartment until they heard from Sharon Mandel, Jordan's friend from the *Wall Street Journal*. Langford related Dr. Royce's reservations about going to the press, but they had tentatively planned to meet with the reporter that evening anyway, if she was available. Sharon promised to call and confirm. Jordan knew her friend would hold off on the story until they had more facts.
"I wonder if she already called," Jordan said.
"Who—Julie?"
"No, Sharon," she said. "I know she said she'd phone around six, but she might've called early. Hand me the car phone and I'll check my messages."
"Did you get through?" he asked.
"I think so. It clicked over after the second ring, and I got my recording. But when I tried to play it back,

there was like a pop. And then, nothing.''

"That's weird,'' Todd said. "Try it again.'' She did; but now, however, her phone didn't ring at all.

They reached her apartment just as the first fire truck arrived. Outside, a crowd of a dozen onlookers had gathered in the street. Jordan was surprised and worried to see the police and firemen entering her building. Langford slowed the car, then double-parked. He and Jordan looked upward, in the direction people were looking and pointing. From a shattered window on the fifth floor, thin wisps of smoke wafted skyward.

"My God,'' she cried. "That's my apartment!''

They both leapt from the car, leaving it haphazardly parked. They ran through the gathering throng, but were stopped at the building's stoop. A uniformed policeman was stopping anyone from entering. The building's residents were being evacuated as a precaution. Jordan was verging on a state of shock. Her first thought was of Julie. When the cop told her the apartment had been unoccupied, she was immensely relieved. Yet when the detective in charge learned that Jordan lived there, the questioning began in earnest.

An hour later, the fire trucks left, and the crowd had dissipated to a handful of hangers-on. Julie had been located at her boyfriend's apartment. The fire marshal declared the building safe, and the residents were allowed to return to their homes. An exhausted Jordan sat on the sofa in the living room, brushing at the coating of soot. She patiently fielded the last of the detective's questions. Finally, he closed his notebook and left, with the comment that a forensics team would be arriving soon.

Her apartment was a shambles. Furniture was upended, books were jostled from their shelves, and fragments of plastic and glass were scattered everywhere. With Todd holding a protective arm around her shoulder, they slowly walked from room to room, surveying the destruction. Jordan's face was pale, with the thousand-yard stare of the shell-shocked. Every few steps, she shook her head.

"I just can't believe it," she kept repeating.

The bedroom had absorbed most of the damage. Almost nothing in the room was recognizable. The bedframe, chair, and dresser were reduced to splintered pulp. The mattress and linens were scorched heaps of charred fabric. Shards of mirrored glass punctured the walls like shrapnel, and razor-sharp plastic slivers of former telephone or computer littered the rug like deadly tinsel. Interestingly, the damage seemed to have been directed upward and outward, from the area of the night table. The wall directly behind it was virtually unscathed. Worse than the debris, however, was the fact of what had happened. According to the fire chief, the explosion was caused by a bomb.

"He could have been way off base," Langford reassured her. "Sometimes the cops say things like that just for shock value, to see what you're going to say."

Jordan's expression hardened. "Todd, take a close look at this room. This wasn't some little wiring problem, and you know it. Everything's blown to bits."

"It could've been an accident," he said, opening the door to her clothes closet. "It's a stretch to say it's intentional."

Jordan shook her head. "Forever the optimist."

"But who'd want to hurt you or Julie? Neither of you has an enemy in the world." He paused. "Where'd you say the ledger was? I want to see if it's safe."

"Top shelf, under those sweaters." She clenched her fists. "You know, it could've been *anyone*. It doesn't have to be an old boyfriend, like the cop said. There are plenty of sickos out there."

He forced his voice to remain calm. "Jordan."

"Who knows? Much as I hate to admit it, maybe they *were* after Julie. With a body like hers, she attracts her share of perverts. Once this guy was even stalking her.''

''Jordan.''

''Maybe it was one of our freaking neighbors, who didn't like our music. Maybe we were late with our rent,'' she said, her voice rising, ''or maybe someone just wanted to have a little fun! Hey guys, we got nothin' better to do, why don't we blow the shit out of Five-F! Jesus!''

''Jor . . .''

''*What* already? What?''

''The tapes and the ledger,'' he said softly. ''They're gone.''

The speed with which any remaining color drained from her face was dramatic. Her mouth fell open, and the pulse in her neck began to flutter wildly. Her fear-driven heart felt as if it wanted to erupt from her chest. Somehow, she willed her limbs to function, and she shuffled woodenly to the closet. Staring at the ransacked shelves, she understood.

For Josh Meyerson, the three months since he'd begun work in the hospital had been an incredibly enlightening experience. No longer a shy and sheltered young man, he'd made eye-opening discoveries about the world. But perhaps the most surprising discovery had been Todd's revelation about Fletcher's discovering cognopsin, and about Dr. Fine.

Flattered that Langford had chosen him as a confidant, Josh truly wanted to help. He'd already looked at the charts and come up with nothing Todd and Jordan didn't already know. He was on call and the ER was quiet, so he wandered up to Dr. Fletcher's lab. If the door were open, he could have a look around.

To his surprise, it was. But an even greater surprise was to see Mike Molloy sitting at Dr. Fletcher's desk. When he saw Meyerson, Molloy turned off his computer.

"I didn't think you'd be here, Mike. I thought you found a job someplace else."

"Nah," said Molloy. "Still looking. I was just finishing up a few odds and ends. What brings you up here?"

Josh gave him the rough details of what he was working on with Todd.

"Well," said Molloy, rising to leave, "I hope you find what you're looking for. Make yourself at home. I don't mind telling you, after what happened to Fletch and Dr. Fine, this hospital gives me the creeps."

Josh spoke up before Molloy reached the door. "Mike, there's something I want to ask you. You know about this experiment Dr. Fletcher was working on, right?"

"I do now."

"Todd told me you weren't aware of Fletcher's discovery," said Josh. "He didn't share what he found out as he went along?"

Molloy hesitated at the doorway. "Some people can spend their whole lives in the dark, Josh. I was like that with Fletch. I never asked much, and he kept things to himself. Does that answer your question?"

A brooding Meyerson watched Molloy leave. No, he thought, it does not.

Outside the Brooklyn social club, the four men formed a huddle. It was early evening, and there was an unexpected chill in the air.

"Let me see if I got this straight," said Anthony. "This is the same girl you were tryin' to nab?"

"That's right," said Merendino.

"And somebody put a bomb in her apartment?"

"You got it," said Vito.

Anthony rolled up the collar of his windbreaker. "What's the word out on the street? What does Vinnie say?"

"He don't know nothin'," said Vito.

"What, is everybody asleep?" said Anthony. "Who's tryin' to knock her off, another wise guy? What's this girl got anyway, besides this stuff in her spinal fluid?" His question was met with blank stares.

"So far as we know," said Merendino, "she's just a medical student. We don't know why someone would want to rub her out."

"Now that's just great," said Anthony. "I feel like I got my thumb up my ass. Listen to me, Vito. Call Vinnie and tell him to find out what the fuck's goin' on. And how's he doin' findin' another source for the stuff?"

"Still workin' on it, Anthony," said Vito.

"Workin' on it ain't good enough," Anthony continued. "Sal wants answers—now. Tell Vinnie to get in touch with that hospital contact of his. Make sure he meets with the guy, noon tomorrow at the latest. Tell him to remind this guy that we own him. He owes us big time, and we always collect on our debts!"

As evening gave way to night, Todd and Jordan locked themselves in Langford's house. They couldn't think of anyplace else to go. Having suppressed an impulse to drive all the way to the Canadian border, they needed a place to regroup mentally. Once there, they paced nervously from room to room, dutifully followed by Hondo, Langford's German shorthaired pointer. Sensing something was wrong, the dog wouldn't let Langford out of his sight.

Several years before, when he moved into the house alone, Langford had acquired a used .22-caliber Iver Johnson automatic, which he kept in his night table. Now he loaded the magazine and put a round in the chamber. Self-consciously, he stuck the pistol in his waistband, feeling foolish but safe. They had no game plan. Exhausted and on edge, the first order of business was simply getting through the night. Tomorrow, they might contact Sharon at the newspaper, or Tom Court-

ney, or both. With nothing to do but wait, they lay in
Langford's bed, fully clothed. Trying unsuccessfully to
relax, they huddled in each other's arms.

In a parked car down the block, the man sat patiently
behind the steering wheel. The windows were rolled
down, and the occasional cool breeze was refreshing.
He waited in quiet stillness until all the lights in the
house were out before he dared move closer. He was
accustomed to long waits.

Trailing the couple north from SoHo proved no problem because he knew where the doctor lived, and Langford's retreat to his own house had been predictable.
Most first-time targets acted similarly, falling back to
the comfort of familiar surroundings. It was obvious
the young physician had never been hunted before, or
else he wouldn't have chosen such an accessible loca-
tion. The suburban home offered everything a hired
assassin could want: remoteness, ease of access, and
ready routes of escape.

As he sat in the car waiting and watching, the man
assessed his options. While luck played a small role,
proper planning was essential to operations like this.
Although his murder of Dr. Fletcher had an element of
opportunism, he'd been meticulous when he'd gunned
down the pharmacist. In this case, he concluded, a frontal assault would probably be easiest. It would be nothing at all to enter the house once they were asleep and
simply gun them down.

It was a tactic that depended on both of them being
in the same spot simultaneously. The problem was,
there was no guarantee they would both be sleeping at
the same time. One might be in the bathroom, or have
gotten up to watch TV. Also, as straightforward as the
house's layout probably was, in the dark, nothing was
guaranteed. No, it would be best to let them come to
him.

But in order to do that, they had to be suitably compelled. And in the past, he found that nothing was quite so compelling, so swiftly motivating, or so horrifying, as a blazing fire. In the dark, an unexpected inferno sent otherwise sensible people into a mindless panic. In retreating from the flames, they invariably rushed for the nearest exit—where he would be conveniently waiting.

When he finished this job, he would deal with the Mafia goons—especially the blond-haired guy with an attitude. It was amazing that they actually thought they could control him. The whole time he'd been feeding them information, he'd been giving that same information to others, as well. The others had profited where the mobsters had not. Did they actually think that, because he'd once been indebted to them, they could make him jump like a marionette? Tomorrow, he'd spell it out for them.

It was after two when he finally went into action. The first thing he did was to shoot out the overhead street lights with a noiseless Hammerli CO_2 air pistol, rendering the street dark for a hundred yards on each side of the house. For the next half hour, he circled the house, making sure the lights were out, the TV was off, and that no one was stirring. The frame building was old. It was built on a poured concrete slab, with a wooden first floor set twelve inches above it. The two were separated by a little-used crawl space. He would direct his efforts there.

He removed a five-gallon gas can from the trunk of his car. It was filled with highly volatile Cam-2 racing fuel. He entered the crawl space on his stomach, lighting the way with a mini Maglite. In addition to a thick veil of cobwebs, the space was littered with two generations of debris, from decomposing tires to discarded children's toys. The man slithered ahead, pushing the junk aside until he reached the vicinity of the master bedroom. There, he assembled a pile of combustible kindling and saturated the overhead floorboards, careful

to avoid dousing himself with fuel. Then, as he retreated from the crawl space, he poured a thin trail of
gasoline behind him.

Outside, he straightened up and caught his breath.
Despite his efforts, his clothing reeked of Cam-2,
which had a cloying, fruity odor. Bending over, he
crouched and tiptoed to each of the home's side and
rear windows, where he spread fuel on the frames. Taking a toothpaste-like tube from his pocket, he squeezed
out a thin layer of flammable gel known as Fire Ribbon,
joining all the windows to the crawl space. Finally, he
returned to the front corner of the house, where he'd
stashed his firearm.

Even though the area was well into the suburbs,
Langford still had neighbors. The man knew there
wouldn't be much time before awakened residents
alerted the police. Two minutes, perhaps three. But it
should be sufficient. Once the house was torched, the
occupants would dash toward the only exit not ablaze,
where he would be conveniently waiting. He picked up
his automatic rifle, a nine-millimeter MP5-N subgun
with a Mickey Finn suppressor and a Hensoldt Aiming
Point Projector. When all was ready, he sank down to
one knee and lit a match.

To Langford, it seemed as if he'd barely drifted off
when he heard a loud boom. The bed shook wildly,
and the air seemed to vibrate. Jostled awake, he bobbed
upright in the bed. Hondo was at the bedside, whining
furiously, tail tucked between his legs. Langford's first
thought was that he must have left the lights on, because the room was brightly illuminated. Beside him,
Jordan propped herself up on her elbow, her eyes wide
with fright. But he had no time to wonder what was
going on. In the flickering orange light, he could see a
smoking vapor rising through the carpet.

"Jordan, quick, get up! There's a fire!"

She struggled to sit upright, still not comprehending,

looking toward the foot of the bed. "My shoes."

"To hell with the shoes," he shouted, grabbing her arm. "Come on!"

Yanking her out of bed, his eyes darted feverishly to the window. Its wooden frame was ablaze, and angry flames clawed at the glass, whose overheated panes began to crack and shatter. Where the fire was coming from, and how had it appeared so suddenly? The room reeked with an acrid odor. With the windows on fire, the only chance for escape lay straight ahead. Without thinking, Langford grabbed the pistol from the night table and jammed it into his waistband. Pulling Jordan up, he stumbled toward the door, with the old dog close on their heels.

The hallway was already thick with smoke. He looked to his right and left, only to find that the fire breached the side windows. The whole house appeared engulfed in flames. That left only the front door. Behind him, Jordan was choking on the smoke.

"Which way?" she screamed.

"Follow me. Keep your head down and hold tight!"

The billowing smoke was caustic and blinding. It irritated their eyes, which began to water uncontrollably. Blinking furiously, Langford staggered ahead in a half crouch. Before them, the faint outline of the front door beckoned. With Jordan close in tow, he stumbled toward it, careening off walls he couldn't see. Finally there, Langford released Jordan and reached for the front doorknob.

He'd forgotten that the door was locked. He fumbled with the brass bolt until he finally turned it over, then pulled on the door again. It gave slightly, still held fast by an overlooked metal chain. The smoke in the room was becoming impenetrable. This time, when he reached for the latch, he couldn't undo it. After swatting at it uselessly, he grabbed the knob in both hands and pulled as hard as he could.

The latch broke free from its moorings in a shower

of splinters. In his near-panic, Langford had pulled so
forcefully that he was unprepared for the door's sudden
movement. It struck him in the cheek. Stunned, he fell
sideways into Jordan, knocking her onto the floor. As
he turned in her direction, something hammered into
the side of his skull. Stunned, he fell to the floor.

Hondo was instantly beside him, licking his face.
Then the dog tensed, lowering his neck as he turned
toward the door. He let out a low and menacing growl,
then slowly crept toward the doorway, fangs bared.

From where she lay two yards distant, Jordan could
hear nothing but the mounting crackle of the flames.
But she could see something through the smoke. A red
laser dot suddenly appeared, a foot away from Langford's head. The carpet beneath it quickly disintegrated
into a circular hole, sending a blizzard of fibers into
the air. A second hole appeared, then another, stitching
a lazy arc toward Langford. At the last minute, Langford realized what was happening. He quickly rolled
onto his back just as something whizzed by his chin.

Old though he was, Hondo was nevertheless a
trained hunter. When he saw the darkened shape fill the
doorway, he took two quick steps and then leapt at the
attacker. But the aiming dot was on his chest before he
was halfway there. Struck in midflight, he gave a little
yelp and then fell limply by the front door.

Jordan watched, paralyzed. She tried to shout, but
the words wouldn't come. Everything seemed to happen in slow motion. Langford began a backward, crab-
like scuttle, away from the front door and back down
the hall. He had retreated about five feet when a figure
suddenly appeared in the open front doorway. The fresh
air rushed inward, sending the smoke swirling about
him. The man was wearing dark clothing and carried
what was unmistakably an assault weapon. From a
barrel-mounted tube, a narrow beam of red light split
the darkness, weaving through the smoke like a cobra.

The sight of the gun infuriated Jordan. Out of the

man's sight, she sprang to her feet, suddenly energized. Her hands searched wildly for a weapon. She picked up the first thing she could find—an umbrella. Propelled by rage, she leapt forward, holding the umbrella over her head like an axe.

Despite the smoke, the man saw her out of the corner of his eye. He swung the gun barrel in her direction, but he wasn't quick enough. The umbrella's metal tip caught him in the temple, spinning him around. Jordan charged ahead, swinging her makeshift weapon with Ruthian authority, raining down a series of strikes against his head and shoulders. The flurry of blows was distracting. The intruder raised an arm to ward them off. The uninterrupted attack forced him down the hall, toward the now-raging fire.

His heel thudded into Langford's leg. He tumbled, tripping sideways. His gun hand collided with the floor, and the weapon skittered from his grasp. But he was now out of Jordan's range. He reached out for the gun handle, his fingers inching slowly toward it.

His head finally clear, Langford realized what was about to happen. If the man reached the weapon, both he and Jordan would be dead within seconds. Without thinking, he slid out from under the intruder and rolled onto his side. Suddenly, he remembered his own pistol. Beyond him, the man's hand closed around the MP5-N's grip.

Langford's actions were pure reflex. Just as the man was straightening up, Langford drew the .22 from his waistband and pointed it one-handed. He fired just before the red aiming dot reached him, pulling the trigger blindly, aiming at the central mass, rapidly snapping off four shots. The muzzle of the assault weapon started to waver, then steadied and continued pointing unerringly in his direction. Langford fired again, then again. The man staggered backward. The sixth and final round caught him in the throat, and he slowly toppled into the flames rising behind him.

His fuel-spattered jacket ignited with a *whoosh*. As the flames began to consume him, an agonizing wail rose from his lips. A trembling hand stretched out in Langford's direction. For a moment, Langford stared blankly back at the man, paralyzed by the sight of a human torch. Then came Jordan's horrified scream. Finally he jumped to his feet and headed for the victim, choking at the smell of burning flesh. But the flames were too intense. The man's head raised up, his hair ablaze, and for a brief instant, his eyes locked on Langford's. Then they slowly rolled back in their sockets, and he slumped forward, motionless. Langford was appalled.

"Jesus God in heaven," he said.

The flames were coming closer. Jordan tugged insistently on his arm, yelling something incomprehensible. Langford looked down at Hondo, who lay on his side, unmoving. Any further delay could prove fatal.

Outside, they staggered away from the house and the inferno. They alternately coughed and inhaled, gulping in lungfuls of cool night air. In the houses on either side of them, lights were going on. Jordan could just make out Langford's features in the darkness. She touched his soot-stained forehead, dabbing at the rivulet of blood that dampened his cheek.

"Are you all right?"

Langford grasped her wrist with a frightening intensity. "That man," he said.

"The bastard was trying to kill us, Todd. You couldn't save him."

"No, I'm not . . . That guy," he said. "I know him."

Chapter Nineteen

THEY REALIZED IT WAS POINTLESS TO STAY. THE BLAZ-
ing house was beyond salvage, and the police would
soon be there with questions they couldn't answer.
They quickly got into his car and sped away, driving
south.

Langford held the wheel tight in white-knuckled
fists. "This has sure been a country-western summer,"
he said. "My best friend is killed, Dr. Fine gets
whacked, and now they're after us. I can't wait to see
what happens next."

"Does it hurt?" Jordan said. "Your head?"

"No, it's numb. I always wondered what it was like
to get shot."

"You're lucky it wasn't an inch lower."

"We're *both* lucky," he said. "We could be roast
pork by now."

"Who was he?"

Langford's lids narrowed. "Mike Molloy. At least,
that's the name he went by. He worked for Dr. Fletcher
as a lab assistant."

"You're kidding! A grad student?"

"Your guess is as good as mine," he said. "I don't
know much about him, and I bet Fletch didn't either.
Molloy didn't say much. The times I was in the lab,
he was kind of just *there*."

"Why would he want to kill us?" she asked.

"I don't think he did. Not him personally. The guy had the equipment of a trained killer, Jordan. I'm sure he was the one who killed Fletcher and Fine, at somebody else's request."

"Dr. Royce?"

"That's where I'd put *my* money," he said. "After all, this didn't happen until after I told him about the ledger and the tapes. But we've done enough guessing for one day. I think it's time we talked to a professional."

The return of Rita's consciousness was abrupt. One minute Rita was asleep, and the next, she was fully awake. Her mind was intuitive, geared toward problem-solving, honed by more than two years of medical training. So, when she found herself alert but unresponsive, she immediately attributed her condition to drug effect.

She realized there must have been a screwup.

Lying there in the darkness, sorting out symptoms and sensations, she tried to figure out why she couldn't move her muscles. Even worse, she couldn't breathe, although her lungs kept filling with air. But the more she heard a nearby rhythmic *whoosh*, the more she came to realize she was on a respirator, which meant, by extension, that she was intubated. This, along with her strange muscular inactivity, meant one thing: that drugs had paralyzed her body.

The most likely drug was succinyl choline. But there was also curare, and pancuronium. It could have been any of them. Of course, they were also probably giving her some kind of hypnotic to keep her asleep. What must have happened, she reasoned, was that they—whoever "they" were—had inadvertently omitted one of her doses, allowing her consciousness to return. Before that, the last thing she remembered was sitting in the hospital bed, holding Adrianna.

The thought of the baby made her heart start pounding. The hardest part of all was not knowing. But Rita accepted her powerlessness, mentally biding her time, keeping attuned to physical sensations. Slowly, her muscular function returned. At first she could wiggle her toes, then her hands, and finally her lips. She knew she had to wait for just the right moment.

She concentrated on her hearing, sifting out sounds. Not far away, there was the sibilant hissing of other respirators, in addition to assorted mechanical sounds she recognized as belonging to resuscitative equipment. No doubt there were other patients in the same predicament as she was. Occasionally she heard the scuffling of footsteps, returning at what she approximated were half-hour intervals. Finally, with the footsteps receding in the distance, she knew the time had come.

The first order of business was her vision. Her lids were kept shut by something sticky, and when she managed to lift her stony fingers to her eyes, she discovered strips of tape. She worked her nails under the edges and carefully lifted off the strips, wincing when they stuck to her lashes. But finally she was able to open her eyes.

After the hours of enforced darkness, even the room's pale light seemed dazzling. Its initial brightness was painful, and Rita had to squint. But slowly, she managed to get things in focus. Looking up, she saw a ceiling of white acoustical tile, interspersed with fluorescent fixtures. Just above her face, there was a corrugated length of accordionlike plastic tubing, one end of which led to a ventilator. Working deliberately, Rita detached the hose from her tube, until she was finally able to take a deep breath of cool room air.

Taking out the tube shouldn't be too hard, she reasoned; she'd seen it done dozens of times. It, too, had anchoring tape—the flesh-colored variety, stickier than the paper. But there was only one strip at the tube's base, securing it to her cheeks. Soon she managed to work it free. Finally, there was only the tube itself,

inside her windpipe, held in place by an anchoring balloon. The balloon was ordinarily deflated with a syringe, and Rita had none. But whatever Rita lacked in
equipment, she made up in determination. Her greatest
incentive was the thought of her daughter. She picked
at the tube's air reservoir, digging in, jabbing with her
nails until she finally nicked it. The latex bulb slowly
deflated. She could feel the tube loosen, wobble in her
throat. Now would come the uncomfortable part. Taking two deep breaths, she exhaled, then forcibly swallowed, yanking at the tube with both hands.

As it passed through her throat, she gagged repeatedly, bringing tears to her eyes. But the tube was out.
After a moment's rest, Rita inhaled cautiously, then
forced herself onto her elbows. Now accustomed to the
ambient light, she looked around. What she saw both
appalled and terrified her.

She was in a large, rectangular room, filled with an
otherworldly, bluish glow. Patients were everywhere,
flat and unmoving, spaced at regular intervals like chess
pieces. They were all unconscious, supine on makeshift
supports. Each patient was intubated, and all had IVs.

She knew this was not the time to figure out what
was going on. Gripped by fear and revulsion, the par-
amount thing on Rita's mind was getting out of there.
Only when she'd returned to the warmth and safety of
her family would she try to piece it all together. Her
legs were bound by black cloth restraints. She quickly
wrenched at the Velcro, tearing the fasteners apart with
a loud rip. There was IV tubing attached to her left
wrist. Rita unhesitatingly pulled it out, sending droplets
of blood and IV fluid across the floor.

Oblivious to the blood that streamed from her hand,
Rita swung her legs over the edge of the bed. She felt
a sharp jab between her legs, then a restraining tug.
Looking down, she noticed a urinary catheter, pulled
taut against her urethra. Like the endotracheal tube, it

would be held in place by an inflated balloon. But this time, her nails would be insufficient to deflate it. Gritting her teeth, Rita took a deep breath and pulled for all she was worth.

As the walnut-size balloon ripped her outer urethra open, an excruciating pain tore through her vagina. Rita winced, clenching her teeth to suppress a scream. Knifelike spasms crested in a wave that only slowly subsided. When it finally did, she slid upright onto the tiled floor. Her knees nearly buckled from weakness and inactivity. As she slowly straightened up, she felt something sticking to her back.

Craning her neck, Rita noticed an ultra-thin tube taped to her lumbar area. She had no idea what it was, but this was no time to be cautious. Reaching around, she tore off the tape, relieved when the tube came with it. Freed of all restraints, she stumbled forward, frantically searching for a way out.

Across the room, she vaguely made out what she thought was a doorknob. Bent at the waist, she staggered toward it, hobbled by pain and weakness. Spurred on by thoughts of Adrianna, Rita lurched unsteadily through the peculiar bluish glow. Her drunken gait made a zigzag path across the tile, and she trailed droplets of blood from her groin and wrist.

The door spelled freedom, its knob meant escape. Indistinct though it was, the door frame's rectangular outline blazed in her mind like a beacon. Beyond the door, Jeff and the baby were calling to her. She stretched her trembling arm out, straining unsteadily for the knob. She could visualize their faces, picture their smiles. Adrianna . . .

The door burst open with a thunderous crash. Rita stopped short, overcome by fear and panic. A tall, white-suited woman stood glowering, filling the room with her malevolent presence.

"What is this, a replay?" she bellowed. "What're you doing out of bed, precious?"

Rita opened her mouth in feeble pantomime, unable to respond. A birdlike fluttering of terror warbled in her throat, rising and falling along with her hope.

"You weren't by any chance trying to leave us?" The woman took a menacing step forward, jabbing a finger emphatically in Rita's chest. Rita's legs buckled, and she sank helplessly to her hands and knees. "You should be ashamed of yourself," the woman continued. "A doctor in training and all. Didn't they teach you anything about following doctor's orders?"

Gazing up in fear and futility, Rita's lips formed a plea. "Please, I beg you—"

"Oh, for God's sake," the woman said disgustedly. She reached toward her belt and unclipped a small black device. "Save your prayers for church." With that, she touched the plastic to Rita's forehead and pressed a button.

A powerful burst of electricity surged through Rita's body, rendering her limp. Rita collapsed heavily onto her side, stunned and unable to move. The woman's strong hands seized her wrists, and Rita found herself being dragged across the cold floor.

"That's a good girl," the woman said. "Now let's get you back to bed before the doctor makes his rounds."

Once in the city, Todd and Jordan checked into a hotel, where the desk clerk looked them over skeptically. They stank of smoke and petroleum, and sooty smudges marred their already disheveled appearance. With her apartment blown up and his house incinerated, their worldly belongings consisted of the clothes on their backs. Their jeans and jerseys were not much to look at. They double-locked the door to their room. Langford immediately took a shower, and then Jordan carefully disinfected his bullet-creased scalp with antibacterial soap. The superficial wound would require little additional care. When he finished, the bedside clock read four A.M. He sat on the bed to make his call.

He hated waking Courtney, but he didn't feel he had much choice. Tom Courtney was the only person he trusted. Moreover, he was in a position of authority, and had city, state, and federal contacts. After Langford outlined the situation for the better part of a half hour, the agent told him to sit tight. The information he'd need would take all morning to gather. He promised Langford he'd ring back as soon as he had something to report.

Langford sat on the windowsill and looked out the hotel window at the sparse early-morning traffic. It was dawn when Jordan finally emerged from the bathroom. She'd been in the shower for an hour, luxuriating in the spray, hoping without success that its warm needles would soothe her frazzled nerves. When she finally got out, she crossed the room to him, trailing curling wisps of steam, head turbaned and body wrapped in an over-size terry towel. Although she'd successfully removed the dirt and grime, she couldn't rinse off the layers of fear and despair. Langford put his arms around her and drew her close. She leaned against him, looking down into the street, watching the distant cars silently pass by.

At length, they retreated to the bed and crawled under the covers. Despite their fatigue, they were both too unnerved to think of either sleep or sex. Neither of them felt like eating. Jordan worked the remote to turn on the TV, clicking from channel to channel, searching for local news. But when she finally found it, there was no mention of a several-hours-old fire north of the city. So they simply lay there, emotionally and physically numb, as she idly switched from station to station.

The minutes and hours seemed interminably slow in passing. At nine-thirty, Langford couldn't stand it any longer. He got up, put on his bedraggled garments, and went out to buy new clothes. Forty-five minutes later, he returned with two pairs of Levi's, underwear, assorted shirts and tops, toiletries, and a pair of shoes for Jordan. It wasn't much, but at least it would last them a day or two. He also bought a box of CCI Stinger .22s at a sporting goods store. After reloading the Iver Johnson, he dumped their soiled clothes in a trash bag. Then he unceremoniously carted it down the hall and dumped the bag into the incinerator.

Although they weren't hungry, they called room service and ordered coffee and a newspaper. Killing time, they read through every section of the *Times*. Finally, shortly after eleven, Courtney called and told them to meet him at a small restaurant on East Forty-eighth.

Vinnie Buonafortuna was in a foul mood, even more irritable than when he'd flunked out of med school in Milan. He struggled to contain his rage. He had a feeling Molloy wasn't going to show up for their noon rendezvous. Vinnie was growing increasingly suspicious of Molloy. Molloy was young, devious, and ruthlessly goal-oriented, a goal which seemed to center around his own accumulation of wealth. Molloy owed them, sure; but they had already paid him a hefty fifty thousand dollars, with another fifty thousand promised for delivery of more of the product. And Buonafortuna *needed* that product. Unless Sal's dementia could be kept in check, they were all going to do some very hard time.

For nearly two years, Molloy had been providing them with information about various research projects in the hospital. Vinnie hadn't agreed with the don about this foray into the medical field, but an opportunity was an opportunity. As it turned out, Molloy had access to something the mob desperately wanted.

Molloy was evasive. Was it possible that Molloy was hiring his services out to others? Word had leaked out that, for a price, Molloy could provide an extraordinary new drug—a drug reputed to increase powers of con-

centration, enhance recall, and heighten mental faculties, which was precisely what the aging Salvatore
Aiello needed. The blond-haired Buonafortuna felt a
growing desperation.

With a scowl creasing his forehead, Vinnie looked
around the gourmet coffee shop with practiced suspi-
cion. He took an indifferent sip of his lukewarm double
espresso. An olive-skinned man approached, wearing a
nondescript windbreaker and black watch cap. He
slipped into the vacant seat across from Buonafortuna.

"Bad news, Vinnie," he whispered excitedly. "Molloy's dead."

Buonafortuna stiffened.

"Somebody shot him at a house in the Bronx."

"What was he doin' up there?"

"The cops don't know, or won't say. It hasn't hit
the papers yet."

"Whose house?" asked Vinnie.

"Some young doc. They can't find him, a guy
named Todd Langford."

"Langford," Buonafortuna said slowly. "The ER
resident?"

"I don't know, Vinnie," Vito said. "What are we
gonna do now?"

"Let me think." Buonafortuna's gaze was distant.
He recognized the name. He'd always been thorough,
memorizing the various details of his jobs—a study
habit he'd developed as a med student. Before he did
the spinal tap on the comatose neuro patient, he famil-
iarized himself with names of physicians he might run
into, and Langford's name had been on the list.

He ran his fingers through his blond hair and stared
out the coffee shop window, eyes narrowed in concentration. According to Joey, Sal's suddenly robust mental powers were starting to falter. Moreover, Merendino
said they had maybe twenty-four hours to give the don
another dose. Now, with Langford . . . here was a distinct new possibility. Maybe Langford also knew about

the compound. While it might have been pure chance that Langford and Molloy worked in the same hospital, it was *no* coincidence that Molloy had, for whatever reason, been in Langford's home. Now Molloy was dead, and Langford was gone. Could Langford lead him to another source while there was still time?

"This is what I want you to do, Vito," said Vinnie. "We have other contacts up at Metropolitan, right? Switchboard people, security?"

"Lots."

"Tell everyone to keep their eyes and ears open. If anyone hears anything from or about Langford, I want to know about it, all right? If anyone goes to meet him, get in your car and trail him, okay?"

"You got it," said Vito.

"We're sure Langford ain't dead, too?" Vinnie asked.

"Nope. But the cops don't know where he is."

"Then we gotta find him, Vito," said Vinnie. "We gotta find him before they do."

The sandwich shop was crowded with midtown and UN types. The three of them squeezed into a small table in the rear and ordered lunch. Courtney produced a driver's license photo of Molloy and slid it across the table to Langford.

"This the guy?" asked Courtney.

"That's him," said Langford.

"His name seems to be legit. He came to the city two years ago, right after you started your residency."

"Is there any connection?" asked Jordan.

"I doubt it. He was freelance. He was a small-time operator before he started working at the hospital."

"Why would he want a job there?" she said.

"It's a great front," Courtney replied. "Very respectable, regular hours. His bachelor's degree is phony, but he *was* a bio major before he dropped out of the University of Indiana. He was also a gymnast.

Under his lab coat, he had the physique for work like this.''

''He took Killer 101 at Indiana?'' said Todd.

''No, that was courtesy of Uncle Sam. After school, he was an Army Ranger before he moved on to SO-COM, the Army's Special Operations Command. They teach black ops, high-tech weapons, that sort of thing. One training mission, two guys died. They thought Molloy was involved but couldn't prove it. Anyway, he got a less-than-honorable discharge and became a drifter. Then he put all those tax dollars to work and went into business on his own.''

''You think he could have done this, then?'' said Todd. ''And Dr. Fletcher and Fine?''

''No question,'' said Courtney. ''The guy had all the tools and training to be a stone-cold killer. I think you wound up doing the cops a big favor.''

''But how did he come to work for Dr. Royce?'' asked Jordan.

''Word on the street is that Molloy had mob connections. It seems that when he came to New York, he did a few jobs for them, lightweight muscle. In return, they were the ones to land him the hospital job, through their union connections. So he owed them. But as for working with Dr. Royce—if he did—he probably arranged that on his own. The Mafia doesn't like competition.''

''What do you mean, '*if* he did'?'' Todd asked.

''It means I think you're sincere, but it doesn't mean I have to buy it,'' said Courtney. ''Whatever the truth is, as your friend, I'm happy to help out, whether I believe it or not. This guy Molloy, sure. He was a low-life. But Royce? He sounds too good to be true. So far, I haven't heard anything which makes me think Molloy was working for Royce.''

''But it *had* to be Dr. Royce, don't you see? He was the only person I told. How could it be that I confide in him, tell him everything—and the next thing you know, Jordan's place blows up, and Molloy sets my house on fire? You call that coincidence?''

Courtney made a palms-up gesture. ''That's what the cops would say. You have absolutely no evidence linking Royce to what happened. And hearsay doesn't get you far in court. Even if you had that conversation of yours on tape, it's circumstantial. No cop in his right mind would act on that.''

''But he tried to kill us!'' Jordan said.

''No, Molloy did. And thanks to you, he's dead.''

Langford grew exasperated. ''This is insane. What are we supposed to do, just sit around twiddling our thumbs?''

''Look, Todd. I'm going to say this as your friend. It should come as no surprise that the cops want to talk to you guys. It's not every day someone's found shot and burned to death in your home. And at least one of your neighbors thinks he saw you leaving the scene. It's just a matter of time before they find you. Why don't you go to the police and tell them what happened?''

''And throw ourselves on the mercy of the court?'' Todd shook his head. ''You've just finished telling me the cops aren't going to believe a word I say, but you want me to try out my story on them anyway? Why the hell would I do that?''

''You know why,'' said Courtney. ''It looks a lot better if you go to them than if they have to come to you. What other choice do you have?''

''Well, Tom, this is the way I see it. Royce has connections. Once we turned ourselves in, we'd be signing our own death warrants. Strange things have been known to happen in police stations. We just don't want to become statistics.''

''That's a little far-fetched, don't you think?'' said Courtney.

''So is having your apartment bombed and your house burned down.''

*   *   *

It had been only a little more than twenty-four hours since he'd confided in Royce, and Langford felt exhausted, strung out on mayhem-induced adrenaline. His mind was in such turmoil that he was unable to relax. By now, the people who wanted them dead knew they weren't. What would they do next? If he and Jordan were considered loose ends a day before, they were even more of an inconvenience now.

"You think we should just head out to the airport?" he suggested.

"What are we going to do for money?" Jordan asked.

"Hmmm. You have a point there." He'd forgotten that his wallet, as well as her purse, had been on top of the bedroom dresser the night before, and were now consumed by flames. All of their credit cards were gone. "Did you have any spare cash in your apartment? An ATM card, or something?"

"No. It was all in my purse. What about you?"

"I'm pretty sure I have a duplicate Visa card in my locker at the hospital," he said. "I have a hundred dollars in traveler's checks there, too."

"Is it safe to go back to the hospital?"

"Absolutely not," he said. "I'll call Josh."

He phoned the hospital from a public booth and had Meyerson paged while Jordan watched nervously from their nearby table. It took a minute for the resident to answer his page. But when he did, Langford was warmed by his friend's enthusiasm.

"Hey, you little rodent," said Todd. "I want you to do a favor for me."

"Jesus, Todd, is that you?"

"Stop shouting, for God's sake," said Langford. "I'm in enough trouble as it is without having the whole world know I'm on the phone with you."

"Where the hell are you? Man, everyone and his neighbor's looking for you!"

"Like who?" asked Langford.

"The cops, for starters. I don't know if you're ready for this, but they say your house got torched. And P.S., there was some dead guy inside."

"I know all about it."

"You do?" said Josh. "Are you and Jordan in some kind of trouble? Christ, it's just like Bonnie and Clyde! What's going on?"

"I'm in a shitload of trouble, but I can't talk about it right now. Who else was looking?"

"Some of the nurses," said Josh. "A few people I never saw before, wise-guy types. Dr. Royce and Dr. Hobson."

Royce and Hobson. "Look, Josh. You're going to have to trust me on this."

"Sure, run it by me."

"I can't go into details," said Todd, "and I'm a little pressed for time. All I can say is we haven't done anything illegal, and you won't get in any trouble. But I need your help. Can you keep it to yourself?"

"Hey, Todd, this is Josh you're talking to. What do you need?"

Langford relayed the combination to his locker and told Meyerson what he needed. It was lunchtime, when the ER was generally slow. Meyerson shouldn't have much trouble taking off for a while. After once again making him promise to keep his mouth shut, he told Josh where he wanted to meet.

At twelve-thirty, he and Jordan left the restaurant for the short walk to the corner of Second Avenue and Forty-fifth Street. The sidewalks were still reasonably crowded. Although they had little trouble losing themselves in the lunch-hour throng, they looked about furtively as they walked, eyeing each stranger they passed and nervously glancing over their shoulders. At the corner, they hid in the shadows of an overhanging awning.

Meyerson arrived precisely on time, at twelve forty-five. The yellow cab rolled to a stop on the southwest side of Second Avenue, across the street from their refuge. Dressed in his whites, Meyerson got out and looked around as the cab sped away. Despite the clandestine nature of his mission, his face radiated its usual smiling enthusiasm.

"Josh!" Langford called. He stepped out into the sunlight and waved his arms. "Over here!"

Meyerson finally saw them and raised his arm and the thin manila envelope he was carrying in reply. When the southbound traffic passed, he stepped out into the street and sauntered toward them. If he was worried, he didn't show it. His gait was relaxed, and his lips had an easy, outgoing grin. He seemed eager to see them.

"Hey, you two outlaws," he called. "Where do I collect the reward?"

He was only fifteen feet away when they heard the car. It was the high-pitched, roaring sound of a floored accelerator. What happened next took less than two seconds and seemed to occur in slow motion. Their heads swiveled sideways in the direction of the onrushing vehicle. As they stared at it, unable to process all the sensory input in such a frighteningly short time, the car jumped the curb and headed straight for them.

There was no chance to shout a warning, or even scream. Jordan's arm automatically started to rise in a reflex response, and Langford's mouth rounded into a perfect oval of astonishment. Only Meyerson reacted unexpectedly, in a behavior born from years of play on a Brooklyn soccer field. He leapt forward, stretching his arms out before him. His upraised palms struck his friends in the chest with a perfect stiff-arm, knocking them backward.

As Jordan was shoved out of the way, she felt the vehicle's front fender graze her thigh as it rushed past. Not two feet away from her, the car's hood buckled as it collided with Meyerson's hips. There was a nauseating thud, and he was catapulted through the air in a

sickening white blur of cartwheeling limbs. As the vehicle sped by, a loud *whoosh* of passing air seemed to
suck the breath from their lungs. They watched Meyerson's grotesquely shattered torso smash into a light
pole fifty feet away, then collapse heavily to the concrete. The car, now well beyond them, skidded off the
sidewalk and careened back onto the avenue. In a blur
of burning rubber, it accelerated out of sight.

For several seconds, Langford felt as if he were cat-
atonic. Having regained his balance, he stood there in
near-paralysis, unable to believe his eyes, looking first
at the disappearing vehicle, and then at Meyerson's pathetically ruptured body. But then Jordan's delayed and
horrified cry finally galvanized him into action. He
sprinted toward his friend, his heart pounding in fear
and urgency.

Meyerson's lifeless body resembled a discarded marionette. His arms and legs stuck out at peculiarly frightening angles to his trunk. His pulverized spinal column
had absorbed the brunt of the impact with the metal
stanchion, and as his shattered vertebrae collapsed, his
back was bent nearly in two. Langford drew to a halt
and knelt helplessly beside his friend.

There was absolutely nothing he could do. Pools of
blood coalesced into a widening crimson lake. There
was a deep, purplish concavity in Meyerson's skull
from a facial fracture. Beneath half-closed lids, his
sightless eyes peered up at the sky. Langford automatically felt for the absent cervical pulse, and then he
closed Meyerson's eyes.

"Shouldn't have listened to me, man." He shook his
head, fighting back the tears. "Jesus, Josh. I'm so very
sorry."

A crowd was beginning to form. Drawn by morbid
curiosity, they leaned forward, staring at the crumpled,
lifeless body. As Langford stood up, he eased the envelope from Meyerson's twisted fingers. Then he
turned to Jordan, grabbed her icy hand, and they fled.

*   *   *

Eyes nearly bugging out of his head, Vinnie Buonafortuna screamed into the phone. "Whaddaya mean,
the accelerator got stuck? I never hearda such bullshit!
I wanted you to follow people, not run them over!"

"I'm sorry, Vinnie. It won't happen again."

"Of course not, you dumb fuck, the guy's dead!
What happened to Langford and the girl?"

"I don't know," said Vito. "I didn't stick around to
find out."

"Okay, okay," said Vinnie. "Put the word out on
the street. I want everybody lookin' for those two,
y'hear me? Everyone!"

Chapter Twenty

THEY RAN FOR THEIR LIVES, SPRINTING DOWN THE street, putting space between themselves and the death scene. They'd gone several blocks when the wail of sirens grew louder behind them. Breathless, they slowed their pace, inhaling deeply. They continued heading east, crossing First Avenue and the FDR Drive. Finally, on the promenade by the East River, they dared sit on a park bench to rest, but they couldn't stop looking over their shoulders.

"I don't understand," Jordan said morosely. "How did they find us?"

"Someone must have been listening in on my conversation with Josh. Or else they followed him. Same result. What bastards!"

"But how could they know you'd call?"

"The hospital's a small world, Jordan," he said. "Everyone knew Josh and I were friendly: More than friendly, shit. I really loved him. I guess they figured that sooner or later, I'd get in touch with him. And they were right." He took a deep breath. "We've got to leave, somehow. Get out of the city."

"Just how are we going to do that? If they knew about Josh, they're sure to be watching the hotel and the car."

"So we'll take a cab to the airport," Todd said. "Get on the first plane heading south."

"And what if they're watching the airports?"

"I don't know, Jordan. I just don't know." He ran trembling fingers through his hair. "I'm having a hard time figuring all of this out."

They huddled on the bench like frightened children, staring suspiciously at the passersby. Jordan reached out and stroked the back of his hand in reassurance. She nervously looked up and down the promenade, then back toward the East River Drive walkway. "We need answers, Todd. And the only person who has them for sure is Dr. Royce."

"Come on, Jordan. I already tried talking to him, and you see what it got us."

"I wasn't thinking of that," she said. "You know what they say, about the best defense being a good offense? We can't just sit around here doing nothing. There might be another place we can find out what we want. And I think we owe it to Rita."

"Where?"

"The clinic," she said. "I think it's time we made a visit to Eastgate."

"Agent Courtney."

"Tom, it's Todd Langford. Can you talk?"

"No problem on this end," said Courtney. "Where are you? Are you still with Jordan?"

"Yeah, we're in midtown. Things are getting a little chaotic."

"Is that what you call it?" said the agent. "I heard about Meyerson. People around you seem to have a bad habit of winding up dead."

"You *know* we had nothing to do with Josh's death."

"My opinion doesn't count. And now the cops want to talk with you more than ever." He lowered his voice. "I don't suppose you'd reconsider turning yourselves in?"

"Not a chance!" said Todd. "Sorry, but we just

don't trust the police. I trusted Dr. Royce, and you see where that got me.''

"This may come as a surprise to you," said Courtney, "but your pal Royce has been in a well-attended medical conference today. Supposed to go on all night. If he's such a bad guy, he sure knows how to keep his nose clean.''

"That's his style, don't you see? Low profile when it suits him, high profile other times. Tom, I need a favor.''

Moments later, Courtney rang off, feeling uneasy. What Langford wanted was simple enough, but it would take a couple of hours. And providing him with it wasn't illegal. Anyway, he owed the doctor for saving his son's life.

But right now, he had more important things to concentrate on. For days, word had been coming from his mob informants that something big relating to Salvatore Aiello was going down. Specifically what, no one seemed to know. Yet it was the kind of talk that made Courtney alarmed. On top of that, one of his contacts thought he'd seen Vinnie Buonafortuna, one of the don's henchmen, in midtown Manhattan. He'd even taken a picture.

Courtney studied the long-distance photo. It was indistinct, but it was unquestionably Buonafortuna. The straight blond hair and coarse stubble of a beard made him appear all the more brutal. The man was ruthless, every bit as much of a killer as Molloy had been. From a desk drawer, Courtney removed a Wilson Combat Compact Tactical Elite .45 auto and checked the magazine. It was loaded with high velocity Cor-Bon hollowpoints. He reinserted the clip in the mag well and holstered the piece in Milt Sparks leather. Putting the photo in his pocket, he got up to begin the search.

Jordan and Langford spent the day losing themselves in crowds. They weren't comfortable staying in one place more than fifteen minutes at a time. Leaving the promenade by the river, they took a cab to the Guggenheim Museum. After wandering around, they left, crossed Fifth Avenue to the park, skirted the reservoir, and headed diagonally south to Columbus Circle. From there, they walked to the New York Public Library and lost themselves among the shelves, killing time. Finally, it was four-fifteen.

Courtney told them they could pick up what they wanted at one of the Building Department's branches in a municipal office near City Hall. The blueprint copies would be ready at a quarter to five. They flagged down a cab and fought the early rush-hour traffic going downtown, arriving a few minutes before five. They prayed they weren't late. But Courtney was as good as his word. Ten minutes later, they paid the fee and left the building with plans to Dr. Royce's clinic.

Joey wore many hats: laborer, clerk, and soldier. Most recently, he was bodyguard to Salvatore Aiello. But he loved the streets in which he'd grown up, and today he was a cab driver. He was also an expert lookout, with trained eyes and ears. He'd been given photos of the man and the girl. Although it would take an incredible stroke of luck, they were now his highest priority.

He took a fare across Central Park South to Lincoln Center. He cruised up and down Broadway, then slowly wound around Columbus Circle. His practiced gaze carefully scanned the crowd. Suddenly, he did a double-take. Twenty yards away, a casually dressed couple was hurriedly walking across the street, heading for Eighth Avenue. Joey cautiously checked the photo, then glanced back at the couple. He switched on his off-duty light and slowly followed, keeping a discreet distance. Although they were taking pains to remain inconspicuous, they occasionally turned their heads. It was them, all right. Smiling to himself, Joey pulled out his mobile phone.

Fifteen minutes later, he spotted the two men he'd called on the corner of Forty-sixth Street. He pulled over to let them in. Vinnie Buonafortuna entered first, followed by Vito.

"Where are they now?" Vinnie asked.

"One block from here," said Joey. "Walking down Sixth."

"Don't follow too closely. Get near enough for Vito to get out and tail them. I'll stay in the cab with you. Is there anything else I should know about them?"

"They're frightened, Vinnie," Joey said. "That makes them a little more observant than usual."

"Then we'll keep off their ass. Good work, Joey. Let's find out what this Langford's up to. I want him to lead us to the drug."

Chapter Twenty-one

COURTNEY'S VOICE CRACKLED IN THE HEADPHONES. "Johnny, what's your twenty?"

"Apartment building on Ninety-second and Lex," he said into the mouthpiece. "Heading up to the roof for a look-see. They still in the restaurant?"

"Roger that," said Courtney.

"And our friends?"

"In a cab that keeps circling the block," Courtney said. "The point man's on the corner of Ninety-first, across the street from them. Reading a paper."

"Copy."

Johnny Armstrong was a retired FBI SWAT team leader who now freelanced for various government agencies. Although his primary job was security, he also did tactical work. A longtime friend of Courtney's, he'd been eager for an assignment.

Their targets were several Mafia enforcers wanted for questioning by various agencies, most notably the Department of Justice. One in particular, Vincent Buonafortuna, was very familiar to Armstrong from his days in the Bureau.

Reaching the roof, he went to the southwest parapet and peered over. He had an unobstructed view of the restaurant a block away. He put the compact Zeiss binoculars to his eyes and glassed the area. The point man, a scruffy-looking character in a windbreaker, was clearly visible on the sidewalk, pretending to read *USA Today*. Armstrong grunted to himself and bent over to open the black transit chest.

Inside the sleek gun case was an Accuracy International AWP sniper rifle. It was .308 caliber, and the barrel's one-in-ten twist was the perfect platform for Federal Match 168-grain high-energy hollowpoint boattails. He carefully removed the weapon, opened the bipod, and set the unit up. After inserting the loaded box magazine, he flipped up the protective scope covers and put his cheek to the comb, near the eyepiece. The experimental Schmidt and Bender 3-12 × 50-mm had built-in night-vision capability. Although it made the unit top-heavy, it offered a superb field of view, and within seconds, the scope's reticle was centered on the point man's forehead.

"In position," he said. All he had to do was wait.

"Copy," Courtney replied.

Courtney was waiting inside the Ninety-first Street entrance to the YM/YWHA. He checked his watch: six-ten P.M. He was still trying to figure out what was going on. It was soon clear that Buonafortuna was not alone. Two other men accompanied him, one in the cab, the other on foot. And while Courtney was convinced his team could take them anytime, it would probably be messy. The three mobsters were assumed to be armed, and a Manhattan shootout was in no one's interest. Everything considered, it would be best to tail them for a while.

But the greater surprise came when they began surveillance. It was soon apparent that Buonafortuna was also on someone's trail. And whereas the object of the henchman's interest would ordinarily be of no concern, Courtney was shocked into near-speechlessness when it became clear that Buonafortuna's quarry was none other than Todd Langford. Worried and confused, Courtney had his team sit tight. Until he learned more about what was going on, all he could do was wait things out.

                              *   *   *

In the booth at the rear of the restaurant, Jordan and
Langford pored over the building's blueprint. Eastgate
was obviously a work in progress. It occupied five
floors of what had previously been a run-down Ninety-
fourth Street tenement. Before they went to the restaurant, they had a cab circle the clinic block. The
building's exterior seemed to have undergone little
more than a facelift. The side fronting the street was
covered with stuccolike brick face. An elaborate steel-
and-enamel sign hung over a modern revolving door.
The rear of the building, however, showed the ravages
of seven decades of wear. The brick and concrete were
unretouched, discolored by an ample coat of soot and
dust.

"Do you know anyone who's been inside the clinic
and seen the patients?" Jordan asked.

"Not a soul. Even after that article in the *Times*,
there hasn't been a tour yet."

"That's weird," she said. "You don't suppose we
could just go through the front door, huh?"

"Not if we want to stay alive."

"You think there's a guard?"

"It wouldn't surprise me," he said. He could sense
her uneasiness. "They probably don't have a big staff,
but there are sure to be some sort of medical personnel.
I don't want to run into someone like the driver of the
car that nailed Josh."

"I really want to find out what happened to Rita, but
what else are we looking for?" she asked.

"Answers. Answers we can't find out on our own,
and answers Royce wouldn't give me. You called it his
hidden agenda." He gave her a long look. "You having
second thoughts about this little venture?"

She bit her lip. "I won't bullshit you, I'm scared. A
big part of me wants to be anyplace but here."

"You want to forget about this?"

"We can't," said Jordan. "I wish there was an alternative, but we don't have a choice. We can't keep running forever. Until we find out how everything's related, we're just sitting ducks."

"Okay. Let's go over these plans once more."

They'd been halfheartedly reviewing the architectural drawings for an hour, but now they turned to them in earnest. The building's centerpiece was a newly installed elevator. The elevator's housing, motor, and mechanical controls were in a metal enclosure on the flat, tar roof. According to the plans, patients were to be cared for on the third and fourth floors. The unoccupied fifth floor was reserved for future expansion. Administrative offices were on two, and the ground floor was a waiting and reception area.

Much as they'd studied the plans, they were at a loss as to exactly how to proceed. It became apparent that the only way to answer their questions would be to get a firsthand look at the building's interior.

"Breaking and entering wasn't exactly what my parents had in mind when they sent me to med school," said Jordan.

"I hear you. But like you said, we don't have another option. What looks like the best way in to you?"

"Wherever we can get in without being spotted. Looks like a couple of possibilities. There's the fire escape. And there are the exterior stairs in the back," she noted, "that lead to something belowground. A basement, I guess. I wonder if anything's open."

"We'll just have to find out. I bet that at least one entrance is unlocked. My biggest worry is that they might be alarmed, but I don't think there's anything we can do about that. But what about that elevator structure? It's got to have an exterior door. You have any preference?"

"Looks to me like a coin toss," she said. "But see these lights? We couldn't tell during the daytime, but they're arranged to light up the whole backyard.

They're probably on a timer. I'm not sure I want to stroll through the floodlights.''

He studied the diagram. "What about the roof? I can't see any lights up there."

She nodded. "I guess that decides it."

They waited until it was dark. Staying in their booth, they toyed with their coffee, playing with uneaten cheesecake. Finally, by eight, it was totally dark. Langford paid the bill and led the way outside.

In the street, they looked furtively from one side to the other. Traffic was sparse, and there were few passersby. Nothing seemed out of the ordinary. Still, they both kept a wary eye, sliding under awnings and around doorways, trying to remain inconspicuous. It was nerve-wracking. Their destination was a tavern near the corner of Ninety-fourth and First.

It took ten minutes to painstakingly traverse the streets and avenues. They wore the pinched expressions of undiscovered fugitives, fully expecting their names shouted out at any moment. They reached the bar and paused. Finally, with one last look around, they entered.

A minute later, Vito emerged from the shadows of an unlit doorway half a block away. He had little trouble remaining unseen. Years of tracking and clandestine pursuit in the streets of Newark, Philadelphia, and New York had earned him the nickname "The Shadow." Keeping his eyes on the tavern's entrance, he raised his arm. Seconds later, the cab with Joey and Vinnie pulled up alongside.

"What are they up to?" asked Vinnie.

"I'm not sure," said Vito.

"Keep an eye on them. If we don't find out what they're doing soon, we'll pull them over for a little chat."

"Don't worry, Vinnie. We'll find out."

*   *   *

"You on them, Johnny?" Courtney asked.

"Roger," Armstrong replied. He wore magnified Litton night-vision goggles, with an image intensifier. When the targets began moving, he quickly broke down his equipment and put it in the travel case. Within thirty seconds, he was on the move. He was now around the corner of Ninety-fourth, peering down the block. "I have them at two hundred meters and not moving."

"Copy. We're go on your signal." Courtney had a dilemma. His team could take the mobsters anytime they wanted. Their assets were in place, ready to move in on their command. Still, as long as they held the upper hand, he felt safer waiting. There was much to be gained, and seemingly little to be lost.

It was a quiet evening in the bar. The grimy tavern seemed to cater to a low-class clientele. The rush-hour crowd, if there had been one, was gone. A handful of patrons were halfheartedly watching a football game on TV. Seeing the young couple enter, a burly bartender disinterestedly leaned their way.

"Help you folks?"

Jordan sat on a stool while Langford bellied up to the bar, eyeing the beer taps. "A couple of Lites." He threw a five on the counter.

The bartender drew their beers, made change, and went back to his perch. Having sized them up, he just as quickly tuned them out. After a few minutes, Jordan nonchalantly got up and walked toward the ladies' room, mindless of the eyes that pursued her. Langford followed a moment later.

Jordan locked the door. She turned on the cold water, wanting the familiar gurgling noise to disguise the sound of her movements. The room's small, chest-level window was between the sink and the commode. It had smudged, opaque glass and a simple locking latch. It didn't appear to have been opened in years.

She undid the latch and pushed it up. The window barely budged. In the clutches of layered grime and dried paint, it wanted to remain frozen. But Jordan was determined. Pushing with all her might, she fractured the gluelike moorings. The window came free with a sharp crack and slowly rattled upward with a creaking groan. Finally she got it open about a foot, on a level with her head. Glancing back at the locked bathroom door, she set to work.

She overturned the wastebasket to use as a step stool. Placing it under the window, she stepped up and worked her head and shoulders into the opening. She shimmied through it, wriggling up and out until her upper torso squeezed past. Then, twisting her hips and thighs, she squirmed forward. Perched on the windowsill, she caught her breath and gazed into the alleyway.

It was only four feet wide, dark and deserted. On the other side was the Eastgate Clinic. Jordan swung her legs over, dangling them free. Releasing her grip, she slipped to the concrete below.

Eight feet away was the window to the men's room. She crept to it and rapped on the windowpane. Seconds later, the window rattled open, and Langford's face appeared in the opening.

"Coast clear?" he asked.

"So far. The fire escape's right here," she said.

"On my way."

Pressing himself up like a gymnast, he squirmed through the window. Dropping down beside her, he eyed the fire escape. It appeared to be a fire department-approved, standard metal exterior stairway. Langford walked under it and pulled the chain, freeing the lowermost rungs, which slid to the street level with a rickety clang. He took hold of the ladder.

"Okay, here goes," he said. "Ready?"

"Right behind you."

He led the way. They slowly climbed up, one story

at a time. But careful though they were, it was hard to remain silent. Each rusted, wobbly rung gave a telltale creak and moan. On the horizontal landings, they were careful to stoop as they passed the windows. Jordan's heart was racing. It seemed as if they were making a frightful racket, and she was afraid someone inside the building would hear them. But there were no sudden shouts, and no interior lights went on. Eventually, they made it up all five flights unnoticed.

The fire escape ended in a ladder that led to the roof. They climbed up and swung themselves over onto the tarred surface. The black pitch, still sealing in the daytime heat of the sun, felt warm against their shoes. The roof was as deserted as the alleyway. Beyond its boxy perimeter, muffled city street sounds reached up to them. Jordan apprehensively looked at the adjacent roof. In its very center, the newly constructed elevator housing marked their destination.

"How are we supposed to get over there?" she asked, looking across the gap.

"It doesn't seem that far."

"Maybe not to Carl Lewis," she said, "but we're sixty feet up. Isn't there some way we can cross over?"

"Come on, Jordan. We're going to have to jump it. It looks farther than it is. Trust me, a five-year-old could do this."

"Now that's encouraging. I suppose you want me to go first?"

He walked over and reassuringly rubbed the nape of her neck. "You're gonna do fine. Just follow my lead, huh?"

She nodded, forcing a hopeful smile. The bordering brick wall was three feet high. Without hesitation, Langford stepped atop and leaped, pushing off with his left foot. He easily bounded to the adjoining parapet and skipped off onto the roof. Then he turned around, beckoning with his arm.

"Piece of cake, Jordan. Don't think about it. Come on, up and at 'em."

Legs trembling, she shuffled to the brick border. Despite her waning confidence, she knew she had no choice. Looking directly at Langford, she sat on the wall and carefully assumed a kneeling position. Then she slowly rose from her crouch, struggling to remain steady, peering across the intervening space as if it were the Great Divide. Fighting for balance, she chanced a look down and was almost immediately overcome by a wave of vertigo.

"Don't look down, Jordan! Keep your eyes straight ahead! You can do this!"

"My legs feel like jelly."

"Don't think about it," he said, reaching toward her. "Just do it!"

She did. With all the strength she could muster, she sprang through the air toward his open arms. Her graceful leap easily breached the gap, and his waiting embrace almost immediately enveloped her. She clung to him, breathing heavily, her whole body shaking.

"What'd I tell you?" he whispered in her ear. "Was that a piece of cake, or what?"

"More like day-old bread," she said. "I hope the rest of this gets easier."

"Let's find out."

Crouching, hand-in-hand, they stole across the roof. The enclosed elevator shed was forty yards away. When they reached it, they straightened up, hugging the shed's walls.

The elevator building was a square hut, fifteen feet wide and ten feet high. The coolness of the steel walls penetrated their clothing. With Langford in the lead, they slowly navigated the building's perimeter and they came to a heavy fire door. He cautiously tried the knob.

It was locked. Slowly and carefully, he wiggled the door handle, but it wouldn't give. He looked at Jordan and shook his head.

"Is there any way around it?" she said.

"No, it's shut tight. Brand-new construction. We'll have to find another way."

They both looked out over the expanse of roof. As far as they could see, the roof was uniformly flat, without interruptions. Nowhere was there a trapdoor, stairs, or skylight.

"This doesn't look too promising," she said.

"There's *got* to be a way in. Let's try over here."

He crept across the roof. She followed close behind, to the roof's edge at the rear of the building. Keeping low, they peered over.

Ten feet beneath the roof, two large halogen floodlights were bolted to the side of the building. They illuminated the entire brick exterior, as well as the concrete courtyard below. Not far away, a fire escape zigzagged downward, the rungs of its ladder taking on an otherworldly shine in the lights' orangish glow.

"What about the fire escape?" she asked.

"Too obvious. Once we're in the light, they could spot us a mile away."

"But the lights don't begin until the fourth floor," she pointed out. "The windows right below us are still dark."

She was right. All of the fifth-floor windows remained in the shadows. Three feet beneath each window frame, the horizontal upper landing of the fire escape traversed the width of the building. At each of the landing's corners, an extension ladder led up to the roof. He thought it just possible that one of the darkened windows might be unlocked.

"Worth a shot," he said. "Go ahead."

This time, she led the way. Reaching the ladder's curved overhang, she stepped over the parapet and onto the upper rung, descending backward. The metal was old, but sturdy. Langford followed close behind. She reached the landing and paused, waiting for him to catch up. Seconds later, he was beside her, giving her shoulder a reassuring squeeze.

She moved ahead slowly. There were ten windows on the floor, each completely dark. She prayed the top floor was still unoccupied. The windows were large, three feet by six, double sash. She peered in.

"See anything?" Langford whispered.

She shook her head. "Dark as a tomb in there." She pressed gingerly against the lower sash's top frame, lifting upward. The window wouldn't budge. In the dim light, she could make out its simple semicircular latch. The window gave an ominous creak. Jordan froze, expecting the interior light to go on any moment. But nothing happened.

"Try the next one," he said.

She slowly moved on, trying each window in turn. Behind her, Langford repeated the attempt, putting all his weight behind it. But none of the windows moved in the slightest. By the time they reached the end of the landing, they were desperate.

"Now what?" she said. "We're getting nowhere fast."

A sultry night wind gusted across the landing, blowing dust into their hair and eyes. Langford blinked and turned his head away, waiting for it to subside. Then he grabbed his T-shirt by the hem and pulled it over his head, exposing the gun tucked into the waistband of his pants. He pulled it out and wrapped the pistol's butt in the shirt's soft cotton.

"What're you doing?" Jordan asked.

"We're not going to get in unless we break the damn windows. You with me on this?"

Her lips tightened into a determined line, and she gave an apprehensive nod. Holding the pistol by the muzzle, he placed his left palm flat on the upper pane to reduce vibration. Then he swung the pistol like a hammer, breaking the glass in the lower corner. The pane made little noise when it shattered. A large triangle of glass fell into the room, striking the floor with a muffled tinkle. Langford quickly repeated the process, knocking little segments loose as he worked toward the middle of the sash.

Finally he was able to reach inside to open the latch. He stuck the gun back in his waistband, pulled on his shirt, and pushed the window open. The lower sash moved with a sticky creak, and the warped wood vibrated as it rattled upwards. He climbed in, then turned around to help Jordan.

They stood where they were, acclimating to the dark. The room had a musty odor, mixed with the smell of recently drying paint and mortar. From the outside street light, they could see that the entire floor looked like an empty loft under renovation. There were no furnishings, fixtures, or people.

They walked across the room in measured silence. Underfoot, the old hardwood floor occasionally groaned at their passage. All their senses were heightened. They were still unsure precisely what they were looking for. There was an occasionally dislodged ceiling tile on the floor, or loose wire, or stray piece of insulation, but no answers. Yet they'd expected this. The answers they wanted—if available—would be found two floors below.

They came to a metal fire door that was ajar. They slid past it, their apprehension mounting. The door opened onto the landing. The stairwell beneath it was black and claustrophobic. Langford pulled out a slender penlight. Its illumination was dim but adequate. Below, they thought they could make out the fourth-floor landing. Like the one above it, it was bare.

"See anything?" Langford whispered.

"Not much. Can't hear anything, either. That's a patient floor, right?"

"Supposed to be," he said. "Let's see if we can get a look."

They descended sideways, their hands brushing the

walls for support. Reaching the fourth floor, they found the door locked. Langford shined his penlight around the edges. The metal door was newly installed. There was a keyhole, but no doorknob. A fire door, it opened only from the inside. Langford tried working his fingers into the slit between door and doorframe, but the opening was too narrow, and he couldn't gain any purchase. Exasperated, he stepped back and exhaled deeply.

"I should have known it'd be locked."

"No one said this would be easy," said Jordan. "But we've come this far, and we can't back out now. Should we go down one more flight?"

"I'm sure those doors are locked, too. What about the elevator?"

"What about it?" she said.

"We didn't check it out. Let's go back for a look."

They purposefully retraced their steps, walking in silent haste. Back on five, Langford switched off his penlight and put it in his pocket. The dark outline of the elevator shaft was faintly visible in the center of the room. As they started toward it, there was a muffled sound behind them. Langford started to turn in its direction when the cold, hard metal touched his temple.

A bright light suddenly shined in his eyes. Its almost painful glare made him wince. He blinked and averted his gaze, looking downward, fighting the icy terror that gripped his heart.

Chapter Twenty-two

A VOICE CAME OUT OF THE FETID DARK. "HEY, BIG stuff." The intense light was unwavering. "I don't know what you're doing here, Langford, but you're gonna talk to me."

Langford's fury outweighed his fear. "Take that goddamn light out of my face."

Vinnie's voice was flat as he called out, "Vito."

The pressure of the metal lessened for a fraction of a second. Before Langford could react, it suddenly returned, smashing into the side of his head with force and rage. Painfully stunned, he staggered and fell backward, sinking to his hands and knees. A searing ache jolted his brain, which felt as if it had been split by an axe. Something warm trickled down his cheek and onto his nose. When he dared open his eyes, he saw the light still playing around him. He could see his blood forming a crimson pattern on the hardwood.

"Get up."

The words were harsh and guttural. Langford pushed upward with his hands, struggling with a shimmering wave of nausea. When the strength returned to his legs, he forced himself to stand. Rising up, he could see Jordan out of the corner of his eye. A hand was clamped heavily around her mouth, and her eyes were wide with terror.

With the light shining in his face, it was impossible

to see his assailants well. He thought there were two of them. One had blond hair, and Langford got a vague impression of a second, olive-skinned man. But it was indistinct, a blur.

"Better think before you open your mouth, Doc. You and this woman don't mean shit to us. We can kill you both in a heartbeat. Don't fuckin' provoke me. Now, listen real close to what I'm askin' you. What was Molloy doing in your house last night?"

Langford's mind was working furiously to come up with a plan. The wound in his scalp pulsated mercilessly. He touched the area with his fingertips. It was virtually the same spot where Molloy's bullet grazed him. He tried to stanch the blood with his hand.

"He was trying to kill us," Langford said slowly.

"No shit? Why would he want to do that?"

Langford was tempted to retaliate with a wise-guy response, but he could just make out a gun pointed in his direction. He had no doubt they were serious about killing them. Instead, "I don't know."

"He didn't say anything to you?" the man asked.

"He tried to burn us alive."

"Did you know Molloy? Before last night, I mean?"

"He was a lab assistant in the hospital where I work."

"That right?" the man said. "A hit man in a medical lab? I'd say you were shittin' me, if I didn't know it was true. But everything else is making no sense to me, Langford. I'll put it to you another way. A little while ago, the guy we work for started goin' a little goofy upstairs, y'know? Now, this is a very important guy. He starts mumblin' peculiar things in court, say, and we could all be in hot water. Then, somethin' wonderful happens.

"Your friend Molloy puts us onto this new drug, and pretty soon the old guy gets a shot or somethin'. Suddenly, he's his old self again, maybe even better than before. Real sharp. Our problems are solved. But the trouble is, this shot's startin' to wear off, and he needs another dose. Molloy called this stuff cognopsin, and—''

''Cognopsin?''

''Oh, I'm ringin' a bell, am I?'' the man said.

''I know what it is,'' Langford carefully replied. ''It doesn't surprise me Molloy had access to it. He worked in the lab where it was discovered.''

''It's some kinda wonder drug?''

''Something like that.''

''Then you're in a position to help us, Doc,'' the man went on. ''Molloy's departure kinda left us in a bind. You see, we need this stuff, and we need it right now.''

Despite Langford's mental fuzziness, words and phrases stimulated his brain. Cognopsin and memory . . . moribund patients, the Eastgate Clinic . . . a valuable product, bribed ambulance attendants . . . all were compelling components to a puzzle that was nearly ready for his mind to assemble.

''I guess you assume I have it, huh?'' said Todd.

''I hope so, for your sake.''

He was skating on thin ice, and he sensed the foreigner's patience was near the breaking point. On the other hand, a little more provocation might throw him off guard. ''And you expect me to give it to you? Just like that?''

''It all depends how much you want to live.''

The gun was thrust into his face, and he heard the metallic snick of a hammer being drawn back. ''All right already, take it easy. I'll get it,'' he said, raising his hands submissively. At the same time, he took a step backward, to the very edge of the landing.

The man with the gun released his grip on Jordan's mouth and started after Langford. In the darkness, Langford pretended to stumble, lowering his shoulder. The gun was no longer pointed at his skull, and he reacted instinctively.

Reaching over his right shoulder with his left hand, he seized the gunman's wrist and pulled hard. Simultaneously, his right hand smashed into the man's triceps. The gun fired down the stairwell, a surprisingly muffled pop. Langford pulled and lifted, using his back for leverage, trying to flip the assailant over his shoulder. He felt the gunman lose his footing and fall forward. Langford bent and pivoted, twisting his torso. But as the man began hurtling over him, his toe struck Langford's heel. Thrown off balance, Langford toppled forward, following the stranger headlong down the darkened stairs.

He somersaulted into the blackness. He heard Jordan's scream and the sound of his own gun tumbling down the stairs with him. His shoulder scraped heavily against the steps. Before the pain hit him, he was off again, tumbling willy-nilly toward the next floor. As he rolled head over heels down the stairwell, he heard a sickening bony snap just before he finally thudded into something firm and resilient.

In a moment of clarity, he realized that what stopped his fall was the gunman's body. The two men lay together like twins, chest-to-chest on the fourth-floor landing. He felt the stark outline of the man's weapon against his ribs. Heart pounding, his fingers were on it in a defensive flash. Several feet away, the bright oval of a flashlight's beam moved across the wall, inching toward him. He wrestled with the gun, wrenching it from the gunman's grasp. To his astonishment, his assailant's unresisting fingers were like putty. He pulled the gun free just as a flashlight beam settled on the other man's face.

The man had heavy facial stubble, with a dark, olive face. The bags of his lower lids were brown crescents beneath onyx eyes. But those eyes were glazed and lifeless. His head listed heavily to one side, above a grotesquely fractured neck. A cry bellowed in the darkness.

"Vito!"

Langford didn't hesitate. He raised the stranger's gun as fast as he could, swinging it in an arc that pointed up the stairs. Following the beam of light, he fired three times in rapid succession, expecting to be stunned by the pistol's roar. Instead, he heard oddly mechanical reports, a kind of hissing click. The ejected shell casings were thimbles of glittering brass, outlined in the whitish beam. And then the flashlight disintegrated. Struck by one of the shots, it burst apart in a blizzard of aluminum, casting the stairs into darkness.

He heard the stranger groan, followed by a scream. The warbling cry was unmistakably Jordan's voice, and he was terrified that he might have shot her. He'd been so intent on retaliation that he hadn't thought about her. In the impenetrable blackness, the only sound was his breathing, and the hollow thumping of his heart. But then he heard a scuffling and the indistinct sound of retreating footsteps.

"Jordan? Jordan!"

"Todd!" she cried. "My God, I thought—"

"Are you all right?"

"I'm okay," she said. "What about that man? I can't see a thing!"

"He's dead. Broken neck." He fumbled in his pocket for the penlight, found it, switched it on, and shined it on the man next to him. The cadaver was silent and unmoving. He shined the thin beam up in her direction. "What happened to the other guy?"

"He ran that way," she said, pointing in the direction he fled. "What did you hit him with?"

"With this. I lost the twenty-two" He shined the penlight on the dead man's gun. Although it hadn't sunk in until now, he realized he was holding a silenced handgun. It was a compact nine-millimeter Beretta Cougar, barely larger than his palm. An outrageously small suppressor bearing the name Aurora was attached to its muzzle. Little more than three inches long, the silencer obviously worked. Langford rolled onto his knees. "How bad was he hit?"

"I'm not sure. But he's alive, and he's bleeding."

Langford started back up the steps, holding the penlight in one hand, the Beretta in the other. Reaching the landing, he directed the beam to the floor to find a faint but distinct blood trail. Jordan dabbed at the cut in his scalp.

"How does it look?" he asked.

"You'll be okay. I don't know how many of your nine lives you just used up. Who were those men, Todd? What was the first one saying about cognopsin?"

"Something about an old guy they'd given it to, courtesy of Molloy. Whoever those guys were, there already seems to be a black market for the stuff! Christ, we don't know diddly." He headed through the doorway, into the room. "Come on, let's go."

"Where are we—"

This time, it was Langford's penlight that went flying. The muffled gunshots came from the direction of the windows. One of the slugs struck the Beretta just above the trigger guard. His hand felt as if a sledgehammer had hit it. The pistol was wrenched free, smashing into the penlight as it tumbled into the shadows.

Langford cursed his stupidity. What in God's name had he been thinking? How could he so confidently presume that one of his haphazard shots had put the man out of commission? Grabbing Jordan by the arm, he pulled her across the floor.

Jordan ran as fast as her legs could carry her. There was a furious buzzing above and behind her, like restless bees seeking to destroy her. She plunged blindly after Langford, racing into the safety of the darkness. It was disorienting, like a nocturnal high-dive into an unlit pool.

But darkness was their sanctuary, their ally, covering

them like a shroud. They headed for the center of the
room, away from the windows and their light. The middle of the room was an ebony cocoon. They finally
stopped running, arms outstretched like blind men.
Their fingers grazed upright metal walls, cool and
smooth.

"The elevator!" Langford shouted.

He'd intended to keep his voice to a whisper. But to
their adrenaline-charged hearing, it sounded like a
scream. A new volley of silenced gunshots punctuated
the darkness. Ricocheting slugs clanged around them,
pinging off the metal with an insistent whine. The ric-
ochets were getting dangerously close, peppering them
with stinging slivers of copper and lead.

Langford's fingers clawed at the metal. His nails slid
across the smooth surface until they located the seam
where the elevator doors closed. Sinking his fingers
into the rubber bumpers, he pried at the doors with all
his might. The heavy slabs seemed glued closed. He
grunted, the sinews of his wrists straining with the effort. Finally, the doors began to give—slowly, at first,
but then more rapidly.

Beyond the half-open doors lay a yawning chasm of
emptiness. His heart sank. He hoped they'd find a vacant cab, unoccupied and unlit, ready to power up for
a downward descent. Instead, there was nothing. Langford moved his hands before him, as if waving through
fog. He felt as if he were standing on a precipice on
the edge of an abyss. Directly behind him, Jordan clung
to his arm.

A bullet hit the door, inches from his head. Jordan
stifled a cry, verging on panic. Langford's sneakered
toe wiggled unsteadily in the elevator opening. He
leaned forward, fighting for balance. Suddenly, his
searching hand found something cold and slippery. His
fingers instantly went around it. It was a thick length
of elevator cable—cold, taut, and lubricated. There was
no time to hesitate.

"Jordan, put your arms around me! Grab on and hold tight!"

It wasn't clear whether or not she understood what he intended. But she responded with alacrity, encircling him with her arms and legs like a koala bear. Langford pushed off with his foot, toward the center of the elevator shaft. There was a brief but dizzying moment when both their bodies bridged the gap, supported by nothing. But then he found the cable, gripping it like a lifeline in both his hands.

His breath came in spasms, a fiery heat in his lungs. Jordan's chest pressed into his back, and her face was wedged into the hollow of his neck. She clung to him, not daring to let go. Langford rested there for a moment, until another bullet twanged overhead, shockingly close. It was all the stimulus he needed. Relaxing his grasp, he let gravity take over.

They slid downward in the darkness. They could see absolutely nothing, and the terror of disorientation was compounded by the fear of impending free-fall. The braided cable slid inexorably through Langford's fingers. He could no longer stop even if he wanted to. The speed of his slide increased, and they began a dangerous swoop downward. He quickly wrapped his knees and calves around the cable to slow their descent.

He tried tightening his grip on the cable, but to no effect. The thick lubricant provided no leverage. But just as he was beginning to fear for their lives, his feet struck something firm and horizontal. They were enveloped in impenetrable blackness.

Chapter Twenty-three

VINNIE BUONAFORTUNA SAT ON THE FLOOR, HIS BACK against the wall. His knees were bent up in front of him, and he held the silenced nine-millimeter Glock automatic in both hands, the elbow of his right arm steadied on his raised right knee. He had lost them. He'd caught sight of them for a moment, as they dashed across the floor. Silhouetted against the window, their moving bodies made easy targets. Ordinarily, it would have been impossible for him to miss.

But he'd never before shot with a shattered elbow. His lower humerus had taken a slug just above the olecranon fossa, pulverizing the bone. While not life-threatening, the injury was painful and bled profusely. With the tiniest movement, the wound throbbed mercilessly, slowing his reactions and throwing off his aim.

He should never have allowed it to get this far. Langford was obviously emotionally attached to the woman. He should have taken the girl first, threatening and torturing her until the man was intimidated into cooperation. But what was done was done. He'd planned to kill them before, once he had what he wanted. The recent events would only speed up the process.

He had serious doubts that Langford had the product. The expression on his face said as much. The doctor had heard about cognopsin, for sure. But why Molloy had tried to kill him, and where the drug was now, were

questions that appeared to elude Langford. No matter.
He spoke into his small handheld radio.

"Joey, listen up. Everything all right outside?"

"No problem, Vinnie."

"Good," said Buonafortuna. "Get your butt in here.
We've got a problem. Come up the fire escape as soon
as you can, and bring a light."

"What're you talkin' about, Vinnie?" said Joey. "Is
Vito there? Is—"

"Don't give me bullshit questions, Joey, just do it!
And bring the Benelli with you!"

"Shots fired," Armstrong said into his mouthpiece. "I
repeat, shots fired."

"Run that by me again?" Courtney said.

"I have flashes on my night vision. On the infrared,
it's a muzzle flash signature, fifth floor, rear. There
goes another one."

"Shit!" said Courtney. "Who's the shooter?"

"Our friend Mr. Buonafortuna. Sitting on his ass in
the corner, firing into the middle of the room. His
weapon's suppressed."

"What about Langford and the girl?"

"No go," said Armstrong. "Thought I acquired
them a few seconds ago, but I can't say for sure. If
they're what he's aiming at, I don't think they're hit.
The bad news is, he's still firing."

"You're just filled with good news. Are—"

"Hold on, Lead," Armstrong interrupted. "I've got
a cowboy on the move, going up the fire escape. Looks
like the driver. He's packin' heavy, a twelve-gauge."

Courtney frowned. From his position three hundred
yards away, he quickly assessed their options. They'd
identified the cab driver as Joey LaRocca, a role-
playing thug wanted for mob-related activities in three
states. The man was little more than a street-level killer.
If he was called into the fight with a shotgun, little good
could come of it. Besides, Courtney wanted to *question*

Buonafortuna. Once LaRocca was in play, they
wouldn't have a choice. It was time to even the odds.

"Can you take him, Johnny?"

Armstrong peered intently through the scope.
"Roger that."

Courtney had a dilemma. The men he was tracking
would shoot him in cold blood, if the need arose. But
ordinarily neither he nor his men would fire unless fired
upon. Yet when he'd been rehired as a Special Agent,
he'd done so on his own terms, and he'd extracted a
concession from his superiors at Justice to liberally use
force in threatening situations. And the situation right
now warranted action.

"Do it," Courtney said.

Armstrong's night-vision equipment had both active
and passive infrared capabilities. He was one hundred
twenty yards away, on the roof of a building on Ninety-
fifth Street. Everything being equal, he would have preferred a head shot, as destruction of the central nervous
system was the surest way to neutralize the quarry. But
the target was moving, going hand-over-hand up the
fire escape's ladder. He therefore centered the cross-
hairs on the man's back. In one fluid movement, he
thumbed off the safety, put his finger in the trigger
guard, and squeezed.

The rifle bucked, sending the thirty-caliber projectile
downrange at twenty-seven hundred feet per second. It
instantly transected the spinal cord at T-3. Mushroom-
ing perfectly, the expanded slug departed the front of
the man's chest in a gaping three-inch exit wound just
above the sternum. The nearly lifeless body slumped
heavily, collapsing in an unsteady heap on the railing,
from which it quickly toppled to the ground.

"Splash one," said Armstrong. "Target down."

"Copy that, Johnny. Good work. Keep an eye out
back. I'm going to look for a way in the front."

*   *   *

In the tomblike recess of the elevator shaft, Langford bent his knees, absorbing Jordan's weight. He eased his hands under her buttocks and helped her slide off. She regained her footing but held onto him, unsteady and disoriented.

"Where are we?" she whispered.

"On the roof of the elevator cab. I don't think we slid too far. Two floors, max."

"I can't see a thing," said Jordan. "Do you still have that little light?"

He shook his head. "It's history. Just as well. I wouldn't want to give him something to shoot at. Bend down. There's got to be an opening in this thing."

They knelt, sinking onto hands and knees. The total blackness was suffocating. Jordan found it impossible to move about without feeling as if she were going to topple over. Her sudden blindness was unnervingly confusing. She found herself pressing tightly into Langford. The sense of touch and bodily contact was reassuring.

Her fingers scratched spiderlike across the elevator's metal roof. She was looking for seams, cracks, or recesses—anything that could gain them entrance into the elevator. But the cool metal seemed uniformly smooth and featureless. Finally, near the juncture of roof and wall, she found it.

It was a trapdoor, about eighteen inches square. There was a small depression in the metal, a fingerhold for lifting. Jordan hooked it with her index finger and pulled. The door swung smoothly up, leaving a four-sided portal in the darkness. Her voice was an excited whisper.

"I think we're in business! Give me your hand!"

She guided his fingers to the aperture. Langford followed its contour, feeling around the edges of the square.

"A ceiling escape hatch, great," he said.

He stuck his head into the opening. He could see

nothing. The power to the cabin had been turned off. The elevator doors seemed closed. But he could just make out a thin, vertical line where they met in the middle. No doubt the floor beyond the doors was illuminated.

"Just might work," Todd said. "Let me go in first."

Swinging his legs over and through the aperture, he dangled on the edge. Placing his flattened palms on opposite metal edges, he supported his own weight vertically, like a gymnast. Finally he let go, falling through the small opening. He hit the floor with a metallic thump. Rolling onto his side, he quickly righted himself and stood up, arms extended roofward.

"Come on," he said, "I've got you."

She sat on the edge of the trapdoor, pushed off, and fell forward. He caught her and lowered her silently to the floor.

"Where to from here?" she asked. "Will this thing go down?"

"No, the power's off. Somebody's got the key."

"This might be a patient floor." She apprehensively squeezed his arm. "What do you think, Todd? We've come this far. May as well take a look."

He felt uncertain. "There could be trouble out there. What do you want to do, just barge on in?"

"For God's sake, Todd, I want to stay alive, not commit suicide! But you pried the doors open on five, right? Why should these be any different?"

She was right, and he knew it. Nodding, he placed his fingertips into the gap between the doors and tried inching the doors apart. At first they hardly budged, sticking together with gluelike adhesiveness. Then they decided to separate, in grudging increments. The gap was an inch wide when the outer doors also gave way.

A bright light suddenly streamed toward them. Their eyes acclimated to the glare, and Todd pressed his face to the gap, trying to get a better view. In her chest, her heart had begun to thud.

"See anything?" she asked.

"Not yet." He adjusted his line of sight. "But I want to make sure we don't bump into anybody." He paused for a deep breath, then swallowed, his throat dry. Beyond his fear of discovery were the uncertainties about what they might find in the clinic. The possibilities were frightening.

"Can you see Rita? Are there any patients?"

"Not that I can make out," he said. "No people at all. So far, it looks like we're facing a big interior wall."

"What's a wall doing there?"

"Hold on, Jordan. Let me get my bearings." He continued turning his head, trying to see all around. "I've got to open this up a little. I think we're okay. You ready?"

She nodded. "Go for it."

His hands were shaking. Ever so slowly, careful not to make a sound, he pried the doors farther apart. The space widened to six inches, then twelve. Jordan's heart beat wildly. At any moment, she expected another face-to-face encounter with someone determined to kill them. But as the fluorescent light streamed over them, she saw that the area ahead was featureless and unintimidating. Indeed, the only thing visible was a flat gray wall, ten feet away. It rose to near–ceiling height, creating a hallway just beyond the elevator. The corridor beckoned.

Langford squeezed past the doors and took Jordan's cold and sweaty palm. They walked like Indians, slow and wary steps on the balls of their feet, down the brightly lit corridor. After proceeding a few nerve-wracking feet, they halted and nervously looked up.

The interior wall did not quite reach the ceiling. A bluish light radiated from the narrow space. Its pale neon glow bathed the tiles like a pastel Caribbean tide. Jordan's fear was beginning to overwhelm her, and she squeezed Todd's hand for reassurance.

"What *is* that light?" she said.

The limpid, greenish-blue color was somewhere between turquoise and aquamarine. It seemed inappropriate, out of place and terrifying. He could think of no
use for it in a chronic-care facility. It didn't resemble
anything with which he was familiar. But then, *nothing*
in this place looked familiar. He was starting to wonder
precisely what in God's name was happening at Eastgate.

"Your guess is as good as mine," he said. "But I
want to get a look in there. Come on."

They made their way to the end of the hall, then
stopped. Langford cautiously peered around the corner.
Beyond it lay yet another hall, similarly empty, unmarked and featureless. But in the center of the corridor
was a door—or rather, a wide, portallike opening. More
of the eerie bluish light radiated from within.

"There's something here," he said cautiously.

"What?" said Jordan.

"I think it's what we're looking for."

She anxiously followed him. Their stealthy footsteps
made no noise in the carpeted hallway. Beyond them,
the blue light beckoned. They felt strangely drawn to
it, like unsuspecting moths. The glow in the hall brightened. Finally they drew abreast of the doorway's border. Langford nervously peered past the door.

He stepped into the opening and looked around in
mounting shock. It was like something out of a dream.
Watching his expression, Jordan grew perplexed, and
more than a little frightened. Seconds later, she stood
beside him in open-mouthed wonder.

They were in a patient treatment area. The room was
a huge square, roughly sixty by sixty feet. And it was
filled with patients, about two dozen in number. Spaced
ten feet apart, they formed neat, even rows, a phalanx
of comatose human flesh. Jordan's gaze immediately
flitted about, searching in vain for Rita.

The light was coming from individual fixtures recessed into the ceiling above each patient. The purpose of the lighting soon became apparent. As the beams radiated downward, they enveloped each patient in a bluish mantle. Langford now recognized the lights as cobalt vapor lamps, an experimental form of anti-microbial lighting, the latest in antisepsis.

The scene was surreal. All of the patients were na-ked. They lay on their backs like sleeping astronauts, facing up, knees slightly bent, arms at their sides, awaiting a blastoff that would never come. At first glance they appeared to be floating, suspended four feet off the ground. But on closer inspection, they were sup-ported by nearly transparent acrylic cradles, which arose from circular hydraulic columns built into the floor.

Each patient was little more than the sum of his tubes. They all had a minimum of four: an IV, dripping into a forearm; a urinary catheter, taped to the inside of the thigh, draining into a collection bag near the floor; an endotracheal tube, hooked to a nearby respi-rator; and a nasogastric tube, used for nourishment. The room's climate-controlled air was warm and humid. There was a slight, almost tropical breeze from contin-uously circulated air.

But the room reeked of death.

Jordan was astonished and appalled by the grotesque spectacle of so many comatose individuals, lined up in orderly rows, their eyelids taped shut to keep their cor-neas from drying out. In the background, the sibilant hiss of the respirators was an uneven symphony punc-tuating the silence.

She and Langford walked into the room with near-catatonic slowness, mesmerized. The putrid stench of infection and decaying flesh was everywhere. Sickened though they were, they felt compelled to see more. They were drawn steadily ahead, iron filings to a mag-net.

"Just whose idea of chronic care is this?" Jordan

asked. "And Royce and Hobson are supposed to be some kind of humanitarians? These people are as good as dead!"

"This is a travesty, Jordan." He inched steadily forward, attracted to the nearest patient. His jaw dropped. "Sweet Jesus," he managed. "It's Conchita!"

"Who?"

"An abortion patient," said Langford. "Her mother works in the hospital. She had an emergency hysterectomy, but she arrested on the operating table. My God, what *happened* to her?"

They halted inches from the acrylic supports. Langford gazed in disbelief at the surgical incision in her lower abdomen. In the pale-blue light, the scar seemed unusually ragged. It was held together by stainless-steel staples which extended from umbilicus to pubic hair. The gaps between the clips oozed serum, which ran to her flanks in sticky rivulets. Between her breasts, still swollen by pregnancy, the skin was bruised. Her ecchymotic, misshapen sternum showed the ravages of the external cardiac massage used to save her. Above it, on Conchita's stiff and leaden face, secretions congealed around her lips and nostrils.

"She looks so young," Jordan said, her voice still trembling.

"Seventeen, I think."

"She's a mess. What's *wrong* with this place?" she said. "Why aren't they doing anything to clean her up?"

Langford checked the label on the IV. "Levophed and lidocaine. Christ. No antibiotics." He shook his head. "They don't give a damn how she looks. If these are the only drugs, all they want to do is keep her alive."

"That's horrible! These are human beings, not lab experiments!"

"She's terminal, circling the drain, Jordan," he said.

"They're doing enough to keep her heart beating, but not one thing more."

"How much longer can she last like that?"

"A week, maybe two," said Langford. "What I don't understand is why. I . . ." His voice abruptly trailed off as something caught his eye. Bending over, he frowned as he saw a thin plastic catheter leading away from the body, toward a stoppered beaker on the floor. Kneeling beside it, he watched a slow trickle of clear fluid enter the container, a drop every few seconds. He traced the catheter upward with his finger, to a spot where it was heavily taped to the patient's lower back.

Langford was incredulous. "I don't believe it," he said.

"What's wrong?" she asked hoarsely.

"This is a lumbar puncture catheter," he said, straightening up. "That beaker's filling with spinal fluid! And I'm not talking about a simple spinal tap. The damn thing's collecting it, draining every ounce she can produce!"

Mortified, Jordan couldn't believe what was going on. "But why?" she asked.

His jaw muscles clenched. "I'm not sure, but I'm starting to get an idea. I don't have a very good feeling about all this." His eyes moved to the next patient. "Let's take a look over there."

Ten feet away, a middle-aged black man lay suspended on his cradle, head swathed in bloodstained bandages. Langford thought he recognized him as a trauma patient whose head had been caved in by a hammer. His fractured right arm was still wrapped in a temporary plastic cast. Approaching the cradle, they both peered beneath it.

"Oh, no," Jordan said when she saw the indwelling spinal catheter. The beaker was two-thirds full. Langford straightened up in mounting fury. Everywhere he looked, the moribund patients—barely kept alive by

machines, drugs, and gadgets—were being drained of
every milliliter of their cerebrospinal fluid. Slowly he
began walking through the room, shocked and enraged.

"This is no chronic-care facility," he said. "It's a
goddamn production line!"

"They're collecting everyone's spinal fluid?"

"Right," he said, "and from people who can't possibly complain—a room full of unconscious trauma patients!"

"But what would they want with all that . . ." Her
voice stopped as she followed her line of reasoning to
its logical conclusion. They both looked at one another,
eyes wide with disbelief. "Cognopsin," she finally
said. "This is where they get the cognopsin!"

"They have to keep them critical," Langford said.
"Alive, but just barely."

"They're not really trying to administer any care at
all, are they?"

"This isn't medical care." Langford snorted. "It's
just a form of prolonged murder."

"So all that mumbo jumbo about why the clinic was
started was bullshit?" she asked. "The only reason this
clinic was built was to extract their CSF?"

"That's what it looks like to me. They collect it here,
but they must process it on another floor. They probably refined Dr. Fletcher's technique for extracting the
cognopsin."

They walked slowly through the room, from one
moribund patient to another, searching for Rita. But she
was nowhere to be seen. Langford was depressingly
familiar with many of the patients. At one time they'd
been people he'd desperately tried to save. But now,
none of them were receiving the slightest treatment for
their wounds, fractures, or injuries.

"That man who shot at you upstairs," Jordan said.
"How did he know to come here?"

"I don't think he did," said Todd. "He wanted the
cognopsin for whatever's wrong with his boss. I doubt

he knew this is where it's made. I think he was following us."

"He wanted us to lead him to it?"

"Right," he said, still looking about. They had nearly reached the last row of patients. "Molloy probably got them the first dose, and then was stringing them along about getting another. I guess the blond guy associated me with Molloy. He was just lucky. Or maybe unlucky."

"You don't think he's working for Royce?"

"No," Todd said. "It doesn't look that way to me, and—"

Suddenly, he abruptly stopped speaking, and his jaw dropped. Jordan looked at him, then followed his line of sight. When she saw it, she gasped.

They had finally found Rita.

She lay in the last cradle of the last row, pale and still, sightless eyes held shut with tape. They moved toward her with faltering hesitation, like mourners. Like the other patients, Rita was naked, hooked up to an array of plastic tubing. The surgical incision was on her abdomen, pink and angry. Jordan realized that her hands had balled into fists, and she forced herself to relax her fingers before touching her friend's cool cheek.

"Poor, dear Rita," she softly intoned, "what have they done to you?"

"Same as they did to everybody else. Come on, Jordan. We can't help her here."

"There must be something we can do!"

"Maybe, if we get her out of this place," he said. "Right now, we're no use to anyone."

She nodded, realizing he was right. They had their answers. Moreover, they knew that *someone* had to be working in the building. Further procrastination wasn't safe. Moving on, they came to a doorway and paused. Todd decided it would probably lead to the stairwell. But Jordan was still distracted.

"What happens if they can't keep Rita or the other patients alive anymore?"

"They probably just pull the plug on 'em," he said.

"What do they do with the bodies?"

"Good question."

She shivered. "Let's get out of here, Todd."

"And go where?"

"The police. We learned what we set out to, and it's the first step in helping Rita. It's time we took Tom Courtney's advice. Once the cops learn about the horror show in here, we'll be in the clear."

He nodded reluctantly. "I suppose. But it'd sure be nice to have something to show them. Like cognopsin powder, or injection. I wonder if—"

The door began to open before them. Large and heavy, it moved slowly. They quickly ducked behind it, pressing themselves against the wall, their hearts pounding and nerves frayed.

A woman entered. Middle-aged, tall and large-framed with blond hair going to gray, Langford thought he recognized her as Mary, a nurse from one of the psych units. But it was hard to tell. A mask shielded her face, and she wore loose green scrubs. Before the door closed behind her, they ducked out of the room.

The stairwell was dark, and they carefully negotiated the first few steps.

"You okay, Jordan?"

"Right behind you," she whispered. "Just keep going."

She pressed her fingers to the small of his back, following his lead. They knew there had to be a light switch somewhere, but they couldn't find it. At the base of the steps, they came to a landing. Blinded by the darkness, they groped at the walls Suddenly Jordan's fingers struck something cold and rubbery. Startled, she lost her balance, and her flailing arms dislodged the object she'd contacted.

It swooped down and enveloped her like a shroud.

It was suffocating her, pressing against her sickeningly, wrapping itself around her neck and face. She smelled the stench of putrefaction and death, and in that one, terrifying moment, she realized that the object hugging her was a cold and lifeless cadaver, come to embrace her in a macabre dance of the dead.

Chapter Twenty-four

BUONAFORTUNA WAS STARTLED BY A WOMAN'S TER-
rified scream.

Everything had been silent before that. When Joey
didn't show up, Vinnie's instincts went on alert. When
the ache in his arm reduced to a steady but bearable
throb, he'd finally gotten up. Anticipating trouble, he'd
kept away from the windows. Instead, he'd slowly
skirted the inner area of the fifth floor, locating what
appeared to be an elevator shaft, dark and unlit. He'd
been standing there contemplating his next move when
the scream filled his ears. It seemed to come from the
stairwell below him.

In spite of the now-closed door on four, the nurse
heard it, too. She pushed the door open; the stairs beyond it were dark. She saw a blur of movement to her
left and looked up. As the room light spilled into the
landing, a man came into view, walking down the
steps. She didn't recognize him.

"Who the hell are you?" she said.

She felt, rather than heard, his reply. He raised his
right hand and pointed something her way. At the very
instant that she heard a soft plop, she felt something
like a closed fist ram into her chest. As she was
slammed against the wall, she remembered being startled, her mouth fell open. Before she could say anything, her world went dark. The second bullet entered

her skull over the bridge of her nose. As the lead slug shed its copper jacket, it liquefied her brainstem. The woman's legs buckled, and she slid silently to the floor.

On the landing one flight below, Langford heard the noise from above. He fumbled wildly, found a doorknob, and yanked it open, pulling Jordan to him. In the sudden light from the doorway, he watched as the dead body slithered off her, as she fought to free herself. The limp and bloated cadaver fell away in a heap. Langford pulled her roughly through the third-floor doorway. Looking back at the lifeless body, he was astonished.

"My God, that was the jumper!" he said. "Now I guess we know what they do with the bodies."

Jordan was mute. In the icy grip of panic, she wore a pasty, white-faced expression of horror. As the door closed behind them, Langford looked for some way to bar it. He spotted a large broom propped against a nearby wall. He wedged its handle between the metal door and its horizontal opening bar.

"Come on," he said, putting his arms around Jordan. "That broom won't delay him long."

Slowly Jordan found her voice. "They just hang them up like that? Like a side of beef?"

"Maybe they have a storage problem," he said.

They saw no sign of life. Are there any other employees? Todd began to wonder. The floor-through, loftlike room was a warehouse: medical supplies, sterile cloth and paper products, irrigants, tubing, dressings, and fluids were stacked on metal shelves. There seemed to be enough to attend to the patients' needs indefinitely.

On the far side of the room they finally found what they were looking for—the high-tech medical lab, with slate-gray countertops covered with glassware. Everything was automated. There was row upon row of flasks, beakers, and distillation apparatus. Each container was carefully labeled.

One piece of glassware fed another, continuously removing impurities and contaminants, until what remained was devoid of cells, drugs, infectious agents, and extraneous molecules. The final distillate was identified as liquefied cognopsin: eighty percent water and twenty percent protein. When the water was removed, what remained was cognopsin in its purified form—a crystalline, white powder. It formed a tiny mound at the end of the workstation, falling like grains of powdered sugar from a sterile conveyor. Everything worked in synchrony toward the final goal, the purification of cognopsin.

"So that's it," Jordan said. "It all comes down to a little pile of powder."

"And worth killing for. These few grams probably would be worth millions. It'd make thousands of doses when it's reconstituted. Where do they store it?" Looking around, he spotted a rectangular, waist-level, ten-foot freezer. He walked over and lifted its heavy cover.

A frozen mist wafted upward. The freezer was filled with lift-out aluminum storage racks. Each rack contained hundreds of rubber-stoppered ten-cc clear glass vials filled with a snowy powder. Langford picked one up and read the label: "Cognopsin, one gram."

"Freeze-dried?" she asked.

He nodded. "For long-term storage." He grabbed a handful of vials and gave several to her. "Stick these in your pocket. Now let's get out of here before we run into that guy again. We've got what we came for."

"Fine with me," she said, letting out a deep breath. "But too bad we don't have anything on paper. I wonder where they keep their records."

From out of nowhere, a voice boomed behind them. "Second floor. Not that you'll ever see them."

Startled beyond belief, Langford recognized the voice even as he turned. The deep, mellifluous tones and precisely enunciated words belonged to Dr. Hobson. He was holding open a door, an entrance so cleverly built into the wall it was nearly impossible to detect.

"Why am I not surprised to find both of you here?" he went on. "You're remarkably persistent. And resilient. Exactly what does it take to destroy you?"

Hobson held a heavy revolver, pointed at Langford. Was this the same chief of emergency medicine, Langford wondered, he respected, even revered? And was Hobson aware of the blond-haired assassin still loose in the building? He was furious, and it took him a moment to speak. "More than you've got."

"So it would seem," said Hobson. "Those are bold words. Or maybe you've just been incredibly lucky. Now, if you don't mind, put those items back on the freezer and come downstairs with me. At these prices, we can't have you pilfering the merchandise."

They both did as they were told. "That's what this is all about?" Jordan asked. "Money?"

"My dear girl, you cannot possibly understand."

"We understand that all your speeches about a chronic-care facility were bullshit, a smokescreen," said Langford. "Both of you guys probably planned this from the start!"

"Both?" Hobson said, puzzled. "Oh, you mean Royce?" He shook his head with a sardonic smile. "He doesn't get it any more than you do. Royce is every bit as much a do-gooder as poor Dr. Fletcher," said Hobson. "I rather enjoyed his looking like the heavy, but the fact is, he doesn't even know this room exists!"

"How can you do this to people?" Jordan asked. "What happened to saving lives?"

"I'm doing nothing more than shaking apples loose from the tree," said Hobson. "All the patients here are as good as dead anyway."

"Rita wasn't!" Jordan shot back.

"Ah, yes," Hobson said. "That *was* something of a

mistake. First Dr. Fine gave her the cognopsin in error.
Then that idiot Royce had her transferred here. But all
that no longer matters. Right now, I'm merely pro-
longing her life for a useful purpose.''

"Useful to whom?" Langford countered. "Whatever happened to death with dignity?"

"Please," Hobson scoffed, waving the gun. "Don't
waste my time. Downstairs."

Langford was desperate to buy time. Once they
moved, they were finished. But here, they had a chance,
because Hobson didn't dare shoot and risk damaging
his precious merchandise. "I thought you were at an
all-day medical conference."

"As a matter of fact, Royce still is," said Hobson.
"Ever the dedicated clinician. But I had a little inven-
tory to go over. And you two . . . what? You presumed
you could sneak in undetected, is that it? Did you think
I'd leave this place unguarded? The staff is small, but
hardly nonexistent. Before your departure, you're going
to tell me precisely how you broke in here."

Langford seemed to ignore him. "How're you going
to market all this?"

"I'm going to sell it, of course," said Hobson. "Do
you have the slightest idea how much some senile, dod-
dering Arab sheik would pay for this? Not to mention
the average guy on the street who wants to get smarter
for a couple of weeks. What's it worth to a Wall Street-
er in a tough market, or even a college student at finals?
I don't have to market the stuff. Cognopsin markets
itself. In fact, my first shipment's tomorrow night.
Which explains what I'm doing here after hours, much
to your chagrin. Now," he said, indicating the doorway, "if you don't mind."

"We're not moving," said Todd.

Hobson lifted the revolver and pointed it at Jordan.
"Either get your asses through that door right now, or
I'll blow an enormous hole in her."

Langford knew he would. Hobson's unctuous composure was giving way to nervousness. There was no question he was prepared to carry out his threat. Langford looked at Jordan, then deliberately walked toward the door. Hobson gave them a wide berth but kept the gun pointed directly at Jordan's head.

"That's much more reasonable," he said. "And consider this, Miss Parker-Ross. Among so-called normal patients, your spinal fluid alone contains elevated amounts of cognopsin. I want to know why, and I want to know what special talents it's given you. I'm beginning to suspect they had something to do with how you tripped up Dr. Fine."

A figure suddenly appeared in the door. It was Dr. Royce, his face etched with disbelief.

"What in the world's going on here? And where's the nurse?" Royce asked.

"Conference ended early, did it?" said Hobson. He pointed the gun barrel at his partner. "I guess you're going with them. Now shut up and follow them down the stairs!"

Vinnie Buonafortuna had finally given up on the barricaded door. Langford's obstacle had proven too effective to overcome one-handed. The pain in his left arm was intense. But worse than the pain was the bleeding. Bending over the dead nurse, he tore a wide strip of cloth from her scrubs and fashioned an ersatz dressing. He wrapped it around his arm like a tourniquet, using one hand and his teeth to sink the knot. Then he continued down the stairwell to the landing below.

He pushed open the fire door and discovered that the next floor was primarily administrative. There were desks, an occasional computer, and papers strewn haphazardly about several offices, all vacant. In the largest room there was a long conference table, topped with empty cardboard boxes. Rolls of tape and address labels lay beside the boxes.

On the wall beyond the fire door, there was a second carefully hidden door. Buonafortuna cautiously opened it and walked past. He came to a lighted stairway and paused for a moment, listening He could make out several voices one flight above, one voice inquiring about Jordan. Then Vinnie carefully started up the first step, just as Langford and Jordan were coming down.

Langford saw him and halted, raising his arms submissively. Jordan sucked in her breath sharply, startled and afraid. It was hard to tell who was more surprised, they or the gunman. Behind them, Royce stared incredulously at the blond-haired stranger.

"What the hell?" Royce asked.

Angered by what Hobson was doing, Royce was now enraged by the sight of the gunman. He suddenly snatched the gun from Hobson's hand and pointed it down the stairs. But his reflexes were no match for those of Buonafortuna. Ordinarily, Vinnie used a two-hand combat stance, but even with one bad arm, his response was lightning quick. The Glock came up smoothly in his right hand. In the haste and confusion, he didn't get a good sight picture. But it was more than adequate. He squeezed the trigger twice, a perfect double-tap. Both bullets caught Royce in the face.

The physician was knocked backward. A baseball-size wedge of skull was torn away, loosing a grisly spray of hair, brain, and scalp. The particulate debris rained down on Hobson, covering his face and shoulders with a gruesome crimson splatter. Then, in an agonal reflex, Royce's fingers tightened. His revolver fired, filling the stairwell with an ear-splitting roar.

Jordan screamed as the bullet zinged harmlessly past her, punching a neat hole in the wall. Langford's arms went protectively around her. They watched Royce slump to a sitting position against the wall, trailing a garish scarlet smear. Hobson remained standing, wiping specks of blood and skin from his eyes. He gazed down at the stranger, whose gun was now pointed his way.

"I don't know who you are," he said with equanimity. "What are you doing here?"

Buonafortuna's words were straightforward. "This your building, pal?"

"In a manner of speaking."

"Good. Listen carefully," said Vinnie. "I'm interested in a drug called cognopsin. I followed these two . . ."

"Cognopsin, you say?" Hobson said with a smile. "You've come to the right place. I happen to have the world's largest supply. In fact, the *only* supply."

"Where is it?"

"In there," Hobson said, inclining his head toward the open door behind him. "Might I inquire how you happen to know about it?"

"No, you might not. Now get all your butts back in there," Vinnie said, flicking the gun barrel. "Very, *very* slowly. And as for you," he said to Jordan, "on the stairway, I heard this man refer to special talents. What's he talkin' about?"

Frightened though she was, Jordan was also infuriated by the unnecessary brutality. She glared at him. "Why should I tell you?"

He pointed the gun in her face. "Because if you don't, I'm gonna pull the trigger. Now keep going, up the stairs."

They slowly ascended—Hobson reentering the room first, followed by Jordan and Langford. Buonafortuna closed the door behind him. Jordan's defiant staring perplexed Langford. "I'm not sure what you heard," Todd said, "but she doesn't know anything."

"Like hell I don't," she said.

"Jordan—"

She gambled, deciding to take a stand. "But I want something in return. If I tell you, you're going to—"

"Watch your mouth," Buonafortuna said. "I don't

wanna hear anything out of you except an answer to my question!''

"Go to hell.''

His reaction was swift and furious. With a blinding backhand swipe, the silenced pistol smashed into her temple. The vicious blow knocked her off her feet. Jordan collapsed to the floor, bloody and unconscious.

Chapter Twenty-five

"JORDAN!"

Langford started for her but was restrained by Buonafortuna. Pointing his pistol at Langford's head, he asked, "Where the hell you goin'?"

"Jesus Christ, you might have killed her!"

"Maybe I did. She's gotta learn to listen." He stepped back, holding the pistol midway between Hobson and Langford. "Now where's the drug, and which of you is gonna give it?"

"Give it?" asked Langford. "To who?"

"To me, asshole," said Buonafortuna. "I saw what it did for Sal. If it can do that to an old man, imagine what it could do to a guy who's still got some smarts."

The noise Courtney heard was unmistakably a gunshot. Loud and booming, it sounded like a .357, or maybe a .44 Magnum. He had to get inside the building. He'd been hesitating at the front entrance, deliberating how to get in. The front door was locked. Now he charged it like a linebacker, lowering his shoulder and ramming into the front panel. But the recent construction was strong and solid. Courtney bounced off awkwardly. He had to consider other options—fast. He barked into his mike.

"I need a ram or a sledgehammer over here, now!

Keep alert, people, we have a possible hostage situation. And Johnny, you see the perp?''

"Still down the stairwell."

"Don't let that sonofabitch sneak out the back!''

The smug, complacent expression never left Hobson's
face. Casually he went to the freezer and picked out
one of the vials. From a supply cabinet, he removed a
sterile five-cc syringe and small stoppered bottle of
bacteriostatic water. Using the syringe, he dissolved the
freeze-dried powder in an appropriate amount of dilu-
ent. As Hobson worked, Buonafortuna pointed the gun
at Langford.

"No games," the gunman told Langford. "Let's try
this again. What kinda talent does the girl have?''

Langford knew evasion was pointless. "She could
tell when people were lying."

"No shit?'' Buonafortuna shoved the gun closer to
Langford's face. "I'm warning you, bright boy."

"That's very interesting," Hobson interjected. "And
I bet it's true. I've known people with that kind of
knack. It would explain how she tripped up Dr. Fine.
He told me he thought you were wise to him somehow."

"That's it?'' Vinnie scoffed. "She's some kinda lie
detector? That's the craziest thing I've heard today!''
He turned to Hobson. "A pretty big shot, Doc. You
gonna give the whole thing?''

"Goodness no," said Royce. "This is a multi-dose
vial. The standard dose is half a cc, a hundred milligrams." He turned back to the closet to get a smaller
syringe for the injection.

Langford was frantic. Jordan might be seriously hurt
and need help. Once the stranger received the cognopsin, he'd have no use for any of them. Apparently,
Hobson—ever the dealmaker—was confident he could
convince the gunman otherwise. Langford doubted it.
He had to do *something* if they were to stay alive.

"This man asked you to give him a shot," he calmly directed to Hobson. "Half a cc won't help him. He needs a full dose."

Hobson's stare was withering. "I don't know what you're up to, but you're risking getting both of us killed."

"I'm trying to stay alive, Dr. Hobson," Todd said. "You know as well as I do that it's one dose per bottle."

"Don't listen to him!" Hobson thundered. "He doesn't know, and neither does the girl! We calculated the amounts with Dr. Fine! This is what we gave all the test patients!"

She heard them from afar, darkly, as if through a tunnel. The feeling that settled over her was warm, familiar, and comfortable. Her soul was liberated, free to roam in that subliminal state of vibrant awareness. Her head ached, but there was no real pain. She was in the zone. Though not quite conscious, she heard the voices. Her brain sifted through the words, and she understood what was being said.

But try though she did, she could not tell who was lying.

The confusion was plain on Buonafortuna's face. He looked back and forth at both men, unable to tell which of them was telling the truth. "I'm really getting tempted to shoot both you turkeys. I've had plenty of experience with needles, and I'm sure I could figure out how to inject myself."

"But can you afford to screw up?" Langford calmly asked. "You've got a lot riding on that injection. All you have to do is check the bottle. Multidose vials say so on the label."

"That's ridiculous!" Hobson fumed. "These are our own labels, not some printed up by a drug company!"

"A full dose is five ccs," Langford repeated. "Don't sell yourself short."

"You're trying to kill him!" Hobson thundered.

"Give me that!" Buonafortuna snapped. He snatched the bottle from Hobson and read the label. His face darkened. "There's nothing here about more than one dose!"

"Of course not," said Hobson. "This wasn't written to please the FDA!"

Just then, Jordan stirred. All three men turned to watch as she painfully rolled onto her side, her lids fluttering open. Her mind was blank. She touched the side of her head, felt the welt there. Through still-glassy vision, she looked back at the man staring at her.

"Special talent, huh?" Buonafortuna said. "We'll see. Can you hear me, sweet cheeks?"

Jordan managed a silent nod.

"Listen to these two guys real careful," he continued. "Seems they have different opinions. Once you hear what they have to say, I want you—"

"I heard what they said."

"Is that right?" said Buonafortuna. "What were they talkin' about?"

"The cognopsin dose," she said.

"And you don't happen to know the right dose, huh?"

She nodded her head.

"Then tell me," said Buonafortuna. "Who's the liar?"

Jordan looked from Langford to Hobson. She saw relief in Todd's eyes, relief tinged with uncertainty. Hobson's smile radiated confidence. What she said would be crucial. Her answer could even prove lethal. But she also remembered her wrecked apartment, the attempt on their life, and the shattered body of poor Josh Meyerson. She didn't hesitate.

She pointed a finger at Hobson. "He is."

"No!" Hobson cried, as if in pain.

But it was too late. Buonafortuna's gun turned his way in mid-scream. The silenced Glock coughed once, and the hollowpoint caught Hobson in the neck. The copper-jacketed slug transected the right carotid and chipped off the transverse process of C-3 before exiting the upper trapezius muscle. Hobson's hands were halfway to his face when he saw the blood gushing from the severed artery, a crimson geyser that arched like an opened faucet.

Hobson's legs buckled. He fell to his knees, his expression a mixture of astonishment and incredulity. He tried to stanch the blood with his hands, but it was hopeless. The scarlet gore only welled up between his fingers. His lips moved, but no sound came out. Then he looked up at the assassin with a curious expression that was part inquiry, part plea. Vinnie fired once more, hitting Hobson in the head. The older man fell heavily onto his side, his life seeping out onto the floor.

"Now, let's get to work, *capisce*?" said Buonafortuna.

"I don't believe you just did that," Jordan whispered in horror.

"Believe it. I don't have time for conversation." He tossed Langford the vial. "Now, Doc, the injection. How long'll it take to work?"

"In the clinical trials," said Todd, "most patients improved overnight. Maybe twelve hours."

"That long, huh?"

"It's not the same as speed," Todd said.

"What would happen if you doubled the dose to two vials?"

Langford shot a quick glance at Jordan, then looked back. "Probably nothing. But we never tried it."

"Then try it now! Christ, what've I got to lose?"

Langford assembled the required paraphernalia. He returned to the supply cabinet and opened a larger sterile syringe, filling it first with the five ccs Hobson had dissolved, and then repeating the process with a second vial. Finally, he held up the ten-cc syringe and squirted out the air bubbles. "Ready?"

"You wouldn't try to fuck with me, would you?"
said Buonafortuna.

"Like I said," Todd replied, "I want to stay alive."

"Good. Do the right arm. And if you even *think*
about a trick," Vinnie said, pointing the gun at Jordan's
head, "I'll kill her." With obvious discomfort, Buonafortuna transferred the Glock from his good arm to the
injured left hand. Then he held his right arm out
straight.

Langford rolled up the man's sleeve and tied a tourniquet around the biceps. The forearm veins were
prominent and distended. With a fingertip, Langford
tested the large cephalic vein in the antecubital fossa
and judged it acceptable. He wiped it with an alcohol
swab.

"The solution might feel a little cold going in."

"Just do it," said Buonafortuna. "I'll be watchin'."

Langford eased the needle under the skin, sliding its
tip into the vein. The stranger didn't flinch. After as-
pirating a small amount of blood, he began to inject.
The clear liquid flowed freely. After a few seconds, he
withdrew the needle, covered the puncture site with the
swab, and bent up the arm.

Buonafortuna replaced the gun in his right hand.
"You did good, Doc. Now, tell me again: how long'll
it take?"

Langford had no idea. Everything he knew about it
was anecdotal, reports from the nurses. Of course, the
overnight time frame they'd alluded to referred to a
dose of one hundred milligrams, not two grams. Langford was just as curious about a dose twenty times normal as Royce had been. He felt he had to say
something. "Within an hour, I imagine," he guessed.

"Great. Now help this lady up. Then we'll all sit
down and wait."

Langford helped Jordan to her feet, checking the
knot on her temple, which was considerably swollen,

but not bleeding. "Doesn't look too serious. How's it feel?"

"I'll survive." She looked at Buonafortuna. "You don't have to pretend for my sake. I know you're going to kill us anyway."

He laughed. "Lady, you ever heard the St. Francis prayer? I'm just a channel for the will of God. Whatever happens to you's up to Him. But why should I be deprived of your company?"

Jordan and Langford sat on lab stools. Across from them, Buonafortuna leaned against a countertop. His shattered, hastily bandaged left arm occasionally dribbled blood, but the pain no longer seemed to bother him.

"Just to pass the time, why don't you satisfy my curiosity?" Buonafortuna went on. "This is pretty damn neat, this ability you got. It could prove real helpful. People would pay through the ass to have a fraction of your talent."

"Is that why you're keeping us alive?" asked Jordan. "To sell me to the highest bidder?"

"Now there's a thought." Vinnie chuckled. "I imagine there'd be a lot of buyers. Wealthy buyers. Heads of state, y'know, maybe entire governments. Definitely worth considering."

Langford stared fixedly at the gunman. Something odd was happening to him. His eyes were taking on a certain glint, a decidedly maniacal gleam. Was he becoming shocky from blood loss? But he didn't seem to be bleeding that badly. He decided to humor him.

"She'd command a pretty steep price," Todd said.

"I beg your pardon?" Jordan said.

"Oh, you got that right," Buonafortuna agreed with a smile. "But her real beauty," he said, carelessly tapping his skull with the silencer, "lies here."

Jordan was perplexed by the man's peculiar smile. "Why is getting this shot so important to you?"

"What're you, an idiot?" asked Buonafortuna, grinning strangely. "I've seen what this stuff did for Sal. Why should he be the only one on the receiving end? You think I always want to be doin' his nickel-and-dime legwork?"

Could it be the cognopsin? Langford wondered. The proper amount would dramatically improve cognitive performance. But what happened when twenty times the normal dose went to work on the human brain? Could it work this fast—and this intensely? "So you want to get a piece of the action, is that it?" said Todd. "Sort of like cocaine, where you take a little taste first before you deal it?"

Buonafortuna tilted his head back, emitting a high-pitched howl of laughter. "That's what you think this is about, a drug deal? That's fuckin' priceless!"

What was happening had to be drug effect. The killer was undergoing a profound, progressive change. Some of it was physical: the tightly constricted pupils, the flared nostrils, and the beaded perspiration on his upper lip. But for the most part, the changes were mental, and emotional.

The brain was divided into various areas, or loci, which governed affect, behavior, and mood. There were centers for satisfaction, fear, and sleep. But at that moment, the cerebral center responsible for humor was being repeatedly stimulated by the cognopsin. Neurons fired over and over again, causing the man's extreme behavior. But his bizarre antics were only one step removed from lunacy.

Good Lord, Langford worried. What's going to happen next? "You know," said Todd, "I bet if you played your cards right, you could even be the next don."

Jordan quickly caught on. "You're onto something, Todd. Someone as sharp as he is could definitely go right to the top."

Buonafortuna's eyes were now rapidly flitting from side to side. He had begun to drool. White spittle formed at the corners of his mouth, and his throat seemed to be filling with fluid. Even though he swallowed repeatedly, a trickle of saliva snaked down his chin. His eyes widened grotesquely, and his speech became rapid-fire.

"The top, the top, the top! Don't you see the beauty of it?" Buonafortuna said, eyes blazing. "A guy like me, flunked outa med school, runnin' numbers and crackin' heads for those goons, winds up bein' the head of the whole damn syndicate!"

From frontal lobe to cerebellum, neurotransmitters flowed liberally from cell to cell. Synapses repeatedly fired, sometimes asynchronously, sometimes in concert. The brain's millions of neurons reached a fever pitch of excitability. A twitching began in his lower limbs, and his knees started to shake. Langford was sure it wouldn't be long before the man lost it entirely. But he still had a weapon, and a madman with a gun was an unpredictable quantity.

Fighting disorientation, Buonafortuna glanced down at his trembling hands. In his diminished awareness, he suddenly realized what was happening to him. His fury rose in him, and he glared at Langford. "You bastard," he said, raising the gun.

But as Langford and Jordan watched, his body suddenly went into spasm. Overwhelmed by the massive amount of cognopsin, his entire CNS was short-circuiting. His eyes rolled upward in their sockets, revealing the bloodshot undersides of his sclerae. His back arched, arms bent at the elbows at a ninety-degree angle, and his hands flexed at the wrist, praying mantislike. The silenced Glock was still in his grasp, pointing toward the floor. Jordan grabbed Langford's arm.

"What's *happening* to him?" she screamed.

"A grand mal seizure. Keep back, he's still dangerous!"

Buonafortuna's teeth were rigidly clenched. His jaw

muscles spasmed, and his lips stretched back painfully, baring his teeth in a macabre rictus. Sputum gushed forth, spewing from his lips in a pinkish froth. His unbalanced body jerked, prancing like a marionette.

Suddenly, the door burst open in a crash of splintered wood. Three uniformed men burst into the room, wearing assault vests. One of them, whom Langford recognized as Tom Courtney, was aiming a pistol at the gunman.

"Drop your weapon!" Courtney commanded. "Put it down, *now*!"

But the gunman could not. In the throes of a convulsion, his body was frozen by muscular contractions, a grotesque human pantomime. Although he tottered precariously, on the verge of collapse, his right hand was welded to the gun. As team leader, Courtney was the first to fire.

His one-hundred-eighty-five-grain hollow point, moving at eleven hundred fifty feet per second, took off the top of Vinnie's head. He fired twice more as the men beside him opened up. In the close confines, the sound was deafening. To Jordan, the whole room seemed to explode. She let Langford's hand go and squeezed her eyes shut, pressing her palms to her ears. It was all over in an instant, but not before Buonafortuna's body was shredded.

The sudden silence was nearly as overwhelming as the gunfire. Spent shell casings lay everywhere, and the room was filled with an acrid gray haze. A man with a pump shotgun stepped forward. Standing over what was left of the gunman, he kicked the Glock away. Buonafortuna's entire arm came with it. Severed at the shoulder by eight pellets of double-ought buckshot, it broke free cleanly, like a claw plucked from a crab shell.

Courtney thumbed on the safety and holstered his weapon, then looked at Langford and Jordan, sizing up their injuries. He spoke into his mike. "We're secure,

Johnny. Get some medics up here on the double." Then he waved his hand, parting the smoky residue as he walked toward his friends. "You guys okay?"

Langford nodded, inhaling with relief. "We'll be all right. How'd you know we were here?"

"It's a long story."

From across the room, another officer called to them. "Better take a look. We've got a live one here."

They all ran to where Hobson lay on his back in a pool of blood. The arterial spurting, diminished as the blood pressure dropped, was still a noticeable flow. Langford knelt by the stricken man and tore off a strip of his shirt. His medical training was every bit as ingrained as the actions of the assault team. It didn't matter that Buonafortuna's second shot had destroyed Hobson's cerebral cortex. The victim's heart still worked, even if his brain did not. Langford folded the cloth and placed the makeshift dressing on the neck entrance wound, stopping the blood flow.

"Set up an IV, Jordan," he said.

Her lips tightened, a tense line of bitter resentment. She touched the knot on her head, but it didn't hurt. The real pain she felt was inside, a churning tide of hatred, and revenge. "Why don't you just leave him alone."

"You know we can't do that," said Todd. "He's got almost no volume. Probably an exercise in futility, but what the hell."

"Who is that?" asked Courtney.

"This? Dr. Hobson, or what's left of him."

"And the one at the top of the steps?" asked the agent.

"Dr. Royce," said Todd. "The guy you just killed shot them both."

"Try to keep him alive, will you?" said Courtney. "The press is going to have a field day with this. Before they do, you and I better have a little talk."

Epilogue

TWO DAYS AFTER THE MASSACRE AT EASTGATE, THE three of them stood by the kitchen countertop in Jordan's new apartment, drinking coffee.

"They finally had to put Aiello in protective custody this morning, in the prison infirmary," said Tom Courtney. "He's pretty incoherent, but when he babbles, he's telling us just what we want to know."

"You're building cases against the rest of his family?" said Jordan.

"What's left of it. With the don behind bars, and Buonafortuna and the rest of his crew dead, the pigeons are leaving the roost. It'll take years for the syndicate to recover."

Todd shook his head. "I'm still confused. If Molloy had all these Mafia ties, how did he fit in with Dr. Hobson?"

"The way we see it," said Courtney, "Molloy was an opportunist. Most of what he did was mob related, but he saw the potential for a big score in cognopsin. He probably leaked word to Hobson right after Fletcher made the discovery."

Jordan was perplexed. "How could he know Hobson'd be interested?"

"It takes one to know one," Courtney said. "Maybe it was something Hobson said in passing, or the look in his eye. But Molloy knew he'd found his mark."

"And all along, we figured it was Dr. Royce," said Todd.

Courtney nodded. "An image Hobson was happy to cultivate."

"Dr. Royce was really in the dark?" Jordan asked.

"It looks that way," Courtney agreed. "Royce was full of bluff and bluster, but deep down, he was a dedicated researcher. We think he honestly believed the only way to get the needed data about cognopsin was to study its effects on patients at Eastgate. We don't think he had the slightest inkling about Hobson's profit motive."

"So, it was Hobson who told Molloy to kill Dr. Fletcher and Dr. Fine?" Todd said.

"Correct. They'd outlived their usefulness to him. We now have witnesses who place Molloy in the parking lot the day Dr. Fine was shot."

"But what about Josh?" said Jordan. "Wasn't Molloy already dead?"

"Right," said Courtney. "That was Mafia, one of Buonafortuna's goons." He put down his cup and paused. "Now I have a question for you. What happens with the cognopsin?"

"You gave all the vials to the FDA," said Todd, "and we turned over the records. After their investigation, they'll probably start legitimate testing in about a year. Jordan and I already outlined the research paper. We'll make sure Fletch'll get the credit he deserves."

"Then I guess that's about it, kids," Courtney said, getting ready to leave. "When're you going back to work, anyway?"

"Tomorrow," said Langford. "Jordan's been helping out in the ICU, and they gave me the whole week off. We'll have you back here sometime, Tom. After we get some furniture in the place."

Their new home was another apartment in Jordan's building. Fearing a lawsuit over lax security, the landlord had made it available with alacrity. Julie moved in with her boyfriend. Although the newer apartment was smaller, a one bedroom, it had a spacious living room with a large, working fireplace. Now, despite the remaining warmth of October, the hearth was ablaze.

Langford sat cross-legged on the Oriental rug, the room's only furnishing other than the bed. The nearby fire baked him in its dry heat. A small puppy was asleep in his lap. It was a gift from Jordan. The seven-week-old German shorthair was almost pure chocolate in color. Curled in a contented ball, it occasionally twitched an ear as it slept. Langford stroked its warm fur, as smooth and soft as velvet. Jordan looked on serenely.

"Decided what to name him yet?" she asked.

"What's wrong with 'Boy'? He responds to that pretty well."

Jordan leaned toward the dog. "You awake, Boy?" The puppy lazily opened one eye and lifted an ear. It looked at her, saw no reason to stir, and went back to sleep. "Well, I guess that settles that."

He stroked the puppy's head contentedly. "This is the best gift I've had in a long time." He kissed Jordan on the cheek. "Thank you for that."

She snuggled against him. "We have a lot to be thankful for, don't we?"

"That we do. We're very, very lucky."

"Do you think what Dr. Swenson said yesterday is true?" she asked.

"About your exam being normal? Why would you doubt it?"

"I don't," Jordan said. "It was just that . . . It's so strange, what cognopsin did to me. I guess I'll always have this knack about thinking I can tell when people are lying, but to have it so enhanced? I really didn't want that power, when I had it. I fought it, I resented it. For a while, I felt like a freak. But now that it's gone . . ."

"You miss it?" Todd said.

"I guess what I miss is the opportunity. It opened up a whole new world for me, Todd. It was a window into my soul."

"In what way?"

"It's like this," she said. "I've come to think of consciousness as a place, a place in my head. It's a pit stop, a way station on the journey from sleep to wakefulness."

"Getting poetic in our convalescence, are we?"

"I was able to go to that place, Todd. And what I found there was just the tip of the iceberg. You and I, we all have tremendous powers waiting to be developed. It's inside us, don't you see? We have this untapped potential. In my case, cognopsin was the key."

"Could be a dangerous key, if not used properly," he said.

"Hmmm." Jordan put her head on his shoulder and looked into the fire. The flames were golden, sparkling fingers of heat. A draft fluttered, and the flames soared richly. One of the logs hissed, then popped in a thin wisp of quickly consumed white steam.

She wondered if he could ever truly understand. She had been to a place few people had ever visited, and she had returned to tell the tale. But although she could discuss it, she couldn't describe it. Words could not do justice to what she had seen there.

For, like the hearth, her soul had been touched by fire, and her mind was still ablaze.

It was a crisp, clear, early November morning, golden around the edges, with enough humidity to turn one's breath into a frosty vapor. From Rita's Mount Sinai hospital room, Jordan had an unobstructed view of eastern Central Park. Across Fifth Avenue, a recently fallen patchwork of red and yellow leaves covered the grass like a quilt. After Courtney arrived at Eastgate, she and Todd had quickly given Rita a booster of cognopsin before Rita was rushed back to Met. Being young and without a chronic disease, her body mended on its own. Once she'd recovered, Jeffrey Donninger requested that his wife be transferred to Sinai.

Owing to luck and a good tissue match, no sooner had she emerged from her ordeal at the clinic than a kidney had been located. Sinai's transplant team performed the surgery at ten in the evening. Rita was now twelve hours post-op. Other than for some facial puffiness, she looked to be the picture of health. Jordan thought it amazing that her friend hadn't died of kidney failure while at Eastgate. She reached over the bed rail and took Rita's hand.

"I can't stay long, Reet. How're you feeling?"

Rita managed a smile, squeezing Jordan's fingers. "Pretty darn humble," she said, her voice hoarse. "Grateful to be alive, and to have a friend like you. Did you see the baby today?"

"Yes," Jordan nodded, "on my way up here. "God, she's gorgeous. Did you ever think motherhood would turn out like this?"

Rita shook her head, her eyes growing heavy with thanks and tears. "No," she said softly. "Not in my wildest dreams."

They were standing just inside the doors to the ICU, wearing regulation yellow paper over-gowns. The reporter clicked her ballpoint, folded up her notebook, and then shook hands.

"Appreciate it, Jordan. I owe you one. This is going to make one hell of a story."

"What you've been writing all week ain't too shabby," said Jordan.

"The wrap-up's the most important piece, after the intro. It's a hook-'em, land-'em thing. This will tie all the loose ends together. You know," said Sharon Mandel, shaking her head, "greed is such a baffling motive. Hobson could have taken the high road. If he'd gone public and done things the normal way, it might have taken a little longer, but he'd still have made tons of money. Go figure.''

"Patience is one thing they don't teach in med school.''

"Oh, but what they *do* teach . . .'' said the reporter. She gestured toward the nearest ICU bed. ''Most people have no idea how far medicine's come. These machines are incredible—and the drugs? To keep people alive days, even weeks at a time? It's mind-boggling.''

"It's progress, Sharon. Every patient deserves the best possible shot at survival.''

"Even Dr. Hobson here?'' the reporter asked.

Jordan replied softly, "Especially Dr. Hobson.''

For the last time that morning, the reporter turned to look at the prostrate form of the former chief of emergency medicine. Head swathed in bandages, with countless tubes protruding from his body, he seemed attached to every life-prolonging device imaginable. One week after his injury, he looked grotesque. His swollen lips were cracked, bloated like sausage skins. His flesh had turned a deeply cyanotic, almost purplish hue. Yet despite his prolonged terminal state, death was not an option.

"How many times did you say he's been resuscitated?''

"Twelve, at last count,'' said Jordan.

"Whew. That must be some kind of record,'' said the reporter.